HOMESICK

Marc Raabe owns and runs a television production company and lives with his family in Cologne.

Also by Marc Raabe

Cut
The Shock

HOMESICK

MARC
RAABE

MANILLA

...ny in 2015 by Ullstein Buchverlage GmbH, Berlin

First publi/edition published in Great Britain in 2018 by
MANILLA PUBLISHING
The)–81 Wimpole St, London W1G
www.zaffrebooks.co.)5

Copyright © Msabel Ade...

English tra...

A CIP catalogue record for this book is
available from the British Library.

ISBN: 978-1-78576-726-5

Also available as an ebook

1 3 5 7 9 10 8 6 4 2

Typeset by IDSUK (Data Connection) Ltd
Printed and bound in Great Britain by Clays Ltd, Elcograf S.p.A.

Manilla Publishing is an imprint of Bonnier Zaffre,
part of Bonnier Books UK
www.bonnierzaffre.co.uk
www.bonnierbooks.co.uk

I is another.
Arthur Rimbaud

Prologue

September 1981

There was still enough air to breathe.

The pages of The Black Jaguar *lay open next to his bed, under a well-thumbed copy of* Batman *magazine. Typical reading material for a thirteen-year-old. The light had been out for a while. The duvet rose and fell like a soft swell.*

Suddenly he found himself gasping for breath.

Just before he woke up, he dreamed he was drowning. A recurring nightmare.

When he was a small child, he fell into the ice at the edge of a nearby lake. It was dusk, and a blanket of fresh snow had buried everything under a pure, deceptive cover of powdery white. The mountains stood out sharp and clear against the backdrop of an empty sky. The ice gave way without warning. Black water closed in around him, like a clenching fist, and the ripples sloshed together over his head. His padded coat was soaked and heavy, dragging him down like a life jacket filled with lead. He sank to the bottom, crippled by the shock.

His mother had come to his rescue that time, literally at the last second. But in some of his dreams her hand morphed into a powerful male hand with a crescent-shaped scar on the back, grabbing him and pulling him out of the water like a little kitten.

Ever since then he had avoided water any deeper than his hips.

But there wasn't any water here in his bedroom.

He was lying in his bed.

Someone was pressing a pillow into his face.

He frantically gasped for air, only to get a mouthful of cotton instead. The tip of one of the feathers pierced through the pillow and cut his lip. The pillow pressed his nose against his face, making his body cry out for oxygen. Blinded by panic, he tried to wriggle out from beneath the pillow, frantically waving his arms and trying to break free. Someone was sitting on top of him, pinning him down with the weight of their whole body. His lungs felt like they were about to burst. He clenched his fists and lashed out.

Suddenly the pressure eased.

He snatched the pillow away from his face and gasped for air to cool his burning lungs. There, in the pale moonlight, he saw the vague outlines of a figure, barely a silhouette against the cold lustre of the wallpaper. Wriggling around on top of him was a body with a misshapen, insect-like head. He almost forgot to defend himself for a moment. The figure got up, hissing as he breathed. Its shadow looked like something from Batman's Gotham City. The head was strangely smooth. Staring back at him instead of eyes were two circular pieces of glass the size of fists. He could see his own pale face reflected in them. A black oval protruded from the space where a mouth and a nose should have been.

He was about to scream, but a sharp blow to the temple from his left stopped him before he could make a sound. Faint stars shimmered, then the second blow struck him. He lost consciousness. Everything went dark, like a fuse had blown.

For a while there was nothing.

He woke up when he felt the floor shaking. No, trembling. He lay curled up like an embryo, his ears ringing and ribs aching.

Every now and again he felt a harsh jolt, sometimes two in quick succession. He tried to move his hands and feet but realised they were tied. There was a sheet of tarpaulin tacked down overhead, and when he tried to stretch his body, he found there was only so far that he could move. He realised he was freezing cold and wearing nothing but his underpants. The wind pushed through the gaps. The air smelled of exhaust fumes, which he guessed were coming from a moped judging by the high-pitched buzzing of the engine, like a circular saw. He screwed up his eyes and fantasised for a moment that it was all just a nightmare.

How could this be happening? He had only just been in bed, fast asleep!

'Wake up, please let me wake up,' he quietly begged.

The sound of his own voice brought him back to reality.

This wasn't a dream.

He wasn't going to wake up.

His throat became constricted. He tried to breathe through the fear. He was thirteen! He was too old to just give up. Yes, he'd given up before – back then, under the ice.

But never again.

He felt his way along the boards around him as best he could, even though his wrists were tied in front of his stomach. It seemed he was in some kind of flat-bed trailer. The tarpaulin was pulled tight overhead; presumably it had eyelets and was fastened on the outside with a rope. There was a hook protruding from the board in front of him, possibly for securing loads.

He tried to locate the knot between his wrists, but he couldn't see much in the darkness. When he twisted his wrists against each other, he felt a thick, bulbous knob, like several knots on top of one another. He thought about one time when he'd tied his shoes in a double knot and had to unpick it with a fork when he couldn't get them off.

He lifted his hands up and pressed the knot into the sharp end of the hook. He carefully tugged at the knot with his hands, then he pulled it away from the hook and pushed it back in again. A damp film of sweat crept over his skin in spite of the draught. The knot became looser and looser.

Suddenly the trailer started juddering, as if it was being pulled along a path full of bumps and potholes. The loading platform banged against his body. The whirring gave way to a sombre rattling sound and finally fell silent.

Someone folded the trailer stand down.

The air smelled of damp earth, resin and fir trees.

The rope purred as it came loose from the eyelets. The cover was cast aside, revealing the silhouettes of trees against a torn sky. The insect head leaned over him.

'Get out!' The voice had a strangely hollow and metallic tone. And it sounded like it was coming from a teenager like him. A boy.

'I can't,' he replied, pointing at his feet with his chin.

Without saying a word, the boy unfastened the ties around his feet and bound his legs together instead, so he could walk in very small steps. Then the boy stood back and observed as he struggled and stumbled his way out of the trailer. He straightened himself up, panting.

A clearly defined crescent moon briefly emerged from between the wisps of cloud. The boy was holding a knife in his fist. Its blade gleamed in the moonlight.

'That way,' the boy said.

'What . . . what are you going to do with me?'

'Sir!'

'What?'

'You have to call me "sir"!'

He gulped. 'What are you going to do with me, sir?'

'Just shut up and move.'

The boy shoved him and made him walk ahead. Leaves rustled on the ground as he shuffled along. Stones and hard branches jabbed the soles of his bare feet. The boy's breath hissed softly through the mask. There was no path, just a short zigzag line through the trees. He thought he could hear a waterfall rushing down in the distance. He wrung his hands, turned his fingertips inwards and tugged at the knot. The rope would be loose before long. His heart was pounding wildly. If only the boy didn't have that knife!

Then he saw the hole. Suddenly he was standing right in front of it: a gaping black hole in the forest floor. Rectangular, like a grave.

He stopped dead in his tracks.

'Over there,' said the boy.

'You want to kill me?'

'You've been dead to me for a long time.'

'What do you . . . what do you mean, sir?'

The boy behind him said nothing.

He gave a desperate jerk with his arms. The cords chafed his skin and the knot tightened again. This couldn't be happening! But wasn't the rope looser? 'Please . . . let me go,' he whimpered.

'No,' the boy snapped.

He made one last attempt to break free from the knot by squeezing his hand as tightly as he could, then forcing it through the loop. The rope burned like fire as it chafed against his skin. Suddenly his hand was free. He spun around with his fist clenched and punched the other boy in the stomach. The knife fell to the ground as the boy staggered backwards, gasping for breath. He quickly bent down and picked it up. The handle was warm from the heat of the other boy's hand. Or was it his own hand, still burning from the rope?

'Stay where you are,' he hissed.

The other boy stood stooped less than three steps away against the trunk of the next tree, glowering at him with his insect eyes.

He bent down and reached between his feet, his fingers trembling as he cut the rope.

That very instant, the boy pounced on him. They fell to the ground, wrestling for the knife. The moon illuminated their hands – and suddenly he froze. He knew those hands! They were . . .

The boy snatched the knife right out of his hands. He instinctively turned around to get up and run away but was stopped dead by a hot, overpowering pain in his back. He cried out in agony. All the strength drained from his body. He fell to the ground on his stomach, right next to the hole in the ground. A boot pushed against his pelvis and bumped him to one side, defenceless. He rolled over the edge like a useless bag of bones and fell into the pit. His head banged on a stone as he hit the ground. He lay there motionless.

For a while it was completely silent. He felt like he had gone deaf, like he was locked up somewhere outside of his body while it raged with pain. The trees above him were clouds of black leaves. A voice seemed to whisper directly into his brain from the sky.

'Ma?' he whispered.

But there was no answer.

'Maaaaaa!'

He saw the figure appear in a blur at the edge of the hole in the ground. A huge black insect holding a shovel in its hand. The first scoop of soil hailed down on his face, drawing a curtain on the sky and burying the last glimmer of hope.

Thirty-two years later

Chapter 1

Berlin – Saturday, 5 January 2013, 3.18 a.m.

Jesse woke from the dream with a jolt and sat up straight in his bed.

Darkness surrounded him. He was sweating.

It took him a moment to realise that he was no longer a young boy, but a full-grown man. Christ, it had all been so close and so real. He felt like he could still taste the soil in his mouth. The old scar on his back itched like someone had been scratching it. But the scream he had heard wasn't coming from inside his dream. It was the cry of a young girl.

He threw the duvet to one side, planted his feet on the floor and stood up.

Cold laminate flooring. Fresh air on his damp forehead. The floor was dry, firm and light. Forty-five years old and he was still having the same old nightmare. It started with the insect man shovelling earth onto him and ended when he was just about to suffocate in his grave. That was it. Nothing else. No location or time, nothing before or after it. There was just one variant of the nightmare, when he was drowning in a frozen lake.

The girl's scream was preying on his mind. He pushed the handle on the bedroom door and, rushing through the hall past the last of the boxes he still hadn't unpacked, he tripped over his doctor's bag by the coat rack. He always left it there, packed and ready to go. He cursed and kicked it aside, noticing the colourful beam of light shining through the crack under the door. Another three strides and he made it into the bedroom.

'Isa,' he whispered.

The little girl with a shock of tousled blond hair was sitting bolt upright in her bed with her eyes fixed on the window directly opposite.

'Isa!'

'Shh,' she whispered without moving a muscle. 'Dad, there's someone there.'

Jesse glanced at the window. 'Over there?'

'Where else?' Isabelle whispered, her voice positively brimming with exasperation. Adults were so incredibly slow sometimes.

Jesse gave a quiet sigh and walked over to the window. 'What did he look like?'

'He had a dark mane and wild eyes.'

'Wild eyes?'

Isa nodded. 'He looked at me.'

Jesse opened the window. Fresh air rushed towards in. He leaned out over the window ledge and looked right and left at the street below. 'No monsters anywhere. Want to come and see for yourself?'

Isa shook her head. Wisps of blond hair waved back and forth. 'It wasn't a monster.'

Jesse smiled. 'So then what was it?'

'I don't know. Something a bit like a monster,' she whispered.

Jesse nodded and carefully closed the window. He walked back over to her and sat on the edge of the bed.

Isabelle budged over to make room for him on the crumpled bedcover. Jesse smiled, swung his legs onto the bed and lay down next to his eight-year-old daughter.

Isa curled up and silently pressed her head against his armpit. She sighed as she inhaled and exhaled, like she'd been short of breath for a while. Jesse could feel her heartbeat racing beneath her delicate ribcage.

'Dad?'

'Hmm?'

'You won't leave me here by myself if I fall asleep, will you?'

'Hmm,' Jesse mumbled wearily. The heat from the bed and the presence of his daughter were helping to still the reverberations of his own nightmare, one that had been haunting him for as long as he could remember. He hated waking up and having to make sure he wasn't drowning or buried beneath a layer of earth. Sometimes, when the dream was longer and began differently, he could observe himself as if separate from his body. It was like he was standing right there watching his mirror image: a small boy playing on the banks of a frozen lake. Sometimes they even spoke to each other. Words from Jesse to Jesse.

Jesse didn't know which part of the dream was from his past and which part was a fantasy. His memory was cut off when he had his accident at the age of thirteen. Since then, his life had been divided into the *before* and the *after*. Everything from *before* the accident was shrouded in darkness, even the things the others told him about it in the children's home. Little by little, he crudely pieced together the fragments of his life to make some sense of it all. His father was the captain of a ship, they said, but nobody knew anything about his mother. He didn't much like the things they told him about himself. Some of it made him feel ashamed.

For a moment he found himself wondering who needed who more. Did Isa need him – or did he need Isa? Strands of her hair tickled his cheek. The scent of pine needles and damp earth lingered in her hair after their day out in the woods. Good thing Sandra wasn't there. As far as Isa's mother was concerned, children's hair should smell of shampoo, not the forest. Ever since their time together as kids at Adlershof children's home, Sandra saw the forest as another word for prison, unlike cities, which were her definition of freedom. For Jesse it was completely the opposite.

'Have you brushed your teeth?

Isa didn't respond. Her breathing was suspiciously even, like it always was when she was pretending to be asleep.

'Oi!' he whispered in her ear, gently tickling her on the hip. His daughter giggled and squirmed under the sheets. 'That's enough. Up you get now – go clean your teeth.'

'Oh, Dad! But I'm sooo tired.'

'I know. Me too,' Jesse yawned.

'I could always brush my teeth tomorrow instead.'

'Or next week, huh?'

'I'll be at Mum's then. I always have to brush my teeth a thousand times when I'm there.'

'Well, then, I suppose you're getting off pretty lightly if you only have to brush them three times when you're here. So off you go!'

Isa threw the covers off in exasperation and clambered over Jesse, making sure she gave him a hefty jab before she climbed out of the bed. He quickly dodged her, protecting the old scar on his back, but she caught him between the ribs. 'Ouch!' Jesse grinned. 'Should I come with you?'

'Nope.' Isa trundled over towards the bathroom with an air of defiance, her bare feet slapping on the floor as she padded along. The bathroom door creaked as she closed it behind her.

Jesse gave a weary sigh. His eyes skimmed the walls of Isa's room, the only one in the flat he'd finished decorating so far. Colourful glowing fish floated idly around the room, projected onto the wallpaper by a small lamp with a rotating shade. He had given the lamp to Isa as a gift six months ago, the first time she stayed overnight with him in his new flat. That wasn't long after he separated from Sandra. One time, Isa woke him up in the middle of the night because she thought the fish were dead. He brought them back to life by changing the light bulb.

Jesse's eyelids drooped. He dozed off.

When he opened his eyes again he felt cold. The bed next to him was empty. The flat was completely quiet.

'Isa?'

No answer.

He swung his legs out of the bed, shivered and rushed over to the bathroom. No beam of light under the door. No noise.

Silence.

Cold air gushed towards him when he opened the door. The bathroom was empty and dark, except for the faint glimmer of light from the yard shining through the frosted window. He ran his thumb along Isa's toothbrush. It was dry.

A quiet thud made him turn around. The sound of wood on wood. The window flapped in its frame and the handle was in the unlocked position. Had *he* left the window open? It was unlikely to have been Isa, particularly after the episode with the monster – or whatever it was she thought she'd seen.

Jesse tried to remain calm. He opened the window and looked out. The night sky was clear and there was not a single cloud above the grey, abandoned yard. 'Isa?'

Silence.

Why the hell was the window open? He felt like a band of iron was tightening around his chest. Jesse turned around, rushed into the corridor, tore the living room door open and flicked on the light switch.

He squinted. No Isa.

He tried to stay calm, but his heart was pounding.

Onward to the kitchen. Door open, light on.

He stopped in the doorway and let out a deep breath. The tension drained from his body as he sighed. It made him feel dizzy with relief.

There she was.

Isa was sitting on the floor next to the table, with her back against the radiator and her chin on her chest. The corners of her mouth were smeared in brown. The jar of Nutella she'd evidently polished off was on the floor next to her with a spoon sticking out of it. Isa's small ribcage rose and fell peacefully in perfect time with her breathing.

Jesse nestled in beside her by the warm radiator, her narrow shoulder blade resting against his upper arm. Their figures were reflected in the glass of the kitchen door. It was almost as if they had been fused together. He saw himself with his short, clean-cut blond hair and receding hairline, his brown eyes shining back at him as he sat there in his black T-shirt and bare legs. Isa's hair was the same shade of blond as his, with the same characteristic cowlick. Like so many times before, Jesse found himself wondering what he had done to deserve her. He knew there were many things Sandra wouldn't forgive him for, particularly his absence, his self-absorbed ways, his restlessness and his selfish decisions. He had always been afraid that Isa might feel the same as Sandra, that she would adopt her mother's point of view. The greatest of all the fears that hounded him was that maybe he really didn't deserve her.

Jesse sighed.

He hated cities with a passion, but he would even have moved to New York for Isa. So when Sandra decided to move to Berlin after they broke up, it probably wasn't the worst thing she could have done.

Chapter 2

Garmisch-Partenkirchen – Saturday, 5 January 2013, 4.21 p.m.

The wind whistled furiously as it battered against the walls of the west wing. Artur Messner couldn't help but think it sounded like it was trying to avenge the ugly stories that had played out behind the walls of this building. He hated these old walls. But he needed them too. Those were the two sentences Artur Messner would use if anyone ever wanted to know his definition of home. But nobody asked him these days.

They would probably have to carry him out of here in his beloved burgundy wing chair sooner or later. He jerked and swivelled the heavy armchair as he sat in it, edging it closer to the dormer window to look outside. He needed something to stop him glancing back, over his left shoulder, into the dimly lit room. But not because he found the furnishings ugly; things like that ceased to matter so much with old age. A threadbare oriental rug, a makeshift row of kitchen fittings and a tiny television on top of the fridge.

No, it was the package on his dining table. The package was the thing he didn't want to look at. He wished he could have just thrown it out of the window.

A frosty wreath framed the view over the billowing treetops onto the frozen lake. Muffled cries rose through the building at regular intervals and echoed through the long corridors. Charly had run away for the third time and they were still desperately trying to find her. They would have to tell the police eventually. Artur was fully aware of what an ordeal that always turned out to be.

Artur Messner was seventy-four. He regretted many things in his life, including his marriage to Hannelore. Six years after the wedding, she had an affair with a Canadian ski jumper during the traditional New Year ski jumping event at the Four Hills Tournament in Garmisch. It wasn't his wife's first affair. She couldn't cope with the 'miserable life' she said Artur offered her. She left for Canada two months later, without so much as a second thought, and never came back. She left their son Richard with him, saying the two of them were just the same and belonged together.

But nothing hurt Artur more than having to hand over the reins of Adlershof to Richard seven years ago. If only he didn't have this damn rheumatism. Almost thirty years of pain and high doses of cortisone had taken their toll, and his body was worn out and frail.

And he had *this* to deal with.

Even without turning around he could see the package staring at him from its perch on the top of the table. Nothing compared to *this*. Not his loveless marriage, nor his bitter end as the principal of the boarding school and children's home, nor the excruciating pain he constantly had to endure.

He stared at the lake stubbornly. The sun was disappearing behind the tops of the Wetterstein mountains, casting a cold, ever-expanding shadow. The fading light turned the snow blue and the rest of the landscape to black. Artur thought about just throwing the package away or burying it somewhere on the hillside, as far away as his old feet would carry him. But how was he supposed to bury it if he didn't even dare to touch it? This damn package was turning him into something he never wanted to be: a coward.

It had come with the mail around midday. Philippa brought it up to him with his lunch – well, if you could call the spartan diet crap she served him lunch.

The package was roughly half the size of a shoe box and came wrapped in smooth brown paper. Philippa gave a tight-lipped smile as she placed it on the table in the middle of the room, the kind of smile that said she wanted to express a warmth she'd lost over the thirty-nine years of her life. Although Artur wasn't particularly fond of Philippa, he was grateful that his son had appointed her. It was one of the few choices Richard had made that he could actually understand. It was difficult enough to find good staff for a home, but finding good staff who didn't crack under the pressure was even harder.

When Philippa left the room, he was left with a choice: either open the package or eat lunch first. Had he succumbed to curiosity, he would have started with the package. Mail like this was something of a rarity for him. Still, he chose to eat lunch first.

His fingers were positively trembling later that day when he opened the package. He put it down to the arthritis, trying not to admit to himself how nervous he was. He was partly nervous out of excitement, and partly because the package unsettled him for some reason. Well, he hadn't been expecting any post or gifts, after all. And it wasn't like he was particularly popular with the former pupils of the combined children's home and boarding school. In a moment of wistful nostalgia, he found himself thinking about Christmas and his childhood birthdays.

Good grief, how long had it been since someone had given him a present?

The paper rustled as he unwrapped it. There was no sender, just his name, Artur Messner, written in pointy block capitals above his address. He peeled the paper away to reveal a cardboard box, then he opened the lid and found a white container inside. An inconspicuous opaque Tupperware box. Perhaps it's something to eat, Artur thought to himself.

He lifted the lid with his thumb and recoiled in shock. What a foul stench! He hesitated for a moment and thought about just throwing the container in the bin. But curiosity got the better of him.

He opened the lid.

Inside was the bloated, pale-green hand. A man's hand.

He felt sick.

Still, he couldn't look away. The large hand was clearly marked with the lines of age and had a striking crescent-shaped burn on the back. Tears welled up into Artur's eyes. He tried to blink them away, but the images were gushing towards him uncontrollably, moving in circles around his brain. He was always forgetting things these days, but he had the memory of an elephant when it came to the past. His last encounter with the owner of this hand wasn't something he liked to recall. He had dismissed Wilbert with a cool farewell – to be on the safe side, he said at the time. But now he knew that fear was the real reason he had sent him away. Maybe he would have been able to stop thinking about it if Wilbert had only been a school acquaintance. But people who hurtle down the closed Olympic bob run by the lake at night and steal motorbikes together are more than just acquaintances.

He snapped the container shut. Who in God's name would do something like this? And why?

He spent the rest of the day in his burgundy armchair, caught between ponderings and memories. Finally, a shrill noise startled him. He reached for his Bakelite telephone with stiff fingers and raised it to his ear. He was glad he still had the old thing. Those new modern phones weighed next to nothing and their buttons were far too small. 'Messner speaking,' he answered.

'*Artur* Messner?' It was the voice of a man and it sounded muffled, as if he was speaking through a handkerchief. It was difficult to judge how old he was. Thirty, perhaps. But then again, he could be fifty.

'Yes, who is it?'

'Did you get the package?'

Artur's hand started trembling. He pressed the receiver closer to his ear. 'Who is this? Was it *you* who sent the package?' Oh dear, how helpless he sounded. He used to be the head of Adlershof, for goodness' sake. Now he was just a doddery old man.

Losing his independence had been an insidious process, but the fact that he'd lost it was a sudden, painful realisation.

'So you *did* get it,' the man surmised. 'And you probably opened it too.'

'Who is this? What do you want from me?'

'All I want to know for now is where Jesse is.'

'Jesse?' And what in God's name was this 'for now' supposed to mean? 'What do you want from Jesse?'

'Just tell me where I can find him.' Something in the man's voice sounded vaguely familiar, but Artur couldn't quite put his finger on what it was. His tone was calm, which only served to make the whole thing seem even more surreal. The contrast between his voice and the gruesome contents of the package was unsettling. The man seemed to think there was no need to threaten him, and in Artur's experience, that could only be a bad sign. From what he had seen, only people who had far from exhausted all their options could be so calm and composed.

'But I have no idea,' Artur said. 'I don't know where Jesse is.' For God's sake! He really wasn't as good a liar as he used to be.

'Should I take that as an invitation?

'I . . . um, an invitation?

'To talk face-to-face. Sometimes it's easier to talk when you look someone in the eyes.' He paused for a second, 'And shake hands.'

Artur's stomach tensed up. *Shake hands?* Was that really what he'd said? Artur had never been the type of person who would be willing to give up their right hand for anyone else, Jesse included. As a little boy, he had been forced to stand by and watch as his father and his older brother Werner were gunned down by an SS captain not long before the end of the Second World War. His mother had finally backed down and told the SS officer what he wanted to know, saving Artur's life and her own.

'I . . . um, I'm not sure if the address I have is still the right one, it's been a while . . .'

'Just give me the address.'

Chapter 3

'Out you get, your highness,' Jesse held the door of his Volvo open, somehow conjured up a tired smile and gave a light-hearted bow in Isa's direction. 'The queen mother awaits.'

Isa blinked and pouted. According to Sandra, she was 'just like her dad' when it came to her grumpy early-morning moods. It had been a cold start to the day for them in many respects. If it wasn't already bad enough that it was Monday, the words 'no more hazelnut spread', 'pit stop at Mum's house' and 'test' only served to make matters worse. Isa's mood was almost as icy as the temperature outside, which was now minus eleven degrees. An area of low pressure from Siberia had covered Germany in snow from the Baltic Sea to the Alps. They were calling it 'System Adrian' on the news.

Isa climbed wearily out of the back seat of the car with the stiff collar of her dark-blue pea coat turned up to her ears. Solitary snowflakes fell from the colourless sky and got caught in her silky blond hair as they twirled to the ground. She had insisted on wearing her red tartan skirt. When Jesse reminded her it was winter, her response was to put on a pair of dark blue tights with the toes cut off so that she could feel the lambskin inside her boots with her toes. That was the most important thing, after all.

Her footsteps crunched in the fresh snow, and Jesse could smell the Colgate wafting in the air as she plodded past him. Had she eaten the toothpaste instead of brushing her teeth? He resisted the urge to comment. His shift in the children's clinic at St Josef's hospital was due to start in half an hour. Best not to part ways on an argument.

He grabbed Isa's bag and followed her to the door. Looming above the brickwork on the ground floor of the apartment building were five floors of grey-tinged stone punctuated by traditional Berlin-style windows and elegant ornamental details. The black Victorian grille in front of the oak door at the entrance exuded the charm of an upper-class London area, even though Berlin Wilmersdorf certainly wasn't a patch on Chelsea or Mayfair. But no doubt that was exactly what Sandra's new boyfriend Leon had in mind when he rented the flat here on Hildegardstrasse. Leon Stein had spent a few years as a choreographer in the West End in London and had all the smug, over-the-top facial expressions to be expected of a dancer. He had squandered almost all his assets and he was hardly ever at home.

Isa had already buzzed upstairs and she was now standing in the open doorway of the apartment building.

Sandra was waiting for her on the third floor. Her blond hair was tied back in a ponytail and her thin, slightly pointed face was flushed from her early-morning dancing exercises and stretches. As usual, her blue eyes looked strained and slightly sad. They used to beam with light, but now they had the same look Jesse recognised in a lot of children who had been taken into care, himself included.

Isa threw her arms around Jesse and hugged him goodbye with all the strength she had in her arms. 'Bye, blue man!' she said softly. He smiled. Quite predictably, everything he was wearing was blue except for his boots. His winter jacket with its fur-trimmed hood was dark blue and his scarf and jeans were slightly lighter. Isa first noticed his penchant for blue when she was just four. Since then, she called him her 'blue man' every time she said hello or goodbye.

'Morning, Mum,' Isa mumbled as she scurried into the flat. She made a point of putting her scruffy Ugg boots away under the coat rack before darting across the whitewashed parquet towards her room.

'Morning, young lady.' Sandra gazed after her, raised her eyebrows and shot a sharp glare in Jesse's direction. Bare toes and no hat. Of course he was in her bad books. He was sure Sandra had noticed the 'eau de toothpaste' too.

'So,' Sandra began. 'Did you get my message?'

'What message?'

'Oh, it doesn't matter.' There was a strange undertone in her voice. Was she annoyed? Or nervous?

'What did you want?'

'Do you ever check your landline these days?'

Jesse shrugged. His house phone was usually on silent and he only really used the answerphone to screen his calls. Sandra completely failed to understand why he didn't feel duty-bound to answer messages. 'Why didn't you call my mobile instead?' he asked.

'You don't use voicemail—'

—and I have no desire to keep running around after you until you finally decide you can be bothered to answer, Jesse thought

to himself, mentally finishing the sentence for her. 'Just tell me what you wanted to talk to me about.'

'I told you, it doesn't matter. It's sorted now.'

There was a brief pause. He started to get annoyed, like he always did when he felt this mix of guilty conscience and rejection.

Isa's head appeared behind Sandra. 'Aren't you coming tonight, Dad?' she said, peering out from the gap between the door and her bedroom.

'Tonight?' Jesse looked from Isa to Sandra in confusion.

The woman he was still officially married to rubbed her right index finger with her left hand, like she always did when she felt awkward.

'*I* heard the message,' Isa smirked, adding fuel to the fire without realising it. Her mother glanced reproachfully over her shoulder, then Isa's head instantly disappeared.

'Do you need me to help?' asked Jesse.

'Help? How about you give me some *support*?'

'If you need someone to look after Isa—'

She wavered, her emotions fluctuating between irritation and – well, what was it?

'When are you going out?' Jesse asked.

'Six o'clock.'

'Is there a problem with me seeing my daughter? Is Leon around?'

'Nope,' a cheery voice replied from Isa's room. 'He's in Chicago'.

'I'm going to look at a little dance studio. I'm thinking maybe I can rent it and teach classes,' Sandra said. She sounded reluctant to tell him about it.

A dance studio. So that was it. 'While Leon is off touring the world making big bucks?'

'Leave it,' Sandra snapped flatly.

'Well, he's away so much—'

'Says Mr Doctors Without Borders himself!' Sandra said.

'At least you seem to be much more understanding of Mr Dancing Without Borders's absence.'

Sandra wanted to answer back, but instead she just stopped and closed her eyes for a moment. She smiled when she opened them and looked at him again. A distant smile. False and cautious. 'Please just leave Leon out of it. I don't want to have to worry about him.'

'Worry? About Leon?'

She looked at him silently and rubbed her finger again.

'Oh, come on!' Jesse said. 'Please tell me you're joking?'

The look in her eyes answered the question for her. For God's sake! Where had all this come from? 'What happened with Markus back then was different,' Jesse said. 'And you of all people should know that.'

'*He* says differently.'

Her use of the present tense didn't escape Jesse: *says*, not *said*. 'Have you been speaking to him?'

Sandra kept quiet.

He sighed and bit his tongue. 'And I'm guessing you've already asked Jule if she can do it?'

'Jule doesn't have time; she's working. But it doesn't matter anyway. Like I said, Isa will be fine on her own for a while.'

Jesse glanced at the clock. Six o'clock was too early for him really. He wanted to see Isa, but he was aware that the combination of 'Sandra like a cat on a hot tin roof' and 'Jesse running late' was a delicate one. 'I'll be there around six o'clock, give or take ten minutes,' he said.

Sandra looked far from happy.

'For sure,' he said.

'OK,' she sighed. 'By the way, I meant to ask: have you been to Adlershof recently?'

Jesse looked at her in surprise. 'No, what makes you think that?'

'It doesn't matter.'

'OK, well, see you tonight, then,' he said.

'Yeah, see you later.' Her voice was calmer now. That was one of the few advantages of their separation: the anger didn't take as long to subside. They could still push each other's buttons, but at least they'd managed to make more of an effort since the split.

The Volvo S60 made a brittle electronic sound when it started up. Jesse had bought the S60 on impulse from a used car dealer when he let Sandra keep the old Volvo estate after the split. He ended up hating the car in just a few weeks. It was too much: too sporty, with too much electronic equipment. The only thing he liked was the sound system, and that was mostly because of the excited look that crept onto Isa's face whenever he turned the volume up.

He cranked up the volume and rolled down the passenger-side window. Icy wind blew into the car. Billy Idol's 'White Wedding' blasted into his ears.

Worry. About Leon. What a load of crap.

Snowflakes drifted into his field of vision. He stared at the windscreen and found himself picturing Markus's stocky body there like a projected image. He saw the dark hair and his razor-sharp parting on that square skull of his. It suited him just as little as his false air of sophistication and his alleged fondness for dance. He was about as stiff as a snapped broom – just who was he kidding?

The old scar on Jesse's back itched again, like it often did whenever his thoughts turned to Markus and the accident. If it really was an accident. He still found that hard to believe.

Billy Idol's voice broke into a scream singing about a new start. Cynical, perhaps? Damn! It was much too late for him to start again. Now going to work again every day was the only thing he had left. Ever since the split he had been feeling more homeless than ever.

Start again.

That was what he did back then, after the accident. Focal retrograde amnesia. One day a light goes off, like someone's pulled a plug out of the socket, then you forget everything and boot up again. If human beings are a sum of their experiences and memories, he must have been completely erased at the age of thirteen. Except for his genes and fundamental skills such as speaking, running, calculating, cycling – oh, and the inability to swim properly. Other people had to tell him who he was. He had pieced himself together from the fragments. And even now, he still had the empty feeling of not really knowing who he was.

The window hummed as he rolled it up. He indicated. The best place to forget about it all was in the clinic at St Josef's. Or on a day out in the forest with Isa.

Chapter 4

Berlin – Monday, 7 January 2013, 3.52 p.m.

There was something not quite right about this girl, that much was clear. Marta was sitting next to Jule like a waxwork in the waiting room at St Josef's. Jule had wrapped Marta's forehead in a makeshift dressing that separated her dark hair into a tight helmet and long straggly strands. The twelve-year-old girl had her freezing-cold hands in her lap and was twiddling her fingers restlessly.

Jule was sick and tired of it all. She didn't know why she put herself through it. It wasn't the children's fault; their parents were the problem. She rarely got the chance to see their faces, but she knew what they were like. All you had to do was take one look at the children to see what kind of parents they had. Their faces when they pushed the door open in the morning and how their expressions changed when it was time to leave to go home again in the evening.

As far as Jule was concerned, parents should work damn hard to make sure they deserved their kids – and very few children deserved parents like these ones had. Over time she felt more and more inclined to believe that staying in a home was the best option for some children.

'Believe me, you're only saying that because you've never lived in one,' Sandra had replied when she said the same thing to her. And no doubt she was right, at least up to a point. What could Jule say about living in a children's home? Unlike Sandra, she came from the perfect family. At least from the outside looking in. Her dad was a dentist and her mother was a housewife. Her sister Angela, ever the conformist, had also bagged herself a dentist, and her big brother Benedikt worked for the CID in Hamburg. Jule hadn't been short of offers to follow in her sister's footsteps. She just chose not to as she found it deadly boring.

Jule saw herself as an average-height woman, maybe slightly prettier than average, with average-length, averagely blond hair, and average intelligence. She was sort of average in every respect. Apart from her intense green eyes, perhaps, and her deep voice, which didn't quite match up with her delicate frame.

She made every effort to overcome this. Her top marks at school were followed by a music degree, which she dropped out of and exchanged for two years on the road as the singer in a band – an average one, of course. Sex, drugs and rock 'n roll. It all sounded promising at the age of twenty-two, kind of like a rebellion. But a couple of years on, the initial appeal had worn off and it began to feel like she was constantly on the run. They had all been dragging a ball and chain behind them for a long time, all with their own unique personalised engraving. Ghosts that appeared in the night.

'I guess it just reached a tipping point,' was her cautious response whenever anyone asked her why she'd left the band. She kept the real reason to herself. Even Sandra only knew half of the story.

She threw herself into her studies after that, much to her parents' delight. Back to the good old picture-perfect world. OK, so it was psychology and not dentistry – but still, it could have been worse. But what *couldn't* have been worse, at least in their eyes, was her choice of job. They had been arguing about it again just two weeks ago, on Christmas Eve.

It was a touchy subject for Jule, hence her highly strung response. She had her own doubts about her job, but for different reasons from her mother, who had no idea what it was like to witness the kinds of things she saw day in, day out. There were children who had faeces in their underwear every day and children who often had nothing to eat because their parents had more 'important' things to buy. And there were kids who got beaten up, sometimes in private, sometimes openly.

The worst thing about it was that Jule didn't know what to do with the anger she felt inside. These children had such gaping voids in their lives it made her lose hope. These weren't the kind of holes you could just patch over. You couldn't hold back the flood either. But you could possibly drown in it.

She sighed and straightened her back in her seat. Tried to smile away the increasingly severe frown around her mouth. For fuck's sake. She was far too given to smiling when she felt bad. She smiled at home, at university and on stage. The laughter lines around her mouth were going to be deeper than the ones around her eyes.

The only person Jule didn't feel like she had to smile around was Sandra. She had been happy to get Sandra's call the night before, despite how late it was, and she was looking forward to seeing her. 'Six o'clock tomorrow at Café Einstein?' Sandra's voice turned serious and quiet all of a sudden, like she was afraid someone might be listening to their conversation. 'There's something I *desperately* have to tell you about Jesse and Garmisch. But please don't say a word to him!' Sandra said. She didn't really know why she said that – it wasn't as if she was constantly bumping into Jesse.

The fact that she wanted to talk about Jesse was nothing new. It had been that way for years – decades, in fact. Jule repeatedly found herself being forced to summon an almost superhuman amount of patience when conversation turned to Jesse. But this time it sounded different, not the usual *Jesse did this, Jesse did that*. It obviously had something to do with one of the old stories from the home, and Sandra had sounded worried – really quite worried.

Sometimes Jule almost envied Sandra's past in the children's home. Sandra had *permission* to feel lost. Unlike her. You weren't supposed to feel lost if things were only averagely bad.

Jule checked the time. Just two more hours and it'd be six o'clock. If they had to keep waiting like this, she'd be too late to catch Sandra. The back of her plastic chair creaked. The functional corridor lighting of St Josef's hospital wiped out all the shadows, including the ones on Marta's face.

By this stage, Jule realised it was quite possible that the girl lived on the streets. She had only been coming to the centre for a few days. Today she turned up with her cheek badly swollen and a blood-soaked handkerchief pressed onto her forehead above her left eyebrow. There was a gash beneath the handkerchief.

When Jule tried to get in touch with Marta's parents, it turned out that the address and phone number she had didn't exist. Perhaps Marta wasn't even her name. Still, Jule gave them Marta's name and address when they registered her at St Josef's. Anything else would have only caused unnecessary problems.

Now they'd ended up here of all places, in the outpatient clinic where Jesse worked. Jesse was the last person she wanted to run into, but St Josef's was the nearest hospital and, given the snow and the travel conditions, that was all that mattered. Perhaps she'd be lucky and get assigned a different doctor instead.

Sandra and Isa popped into her head. A smile flashed over her lips. She was dotty about that little girl and wished she could have been her godmother. Anyway, that hadn't happened. She still had her suspicions that Jesse was the reason why.

She found herself wondering once again whether she would have taken the job working for the youth organisation if she had ever had her own children. The job was demanding, and the money wasn't all that attractive for a psychologist like her. But she didn't have any children. And that was nobody's fault but her own.

She straightened her back again, stretched her neck and tried to ignore the pressure on her bladder. She smiled encouragingly, but Marta didn't even notice.

'Marta? Everything OK?'

'Hmm.'

A nurse was scurrying past them and Jule took the opportunity to ask about the wait. 'Excuse me, do you know roughly how long it—'

'Quarter of an hour,' the nurse called out without even turning around.

Enough time for another quick visit to the toilet. The girl was adamant she wouldn't go with her, so Jule stood up alone and took another anxious look at her – Marta, or whatever her name was. She was wearing a red anorak that was much too thin for the weather. As Jule made her way to the toilet, a doctor came towards her in almost as much of a hurry as the nurse had been. He was wearing a white surgical mask and a surgical cap, with space between them for his eyes, like he was looking out of a helmet visor. Their eyes met briefly. His irises were a dark shade of amber. She wasn't sure if it was Jesse or not. There was no recognition in his eyes.

If Jesse was on duty and had been called to one of the operating theatres, she either had a good chance of avoiding him or they were just going to have a longer wait. Emergencies were always a priority, that was just the way things went.

Chapter 5

Berlin – Monday, 7 January 2013, 4.19 p.m.

Jesse dismissed the two white bones from the screen with a click of the mouse. Next, please! The pace was fast in casualty, but that didn't stress him out like it did most of his colleagues. He enjoyed the variety and liked how the job allowed him to focus on the patients. All of them were emergencies in their own unique way. He would never consider settling down as a general paediatrician or trying to get himself into a senior position. Working in a practice meant you had to appoint assistants and deal with the accounting procedures for medical insurance. He was too restless to work as a senior consultant; he rarely lasted a long time in one place. And he was even less likely to stay if the paperwork was threatening to take up more of his time than the patients.

'Jesse?'

Dr Rahul Taneja was standing in the doorway between the two consulting rooms. Dark rings shimmered beneath her similarly dark brown eyes. 'I need to do an ultrasound in room two, can we switch?'

'No problem.' Jesse logged off the computer and took his keys and his patient cards, then pulled his doctor's bag out from under the table so quickly that it scraped against the metal base of the roller stool. Another scar on the leather. But Jesse liked every single mark. He even took his doctor's bag with him when he didn't need it, like here in the hospital. It made him feel secure. Each scratch was like a diary entry. He liked it when memories had something unalterable about them, something that couldn't be erased.

Quick change. Dr Rahul Taneja pushed a pale-faced boy of around six years old into the treatment room, accompanied by his mother and her anxious, restless eyes. Jesse gave them both a friendly nod as he passed them on his way to consulting room one. His keys clattered as he dropped them next to the keyboard on the plastic-coated desk. The key ring – a small stuffed lion that Isa had given him – landed on its back. His doctor's bag landed in its usual spot right under the table. The noise that erupted from Jesse's stomach sounded like the lion had come to life.

He ignored his hunger and scanned the name and medical history on the patient card on the top of the pile. Then he stepped into the corridor through the sliding door and walked into the waiting area. Fourteen pairs of eyes were staring at him, including Jule's. He'd noticed her a while ago when he'd come to collect another patient, but she barely acknowledged his nod in her direction. Her blond hair was pinned up. Her soft, feminine features and round curved eyebrows looked tense.

'Marta Wilhelm?' Jesse asked, addressing the whole room.

Jule got up slowly, with the same look of displeasure on her face that he was feeling on the inside. Oh great. What the hell was *she* doing here anyway? She knew he worked here.

He looked at the girl standing beside Jule and the doctor in him automatically took over. Pubescent, thin, hungry frame, neglected-looking wintry pale skin, fresh haematoma on her left cheekbone, a dressing above her eye, probably covering the laceration mentioned in the medical history questionnaire. It was obvious that someone had hit her. Her eyes were fixed on the floor, as if the world above the hospital lino was full of incalculable risks.

Jesse sighed internally.

This kind of thing was the reason he did his job. And this kind of thing was the reason he sometimes hated his job. Or at least he hated the feeling of powerlessness. Time and time again he felt overcome with a need to do something to help. Something more than just stitch up a gash on a child's forehead. But most of the time, all he could do was notify social services if he suspected that something was amiss. He silently thanked Sandra for making sure Isa wasn't as lost as this girl.

'Hi, Jesse,' Jule said drily as she passed him on her way into the consulting room.

'Hi, Jule,' Jesse mumbled, then quickly went over to the washbasin and activated the mechanical dispenser with his elbow. Disinfectant squirted out into his open hand. He rubbed it vigorously, almost as if he was trying to wash away his distaste. Then he turned to face the girl. 'Hi, Marta, I'm Jesse. Jesse Berg.' He pointed towards the examination bed in the middle of the room. 'Have a seat.'

The girl flinched, even though Jesse had spoken softly and calmly. She seemed strangely startled and her mind appeared to be working overtime. She walked over to the bed like she was being controlled by someone with a remote.

'Have we met before?' asked Jesse.

She seemed to have composed herself now and gave a faint shake of the head.

'OK, then. So tell me, what happened to you?'

Marta's mouth stayed zipped tight.

'She had an accident,' Jule explained. 'She needs someone to take a look at the wound.'

'What sort of accident?' Jesse asked. 'In the centre where you work?

Jule hesitated and took a moment to think. 'No.'

'OK, then. So how did it happen?' He glanced from Jule to Marta, then back to Jule.

Silence. The only sound to be heard was the buzzing of the cool white ceiling lights.

'Right, then, let's take a look.' He started gently unwrapping the girl's dressing while she sat there on the bed as stiff as a board, with legs like two steel brackets. Her eyes were the only part of her that moved, flitting around the room like she was looking for an escape route. The wound above her eyebrow was relatively fresh, perhaps from that same morning. It was a gaping cut around two centimetres long.

'Don't worry, Marta. We'll get you sorted,' he murmured and gave an encouraging smile. 'But first I just need to stop it hurting so much.' He went over to the shelf and filled a syringe with two millilitres of mepivacaine, keeping his back to Marta so she wouldn't see the needle.

'Do you think you can glue the wound, or— ?' Jule was suddenly standing there next to him. She spoke softly and avoided using the word *stitch*.

'I reckon glue should do the trick.'

Jule stared at the needle. She quickly averted her gaze. Jesse removed the needle from the syringe without saying a thing. He could manage to drip the local anaesthetic into the wound with just the blunt plastic cannula. 'Don't worry, Marta,' he said, then turned around and stopped mid-sentence. Marta was standing in the middle of the room, staring at him.

'Is everything OK, Marta?'

She nodded with a strangely frantic air.

'I just need you to lie down now so I can drip some anaesthetic into your wound and stop it hurting so much. Can you do that for me?'

Marta didn't budge. Her eyes wandered over to the door and then back to Jesse again. Her body was tensed up like a bowstring and her hands were buried deep inside the pockets of her anorak.

Jesse tried to make his body language as unthreatening and reassuring as possible. He let his arms dangle by his sides, smiled at her and stayed right where he was. 'It won't hurt, I promise. Just a couple of minutes, and—'

Out of nowhere, Marta seemed to positively explode. She snatched her hands out of her pockets, made a dash for the sliding door and vanished into the corridor in the blink of an eye.

'Marta!' Jule shouted after her.

The hurried squeaking of rubber soles resonated from the corridor, followed by a startled scream and the clanging of metallic instruments clattering onto the ground. Jesse made it to the door before Jule and ran down the corridor past Irina, the nurse who was standing there clutching her arm with her mouth agape. Silver instruments were scattered all around her feet. 'Which way did she go?' he shouted.

'Er – the waiting room.'

Jesse dashed through the open doorway. Marta was nowhere to be seen. His white doctor's coat was flapping around his legs. Patients were gawping at him. Frank Reutlein leaned forward from inside the glass compartment at the reception desk with a curious look on his face.

'I'm looking for a girl,' Jesse called out as he ran past. 'Dark hair, gash on her forehead?'

'Oh . . . she left, I think,' Reutlein called out from behind him.

A bitterly cold wind greeted him when he got to the door. It was already dark outside. Snowflakes tumbled into the light of the street lamps from the slate-grey sky, and the footprints in the snow carved dividing lines into the footpath alongside Wüsthoffstrasse. Marta was nowhere to be seen.

'Where is she?' Jule appeared next to him. A cloud of warm air billowed out of her mouth.

Jesse raised his hands, completely baffled.

Jule hurried past him and onto the narrow single-lane street, stepping over a ridge of snow between two cars along the way. She looked all around, then headed back to Jesse. 'Great,' she grumbled. 'Just great. Couldn't you at least have taken a dropper out instead of a syringe?'

'You think she ran away because of the syringe?'

Jule brushed a few loose strands of hair away from her face. 'No idea,' she panted.

'There wasn't even a needle on it,' Jesse said.

'Maybe you should have called a woman instead.'

Jesse knew what she meant. Most injuries like Marta's were impact wounds from being hit by men. 'My female colleague's ill. Otherwise I would have called her in.'

'Well, whatever happened to her, you definitely seemed to scare her.'

Her reproach stung.

'You sound like Sandra. Are you the chicken or the egg?'

'Sorry, what?'

'Is Sandra the one who keeps telling you old horror stories about me, or do *you* talk *her* into believing that I'm someone she should be scared of?' She even seemed worried about Leon this morning. Because of me? What a load of nonsense.'

The resigned look on Jule's face became rigid and hard. 'Of course. Clearly there's some sort of conspiracy against you,' she said. 'You know what they call it in psychology when someone projects their own issues onto others? Transference.' Jesse bit his tongue. This risked turning into an argument full of old sensitivities. It was the kind of conversation he no interest in having. He had to get back to the clinic. Besides, he was freezing in his doctor's coat, and the snow was seeping into his medical clogs.

'So what now?' Jule asked. She had clearly arrived at the same conclusion as him.

'I'll get them to make an announcement at the reception desk. Maybe she's still in the hospital. That's about as much as we can do.'

Jule turned to face the clinic with a pensive look on her face. It was strangely quiet: the snow was muffling the noise from the city. A siren sounded the air from A & E. Blue snowflakes fluttered over the roof of St Josef's. 'She isn't in the hospital,' Jule said.

'How do you know?'

'Children like Marta don't just hide around the corner when they run away. They try to put as much distance as possible between themselves and whatever it is they're afraid of.'

Children like Marta. Or like me, Jesse thought. For a brief moment he was overcome with a childish longing for Jule to show him the same understanding she had shown Marta.

'Perhaps she's on her way back to the centre,' said Jule. 'I'll go and see if she's there.'

Jule's goodbye was even chillier than her hello. She pulled her coat around her, put her woolly hat on and trudged down Wüsthoffstrasse towards the centre where she worked.

Jesse looked up to the sky. Gloomy and dark, scattered with white dots. He pushed his concerns about Marta out of his mind. There were other patients in the waiting room who weren't going anywhere. He glanced at his watch: an old classic with a black dial and self-winding system. Artur had given it to him as a present when he passed his exams at the age of eighteen. The watch said it was twenty to five. The second hand was ticking away frantically. He wanted to pick up Isa at around six o'clock. He was going to be late if he didn't get one hell of a move on.

As he made his way back to the clinic, he couldn't stop thinking about the strange look in Marta's eyes. She wasn't staring at the syringe in fear. She was looking at *him*. He didn't like to admit it, but Jule was right. Marta was afraid of him.

Sixteen minutes after he'd left the clinic, Jesse was finally back at his desk. His leather doctor's bag was in its usual spot in the shadows beneath the desk, and his keys were still next to the keyboard. But the lion was no longer on its back staring at the easy-wipe surface.

Chapter 6

Jesse turned the key in the locker door and anxiously glanced out of the window. The lion swung back and forth energetically on the key ring as he opened the mousy-grey door. He was thirteen minutes late already and he hadn't even set off yet. The low-pressure system they were calling 'Adrian' on the weather forecast was baring its teeth. Snow was falling thick and fast, getting heavier all the time. On days like this in Adlershof, the snow used to pile up like a wall against the back door to the kitchen.

He reached for his Caterpillar boots with the kind of automatic motion that can locate things even when the person is half asleep. But instead he found himself grasping into empty space.

He stopped what he was doing, flummoxed.

The locker was empty. Two wire hangers were dangling from the metal rod, rocking from side to side in the draft from the door he'd just opened. His dark-blue coat had disappeared, as had his scarf and his boots. The only trace of his boots was a couple of dirty prints on the bottom of the locker.

He was too baffled to get really angry. Who in their right mind would steal clothes from the doctors' breakout area? And how had they managed to open the locker door? It didn't look like anyone had tampered with the lock. He jiggled his key back and forth in the lock just to check, then stopped what he was doing when the lion caught his eye. When he thought about it, he realised Marta had been standing right in front of his desk with those big eyes and her hands buried deep in the pockets of her red anorak. Bloody hell, was it *her*? Had she pocketed the key while he was getting the syringe ready? She would have had plenty of time to clear out his locker while he and Jule were out on the street looking for her. But what good were his clothes to her? He cursed again when he realised his wallet was in his coat, along with his ID, his driving licence and his bank cards. Things like that were a complete pain in the arse to replace, not to mention the money he had lost.

He contemplated calling the police but gave up on that idea. He did have Marta's patient card with her address and her personal information on it, after all. He checked his watch and felt the pangs of guilt setting in again. Twenty past. Isa was waiting for him, then there was Sandra to deal with. And he still had so much stuff to sort out when he got there. He fished his smartphone out of his pocket and called Sandra on her landline. 'Hi,' Leon's voice rasped through the speaker. 'The Steins are out dancing at the moment. Please leave a message and we'll get back to you as soon as we can.'

The Steins. Dancing. It was bad enough that this guy was sharing a bed with Sandra. But did he really have to call them by his surname? He scrolled to Sandra's mobile number with furious fingers, but she didn't answer the phone. The only person he hadn't called yet was Isa. Leon had recently given her an iPhone as a gift. It was a blatant case of bribery – and a particularly objectionable one at that, considering that Jesse had given Isa an iPod just two months before.

Isa wasn't picking up either.

The wallet would just have to wait. He needed to check on Isa first.

The squeaking of his medical clogs echoed between the concrete walls as he walked towards the car in the underground garage. He opened the boot and put the doctor's bag in the space between two empty drinks crates and a toolbox that didn't have a single scratch yet. He'd borrowed it from a colleague when he moved to the new flat and he still hadn't given it back.

The low-pressure system welcomed him to the road with snow and poor visibility. He crawled along in first or second gear for most of the journey, cursing his summer wheels and the car dealer.

It was just after half past seven when Jesse finally stopped on the pavement outside Sandra's apartment building. He was over an hour and a half late. Heavy snowflakes tumbled onto his face; one melted on his lips. His worn doctor's clogs filled up with snow as he made his way to the front door. Just moments ago, his feet were still warm from the hot air in the car. Now they were getting cold and wet.

He rang the bell and waited for the familiar sound of someone pressing the buzzer or Isa's voice over the intercom. But it remained silent except for the whispers of the falling snow and the muffled bursts of noise from the traffic.

He rang the buzzer again, long and sustained at first, then an impatient staccato. It was quite possible that Isa would fail to notice a firework display on New Year's Eve if she had her iPod on full blast. Suddenly the door opened from the inside. A young man with a pointed nose and a bobble hat pulled right down over his forehead bounced out of the building. He eyed Jesse up with a blank expression, then noticed the doctor's bag and the hospital logo stitched onto it. He let him in.

If you were a serial killer, Jesse thought to himself, *all you'd need to do is carry a doctor's bag . . .*

He took the stairs two at a time. The melody of the doorbell rang out faintly through the white door, but nobody opened. He rapped on the door with his knuckles. The sound of his fist on the door combined with the soft clicking of the lock. The door gave way and swung open a touch. It was pitch black in the flat.

'Isa?'

His voice echoed in the staircase.

Jesse pushed the small lever on the lock with his index finger. He promised himself he'd have a word with Isa. Sometimes she left the door on the latch when she was staying with him, so she didn't always have to think about the 'stupid key' and she could just push the door open instead.

'Hello? Isa? Are you there?' Jesse stepped inside the flat and switched on the light. The hall was ordered and all the doors were closed, except for the one to the living room right at the end. He looked around. A row of shoes under Sandra's coats on the rack. A bowl for the keys and a small stack of mail on the sideboard to the right. Music coming from Isa's room to the left, so muffled it was unrecognisable.

He had to smile when he pictured her there: eyes closed, earphones in her glowing red ears, chin bobbing up and down, completely oblivious to everything around her. Then he noticed the smell. A smell he knew all too well, and one that certainly didn't belong here.

It had to be a mistake.

He looked over to the open door to the living room at the end of the hallway. Sandra had put the beige suede sofa in the middle of the spacious room with its back to the door. Its outlines were clearly defined against the rest of the dark space in the room. The hallway was reflected as a rectangle of light in the shiny new high-definition TV on the wall. Was the smell coming from the living room?

The sandy-coloured runner in the hallway cushioned his footsteps. There was a switch panel on the right, between the sideboard and the kitchen door. Leon was into that kind of thing. Control every single light from anywhere. Jesse pressed the button at the top, and the living room light flickered on with a warm, subtle glow. Ambient lighting. Sandra's choice. The soft music kept rattling away to the left behind him in Isa's room.

The smell was definitely coming from the living room. It was stronger now, and it was unmistakable.

Jesse hesitated. Suddenly his feet felt like lead. A warning voice inside his head was getting louder. The door to the living room was open like an invitation. The back of the sofa obscured his view of part of the floor, but over by the wall underneath the TV he could see the shape of an overturned coffee table. Shards glinted in the beam of the downlights on the flokati rug. He felt hot and cold all at once. He forced himself to move closer. The rug was covered in spatters. Spatters that matched the smell.

One last step, then he was inside the room.

The flokati rug was like a white field with sharply defined contours. Lying there on the floor directly behind the sofa was Sandra. She was wearing light cotton trousers with creases, a matching cardigan that went down to her hips and a champagne-coloured top underneath. The smooth fabric was soaked in dark, merging islands of blood in several places. The right sleeve of her cardigan was in tatters, and there were gaping cuts in her arm and her hand. Sandra's eyes gazed just a hair's breadth past Jesse, staring into the abyss.

For a second, he thought she was looking right at him. Maybe she was just injured and had been waiting for him. Maybe it was just as he had thought: the smell didn't belong here, or it was a trick of the senses.

But it was real. It crept into his nose and his brain and had him gasping for air.

His hands clutched the back of the sofa. A gruesome picture flashed before his eyes. A gleaming rectangle, a woman and a pattern of dark flecks, like he'd seen this all before. He felt sick. His legs gave way and he supported himself on the back of the sofa.

'Isa?'

No answer.

The window and the door to the balcony on the right were closed. Snowflakes were tumbling to the ground in the courtyard between them. He saw his pale reflection in the double glazing.

'Isa!'

Suddenly he regained control of his legs. He burst into the hallway and flung the door of Isa's room open so hastily that it banged against the wall and rebounded. The room was empty. The soft, even beat was louder now and droned on regardless. Isa's forest-green duvet was piled up on the bed. Written on the wall above it in large, spidery red capital letters were the words:

You don't deserve her.

Chapter 7

The words resounded in his head like the tolling of a deadened bell.

'Isa?'

No answer. Just the music in the background, like a ghostly whisper. He tore the crumpled duvet off the sheet and shook it in the air, almost as if Isa could be hiding in there and might fall out. He found her earphones and her iPod under the pillow. The shiny black screen was covered in smudges from her fingers, and the cable connecting the earphones was all twisted, like she had shoved the iPod under the pillow in a hurry. He pulled out the plug and the music stopped dead. The silence was more unbearable than the gentle hum of the beats.

'Isabelle?'

He lifted the mattress, looked under the bed and opened the wardrobe. Suddenly Isa's scent wafted into the air. He swept the clothes hangers to one side, hoping to see her little face staring back at him, hiding from whoever or whatever it was. But all that was there was the plywood panel at the back of the wardrobe. He ran from room to room, rummaged through Sandra's wardrobe, then checked the bath and the dirty laundry basket. They often played hide and seek in the house in Esslingen when Isa was small, and now he was searching every nook and cranny he could think of, hoping to hear her giggling somewhere in a corner of the flat like she always used to when she couldn't hold back any longer.

No such luck.

His eyes rested on the door to the one room he still hadn't searched: the living room, where Sandra's body was lying on the floor. His throat felt tight. He wanted to close his eyes so that he wouldn't have to have to look at her. But that wouldn't help at all. He needed to be sure.

He went back into the living room. 'Isa? Isa, if you're there then *please* come out.' He wasn't religious – the last time he'd been to a church service was decades ago, in the children's home, when they pelted the visiting Catholic priest with fir cones – but he felt like praying now, to someone or something. 'It's me, Isa. You don't have to be afraid.'

The curtains rustled as he raised them and let them fall back into place. He opened the door onto the balcony. The snow outside was pristine and the cold sharp.

He closed the door mechanically, trying to run away from the pain unfurling inside of him. He knelt in front of Sandra and forced himself to look at her, to endure her looking back at him so vacantly. The image of a sheet came into his head, brown, so palpable he could almost touch it. He didn't know why. They hadn't ever used brown sheets for the dead on any of his Doctors Without Borders missions, not in Haiti or Darfur, Sudan. And if he and his team weren't based in the area, then cracked earth and shallow roadside ditches were the only burial sites around. The only sheet that covered everything was the dust. But this wasn't one of his Doctors without Borders missions. This wasn't a foreign country.

This was Berlin. This was Sandra.

He knew it was no use, but he felt for her pulse anyway. The fact that her heart had stopped beating still came as a shock. He forced himself to be calm, to get back on the trail and at least try to stay focused. The doctor in him established that Sandra's skin was cool, but she wasn't *cold*.

She couldn't have been dead for long. If he had arrived on time, maybe she would still be alive, and Isa would still be here.

He brushed his trembling fingers over Sandra's eyelids and closed her eyes. A tide of memories swept over him. Sandra aged thirteen, at Adlershof, when she snubbed and scorned him after his accident. He had no idea what he'd done to her earlier, in the *before*, to make her treat him that way. Then Sandra a year later, at the age of fourteen: those hesitant glances as if to say she couldn't believe she liked *him* of all the people. Their first kiss in the ski room; Sandra fuming with rage, irreconcilable; Sandra's laughter, her forgiveness; Sandra's face at Isa's birth: screwed up in pain, then relieved, drenched in tears of happiness. Almost his entire life had Sandra in it. Except the *before* part, which was so alien to him that he could almost understand why Sandra was so full of contempt for him in the beginning. He was someone else in the *before* part. Someone he didn't understand. Someone who secretly made him feel ashamed.

And despite all that she still chose him, married him and gave him the gift of Isa.

Isa, who had now vanished.

The thought of her iPod popped back into his head. But just where was her iPhone? He snatched his mobile phone out of the pocket of his doctor's coat. Why hadn't he thought of that right away? He scrolled to her name with trembling fingers and called the number. Perhaps Leon's attempt at bribery would come to some good use after all. He listened out in case he could hear the phone ringing nearby. But the only sound to be heard was the ringing tone in his ear. Then a crackling and rustling sound. Jesse's heart skipped a beat.

'Dad?' Isa's voice was just a muffled whisper.

'Isa! Where are you, sweetheart? Are you all right?'

'Dad, shh! You have to be quiet, he—' Something rattled in the background. Then Isa shrieked.

'Isa! What's going on? Can you hear me?'

Instead of an answer, all he could hear was the interference on the line. It was getting quieter with every second. 'Hello? Can you hear me? Are you OK?'

He heard a clicking sound, a loud noise that was gradually getting louder, then a dull thud and more silence. Was that a car door? 'Isa! Say something!'

There was a rustling sound, then the line went dead.

Jesse stared at the phone in his hand, then called Isa again and listened to the excruciatingly even ringing tone for a while until the attempt to connect was automatically terminated.

He lowered the phone from his ear. His head was completely empty. Best not to think about anything. Not a single thing! Every conceivable thought was just too terrible.

The sound of his phone ringing snapped him out of his trance. His hand trembled when he saw the name on the screen and pressed the phone to his ear. 'Isa? Are you OK? What's going on?'

'I . . . I have to tell you . . .' Isa hesitated and sobbed. Jesse forgot to breathe. More muffled background noise, then suddenly he heard the horn from a car driving past at high speed. Of course! She was on a road somewhere, maybe a motorway.

'Don't,' Isa began again, her voice quivering. 'Don't call the police or try to look for me.'

'Don't . . . what?'

'Dad, please, you can't talk to the police, OK?'

'Isa? Who said that? Who says that I can't talk to the police?

'I don't know . . . He has this thing on his head with circles of glass for eyes, like an inse—' He heard a crashing sound. Isa cried out in pain.

'Isa! Is everything okay?' Jesse clenched his fists. It was as if the blow had struck him. 'Hello? Listen to me, whoever you are: leave my daughter alone!' No response. All Jesse could hear was the rustling and the noise from the road – that, and the faint whispering of a man's voice in the background.

'Dad, please,' Isa sobbed. 'If the police come looking for me he's going to kill me.'

Jesse held his breath. 'Isa? Tell me where you are! Who's there with you?

She sniffed. Her distorted breath hissed out of the phone and into his ear. Jesse could clearly see her little fingers clinging to the phone; he heard the rising and falling of her ribcage. Lone cars whipped past Isa on the other end of the line. He could vaguely hear the man's muffled voice in the silence between each passing car.

Isa sobbed again. 'Dad?'

'Yes?'

'You've got to forget about me.'

A truck thundered past. The line went dead that very second. Silence.

He stared at the screen, shaken.

He quickly pressed redial. The phone crackled. A monotonous female voice answered: *'I'm sorry, but the person you have called is not available at the moment—'*

Jesse lowered the phone. Stared into the void.

You've got to forget about me?

He knelt in front of Sandra. Blood was splattered under her chin. There was something expressionless and alarmingly peaceful about her face as she lay there with her eyes closed, all life drained from her muscles.

He leaned over and put his hand on her cheek. 'I don't know who it was,' he whispered, 'but I promise you I'm going to find him and bring Isa back.'

Suddenly Jesse heard a voice in the hallway: 'Sandra?'

He spun around.

Had he left the front door open? A face appeared above the beige horizon created by the armrest of the suede sofa. Jule's face.

'Jesse? What are you—?' Her pupils widened and her mouth opened slowly. Her movements were as slow as her brain, which still couldn't believe what she was seeing.

Jesse got up, dumbstruck.

Jule's eyes darted from Sandra to Jesse and back again. She was dangling a key on a light-brown string in her right hand, and the door to the flat was open behind her. The timer ticked in the staircase and the light went out.

'What . . . what have you done?' Her hand gravitated towards her mouth.

'Me? What do you mean, what have *I* done?'

Jule slowly backed away.

'Jule, wait, let me—'

She turned to face the exit, as if on cue, and seemed to be gauging the distance.

Jesse made his decision in a split second. There was no way he was going to let Jule call the police. Isa would be in danger if she did. He jumped over the sofa. One of his clogs slipped halfway down his foot. Jule started running that second, but it was much too late, and she wasn't fast enough. Jesse stumbled as he caught up with her and tried to hold on to her. She stumbled and ran into the sideboard in the hallway. The stone bowl holding the keys crashed to the floor and the feet of the sideboard scraped over the parquet. Jesse clambered past her to the door and slammed it shut, then leaned against it with his back and blocked her path.

Jule clutched her lower abdomen and leaned against the wall between the door to the bedroom and the kitchen with the look of a cornered animal in her eyes. They stood there face-to-face for a moment, silently sizing each other up and breathing heavily.

'I have nothing to do with this,' Jesse said. 'You have to believe me.'

Jule's ribcage expanded and her eyes flitted back and forth. Her agitated breath in the silence of the flat was unbearable.

Jule suddenly pushed away from the wall and fled into the kitchen, vanishing from his sight. Jesse heard her opening one of the drawers. The clattering of metal was so loud it made him flinch.

'Jule, please be calm. I swear I have nothing to do with it. I only just got here, just like you!'

Silence.

Jesse cautiously moved closer to the kitchen door. 'Somebody's taken Isa. I wasn't trying to hurt you. I just didn't want you to call the police.'

He could hear Jule breathing through the open kitchen door. In. Out. In. Out. Quick and even. Jesse stepped into the doorway. The kitchen fittings gleamed in the glow of the halogen spotlights. Jule stood with her back pressed against the fridge. She brushed a blond strand of hair from her face with her left hand and was holding a carving knife in the other.

'Whoa, whoa, whoa!' He lifted his hands in a pacifying motion. An old memory flashed into his head. He had been up against someone with a knife once before, when he was a young boy.

Why did life always have to be such a fucked-up circle? How come the moments you wanted to forget always came back around?

'Put it away, Jule,' he begged her, his voice strained and hoarse. 'I'm not going to do anything to you. I didn't do anything to Sandra either.'

'Let me go, then!' Jule's voice wobbled. Light bounced off the steel blade. Her grip was so tight that her knuckles were white and her wrist tendons were bulging.

'Only when I'm sure you're not going to call the police.'

'Don't you dare come any closer.'

'Jule, please. I'm not going to hurt you. This is about Isa.'

She gave a short, abrupt shake of the head. She felt for the edge of her coat pocket with her free hand, then she delved inside and fumbled around for something. Jesse already knew what it was before he saw it. He felt hot and cold at the same time. 'Jule, wait!' I'm begging you, please, don't do it.'

Jule pulled her smartphone out of her pocket and held it up so she could keep an eye on Jesse at the same time as using her phone. She held the flat black case with the fingers of her left hand while she unlocked the screen with her thumb. She bit her bottom lip anxiously. Jesse knew that all she had to do was key in three numbers. And press the green phone icon.

Chapter 8

Jesse's eyes were fixed on his opponent, not on the knife in his hand. Jesse was fourteen, but he wasn't stupid or naive. He knew he only needed to look into his eyes to know what move he was going to make next.

A dozen black enamel lampshades were hanging from the ceiling above them. The white inner sides reflected the light from the bulbs into the dining room, and the oppressively heavy beamed ceiling remained dimly lit in the half shadow.

Jesse pivoted with his hands out in front of his chest, mirroring the boy circling around him with a table knife in his hand. The knife had a rounded tip and small, blunt serrated edge – pretty laughable, really. But then again, no more laughable than a stone or a bottle. If you really wanted to kill someone, you could drown them in a chamber pot – Jesse had learned that in the months after the accident. Even if the opponent was as tough as Markus.

A circle of children and adolescents had gathered around them. Sandra, Bernadette, Mattheo, Peter, Richard and Alois were there, along with all the other kids who had conspired against him and kept their mouths shut this whole time. He asked all of them directly, interrogated them to find out if they knew anything about that night, whether they knew how the accident had happened, who was there or might have been there. But none of them said anything. They all stood by Artur's version of events: it was an accident, end of story. Sometimes you just had to keep saying something for long enough and it would turn into the truth.

All eyes were on him. The air was buzzing with excitement, as it always does when a fight is on the cards. But this was more than a brawl, more than just a couple of kids offloading their pent-up aggressions. Everyone in the circle knew that. He could smell Markus's fear. Although Markus was the one with the knife, his forehead was covered in sweat, his breathing was irregular, and his larynx looked like it was about to burst out of his skin when he gulped.

It's him or me, Jesse thought to himself.

They moved in circles, each boy stalking the other. Every time one of them took a step, the other boy followed. It could have almost been a dance, but it was war.

He wasn't like the other boys. Ever since the accident – and he didn't remember anything from before then – he hadn't shot any pigeons or crows. He hadn't trampled on any insects either. The fact that he didn't get scared in moments like these made him feel like there was something amiss with him, like he wasn't quite himself. So maybe it was true what they all said? That he was different before?

Cold-blooded.

Angry.

'I've told you,' Markus hissed. 'One more time and you're in for it.' He twisted the knife in his hand anxiously.

'It won't be the first time, will it? Are you gonna have another go?'

'I don't know why you keep spreading that shit. But if you insist, then why not?'

'I talk shit?' A cold fury took hold of Jesse. 'Me?'

'Mattheo saw you yesterday. So don't try to deny it.'

Jesse could have torn the little snitch to pieces. Or at least shot him a glance that scared the shit out of him. But he didn't dare take his eyes off Markus. 'And what exactly did Mattheo tell you?'

'Think about it. I'm sure it'll come to you, arsehole.'

'I can't think of anything.'

Markus's eyes momentarily flitted to one side – to the girl. Jesse suddenly understood. It was about Sandra. About Sandra and the ski room. Markus was jealous and felt compelled to defend Sandra. But why? He had given her a necklace and they had kissed, that was all. What the hell had Mattheo said to him?

'Markus, leave him alone,' said Sandra. 'Nothing happened.'

'Nothing happened?' snapped Markus. 'I saw you both. You have no idea what he's like.'

'Oh yeah? So what am I like, then?' asked Jesse.

'Like your dad.' Markus spat in his face.

The saliva was hot. Jesse was seething. He hated it when people tarred him with the same brush as his dad. Because it hurt that he couldn't remember him. And because it hurt to hear the stories the others told him.

'You think I don't know what he did to women?' said Markus, spitting with rage.

Jesse's head was ablaze. That was enough. He'd heard that too many times now. So many times that he almost felt like he could remember it.

'Your dad was a fucking psycho and so are you. You always have been!'

Markus's eyes suddenly screwed up, then a split second later he pounced on Jesse. A couple of the girls screamed. He thought he could make out Sandra's voice, but he couldn't understand what she was yelling.

Later on, no one could say exactly what had happened. All the facts had disintegrated into separate fragments that didn't add up. Artur drew a veil of silence over the whole thing, like he always did. The bastard should have been a politician with his talk of unfortunate circumstances! He avoided using the word self-defence, even though it would have been the right term to use, more or less.

Jesse was sent to the hole to survive on a diet of watery porridge for four weeks. Markus was still in the hospital when he came out. He had lost a kidney.

Even though Jesse was a bit ashamed, it seemed pretty fair to him. Sure, he wouldn't be able to prove it because he had no recollection of the accident. But the longer he obsessed over it, the clearer it was to him who must have been behind it.

What was worse, damn it?

Losing a kidney? Or losing your father, your mother and your entire childhood?

He would have chosen a kidney any day if he had the choice, irrespective of whether his father was a psycho. At least you get two kidneys.

Chapter 9

Berlin – Monday, 7 January 2013, 8.15 p.m.

Jule's heart was racing. The hand holding the phone was shaking. Her eyes were fixed on Jesse. The numbers on the dialler were a blur and her thumbs merely grazed the number one.

'Don't, Jule!'

The fridge came on and started buzzing. She pressed the number one again.

'*Jule!*'

'Stay away from me!' Her thumb slid down to the zero, but she hit the hash key instead. For God's sake! Why did they have to make the delete button so ridiculously small and put it so high up on the dialler?

'Jule, please! Just give me *one* minute to show you something.'

'Show me something?' She paused. 'What do you mean, *show me*?'

'It's in Isa's room. He's written something on the wall. Come, I'll show you.'

Jesse raised the palms of his hands and pointed to the kitchen door behind him with his thumbs. Traces of red were stuck to them. His jeans were dark at the knees from Sandra's blood and his doctor's coat gave him a kind of unsettling pathological air. She found herself thinking about one of the stories Sandra had told her years ago, late at night, while opening another bottle of Rioja. A story about the children's home. She was usually stubbornly tight-lipped about her time in the home. Either that, or she would react irritably or even aggressively when Jule tried to talk to her about it. But with Jesse in Sudan on his first Doctors Without Borders mission and Isa still a baby, the red wine and Sandra's frustration at being left alone had opened the floodgates.

'Give me the knife, Jule. I can explain.' Jesse took a step towards her.

'No way.' Jule waved the knife around to show she was serious. A light reflex darted across Jesse's face, making his iris light up in an amber hue. He stayed where he was with his hands up. She decided she wasn't going to fall for it.

'Let me go or I'll call the police.'

She wiggled her thumb and pressed delete to make the hash key disappear.

'Jule, Isa's been kidnapped! Don't you understand?'

'So why won't you call the police?'

'Because the kidnapper's threatening to kill Isa, for Christ's sake!'

Suddenly she felt doubtful. She searched Jess's face for the telltale signs of a lie, but there was no hint that he might not be telling the truth. 'That . . . but that doesn't make any sense. I mean, neither of you are rich. Why—'

'This isn't about money. He wants Isa. He said I have to forget her.'

'Forget? What . . . so what does he want? What is he planning?'

'Jesus! I've no idea!'

'And who is *he*?'

'How should I know?'

Silence.

Jule thought about Leon. Right from the start, he had been trying to buy Isa's love. Then again, sometimes Jesse seemed too obsessed with Isa, especially since he had lost Sandra. What would he do if he felt like he was going to lose Isa too?

'You don't believe me, do you?'

Jule stayed quiet. Was she being unfair to Jesse? But then why had Sandra seemed so distraught on the phone? What had she been so desperate to tell her about him? She knew he hadn't always been psychologically stable. She also knew that he was hard to figure out. Perhaps her best bet would be to lull him into a sense of security. 'All right,' said Jule, trying to adopt the right tone as she spoke. 'Let's just say I'm prepared to believe you—'

Jesse looked her up and down. 'OK, then, come with me. I'll show you.'

'Show me what?'

'Isa's room. Didn't you hear what I said before? The writing on the wall?'

Yes, she'd heard him. But what if it was a trap? 'You go first.' She pointed at the door with the blade.

Jesse nodded. He retreated slowly, making sure he didn't let her out of his sight. Then he slipped into the hallway

Jule looked at her phone. The screen had gone dark. She tapped it and keyed in the final zero. And hit the green phone icon. She pressed the phone to her ear and waited for the call to be connected to the police. But when the ringing tone sounded, she came up with a better idea. She quickly pressed the red phone icon and hung up.

Chapter 10

Snow, snow and more snow. Artur really didn't need the weather forecast to tell him what he already knew. And he certainly didn't need the thriller that came on the TV after it! He switched the channel over to a soppy film, just some harmless old rubbish, then lowered the volume to zero and sank further into his chair.

Artur had been sleeping badly lately, and he was dreading the night ahead of him. The older he got, the more ghosts there were waiting on his doorstep when darkness fell. He used to sleep in short, deep stretches, so the nightmares could only trouble him on rare occasions. Even then, he could wash away most of the after-effects with cold water in the morning. These days, his sporadic pains and the uneven sleeping patterns of old age were making life ridiculously easy for the ghosts.

Wilbert's hand was preying on his mind. Best not to imagine what could be behind it all.

He had been nervously racking his brains, trying to think of ways to get rid of the package. He definitely wouldn't be able to bury the hand outside with all the frost out there – the ground was too hard, and he wasn't mobile enough to carry the container far enough away from Adlershof. Finally, he settled on an interim solution and decided to put the container in the freezer compartment of his fridge, the same place he kept the thin folder containing the last of those sensitive documents. A thick sheet of ice had formed over the top of the protective plastic film since the last time he had looked at the files. Being neglected had its benefits: nobody came sniffing around up here. No doubt the freezer compartment would only be defrosted when he kicked the bucket. Still, he wouldn't be able to keep Wilbert's hand in the freezer indefinitely. And he wouldn't *want* to keep it there, either.

His thoughts turned to the night when Wilbert injured his hand. It was in 1954, just by the entrance to Garmisch. Wilbert was tall even back then: he was nearly two metres tall by the age of fifteen and towered above everyone at school. It went to his head for a while, so much so that he ended up picking a fight with their maths teacher, old Mr Stachl. Nobody else would have had the guts to provoke him. Well, they all knew what Stachl had done during the war. But Stachl was a petty midget, so he really had it in for the lanky young Wilbert. He frequently forced him to stand by the blackboard and made him look like a fool before sending him back to his seat with insults like: 'Your height is only exceeded by your stupidity', which wasn't true, as both Wilbert and Herman, his average-height brother, were actually pretty bright young lads. Eventually Wilbert decided he'd had enough of putting up and shutting up. The next time Stachl had a go at him, Wilbert swiftly nodded, saluted and said: '*Jawohl, Herr Ober-Nazi.*'

The whole class sat there gawping, flabbergasted.

Stachl turned lobster-red, summoned Wilbert over and made him put his right hand flat on his desk. Then he whacked him with the flat side of his wooden ruler until Wilbert's tears ran all the way down to his shirt collar.

Later on, a group of them met up on the corner of Wettersteinstrasse and Enzianstrasse. Artur was there, along with Wilbert, his brother Herman and the Austrian boy from class, Sebi Kochl, whose father ran a lumber mill across the border. He knew a bit about motorbikes; there were three of them in his father's garage.

That same night, they broke into Stachl's shed and stole his pride and joy: a BMW R51/2. It was a shiny black chrome beast of a motorbike, beautiful to look at and outrageously expensive to boot. Artur could clearly remember how uncomfortable he'd felt at the time. But the others had reached a consensus and he agreed with them: the old Nazi was a bastard and had it coming to him. It wasn't far from Stachl's shed to the outskirts of town. With one of the boys to the left, another to the right, and one at the back, they all pushed the heavy machine until they got past the dark houses. Much to everyone's amazement, Sebi Kochl hot-wired the BMW by torchlight on a secluded dirt track by the river Loisach. Of course, Kochl was first up to ride. The rest of them struggled to keep their balance to begin with and Artur very nearly crashed.

An hour later, the tank was almost empty. They scratched the words 'Nazi pig' into the polished paintwork and hooted with laughter as they emptied their bladders all over the bike.

The water level in the river Loisach wasn't all that high at that time. The boys rolled the bike to the riverbank. As they heaved it into the river, Wilbert's hand, still wounded from Stachl's blows, caught the blistering hot end of the exhaust. He bellowed like a bull. His brother, on the other hand, just laughed. Herman was slightly drunk, and the boisterous rivalry between the two of them was an ongoing theme. Wilbert had carried the crescent-shaped burn on the back of his hand like a medal ever since.

Good lord. And now Wilbert was probably dead.

Artur thought about Jesse, let out a moan, then shifted in his armchair and turned off the muted TV. The soppy crap on the screen wasn't doing anything to distract him anyway. Then he did the only thing he thought he could do in the circumstances. He lifted the Bakelite receiver for the fourteenth time that day, looked at his notebook and squinted at the most recent number Jesse had given him: 030 . . . – a Berlin number. The dial whirred back into place after each rotation. He loved that noise. Three beeps, then the stupid answering machine picked up again. No message, just a short silence followed by a single beep. 'Jesse? Are you there?' He waited for a second, then spoke into the phone as loud as he could, not sure how well the thing actually recorded: 'It's me. Like I said before, please get back to me as soon as you can. It's urgent. I—' A loud crackling sound on the line stopped him mid-sentence. He thought for a second that maybe Jesse had picked up. 'Hello?'

No answer.

Artur listened attentively, but there was nothing to be heard. Not even that static you get when the volume on the radio is turned down too low. Artur pressed down on the cradle several times in succession. Still no use. The line was dead. He looked towards the dark window. An endless stream of white snow-flakes tumbled to the ground behind his reflection in the glass. Damn snow. Every few years it was the same old story. At least this time the power hadn't failed. Was that because Richard had had new lines put in? But then why the hell hadn't he replaced the phone line while he was at it?

For perhaps the hundredth time that day, Artur wondered what the man on the phone wanted and how long it would take him to realise that Jesse no longer lived in Esslingen. Artur didn't have Jesse's new Berlin address – and he was glad of it. At least that way he had something reasonably plausible he could tell the man to get him off his back. And it wasn't like the man had asked him for a phone number anyway.

He grinned. Small mercies.

He just hoped it wasn't going to come back and bite him. The man seemed hard and uncompromising, the kind of person who always got what he wanted. He was going to find Jesse sooner or later, and by the time he did Artur wanted to be sure he'd at least had a warning.

But why wasn't Jesse picking up?

Why had he given him this number if he never answered it?

There was a knock at the door.

Before he could even say 'come in', Richard was standing in the doorway. He was wearing his dark green two-piece corduroy suit and a white shirt with edelweiss blossoms on the tips of the collar. The smile on his face looked like it was being held up by his trouser braces. 'Evening, Dad.'

Artur grumbled.

'I see you're in high spirits?'

'What reason do I have to be in a good mood? Oh, and the phone's gone dead again too.'

'Who did you want to call?' Richard asked suspiciously, but without turning his smile down even by a notch.

For a moment Artur wondered whether Richard might have cut off the phone. 'Well, not the police, if that's what you're thinking. Don't worry.'

Richard nodded. 'Don't worry,' he repeated. 'And neither should you. Charly's bound to turn up eventually. It's not the first time she's run away. And you should know by now that you can trust me to take care of business. I'm a grown-up, Dad.' He slid his large, slightly gnarled hands into his trouser pockets. *Damn*, Artur thought to himself, *why did Richard have to be so much like himself?* Even the patches where his hair was thinning were the same: a circle at the back of his head and an ever-expanding forehead. Not much longer now and Richard's hair would be grey instead of reddish brown too.

'So listen, Dad, if anyone's going to phone the police, it'll be me. Agreed?'

'As long as you do it before it's too late,' Artur grumbled.

'Are you really going to bring that up again?' Richard's tone was calm and smacked of the kind of unnatural patience that was enough to get on anyone's nerves. Every inch the principal of a boarding school and a children's home.

'It would have helped Kristina.'

'Nothing could have helped Kristina. She fell into the ice, Dad.'

But only after two days had gone by, Artur thought to himself. But on the other hand, he also knew Richard was right. The police always started sniffing around and asking questions that could make them look bad to the council and the child welfare office, where his old contacts had lost influence. And most importantly, it could ruin the school's reputation with potential 'sponsors'. That's what they called them these days. And these sponsors loved to keep their noses clean. He never had to rely on them in his heyday, always finding his own ways of making ends meet instead. But things were different now. Everything seemed to be more complicated somehow.

The fact that an institution like Adlershof still even had any sponsors seemed like a miracle to him. And to be totally honest, he didn't have the faintest idea how Richard had managed to pull it off. The concept of a combined children's home and boarding school had always ruffled feathers. Then there was the building's reputation as a former Nazi factory, even though that had been an involuntary interlude during the war, and the fact that Adlershof was far off the beaten track. All these things made running the institution terribly hard work for Artur in the years before he retired. Now there was all this nonsense about websites and selling the promise of modern teaching methods, a good digital infrastructure, tennis courts, media training – and so on, and so on . . . He really should have been singing Richard's praises. But he was always so annoyed by the smug way he said 'Dad' that he found it hard to admit he'd consistently avoided phoning the police when he was in charge. And for a good reason.

'Hands off the phone, Dad. Promise?'

The useless piece of crap doesn't work anyway, Artur thought to himself.

Jesse came into his head again. For the first time in his life Artur wished he had a mobile phone, although he doubted he'd be able to work it with those crooked, unsteady fingers of his. All the keys were too close together. Not to mention the technology, which quite frankly baffled him.

Richard nodded at him, as if to say he would be glad if, against all odds, his father would just roll over and leave him to it.

Artur's eyes wandered over to the three photos on the wall next to the door. The picture on the left was of Richard and the whole gang. They were all aged between eleven and twelve, with hats on and their shoes submerged in fresh snow. His son had the same smile in the photo, the only difference being the laughter in his eyes back then. Standing next to him were Jesse and Mattheo, Bernadette, Sandra, Alois, Wolle and Markus. A tight-knit group, at least when they were united against him, the principal. He would never have thought that Sandra and Jesse would be the only ones to end up living their lives far away from Adlershof.

It was one of the few photos from the time before Jesse's accident. Richard and Jesse were never the best of friends. Jesse was too dominant for that. And whenever Richard rebelled and insisted on his rights as the principal's son, the two of them seemed to sort things out in a quiet back room somewhere, and Richard would always come off worse and walk away looking scared and defeated – like on the day of the snowball fight.

The courtyard was covered in a pristine layer of fresh snow almost fifteen centimetres deep, and the children rushed outside to play in it. The low sun pushed between the clouds and shone into the yard. Everything beamed brightly with long, sharply defined shadows. Jesse had divided everyone into two teams: the girls and Markus were with him as usual, and Mattheo, Wolle and Alois were on Richard's team. The wet snow formed firm clumps, and the snowballs were flying back and forth across the yard. The sound of yelling and laughter carried all the way to Artur's window; he'd opened it slightly so that he could keep an eye on them.

The smallest of all the children, Mattheo, was very nimble. He'd come a long way in the last six months and was now bolder and more skilful than before. Jesse underestimated him, concentrated on Richard, and ended up with a firmly moulded snowball right in the face. Mattheo threw his arms in the air in triumph, his face beaming like he'd grown overnight. Bernadette and Sandra broke out into fits of laughter. Jesse ran over to Mattheo without saying a word, then knocked him over and pushed his face into the snow. All the children were yelling. Jesse had a razor-sharp grin on his face, still red from the impact, and he just kept pushing. Mattheo was kicking out helplessly and reaching into thin air with his arms. 'Leave him alone,' Bernadette shouted.

'Why should I? He was asking for it,' Jesse shouted back at her. He let Mattheo catch his breath for a second and pushed him into the snow again.

'He can't fight back,' Sandra objected.

'I think he can. You saw that snowball, didn't you? It was like a stone!'

'Leave him alone, Jesse,' Richard said. He was increasingly getting into the habit of chiming in whenever the two girls were around.

'What's this got to do with *you*?' Jesse shouted and let go of Mattheo.

'I'm just saying leave him alone.' Richard's face screwed up as Jesse stomped over to him. All the yelling had given way to complete silence. Jesse's footsteps crunched in the snow. He looked up for a second and glanced at the window where Artur was standing. The young boy's stare pierced like a hot needle, although he wasn't certain Jesse could even see him behind the glass. Artur briefly contemplated stepping in. But what good would it do Richard if he couldn't stand up for himself?

He decided to wait. To observe.

Jesse squared up to Richard, who in turn instinctively edged back a couple of centimetres so he wouldn't be quite so close. Artur held his breath. This whole thing smacked of an altercation, of angry cries and people getting hurt. But Jesse just leaned over and whispered something in Richard's ear.

Meeting adjourned. Off to the quiet back room.

Wherever the two of them eventually fought it out – if there even was a fight, that is – it happened in secret. Artur was all too aware of the opportunities he'd missed back then. He'd missed his chance to intervene. It had slipped through his fingers. *He* had slipped through his fingers. Even today, he was lost for words when he thought about how little it took for things to be thrown out of joint sometimes. Usually it was enough to just wait it out and do nothing for a while.

Only the terrible accident straightened everything out, albeit in a downright eerie way. At least what he called an *accident*, anyway.

Chapter 11

Jesse had taken a few steps into the hallway and was looking through the door to Isa's room. The spidery red letters positively burned on the wall. All the madness with Jule had distracted him, but now the pain was rushing back in full force. He remembered Isa's narrow shoulders and her little cheeks, thought about how she snuggled up to him and how her sleep-bedraggled hair softly tickled him. He saw her angry little round face as she climbed over him and jabbed him in the side when he ordered her to brush her teeth.

A noise from the kitchen interrupted his thoughts.

Jule! He rushed back into the kitchen and stopped dead in his tracks. Jule had disappeared. The window by the dining area was wide open.

Jesse went over to the window and leaned out. They were on the third floor. How on earth could she . . .

He turned around just in time to catch Jule creeping into the corridor from where she had been standing next to the door. Two swift leaps, and he managed to catch her halfway between the kitchen and the apartment door.

She cried out, dropped the phone and lunged towards him with the knife. Jesse dodged and grabbed her by the wrist, but he wasn't fast enough: the blade went under his doctor's coat and cut him above his jeans. The pain was hot and sharp. He took hold of the hand holding the knife and forced it into the air, twisting her arm. Jule groaned and squirmed under his grip, then dropped the knife. He kicked it down the hall and it hit the apartment door, spinning to a stop. Jule had her back turned to him now. She kicked out behind her but missed him.

'Stop it! I'm not going to hurt you.'

'Let me go,' Jule gasped. Her next kick caught him on his shin.

Jesse cursed and twisted her arm even further. Her body lurched forward. He pushed her towards Isa's room and through the doorway. She stumbled and landed beside the bed.

'Look, for God's sake! Do you believe me now?'

Jule groaned as she straightened up, rubbing her arm. She froze when she saw the writing above Isa's bed. She whispered the words to herself: 'You don't deserve her'. The sound of her reading it out loud made it unbearably real: Isa really had disappeared. She'd been kidnapped, taken by some stranger who wanted to make sure Jesse never saw his daughter again.

'What do you think it's supposed to mean?'

Jesse wished he had an answer, but he didn't. At least nothing that could help.

'And who's the *her*? Isa? Or Sandra?'

'Isa, I guess? It's written above her bed. Jesse felt a nagging pain in his waist. Red blotches of blood were showing through the white cotton of his doctor's coat. He quickly lifted his top and his jumper to check the cut. It was deep enough to cause serious problems if it didn't get sewn up soon.

Jule watched him impassively. If she felt bad about it, she wasn't letting on. 'But didn't you say you spoke to the kidnapper before?'

'Not directly. Isa was the only one I spoke to. But someone was there telling her what to say.'

'You have to call the police, Jesse. You have to tell them about Sandra. And about Isa.'

'No way.'

'I know you're scared something's going to happen to her, but—'

'Just leave it!'

'You could call my brother.'

Jesse knew that Jule's brother worked for the criminal investigation department in Hamburg, but they didn't know each other personally and he didn't think he'd get the discretion he needed from him. Why should Jule's brother risk his job for him? They were dealing with a murder, after all. 'What difference would that make? The police are all the same. He wouldn't hesitate to tell his colleagues in Berlin.'

'I could tell him you just need some advice. You could—'

'For God's sake, no!'

Jule flinched and avoided looking him directly in the eyes.

Jesse calmed himself. He was so close to losing it. If he wanted Jule to trust him he definitely wasn't going about it the right way. 'I don't want anything to happen to her,' he tried to explain.

Jule anxiously bit her bottom lip. God, he hated the expression on her face and the look in her eyes. They were all too familiar. People always used to look at him that way at Adlershof. Whenever he even slightly raised his voice, they looked at him like he was someone to be afraid of. 'Do you still believe that . . . Sandra . . . that it was me?'

'I . . . no, but . . .'

'What?'

There was a long, uncomfortable silence.

'Did Sandra say something to you? Is it because of some old story from the children's home?'

Jule defiantly tried to hold his gaze but he knew he'd hit the nail on the head. '*What* did she tell you? About what happened with Markus?'

She said nothing and just moved her head a touch, somewhere between a nod and a shake.

'And did she ever tell you what *he* did to *me*?'

'I don't know what you mean.'

'I'm saying she didn't tell you the whole story.' He pulled up his top in exasperation and turned around to show her the scar on his back. 'Pretty close.' He turned back around. 'Just a bit further in and it would have caught my spinal column. Any further out and it would've been my lungs or my heart.'

'That was Markus?'

'He never admitted it. He was always too much of a coward for that. But I don't know who else it could have been.'

'But you don't know for certain.'

'Like I said, I don't know who else it could have been.' He sat down by the door.

They sat in silence for a while. The emptiness of Isa's room was clawing at him. He kept his eyes off the wall above the bed and tried to think straight, but he was in a daze. The colourful furniture, Isa's night light at the side of the bed, the stuffed toys and the low desk with coloured pencils scattered all over it: it felt like Isa could just walk back in there any second and start drawing or doing her homework.

'OK,' Jule quietly conceded and straightened her back. 'Say I believe you. Who do you think might have done this? Do you have any suspicions?'

'I'm not sure. No.'

She pointed at the writing. '"You don't deserve her". Sounds like he knows you.'

Jesse nodded. His thoughts were paralysed. His body seemed to be reacting to the stress.

'Sounds like revenge to me,' Jule said. 'Like someone has some unfinished business with you.'

Jesse stared at her.

'What might that be? Can you think of anyone?'

'Nothing comes to mind,' he rasped.

'Something from your past, when you lived in the home? What happened with Markus?'

'No, I reckon we're quits on that one.'

'That's what *you* think.'

'I'm perfectly capable of remembering who I've done something to, as you put it, and knowing whether we might have any unfinished business . . .'

'But this other person might see things completely differently. Sandra said a few things—'

'—but maybe there's one exception.'

Jule raised her eyebrows.

'The *before* part.'

Jule's face was like a question mark.

'Everything that happened *before* the accident.'

'The accident?'

Jesse pointed at his back. 'The scar I showed you.'

'Didn't you say that was Markus?'

'Yes. But they always tried to make me believe it was an accident.'

'So what happened exactly?'

'That's just it: I don't know. It might be a stab wound from a knife. Or maybe a screwdriver. It might even be from a crossbow.'

'A crossbow?' Jule's face screwed up at the thought. 'That sounds ridiculous. Why on earth would it be from a crossbow?'

He shrugged. It was best not to go there right now. Jule probably wouldn't understand anyway. Sandra hadn't understood either, and he was glad to learn she obviously hadn't told Jule everything after all.

'You're saying you can't remember?'

'No, I can't remember the accident or anything that happened before it.'

'How big is the gap in your memory?

'Big.'

'*How* big?'

'I've basically forgotten everything. Focal retrograde amnesia – that's what they said it was.'

'Did you have any injuries besides the one on your back? I mean, it's hardly the most typical link to make.'

'Bruises all over my body, a broken leg and a fractured skull, hence the memory loss.'

Jule was speechless.

The scar on Jesse's back itched, and the fresh wound burned in his side. He turned his back against the wall. The cold helped a little.

'You really can't remember anything from that period? Not even from your childhood?'

'A couple of snippets. Things that other people told me. Like the fact that my dad was an alcoholic. The others in the home couldn't stand me. Apparently I was a bit of . . . well, a bastard.'

'I see. Bastard doesn't exactly sound like language from a children's home.'

'Well, call it what you like.'

She looked at him for a long time, like she was weighing up the things she'd heard about him, everything she knew about him and the things he'd just told her, all the information she had. 'Well, it seems like this is probably connected to something that happened before the accident. Or maybe it has to do with the accident itself.'

Jesse glanced over at the writing on the wall. 'Looks that way,' he mumbled. He always felt empty when he thought about how much he must have forgotten. For a long time Sandra had been his only way of fighting this feeling of emptiness – a temporary remedy, at least. But ever since he'd split from Sandra, Isa was the only one capable of filling the void.

'So, did Isa say anything? Anything that could give us a clue as to who has taken her?'

Jesse hesitated. 'There was one thing. She said he was wearing something which had glass circles for eyes.'

'Glasses? No, maybe a mask?'

A mask? Jesse thought back to when the man hit Isa. What was it she'd said before that? He looked like an inse . . . ? 'Insect,' he mumbled. 'She was going to say he looked like an *insect*.'

'Sorry, what?'

'He didn't let her finish, but I think Isa was trying to tell me he looked like an insect. He must have been wearing a kind of mask that made him look like an insect.'

Jule frowned. 'That sounds a bit far-fetched. What could she have meant?'

Suddenly an image appeared before Jesse's eyes. One that had haunted his nightmares for as long as he could remember. A large insect burying him alive in the dark. He stared at Jule and felt the hairs on his arm stand on end.

'What is it?'

He shook his head silently, his gaze directed at the floor. He'd never thought that his nightmare might have something to do with real life – it seemed too strange – but now suddenly here was something resembling a connection. Isa had been abducted by a man who looked like an insect. So did that mean the dream was real? Some sort of memory from the time before the accident?

Suddenly Artur crossed his mind. He wondered again why he was always so cagey with him and why he always clammed up when the past came up in conversation. Sometimes he claimed to know nothing; other times he said he wanted to protect him. But he didn't need protecting now. He reached for his phone and dialled Artur's number.

'Who are you calling?' Jule asked.

Still unsure how much he could trust her, Jesse kept his mouth shut and listened to the ringing tone. Artur didn't pick up. In the end he decided it didn't matter anyway. Time was running out, and the questions he wanted to ask weren't the kind of things you could clear up over the phone. He had questions he needed to ask Artur and Markus – and any of the others who might still be there.

He gulped. He would have to summon all the experience he'd acquired as a doctor for what was coming next. 'We have to take care of Sandra,' he said.

Jule sighed. She seemed oddly relieved, which Jesse didn't understand.

'Make sure you call one for yourself too,' Jule said, pointing at his waist.

'An ambulance, you mean? We're not calling an ambulance. We're moving her out onto the balcony.'

Chapter 12

Jule's sense of relief vanished. Had Jesse lost his mind? Or had she been right all along? 'You're going to leave her here? On the balcony?'

Jesse brushed his hand through his short, dark-blond hair. His fingers were trembling, but his voice was hard and distant. 'We don't have a choice.'

'Stop saying *we*.'

'Whatever. *I* don't have a choice.'

'Why are you doing this, Jesse? She's your wife, I mean, she was your wife. Separation or no separation.'

'That doesn't come into it. If I leave her here, the smell will take two days at the most to spread to the hallway. Someone will call the police. The balcony is on the north side of the building, it's freezing all the time out there at the moment.'

Jule stood there looking at him with her mouth agape. 'You want to freeze her?'

'She's dead, Jule. She can't feel anything and there's nothing she can do to help us. She can only harm us now. You know I loved her. The police will start asking questions as soon as they find her – and they'll be asking about Isa too.'

'I can't believe that's how you see it.'

'This isn't a matter of morals and decency, Jule. It's about Isa's life. That's how Sandra would see it too. Do it for her.'

Jule shook her head.

'We'll roll her up in the flokati rug and—'

'Not we. *You!*'

Jesse gave a curt nod that made Jule shudder. He changed before her eyes within an instant. He'd never seemed cold before. More uncomfortable in his own skin – a trait she knew drove Sandra to despair at times – but Jule got the impression he was capable of empathy and just didn't always let it show. Surely he wouldn't have become a paediatrician otherwise. But now he was cold and closed off, like a wall of ice. Even the way he spoke was brusque and emotionless.

Jesse looked at her searchingly. 'What if Isa was your daughter? Wouldn't you do anything to find her?'

She nodded instinctively and felt a lump in her throat. 'That's exactly why I'd call the police.'

Jesse gave a stiff nod of the head, like he wasn't at all surprised. His lips formed a pale line on his grey, ashen face. She remembered a photo of her brother from his time in the Bundeswehr, before he joined the police. Short hair, stony expression, military stance. Jesse looked just like that to her. The gentle paediatrician in him had vanished.

'Come with me.' Jesse grabbed her by the top of her right arm, his grip forceful but not rough. She tried to shake him off, but it was no use. He marched her over to the bathroom and secured the window so that she couldn't try to escape. Then he removed the key from the inside of the door and locked her in the bathroom.

Jule sat on the toilet lid. Her legs were shaking. She could hear Jesse doing something in the living room, metal scraping over the floor. Shards falling to the ground. A little later, the sound of dragging and Jesse's heavy breathing. She glanced over at the large double washbasin in the bathroom. Neatly folded hand towels, some perfume and two toothbrushes. One of them large, the other smaller and colourful. She closed her eyes. The sounds continued, conjuring up unbearable images in her mind. The hinge of an outside door creaked. More dragging. Jesse panting. Footsteps. She put her hands over her ears so that all she could hear was the muffled rhythm of her heartbeat. When she took them away again it had all gone quiet.

Very quiet.

Was he going to leave her locked in the bathroom?

She tried to remember when Leon was meant to be getting back from Chicago. Was it this weekend? Or next? She kicked herself. Typical of her to hope that someone else would come along and save the day. Her eyes homed in on the toilet brush and the large white ceramic container. Clean and expensive, just like everything at Sandra's house. Clean for Sandra, expensive for Leon. The thing was probably heavy enough to smash the bathroom window in. Then at least she'd be able to call for help.

The sound of the key turning in the lock put a stop to her escape plans. Jesse's expression was intense and exhausted, like he'd just lost a battle. He was wearing bright-green rubber gloves and holding a bulging bin bag in his left hand.

Now, instead of his doctor's coat, he was wearing a black parka with a fur collar, a clean black V-neck jumper and a classy black shirt, all clearly from Leon's wardrobe, with a fresh pair of jeans and dark, fashionable heavy-duty boots. The only remaining sign of Isa's blue man was his jeans, she thought to herself. The rest of him had morphed into a man in black.

'We're leaving.'

'What do you mean. Where are we going?'

'We're going to find Isa. There are some things I need to clear up.'

'What about your wound?' She pointed to his side, hoping to buy some time.

'My doctor's bag's in the car.'

'I don't want to go with you.'

'Well, you have to.'

'And how exactly are you going to make me?'

Jesse pulled a couple of thin strips of white plastic out of the inner pocket of his coat. Cable ties. They stuck out of his bright green hands like a fistful of skewers.

Her whole body tensed up at the thought of having to go with him. But did she have a choice in the matter? She only came up to just above his shoulders. He was pretty well-built too; she wouldn't stand much of a chance against him. He also seemed to be hell-bent on taking her with him. Something had got into his head while she was locked in the bathroom. She stood up slowly, wobbling at the knees, and pointed at the cable ties. 'It's not going to look good, you marching me through the corridor with those on.'

'I'll be right next to you. Don't even think about running away.'

'I could scream.'

'Isa will die if the police get wind of this.'

'Maybe she'll die if you *don't* call them.'

Jesse ignored her. He glanced into the hallway and picked something up off the floor. It looked like the key to Sandra's new car. 'What kind of car do you drive?'

'Me? A Fiat. Why?'

'And whose is this?' He twiddled the brand-new black key between his thumb and his index finger.

Sandra had told Jule just how much Jesse loved the old estate car. It spoke volumes that he had let Sandra keep it when they separated. Eventually Sandra got sick of the rust bucket, as she liked to call it, and took Leon up on his offer to trade in the old Volvo for a new one. She had clearly done so without consulting Jesse. 'It's Sandra's, I think.'

Jesse pursed his lips. He put the key in his pocket and looked at Jule as if he was trying to stare right through her. 'Give me your hands,' he said. His voice was mechanical.

Chapter 13

Jesse opened the front door. The cold air rushed towards him, as if there was a vacuum in the staircase as big as the one in his chest. Snowflakes floated over the doorstep in the light at the entrance. Like seeing stars in a fainting fit.

He pushed Jule out of the building. Her bound wrists were covered with Leon's coat which was hanging loosely over her shoulders. She shivered and looked up at the grey-orange sky. Light from the city illuminated the snow flurry on Hildegard-strasse, giving it a toxic hue. The parked cars, the pavement and the green spaces were submerged under a featureless layer of fresh snow. The vacuum inside his chest grew larger.

Jesse pressed the unlock button on the key to Sandra's car. The signal lights lit up beneath a mound of snow about twenty metres away. The outline matched an estate car. They stomped towards the mound and Jesse wiped the snow off the model name on the back: Volvo V70, Cross Country. A four-wheel drive family car.

Jesse swept the snow off the passenger door and opened it, then guided Jule towards the leather seat and leaned forward to fasten her seat belt. The wound on the left side of his body was burning. Jule's perfume wafted into his nose. Her breath brushed against his ear. He quickly took another cable tie and tied it around her wrists to the belt across her stomach. He stuffed the bin bag with his blood-soaked clothes into the space on the floor behind her seat.

'Wait here,' he said. He came back after less than two minutes carrying his doctor's bag and two blankets from the boot of his car. He used both his hands to wipe the snow away from the car windows. Then he took a bandage and some medicine out of his bag, sat down in the driver's seat and pushed it back as far as it would go to give himself more room to move.

He started by tearing off the too-small plaster he'd stuck on the cut as a temporary fix. The edges of the wound were clearly swollen. He almost found the stinging sensation a welcome distraction: better to hurt on the outside than the inside. As he dripped the mepivacaine into the wound, his thoughts turned to Marta. Thanks to her, he had no driving licence or money on him. He stapled the cut together with six strips, not stopping to wait for the local anaesthetic to kick in. Even with all his experience, his hands were still trembling. He put a folded sterile compress over the wound and wrapped a piece of gauze dressing around his waist. Jule averted her gaze and stared out of the passenger door. If she was that sensitive, he wondered why she hadn't passed out as soon as she'd seen Sandra's body. Perhaps it would have made everything easier.

She turned around again as he started the engine and cranked up the heating. 'You never told me where we're going.'

Jesse kept quiet and tried to concentrate on the menu prompts for the satnav system. The stupid thing was a newer model than the one in his own Volvo. Annoyingly, it was also a generation more complicated and had a load of extra functions that he didn't understand.

'If you're going to make me come with you, you can—' She broke off when she saw Jesse starting typing the name of the destination into the screen. 'Garmisch-Partenkirchen? You want to go to Adlershof?'

He nodded. He selected the Munich route, but didn't bother entering the exact destination. He did know his way around the place, after all. Then out of nowhere the full address of the children's home flashed up on the screen. He stopped short. Adleshof. Why the hell—?

'That's right up in the Alps,' Jule said, horrified.

Jesse ignored her. There was only one possible explanation as to why the satnav was suggesting the address of the children's home as a possible destination. Sandra must have driven there. 'How long has Sandra had this car?'

'What?'

'The car. How long has Sandra been driving it?'

'I . . . um, no idea. Maybe six or seven weeks.'

'Do you know if she's been to Adlershof recently?'

'Sandra? No. Why would she go there?'

'Exactly. Why would she?' Jesse muttered. As far as he could remember, Sandra had never returned to Adlershof since she moved away. It was the last place in the world she would have gone back to of her own accord. Suddenly he remembered the conversation they'd had that morning when he dropped Isa off. When Sandra had mentioned Markus, he got the feeling she'd spoken to him not long ago. 'That's another reason,' he muttered.

'What kind of reason? What do you mean?

Jesse pressed two painkillers out of the packet from his doctor's bag and swallowed them dry. Then he pushed the seat forward again. The windscreen wipers swept away the remaining snow.

'Seriously, Jesse! That's eight or nine hundred kilometres!'

'Six hundred and seventy-two, according to the satnav.'

'You want to drive seven hundred kilometres *now*, in this weather?'

Jesse indicated and the Volvo crunched its way out of the parking space.

'But Jesse, that's crazy. What do you want to go there for?'

'I have to speak to Artur. And Markus.'

'Who's Artur?'

'The director of the children's home. Or he used to be, anyway. His son's in charge now.'

'What do you think phones are for?'

'In a hundred metres, turn left,' a woman's voice said through the speakers. Jesse glanced at the fuel gauge. Less than half a tank. Shit.

For the next five minutes the icy silence was punctuated only by the smooth, oddly friendly voice of the woman on the satnav. Eventually Jule cracked. 'For God's sake, Jesse! If you're going to kidnap me, then the least you could do is give me an answer. Why are we going to Adlershof? Why can't you just call instead?'

Kidnap. The word stung Jesse. It seemed wrong somehow. But was it really? 'Because I can't get through to Artur,' he said. 'And Markus would just hang up if I called him.'

'What if I call him?' Jule suggested. 'I could try and get him to speak to you.'

Was she being serious? Did she really want to help him? Or was she just looking for an opportunity to call the police? He almost missed the slip road but managed to steer right just in time. The Volvo skidded, then got back on track. Jesse accelerated gently to cut onto the A100. The heavy snow strained his exhausted eyes. He noticed Jule fumbling with the cable ties out of the corner of his eye. She must be thinking he was crazy to be driving to Adlershof.

But he had to go there. He had to talk to Markus and Artur in person. If information was all he needed, he might have just phoned again. He did try to contact Artur in the first place. But wasn't this about more than that? What if Markus still held a grudge? He wanted, no, he *needed* to see his face when he spoke to him. He needed to look into those coal-black eyes, see the two corners of his mouth pointing in different directions, caught somewhere between a smile and a frown. Richard was still there, along with all the things Artur had kept from him.

'Are you even listening to me, Jesse?'

'No,' he said. He had to find Isa. Even if that meant he had to drive to the end of the world.

Chapter 14

1979, Garmisch-Partenkirchen

The two white stone posts and the wide-open wings of the gate almost reminded him of an angel, only with black wings. There didn't seem to be a fence; only the solitary gate on the path.

Ms Wisselsmeier from the child welfare office panted like she was physically carrying them uphill. Her lips were thin, and her breasts came to rest on her stomach whenever she sat down. As she steered the brown Opel Kadett through the angel gate with her stubby fingers, he caught his first glimpse of the children's home. It seemed to emerge from the hill and increase in size as the car moved closer.

He had just turned eleven and thought he was never going to see his father again. He didn't know whether he should feel saved or lost.

His father was the only person he had left. And he wouldn't be so bad if things hadn't taken such a terrible turn all those years ago in Kiel.

He was only three at the time, but he could still remember some moments as if they were photographs. Like postcards on a rotating stand in a souvenir shop. One of the postcards was of his father in his white uniform with a beaming smile, the first time he saw him.

In later years, his father repeatedly told him about that day and how he'd hopped around, ecstatically happy to see him.

Apparently, he kept shouting his name: 'Herman, Herman, Herman!', but without the letter 'R' as he was still so small and couldn't pronounce it properly.

He couldn't remember for himself, but if that was what his father told him, it had to be true. His father told him a lot of stories over the years.

Before finally returning to Kiel, Herman had spent five years as the captain of a ship called the Helgoland, *a former luxury liner that had been converted into a floating hospital and was stationed near Saigon and then Da Nang. The ship had been sent to the South China Sea on behalf of the German government to treat civilian casualties during the Vietnam War. 'The white ship of hope,' he said proudly: that's what the Vietnamese called the* Helgoland. *His mother Gudrun was a doctor. They met on board the ship, but she had to leave when she fell pregnant.*

His mother also appeared on one of the postcards. She was lying on her stomach on the grass wearing a light-green dress, with her head resting in her hands and a smile on her face. Looking into those sparkling blue eyes felt like looking straight into heaven.

But she was never alone in the postcard, because Wilbert had crept into her life and was always sitting there right next to her. Uncle Wilbert, a giant with shovels for paws and a scar on the back of his right hand. He was always there until Herman returned from Vietnam and disaster struck.

Even today, the shots still echoed in his ears. And he could still see the image of Wilbert running away with his father's pistol and the scar on his hand, like a bad omen.

He watched in silence as his father laid his mother's brown coat over her like a sheet to keep from having to look at her eyes or the blood. Her legs were poking out from underneath the coat and one of her arms looked like she was reaching for something. That was another postcard.

Then the police came.

Wilbert had destroyed his family. Wilbert couldn't stand the fact that Gudrun didn't love him as much as she loved his father. He kept saying the same thing over and over.

So where was his brother?

Gone, his father answered. He no longer had a brother.

From then on it was just the two of them. Father and him. Only as time went on, his father was looking less and less like the man with the beaming smile from the postcard. He hated his uncle Wilbert more and more with every passing year. He was the reason his mother was dead and his father had changed so much. And now here he was, at the age of eleven, holding on to the hand of this lardy Wisselsmeier woman in Adlershof children's home. He had been left with no other choice.

Artur Messner welcomed him in the hall. Long dark hair tightly combed down to the back of his neck. Grey-blue eyes and a strangely feeble handshake. Not like Father's handshake. Was Messner deliberately making sure his grip wasn't too tight? Did he take him for a wimp? Perhaps Messner didn't want him there at all. Perhaps children with drunks for parents caused too much trouble. No doubt Wisselsmeier had painted a colourful picture of everything she'd seen. The sparsely furnished two-bed apartment on Kronaustrasse in Garmisch with its fridge full of biscuits and three-day-old scrambled eggs. The captain's uniform on the clothes hanger in the living room, illuminated by the light from a solitary bulb.

It had been three months since the day he took the uniform off the hanger that Saturday afternoon. It was still far too big for him, but he just had to try it on. The window of opportunity came at around one o'clock, just after his father got up and disappeared into the toilet. He was always there for at least an hour.

But not this time.

Father had a kind of sixth sense for these things and could always tell when someone was up to no good. No sooner had he thrown the coat on than the door flew open. Father's eyes fell on the ill-fitting uniform, which sagged around his thin shoulders. 'How dare you,' he hissed.

Best to be quiet. Just let Father do the talking.

'You have to do something to deserve this jacket. Do you think you've earned it?'

No. He hadn't.

'That's the biggest problem with you. That you have to be that way.'

He gulped. There was a bitter taste in his mouth. He knew exactly what his father meant. He wished he could be different – a better, more lovable person. Like a different version of himself – his own better 'brother', to quote his father.

'Your brother, well, he might have deserved to wear it someday. He would also have had the decency to ask me! So tell me again: what should you do?'

'Follow his example,' he said in a strained voice.

'And who can tell you about your brother?'

'You, Father.'

'So, then, who do you have to listen to?'

'To you,' he answered automatically. He hated this 'brother', even though he didn't exist. He wasn't flesh and blood, yet some-how here he was, this invisible 'brother', sharing their home with them. He was always Father's favourite, there was no doubt about that. Sometimes he wished this 'brother' was really here, just for a day. He would have beaten him up and shown him who was really the best.

He was forced to stand in the corner with his face to the wall and his arms stretched out as punishment for his bad behaviour. If he lowered his arms at all, he knew he'd be on the receiving end of a warning rap on the head from his father's knuckles or a punch in the kidneys. But before long, the pain in his arms became so unbearable that he couldn't help but give in and put up with the blows. Beating complete, his father let him put his arms down, but made him stay right where he was without moving a muscle. Later that afternoon when his father went back to the toilet, he left the doors open. The splashes echoed through the hall, making his bladder burn, especially when Father washed his hands. He left the water running for longer than usual that time.

Still, he showed no signs of weakness and asked again. The answer was always the same: his 'brother' wouldn't ask such stupid questions.

Better to fight, then.

Half an hour later the doorbell rang. His legs trembled.

'Stay where you are,' snarled his father. 'And put your arms up again.'

He usually wanted to be left in peace when he had visitors. But the episode with the uniform had changed all that. The laughter at the door was coming from a different woman this time. But it still sounded the same. Sort of dirty. Clean laughter wouldn't have sounded right in this hole.

He wished he could cover his ears. But Father wouldn't allow that, so his ears were invaded by the sound of clapping butt cheeks *and the woman's wailing. He couldn't be sure if she was putting it on or if she was really in pain, just like him.*

Eventually he couldn't take it any more. The worst thing wasn't the sound, but the thought that the two of them could see him standing there, like a scarecrow with a wet crotch, his arms sagging as he tried to keep them out to the sides.

More clapping of bare flesh. More wailing. More moaning.

He could tell from the sound of the bottle being slammed down that his father was drinking the whole time. The moans turned into high-pitched screams. Suddenly out of nowhere he heard a crash and the sound of glass splintering. He glanced anxiously over his shoulder.

His father was lying half on the mattress and half on the floor, surrounded by shards of glass.

He stared at the woman, speechless. The make-up around her eyes was running down her face in black stripes. It was deadly quiet apart from the sound of her snivelling. She rooted around in his father's trousers, pulled a couple of banknotes out, then quickly gathered her things and hurried past him towards the door completely naked, stooped over with her clothes bundled up in her arm.

He stayed in the same spot, unsteady, his arms drooping in pain. A red patch had formed on his father's head between his parting. He wasn't moving. Finally he coughed, grabbed hold of the back of his head and slowly sat up, grunting from the exertion.

He caught him staring at him. 'What are you doing just standing there like that? Your brother would have helped me ages ago!'

He winced. This crappy brother made him feel so bad, like there was something wrong with him. Father was over there bleeding, and instead of helping him, he'd felt something almost like joy. Father seemed to notice and hissed, 'Get out of here!'

He turned around and walked off into the other room.

'And don't you dare take those trousers off, do you hear me?'

Of course he heard him.

He didn't sit on the mattress. The mattress was his home, and he didn't want it to stink. He thought about the woman as he sat on the linoleum floor, staring at the ceiling. She was naked. His father was stronger than her, like a soldier. With big hands, almost as big as that pig Wilbert's giant paws. The woman had put up with it for long enough, but eventually she beat him. No one had managed that before.

His trousers were sticking to his crotch, stinking wet.

She defeated him, *he repeated inside his head.*

If she could do it, then maybe he could as well. Maybe he could win.

A short while later he stood up and took his trousers off, then washed himself while his father was sleeping. Then he got into bed and stretched his legs. The cheap quilt scratched his bare skin. He looked out of the window his father had made him clean the day before. The moon was a pale circle, like someone had shot a hole in the darkness and there was a kingdom of light behind it.

Without his 'brother'.

Chapter 15

A9, just past the exit for Jena – Tuesday, 8 January 2013,
12.52 a.m.

Jesse peered through the windscreen. Snowflakes scurried towards him from out of nowhere, lit up in the headlights and drifted away. The speedo read 105 kilometres per hour and the fuel was running low, much like his concentration levels. He moved his head around, but the exhaustion was too deep-seated to shake off.

He rolled down the window.

Ice-cold air gushed in, stinging his face and startling Jule, who had collapsed into her seat in exhaustion. Jesse felt her eyes on him and was grateful that she was keeping quiet. A couple of snowflakes tumbled into the car through the window. The snow was lighter now and Berlin was about three hundred kilometres behind them. A blue sign with a petrol station symbol on it whizzed past them.

Jesse indicated.

'What are you doing?'

'What do you think I'm doing?' He tapped the brake and moved into the snow-covered exit lane. The petrol station was floating at the side of the road like a spaceship in the Arctic.

The roof was a blue horizontal luminous strip and everything beneath it was drenched in gleaming light. Glistening snow-flakes twirled in the beams from the nearby street lamps. Jesse drove over to the fuel pump right by the entrance to the shop and warily inspected a silver-grey BMW as the owner refuelled. Otherwise, it seemed no one else was here at this ungodly hour.

'I need the toilet,' Jule said.

'I'll make sure you get a chance. Just stay in the car for now.' Suddenly he remembered that he didn't have any credit cards or money with him. 'Do you have your wallet on you?'

She looked at him blankly, then warily.

'Marta stole mine.'

'Marta?' It took her a minute to process the information. Even then, it seemed like she didn't want to believe it was true.

'I'll explain later. Do you have your wallet or not?'

She took a bit too long to think about it.

'Am I going to have to search you?'

Jule sighed. 'Inside pocket on the left.'

Jesse reached inside her coat. She looked away with tears in her eyes as he pulled out the purse. He felt bad for her, but did he really have a choice? There were around two hundred euros in the brown leather purse. At least he didn't have to ask her for the PIN for her ATM card as well.

'Can't you at least untie these plastic things? My shoulders are really tight, and my wrists are aching.'

'Soon,' he said, more abruptly than he intended to.

He inserted the nozzle and filled the tank with diesel. The thick, oily smell wafted into his nose. He couldn't help but picture those children with glazed eyes and corroded respiratory tracts. Just sniff petrol and forget about it all. He had seen that kind of thing every day on his Doctors Without Borders mission in the outskirts of Nyala, the capital city of South Darfur.

He waited for the silver-grey BMW to leave the petrol station, then he went over to the shop, making sure he occasionally checked on Jule while he was away from the car. The skinny man at the cash register was an irritatingly cheery chap in his mid-fifties. He tried to engage Jesse in small talk, but Jesse responded with the bare minimum as he paid for the fuel, two coffees, sandwiches, chocolate bars and a couple of bottles of cola, and didn't hang around any longer than he had to.

Jule piped up again when he started the engine.

'Hang on,' he replied. 'Not here.'

He steered the car away from the illuminated island and towards the car park behind the petrol station. He stopped about a hundred metres away under a faulty street light. Jule looked at the small patch of landscaped woodland on the passenger side.

'If you're quick, the coffee will still be warm,' said Jesse.

'And how do you suggest I drink it?' She shook her wrists at him. Jesse got out of the car and walked over to the passenger side, then cut the plastic strips using the scissors from his medical kit.

'Thanks,' Jule said. 'Do you have any tissues?'

He opened the glove compartment without a second thought. He felt a pang when he saw the packet of Tempo tissues. Sandra always used to keep some in the glove compartment, just in case.

They trudged between the snow-topped trees and bushes in the dark. Jule wandered off ahead and over to the right. He let her go; he'd already crossed enough boundaries with her for one day. It was only when she'd wandered more than ten metres away and he could barely see her between the bushes that he deemed it appropriate to object. 'Hey, don't go too far.'

'Do you seriously want to watch me?'

'I just want to keep an eye on you, that's all.'

'Pretty much the same thing.'

'Stop making such a big deal out of it. There are trees here and it's dark.'

'Oh, in that case, why can I still see you here staring at me?'

For the first time that night, Jesse couldn't help but laugh. It felt inappropriate, but the situation was so weirdly familiar. Sandra and Isa never wanted to use the toilets at service stations. The alternative was to go in a bush or at the edge of the woods. A kind of hygienic emergency backup plan, complete with pocket tissues in the glove compartment. 'If you keep going on about it, I'll eventually have to come over there and drag you back,' he called out.

He turned around and unbuttoned his jeans. The hot urine streamed onto the snow in front of his feet and steamed up from the ground in the reflection of the sparse light. His toes pressed against the leather inside his shoes. They had to be almost a size and a half smaller than his own. Sandra had always claimed not to like men with small feet – something about them toppling over too easily. He quickly buttoned up his fly. 'Jule?'

Nothing but silence from the undergrowth.

He screwed up his eyes and squinted through the black branches in the half-light. The lights of the petrol station were reflected a dull greyish blue on the snow-white ground.

'Jule!'

Still no answer. A metallic thud drifted through the air from somewhere in the distance. Jesse panicked and ran over to the spot where he had just seen Jule. Branches flew into his face as he ran, and the crusted snow crunched under the soles of his shoes. The snow was trodden down where she had just been standing, and her footprints were heading in the opposite direction from the petrol station. Light shone through the tangle of branches above her footprints. It seemed there was another car park nearby.

'Jule!'

He started running with a slightly bent posture, holding his arms out in front of his face for protection. Before he knew it, the trees were behind him and he was stumbling over a kerb that was hidden beneath a snowdrift. In front of him was a sizeable car park. The snow had obscured all the markings, and now there were just a few signposts for HGVs sticking out of it. Swarms of snowflakes hovered in the glow of the street lamps around a dozen parked forty-tonne trucks with glistening white roofs. About thirty metres away, he could see Jule standing in front of the driver's cab of the first articulated lorry in the car park. She was banging on the driver's door with the palm of her hand. A light went on inside the cab.

Jesse ran as fast as he could. A bear of a man opened the door and rubbed his eyes at the woman standing in front of him and gesticulating wildly.

'Jule!'

Her head turned around first, then the long-distance driver also looked over in Jesse's direction. He sluggishly climbed out of the driver's cab and stood up straight next to Jule just as Jesse caught up with her.

'For God's sake Jule, what are you doing?' Jesse panted, trying to pull her away by the arm.

'Leave me alone.' Her green eyes flashed defiantly, confident that she had won. If he didn't think of something immediately, Jule was going to get away and he'd have the police on his back, which meant Isa's life would be in serious danger. The lorry driver glowered at him and gave him the once over. Jesse guessed he must be in his late thirties. His hair was flat and his eyes seemed slightly cloudy, like he'd been drinking. A considerable gut protruded beneath his bulky chest and his upper arms were almost the same size as his thighs. It was hard to tell whether they were mainly fat or muscle.

'Please,' Jule urged him. 'Can I come with you?'

Jesse forced a smile and gave the driver a nod. 'I'm sorry. Sometimes my wife can be a bit—' – he twirled his index finger by his temple – '— she forgot to take her pills today, you see.' He reached out to Jule. 'Come one, love. Let's go. It's for your own good.'

'Don't believe a word he says!'

The man's eyes flitted back and forth between them. He ground his jawbone; the situation seemed too much of him. '*Co się dzieje?*'

A weight was lifted from Jesse shoulders. The guy didn't understand them!

'Do you speak English?' Jule asked,

The giant shook his head '*Polska.*'

'Please! Help me.' Jule rolled up her sleeves and showed him her wrists, urging him to show some compassion. The lorry driver frowned when he saw the marks from the cable ties.

'Jule, please don't.'

The man took a step closer to Jesse and glowered at him. '*Odejdź!*'

Jule climbed into the driver's cab behind the Polish man, who shoved Jesse in the chest, away from the truck. His hands were like two big shovels and the snow was whirling all around him, like a force field. 'We can talk about it, Jule. But please don't do anything stupid! This isn't about you or me. It's about Isa.'

'Give me one good reason why I should play along with this madness.'

'Like I said: Isa.'

'You could have phoned the police hours ago.'

'*Policja?*' The Polish driver gave Jesse another shove in the chest.

'Give me a chance, for God's sake. What if I'm right?'

Jule tried to look over the driver's shoulder. He was standing in her way, blocking her view of Jesse. 'You tied me up and abducted me.'

'Did I have any choice?' Jesse yelled. The Pole seemed to be getting more and more irate each time Jesse said anything.

'What are you hoping to achieve by driving all the way to Adlershof?' Do you seriously think she's there?'

'No . . . I don't know. Maybe. You said it yourself. This has something to do with the past. But I can't remember anything. That's why I have to go there. If I can find out the reason for this, I'll be able to figure out who's kidnapped her too.' He reached out to Jule. 'Come on.'

'*Odejdź!*' The Polish lorry driver knocked Jesse's hand out of the way.

Jesse retreated further, but the Pole followed him.

'What if it's got nothing to do with Adlershof?'

'It does, and you know it! You're just scared. And there's another thing,' Jesse yelled, straining his neck so he could see her better. 'Sandra was at Adlershof not that long ago.'

Jule stopped talking for a moment and seemed to be thinking about what he'd said. 'How do you know that?'

'Adlershof was already in the satnav – the full address. She must have entered it when she went there. I think she spoke to Markus. She said something along those lines yesterday morning when I dropped Isa off. But I didn't quite catch what she meant then—'

The lorry driver's fist rammed into Jesse's stomach without the slightest warning. He felt the strips tearing off the wound, then he doubled over in pain and staggered backwards. 'Jule, please!' he panted and gasped for air.

The Pole seemed to be waiting to see whether Jesse would give up and back down. He towered above him, blocking his view of the driver's cab with his huge body.

'Whatever you do, please just leave the police out of it,' Jesse shouted. He braced himself for another blow, but the lorry driver seemed to be hesitating and trying to get the measure of Jesse. Then he spat in his face. '*Szpetna świnia.*'

Jesse wiped his face with his coat sleeve, then shrank back further and tried to judge his chances against the Pole. Yes, he was a big guy, but he was surely also a bit slow. He slid his hand into his coat pocket and fumbled around for the car key. Sandra's house key was hanging on the key ring too. Small, jagged and sharp. The kind of thing he could use as a weapon in an emergency – he'd learned that in the home. He closed his fist around the inconspicuous piece of metal as the lorry driver edged threateningly closer.

'No, stop! Leave him alone,' Jule yelled. Her voice was so loud that it made the Pole spin around. Jule moved towards him and waved her arms about. 'Leave him alone!' she cried.

The Pole looked from her to Jesse and b..
'*Niewdzięczną suką!*' he snarled.

'Yes, yes! It's OK. Leave him alone.'

The Pole banged his forehead with the palm of h..
then tapped his wrist several times and pointed to Jesse. '*Chc.. ..
wrócić do tego?*'

'Sorry. Really, I'm sorry.'

There was a sinister glint in his eyes.

'Jule, leave it,' Jesse said softly. 'He doesn't understand you.
Whatever you say just gets him even more riled up.'

Jule stopped talking. The three of them stood in the snowstorm, the lorry driver looking angry and confused in between
Jesse and Jule. Jule walked around his huge frame in a semicir-
cle and made a point of standing next to Jesse. The Pole's eyes
glinted with contempt and residual alcohol. His upper body
leaned forward a touch. Jesse wasn't sure if it was supposed to
be a threatening stance or just poor posture. He calmly lifted his
hands and walked backwards with Jule.

'Don't you dare tie my hands together again,' she hissed,
'or accuse me of being scared.'

'OK.' Jesse was careful not to take his eyes off the lorry driver.
His stomach and hips ached with every step he took. The trucker
stayed in the same spot as they moved away, and although he
seemed to get smaller with every step they took, there was
something positively eerie about the way he stood completely
still in the middle of the driving snow.

They trudged through the little patch of woodland in the
freezing cold and made their way to the car, then collapsed into
their seats without stopping to kick the snow off their boots. The
warmth of the car came as a welcome relief. Jesse accidentally put

too much pressure on the accelerator and the tyres hurled fresh snow into the air, the Volvo's four-wheel drive kicking in. They drove past the truck stop, taking one last glance at the man staggering over to his articulated lorry through the swirling snow.

Jesse wished he could just stop for a while to close his eyes and breathe in the silence. But he couldn't, so instead he took a swig of lukewarm coffee and merged onto the A9. The speedometer hovered at seventy kilometres per hour for a while, but that still seemed too fast for him.

'Everything OK?' He asked.

'Hmm,' Jule muttered.

He didn't ask her what he really wanted to know. He was glad she was sitting next to him instead of calling the police on some long-distance driver's phone, but he still didn't totally understand what had happened.

'I need the toilet,' she murmured finally

He would have laughed in any other circumstances. Now he just nodded and thought to himself: *I've got to take a look at my wound.*

Chapter 16

1979, Garmisch-Partenkirchen

He thought long and hard after the episode with the uniform. A whole eight weeks, to be precise. He wondered if he'd gone mad. Lost the plot. But he just couldn't get the woman out of his head. He couldn't stop thinking about that woman and his plan.

He decided to give it a shot.

The following Friday he pulled a sickie. His father was never bothered whether he went to school or not anyway. All he cared about was that he came back on time to do his chores and keep the flat clean.

When his father went to the toilet at around one o'clock that afternoon, he took the uniform off the hanger and put it on again. His father only emerged from the bathroom at two o'clock – and stared at him like he didn't know which of them had lost their mind.

'Take that off now,' he hissed, slurring his words slightly.

He obediently took the uniform off and stood there completely naked except for his underpants.

The trousers were far too long for him and they were now completely crumpled.

The veins in his father's throat and temples popped out. He drove his fist into his stomach.

He fell to his knees and doubled over, wheezing.

'Put your clothes back on. And stand over there.'

'Stand up straight. Arms up.'

He could hardly manage to stand up straight because of the pain in his stomach. His arms were shaking too, sagging like broken wings. Another blow to the kidneys made it even harder. He wished his father was stupid enough to hit him in the face, then everyone could see his bruises and the pain wouldn't run so deep.

'Stay there. Don't move an inch.'

Yes, sir. He tried his best to keep still.

He heard an all too familiar rattling sound behind him. His father put the ironing board up and plugged the iron into the socket. He ironed the trousers and fired off commands whenever he saw his arms started to droop. Until the orders and threats no longer worked, and nothing could make him keep his arms up any more. All the muscles in his body burned and tears ran down his face. Where was the woman? She had to get here eventually! He'd chosen Friday for a reason. The women always came on Fridays, Saturdays and Sundays. No matter how much Father drank, he always stuck to his routine. And the pressure was always at its peak on Fridays.

Had he made a mistake? Was anyone going to come after all?

'Do you know what you've got coming to you?'

He shook his head and pressed his wet, salty lips together. His father turned him around, pushed him against the wall and squared right up to him. He yanked his shirt out of his trousers with his left hand and pulled it all the way up to his neck. His father was holding the iron with his right hand, pointing the smooth, hot metal surface at his bare chest.

'You'll never learn, will you? I wouldn't have to do this to your brother. He wouldn't need telling. But you, you always have to push your luck, don't you?'

His father's breath stank of alcohol and tinned ravioli. The iron was just centimetres away from his chest. For God's sake, when was the doorbell going to ring? Why wasn't anyone coming?

'Come on. Let's have a countdown!' His voice was brimming with excitement. 'How does that sound? You can count, I'll do the deed. Let's start at ten.'

This wasn't part of the plan. He didn't want to count down, but what else could he do? The iron edged closer.

'Ten.'

His voice quivered, like the iron hovering over him.

'Nine.'

He wet himself on the count of eight. He had deliberately drunk so much water this time that his trousers were soon sopping. He silently begged for the doorbell to ring.

'Seven.'

He paused. For too long.

'Go on!' his father whispered in a hoarse voice. 'Your brother and I are waiting.'

'Six.' Oh, how he wished he could press that iron into his brother's face.

'I can't hear you.'

'Five.'

He lost hope and turned around. His father held on to him with his steely grip.

'Four,' he croaked.

His chest felt like it was on fire, like his skin was blistering. He bit his tongue and tasted metal. He cursed himself for being so stupid.

'Keep going!'

He shook his head. He wanted to roar with pain.

'Three,' his father counted. 'Two.'

The doorbell rang.

His father's hand froze. The air smelled of burnt skin. 'Turn to face the wall and stay where you are, OK?'

He left him standing there and walked over to the door.

This time no one laughed when his father opened the door.

'Did someone order extra-large?' his father grunted. The footsteps were getting closer. 'Right, then, let's see what you've got. The top half looks promising enough. Are you shaved?

He glanced over his shoulder anxiously.

The woman on her way into the room had small lips, a round figure and breasts he was sure would flop over her big belly when she sat down.

'Don't worry about him. He's been up to no good.

She looked at his arms. He'd made a point of lifting them again, as hard as that was. Then she let her eyes wander down to his sopping wet trousers. She couldn't see the burnt skin on his chest, but she could see the pain in his face. Her eyes widened and then scrunched up again. His legs gave way and he fell to the floor.

I've won, he said to himself silently.

His plan had worked. His phone call had been successful and social services had arrived in the form of Ms Wisselsmeier.

He left Kronaustrasse that same day. And he took his brother with him.

Chapter 17

Garmisch-Partenkirchen – Tuesday, 8 January 2013, 5.07 a.m.

Artur Messner lay awake. Ghosts, ghosts and more ghosts. He could almost feel them clawing at him his skin, fraying his nerves. If he wasn't thinking about Jesse, he was worrying about Charly. But he blocked Charly out of his mind – he couldn't stop thinking about the container in the freezer compartment. So he got up. That was the only way to escape the prison in his own bed.

He walked over to the fridge in his woollen socks.

Door open, light on.

He squinted and reached for the drinks shelf. The screw cap on the wine bottle opened with a displeasing crunch and the thread crumbled. At one time he would have wiped the fragments of glass away with a towel, but he didn't care about that now. If something ended up in his glass, he would just wash it down with the Riesling. The bottle was almost empty anyway.

He poured the dregs into the first glass he came across and took a hefty swig in the cold light of the open fridge. Surely it wouldn't bother Richard if the electricity bill was a bit higher than normal – not like it used to bother him, anyway. Sometimes Artur really couldn't understand how Richard had managed to find all the money. Looking back now, he really felt like a failure, like everything he'd brought upon himself could have been avoided. How much easier might his life have been if he'd never met Ms Wisselsmeier or agreed to her proposal? But he really needed the money. And he saw nothing wrong with bending the German adoption rules ever so slightly, doctoring the odd file here or there. The whole legal process was so woefully complicated, he felt like he was doing a good deed by circumventing the rules a little. He could still clearly remember the first time: Raphael, 1972, shortly before the Olympic Games in Munich. A good deal, if not equally precarious. In strict confidentiality: an agreement between old friends, so to speak. Sebi and Renate Kochl, a well-heeled couple, were fond of children and very frustrated. No, not frustrated: desperate. Unsurprising really, after three miscarriages and a failed attempt at uterine surgery. The whole ordeal drove Renate Kochl to a nervous breakdown, which led to a spell in a clinic, which of course left its mark on her record. Adoption law gave precedence to stable families, not those with stigma attached to them. So when the Kochls got to adopt little Raphael, it was a miracle of the purest kind. It also landed Adlershof its first profitable donation. And of course, Ms Wisselsmeier got her piece of the pie. He still got goose pimples when he thought about what had come of the whole affair.

The light from the fridge glinted in the wine, shining a golden will-o'-the-wisp on the wall. He washed down the last mouthful. He would need more than that to keep the ghosts at bay. But that would involve going to the kitchen, or maybe even to the cellar. He might as well venture out into the snow and try to get rid of the container and its gruesome contents. Then he could look for the Riesling on the way back to the kitchen.

But what if he couldn't cope with the exertion?

His body tingled. He felt like a little boy about to hatch a risky plan. He glanced over at the freezer compartment, trying to find one last compelling reason that would help make up his mind. The plastic door was light grey. Plain and inconspicuous. Unremarkable, as long as nobody knew what was behind it. The file inside the compartment was covered by a sprawling layer of protective ice. But the container wasn't. How long would it take for Philippa or someone else to come along, supposedly looking out for poor old Artur, then take the container out of the freezer compartment and look inside?

He shook his head. And then he made his decision.

He threw on his parka and a pair of warm trousers, then he pulled his hat down over his forehead and off he went. He was holding a plastic bag with the container and a torch in his right hand and his boots in the other. He quietly shuffled along the old parquet in the hall in just his socks. His skin was tingling. God, he hadn't felt so alive in a long time. Or so depressed. The bag rustled as it swung back and forth.

He pulled his boots on when he got to the kitchen. He sighed when he peered into the pantry. Riesling. But first things first, he had to deal with the container. He unlocked the side exit and cautiously made his way into the small courtyard. It was still snowing ever so slightly. Solitary snowflakes fluttered to the ground in the yellow beam of his torch. The garage and the shed were over to his right, and the bins were straight ahead of him. Perhaps he wouldn't have to walk far after all. The tied-up bag with the container in it surely wouldn't be noticed if he put it somewhere alongside the other bin bags. Then it would be gone with the next rubbish collection.

He trudged over to the bins, feeling conflicted. The bag was like a lead weight. He peered between the boards and saw the metal bins with their lids covered in fresh snow. He tried to push the gate back but stopped, baffled. Crap! A padlock. What was all this nonsense? Did they have to lock the rubbish away these days? Perhaps it was because of the kids. No doubt one of the little rascals had been up to no good. Maybe one of them had done something that meant the rubbish had to be kept out of reach – tipped rubbish into a teacher's bed or something like that. He couldn't help secretly hoping that Richard had been on the receiving end of whatever it was. But he was ashamed of himself for feeling that way.

But where to next? The path down to the lake was too steep for his old bones. How about the cellar – maybe the old part at the back? Then he thought of the gatehouse. The Adlershof caretaker, a fellow called Kawczynski, had lived in that little cottage for years, and of course there was a bin there too. The house was designed in the style of an English country cottage and was maybe five hundred metres up the way. He knew that Kawczynski was a deep sleeper from when he was a little boy.

He plodded ahead, pointing the torch at the ground the whole time. The path had been cleared earlier that evening and was now lined by walls of snow. A solid layer of older snow was visible beneath almost twenty centimetres of fresh snow.

Artur started puffing and could feel himself sweating. *Small steps, slowly does it*, he urged himself, keeping his eyes firmly fixed on the ground. The snow crunched under his weight. A couple of minutes later he looked up and recognised the outlines of the gatehouse. The natural stone wall with the stepped gable cut a clear figure against the white forest behind it. But what was that? There was a light on in one of the ground-floor windows. He turned off his torch, taken aback. The light in the gatehouse went out at almost exactly the same time. The window frame seemed to keep glowing in the dark.

Artur stood in the snow and hesitated.

Was it a coincidence? Or had Kawczynski seen him out there with his torch?

Perhaps I'm not the only one with ghosts haunting them at this time of night, he thought to himself. Or maybe Kawczynski just needed to go to the toilet.

He left the torch off as a precaution and continued to creep along in the dark, then he turned onto the main path about a hundred metres away from the gate. Why did they call it the gatehouse when it was so far away from the gate? He had never quite understood. Maybe that's just the sort of thing that happened when you got an eccentric British woman designing a manor house in the Bavarian Alps around 1906. The narrow cul-de-sac was more slippery than the main path, and the last few metres were a challenge to say the least. The gatehouse was quiet and dark, and the carport looked out of place on the historical façade. The parking space was empty, but he recognised the outlines of three large wheelie bins by the back exit underneath the carport roof.

Artur slowed down and tried to calm his breathing. The cold air tickled his throat and he struggled to fight the urge to cough.

The sound of a car engine seemed to be approaching. He spun around, then saw a glimmer of light appearing over the hilltop. The car headlights blazed onto the main path through the gate. He quickly made his way under the carport and pushed himself against the outside wall behind the bins. The car followed the bend in the road and the beam from the headlights brushed over him. Artur blinked, irritated. Who on earth was out in their car at this time of night?

The car slowed down and turned towards the gatehouse. The headlights shone on Artur's footprints in the fresh snow.

Artur ducked behind the bins as quickly as he could. The carport was bathed in the white halogen light coming from the headlamps. Snow chains were gently rattling as the car ground to a halt just outside the house. It sounded like it had a powerful diesel engine. It had to be a four-wheel drive, otherwise it would have had great difficulty dealing with the mountain roads in this snow.

The sound from the engine died down, but the beam from the headlights remained. First the driver's door opened, then he heard steps crunching in the snow. A long shadow approached on the ground. 'Hello there,' a man's voice called.

Artur held his breath.

'What are you doing there?'

As childish as it was, Artur stayed crouched behind his bin. His knees were aching, and he was fighting back the unbearable urge to cough.

'I've seen you. Come out from behind the bin.'

Artur hurriedly emptied the plastic bag with the container in it in the shadow of the bin, then he reluctantly got up from his perch. His left knee cracked like a twig. The light stung his eyes and cast a cold, hazy white outline around a man's silhouette. He stayed quiet for a moment.

'Hello, Artur,' the man said eventually. He seemed surprised, but not in a good way.

'Who are you?' Artur asked.

'What are you up to?'

'I . . . um . . . nothing. I had . . .' Artur fell silent. He wished he had the eyes of a younger man so that he could see more than a dark shape in a halo of light. 'Where had he heard that voice before? It almost sounded a bit like Jesse's when he first heard it. 'Do we know each other?' he asked.

'We spoke on the phone, not that long ago.'

Artur's stomach tied up in knots. Suddenly the voice sounded much less like Jesse's. The headlights went out behind the man's back, but the outlines continued to glow on Artur's retinas.

Chapter 18

Jesse steered the Volvo around the last hairpin bend on the slope, using the wheel more for support than to steer the car. He had been awake for over twenty-six hours already and the caffeine was no longer working. His gnawing worries about Isa were the only thing keeping him awake. He hadn't taken any painkillers whatsoever in the last few hours, hoping that might keep the tiredness at bay. Just one more drop of mepivacaine when he stitched his wound on a short pit stop.

At least it had stopped snowing. The sky was light already, but shadows were still stretching out over the hillside. The road became narrower again, and a rough black boulder jutted out onto the roadway from the side of the hill, like it had been tossed there by a giant. Jesse nudged Jule with his elbow.

'Hey, wake up. We're there.'

Jule sat up in her seat and stretched her legs out, pushing her feet onto the floor. She had turned down the offer of coffee and cola earlier and had eventually fallen asleep from exhaustion.

'What's all that clattering?'

'Snow chains. I got some at the last petrol station.'

She rubbed her eyes and noticed the time. Eight o'clock. 'Bloody hell, is it that time already? How come it's taken so long?'

'The snow ploughs won't be able to keep up after the volume of snow that fell here last night.'

'Hence the snow chains.'

Jesse nodded. 'It's high season too. Anyone who owns a pair of skis is out and about. The streets are full of tourists.'

'Apparently not here though, huh?'

'No. The tourists don't make it up here. And the next ski slope is pretty far away.'

They drove a few more metres uphill, then suddenly the view opened up onto the mountains. A pale sun was rising over the ridge, pouring a pure, even white haze over the sky and the snow.

Jule had leaned forward and was looking at the majestic white peaks through the windscreen. 'It's . . . amazing.'

'Sounds like you've never been to the mountains.'

'Well, never like this, anyway.'

The gate to Adlershof loomed ahead of them with its black wings.

'A gate without a fence,' Jule muttered.

If you don't have a home, you can't run away, Jesse thought to himself. He drove past the gatehouse on the right and followed the gentle curves of the path.

'Wow,' Jule said, leaning back in her seat. 'It's like . . . we're in the Highlands or something.'

Looming up ahead of them, about three hundred metres away, was the impressive natural stone façade of Adlershof: the central building and the extensions on either side, with their stepped gables and the heavy chimneys, all in the style of an English country house. The snow-topped roofs merged with the wintry landscape.

'This was where you all lived?'

Jesse didn't answer. The sight of the place had taken him back decades. His tiredness gave way to a sudden pang of tension. And not just because of Isa, but because he'd always felt tense, on edge. It was almost like none of it had happened to him, but yes, this *was* where he had grown up. Perhaps he would have had a better opinion of Adlershof if he could remember what had happened before, when he lived with his father. How absurd it was to want to remember something as awful as that, just so he could see this place as something like home.

When the imposing main building was about two hundred metres in front of them, Jesse steered right onto a narrow path lined with snow-covered firs, then into a larger parking area concealed by the surrounding trees. The crunching of the fresh snow under the wheels ceased as he parked the Cross Country. The sudden silence gave free rein to the strange, gnawing feeling inside him.

'Now what do you want to do?'

'Ask Markus a few questions.'

'What is Markus even doing here? Why does he still live here?'

'He's the caretaker.'

'Caretaker? In the home where he grew up? That's—'

'What? Strange?'

'Well, maybe not,' she said, then paused for a moment. 'My dad's a dentist. In Blankenese. My sister works in his practice now. As a dental nurse.'

He looked at her, mystified.

Jule shrugged.

'It might be best for you to stay in the car,' Jesse muttered.

'You've got to be joking. I have to get out of here.'

He looked her up and down. 'Where's that young woman who always smiles and nods so sweetly?'

'She's sitting tied up in a service station near Jena.'

Jesse made a face. 'It's just I don't know how Markus is going to react.'

'There are people inside there,' she pointed at the building 'I'm sure he'll manage to control himself.'

'He doesn't live in the main building.'

'So where does he live, then?'

'In the gatehouse. The little cottage over there near the gate. We just passed it.'

Jule glanced out of the side window, but she couldn't see for the snow-covered firs in her line of vision.

'I'm going to head over there.' Jesse put the key in his pocket, got out of the car and threw his coat on. His breath steamed in the cold morning air. 'If I'm not back in half an hour, head to the main building.'

Without further ado, he slammed the door shut and started stomping through the pristine snow. The firs were positively bending under the weight of the snow, casting a gloomy shadow over the narrow path. Jesse had to strain his eyes when he emerged from the patch of woodland. He turned left and purposefully marched towards the gatehouse. He could see some clearly defined footprints in the snow: they were coming from the main building behind him, then they veered right and continued along the narrow path to the gatehouse. Fresh tyre tracks had dug into the snow beside the building.

The gatehouse looked abandoned. Something about the old building had changed, but Jesse couldn't quite put his finger on what it was. His heart was beating faster with every step he took. Perhaps Markus had already seen him. Would he even open the door?

The footprints led him under the carport. There were more tracks here and it looked like the car had done a U-turn in front of the carport and driven back over towards the main path. Jesse couldn't make sense of the footprints. He was taken aback when he made it to the front door. The weather-beaten oak had been carefully nailed shut with two wide slats of wood in a cross shape. He stared at the 'X' in disbelief. The brass doorbell was rusty and looked like it wouldn't work. He pressed it anyway, but all he could hear was the soft sound of the ice around the frozen buzzer cracking and giving way.

He went up to the window and peered through until the tip of his noise touched the glass, then wiped a circle clean with his hands. Perplexed, he realised that the windows were boarded up on the inside.

The gatehouse seemed to be uninhabited.

The snow behind him crunched, making him spin around.

Jule looked anxious, and a little sheepish. She brushed her blond hair behind her ear with her right hand and then dusted some snow off her shoulders. 'What now?'

'Why aren't you in the car?'

'I was watching you from over there.' She pointed in the direction of the trees. Apparently she had taken a shortcut from where the car was parked.

The sound of a diesel engine approaching at high speed filled the air behind her. A forest-green Toyota Land Cruiser was coming from the main building, and the walls of snow lining the path made it look like it had no wheels. The off-roader stopped around twenty metres away from them, and someone rolled the window down. Smoke billowed up from the exhaust. 'Can I help you?' the voice echoed across. Jesse recognised it immediately. Artur, just a younger version.

'Hello? You're on private land, you know.'

'Richard,' Jesse called. 'It's me, Jesse.'

Richard Messner leaned over the passenger seat to the open window. The diesel engine was gargling away softly. 'Well, I'll be damned!'

Chapter 19

Tuesday, 8 January 2013

Artur opened his eyes. Everything was sort of sticky and he felt dizzy, like he was coming around from an anaesthetic. Good thing he was lying on his back on a soft surface. A heavy old roof beam was hovering above him in the shadows, and above the beam there was a pitched roof. Where in God's name was he? And what had happened to him? The last thing he could remember was leaving the main building and walking down the drive. Then the package came into his head. Of course! Wilbert's hand. He had been trying to get rid of it.

'Are you OK?' The voice was soft – weak and high-pitched. Definitely that of a child.

Artur blinked in confusion. He wanted to respond, but all he could manage was a faint grumble. His throat felt like sand-paper. He tried to prop himself up, but his arms sank into the mattress. No support, no strength.

'Hello?' he rasped.

No answer.

Had he just imagined the child's voice?

He bent his legs so that his withered knees were pointing upwards, then he used his legs to gain some momentum and rolled onto his right side. The edge of the mattress formed a blurry line in front of his eyes. There were floorboards on the other side of the line, so evidently the mattress was lying flat on the floor. He could make out the outlines of a sturdy table, then a chiselled post supporting the roof ridge a couple of metres away. A little girl was sitting on the floor leaning against it with her knees pulled into her chest. She was wearing dark-blue winter tights, children's boots, a mid-calf length skirt with a bold red and blue tartan pattern on it, and a pea coat that was too big for her. Her blond, shoulder-length hair was dishevelled, and her eyes were blue and anxious, with a hint of defiance. The left side of her face looked like she had suffered a blow.

'Where . . . where am I?' Artur asked.

The child said nothing, but stared back at him. How old would she be? Eight? Maybe nine? Artur was beginning to feel nauseous, but fought the urge to throw up. If only he could just sit up!

'Do you feel sick?' the girl asked.

Artur nodded and started racking his brain, trying to work out why the girl seemed familiar to him. Could she be from the home? Bloody useless memory! He recognised hardly any of the children these days, but then again, he barely left his room. 'What's your name?'

'Isabelle,' the little girl said, with a sniff. 'What about you?'

'Artur.'

She said nothing for a moment. 'Are you sick?'

'No, just old. Or – yes,' he corrected himself and tried to sit up again. 'Maybe I'm a bit sick too.'

Isabelle stood up and cautiously edged closer. 'My dad's a doctor.'

Artur pursed his lips, nodded and concentrated on moving his legs over the edge of the mattress so he could stand up. Isabelle observed his efforts with a conflicted look on her face. She seemed scared that Artur might do something to her. But he couldn't even sit up. He felt truly pathetic.

Suddenly the girl moved. She reached for Artur's legs and dragged him over the edge of the mattress, then grabbed his left arm with as firm a grip as she could manage. He could feel her warm hands through his jumper as she pulled at him with all her strength. He pushed his other arm into the mattress and groaned as he sat up. She let go of him as soon as he was upright, as if he had an infectious disease that she was scared she might catch.

'Thank you,' he groaned.

Now he was finally sitting up, he wasn't so sure it had been such a great idea. His circulation took a while to get going. He closed his eyes for a moment, then opened them again. 'Isabelle,' he murmured. 'Where are we?'

'I don't know,' the girl whispered. 'He brought you here too. Like me.'

'Who?'

'The insect man.'

Artur frowned. A pair of glaring headlights appeared inside his head. A silhouette, clouds of breath. 'Insect man,' he muttered. 'Why is he the insect man?'

'Because of the thing on his head. Like a mask.' She drew circles around her eyes. 'With circles of glass for eyes and a sort of filtery-snout thing.

Artur gulped. What on earth had he got himself dragged into? 'A snout?' He tried to imagine what she was talking about. 'Do you know who this insect man is?'

She shook her head frantically.

'How . . . so how did he bring you here?'

'I was lying in bed at home, listening to music, then suddenly he came in. I screamed, but then I don't know what happened next. I woke up in a car – in the back seat, with a hood over my head. My dad called me, but the insect man heard and took my phone off me.'

Oh God, and now this. A kidnapping. Artur was sure he would have had a seizure by now if he wasn't sitting down.

'Didn't you say your dad was a doctor?'

She nodded. 'In Berlin. He's is a paediatrician.'

'Paediatr—' His voice failed him. Isabelle. Berlin.

It all fit together. 'What's your dad's name?'

'Jesse. Why?'

Artur felt a chill down his spine. *Act normal, don't let her see.* But his mind was racing. The package with the hand. Then the phone call from the man asking for Jesse's address. And now he, too, had been kidnapped by this same man, and here he was, sitting with Jesse's abducted daughter.

'Do you have a phone?' Isabelle asked.

Artur snapped out of his thoughts with a jolt. 'Huh?'

'Do you have a phone?'

He shook his head.

Isabelle smiled courageously. Then she sniffed again. 'I had to tell Dad not to call the police. But I didn't tell Mum. I didn't have to tell Mum.' There was a glimmer of hope in her eyes. 'Mum will definitely call the police.'

'Definitely,' Artur said, trying hard to inspire as much confidence as he could with his voice. 'And until she gets here, I'll stay with you.'

Chapter 20

'How long has it been?' Richard asked.

'Since I was last here? About fifteen years? I came to see Artur. You hadn't taken over from him yet,' Jesse replied. His eyes scanned the expensive off-roader. He had tramped over to Richard in the snow and was talking to him through the rolled-down window on the passenger side.

'I see the old man's been keeping you up to date,' Richard said.

'Yes,' Jesse said, even though he hadn't heard much from Artur. Still, it was no bad thing to let Richard think they'd been in touch.

Richard looked at him, clearly trying to reconcile the Jesse from his memory with the Jesse standing in front of him now. It was just the same for Jesse. Richard's receding hairline, the first signs of a double chin, and the same rosy red cheeks. Two white tips of a shirt with embroidered Edelweiss flowers on it protruded over the collar of his dark green coat. Richard used to be ashamed of his father's conservative side – look at him now!

'What are you doing here?' Richard asked.

'I was feeling homesick.'

'Homesick? You?'

'Well, I can't be the first one, can I?'

'No,' Richard gave a joyless laugh. 'But the others are a different kettle of fish. None of them had your brains. Apart from maybe Markus.'

'Speaking of Markus: didn't he live in the gatehouse? Did he move?'

'The gatehouse? Markus?' Richard's tone suddenly changed, like he could sense trouble was brewing. But that was always the case when Jesse and Markus were in the same place at the same time. 'Yes, but he moved out.'

'Did he leave town?'

'No, he didn't leave. He just moved to the north wing.'

'Ah.' Jesse studied the main building down the road. Its contours stood out against the backlight. 'Is he around?'

Instead of answering, Richard gave a brusque nod in Jule's direction. 'Who's she?' Jule's footsteps crunched in the snow behind Jesse.

'A friend.'

'Hmm.' Richard's disapproval was obvious. He was always carrying his moral judgements around his neck like someone trying to sell their wares. 'So how's your wife doing?' he sneered.

Jesse said nothing, trying to fight the image that flashed up in his head. Richard seemed to interpret his silence differently.

'So, is Markus around?'

'He'll be back tonight. Took a couple of days off.'

'Off?'

'Yes, that's what I said. Seems to me like this homesickness is pretty personal.'

Jesse felt Jule's hand on his back. Gentle pressure. A warning. Stay calm.

'What's the deal with the gatehouse?'

'It's being renovated.' Richard was obviously being tight-lipped on the matter.

'And Artur?'

'You're better off asking the old grouch yourself.'

'I will. I just wanted to know if he was around.'

Richard hesitated. He seemed to like this question even less than the one about Markus. 'Philippa is looking for him now, actually,' he finally admitted. 'She went to give him his breakfast and he wasn't there.' Richard laughed. 'But where could he possibly have wandered off to? It's not like there's anywhere he needs to be.'

Jesse nodded, even though he felt like the joke was in bad taste. Richard directed his disdainful gaze at him, suddenly noticing the state he was in. 'You look worn out. Are you OK?'

Jesse couldn't even begin to describe all the things that weren't OK. He desperately needed painkillers for the wound and his body was in need of a break. Not to mention everything else. 'Do you have any rooms free?'

Richard glanced at Jule. 'One room?'

'One will do.' Despite Jule's apparent change of heart in the petrol station car park, he still wasn't sure where he stood with her. Best to keep her close.

Richard raised his eyebrows, then without saying a word, he typed a phone number into the touchscreen display in his car. The ringing tone sounded twice, then a slightly prickly female voice answered: 'I haven't found him yet.'

'That's all right, Philippa, he'll turn up. That's not the reason I'm calling. An old friend has just arrived, with company. Jesse Berg. Could you open Kristina's old room for him please?'

'Kristina? I don't know who she is,' the voice replied.

'Oh yes. That was before your time,' Richard mumbled.

'East wing. Third floor, last door on the left down the hall.'

'The corner room with that awful bed?'

'It's an antique.'

'I think it's hideous. And the mattress stinks.'

Richard grimaced. 'Just do as I say, please,' he replied coolly.

'Fine. Maybe I'll find Charly under the bed, stupid bloody brat.'

Richard clenched his jaw and swiftly terminated the call. 'I have to go,' he said to Jesse. 'You know the way. Do you have bags with you?'

'In the car,' Jesse lied.

'OK, then, cheerio.' Richard waved, and Jesse noticed he wasn't wearing a ring on any of his fingers. So still no wife, then. And from his interaction with Philippa, it sounded like she was just an employee. The window whirred back up and the Toyota drove on. Jesse caught Jule glaring at him, no doubt because of the words 'one room', 'awful bed' and 'stinking mattress'.

'You're not thinking of locking me in, are you?'

'Not after what happened with the lorry driver.' Jesse concealed his lingering doubts behind a strained smile. 'I have to go back to the car. I need my doctor's bag.'

They trudged back to the car and then on to the main building. Soon they found themselves standing in the long shadow of the Adlershof building. Jule looked up at the imposing stone façade apprehensively. The central building had three floors and an attic lined with dormer windows. The stepped gables of the adjoining wings of the building rose up to the left and the right like two huge jagged arrowheads. On either side of the central building were slightly smaller extensions that had been built at a later stage.

'Who would build something like this in the middle of Bavaria?' Jule asked.

'Two English architects commissioned by a British woman. Victoria Aubree Thurgood.'

'Hence the country house effect.'

'People around these parts always called it the English castle. Victoria Thurgood wanted it to be used as a meeting place for artists, but then the First World War broke out just before they could finish it. They say she never saw the building herself. The Nazis commandeered it for the Hitler Youth during the Second World War, then the Allies moved in and took over.'

Their footsteps crunched in time as they plodded through the snow. The large coat of arms at the centre of the facade had taken a battering from the weather and now all the colours were faded. But, judging by the brickwork, the white sash windows and the red and white paint on the shutters, the rest of the building had been recently renovated.

'And who owns it now? This Richard guy?'

'Richard is Artur's son. But as far as I know, Adlershof is owned by a trust that Artur founded. I don't know much about it. I was never really that interested, to be honest. But Artur would never have kept Adlershof running without outside help.'

They entered through the stone archway supporting the large balcony above the entrance. Jesse noticed that the wooden double doors with the familiar herringbone pattern had been painted white. It offended him, like someone had tampered with his memories. But maybe he was being overly sensitive because he just didn't have enough memories.

The well-oiled door swung open smoothly. The sound of footsteps approaching on the wooden steps resounded in the stairwell. Philippa looked them up and down. 'Are you this Jesse Berg?'

'Yes'

'*The* Jesse?'

'If you say so.'

'Don't go thinking you're welcome.'

Chapter 21

1979, Garmisch-Partenkirchen

Artur Messner hadn't had much time to give him a proper welcome. Or perhaps he didn't want to waste his time on small talk. As
they walked through the corridors of the children's home together,
it seemed like Messner was trying to pack as much information as
possible into the short time they had. At most, Messner's sentences
boiled down to a series of key words: children's home, boarding
school below, classrooms in the east wing, west wing off-limits,
share a room with four other boys, ten rules, giving and taking . . .

He could barely pay attention to what the principal was saying
as he trotted alongside him. It was all just too much to take in at
once. He only had eyes for the vast building: a majestic-looking,
almost awe-inspiring ruin that looked like something out of an
old English story. The Canterville Ghost, perhaps. Or like a castle
from the stories about Nessie. Was there even a castle by Loch
Ness, or was he imagining it? For a horrible moment he feared
there was no room for him in such a story, in a building like this.
He felt sort of dirty, like there was something bad about him,
something rotten.

But the more he looked at the building and its battered walls,
the dilapidated railings, the dents and loose floorboards in the

herringbone parquet, the more he could see his place in it. This building was like him. Damaged.

They climbed up another flight of stairs until they reached the landing beneath the roof. The boys' block was on one side of the stairs and the girls' block on the other. Messner assigned him to the dorm opposite the laundry room. Five beds in a row, a long sloping ceiling with dormer windows and wooden floorboards painted in a colour which resembled dried blood. The striped wallpaper was green, white and brown, with roughly cut edges and air bubbles here and there.

It almost felt good when he put his suitcase on the floor. So this was his new home. His new life.

Just as he was about to leave, Messner turned to face him again. 'What your father did to you . . . that was—'

'I know,' he snapped. The feeling of being at one with his new surroundings disintegrated in a flash. There it was again, the filth. For God's sake, why did Messner have to remind him about that right now?

Messner remained in the doorway, trying to find the right words. But there were none, goddam it. 'He can't hurt you now you're here.' From the tone of his voice, it sounded like he believed that was all down to him. 'He'll be punished for what he did to you.'

Like that was any comfort! Still, he nodded.

'And perhaps, you never know, that might help you,' Messner added. He looked like he was waiting for a reaction. But what kind of reaction? Tears? Anger? Maybe even hatred?

This man just didn't have a clue. He didn't feel the slightest bit of hatred for his father. He only hated what he had become. And he hated the man who had made him that way. The man who stole his father's life. Wilbert. It was his fault. He was the one who needed to be punished. And every time his father told him about Kiel, he swore that someday he was going to find him and punish him.

'OK, then. All sorted?'

He gulped and nodded, hiding his rage.

'Just ask your roommates if you have any questions. They'll be able to tell you anything you need to know.'

He nodded again.

'Right, then, I'll leave you alone.'

More nodding. Messner's footsteps on the stairs. Alone, at last.

The air was thick and clammy. Five empty beds and bedding that smelled of the other boys in the dorm, a scent that rose and got caught under the sloping ceiling. He found the slight fug almost pleasant compared to the house on Kronaustrasse. He opened the dormer window and sat on the bed underneath it. It creaked invitingly as he sat down. The pillows and duvets on all five beds were carefully laid so he couldn't tell which of them was free, or if any of them were free, for that matter. Hadn't Messner said something about that when they were walking through the building? He couldn't remember. Perhaps he had to sleep on a mattress on the floor here, too, like he had done in his father's house on Kronaustrasse. He didn't have anything against mattresses, but he did find the idea of the creaking bed by the window more appealing. He looked through the clean window inside the warped wooden frame. No shutters like they'd had on Kronaustrasse. No curtains either. Maybe he'd be able to see the moon at night. And now no one would ever compare him to his brother. Never again.

'Oi, get off!'

He flinched. Standing there in the doorway was a boy roughly the same age as him, with a long face, straight dark hair and squinty brown eyes. He had a self-important look on his face and his left arm was against the door jamb. 'I said get off!' the boy repeated. His voice was unusually husky for some-one his age.

He obeyed but took his time to get up. Well, obviously – he didn't want him to think he was a wimp. 'Is this your bed?'

'My bed. My room. What are you doing here?'

'I'm new.'

'New?' The boy with the thin face made his eyes even smaller and turned his nose up, almost as if screwing his face up might help him think. 'You're in our room?'

'Seems that way, doesn't it?'

Three others appeared from behind the thin-faced boy, who was still leaning against the door. The smallest of them poked his head through the gap between the door and the bigger boy's arm. 'Who's this, then, Alois?' he asked.

'Butt out, Mattheo,' Alois snapped. 'Do you know anything about this, Markus?'

Markus, the boy with thick black hair, shook his squarish head. 'Nope, not a thing.'

He looked the new lodger up and down, but he didn't seem as wary as the other boys. 'What's your name?'

'Jesse.'

'I'm Markus,' the square-headed boy said. 'The little guy's Mattheo, and—'

'What are you doing, a round of introductions?' Alois chipped in.

'He'll need to learn our names if he's going to get the hang of things around here.'

'Yeah, so he knows who calls the shots. I'm Wolle,' the fourth and last member of the group introduced himself. The boy had curls down to his chin, an oddly straight mouth and eyebrows so slanted they seemed to be trying to meet at a point in the middle. He seemed equally as unwelcoming as Alois and Mattheo.

'Hi,' Jesse nodded anxiously. He felt uncomfortable in his skin. 'So which bed can I take?'

'None of them,' Alois answered.

Jesse frowned. 'But there are only four of you, and there are five—'

'Who says we don't need the other bed?'

Alois's smile was disconcertingly thin.

'Exactly,' Mattheo squawked.

'The fifth bed is Richard's,' Wolle explained.

'Who's Richard?'

'Richard's another homie,' Mattheo said eagerly. 'He sleeps here, but only sometimes, and—' Alois poked him in the ribs to shut him up.

'What's a homie?'

'You'll find out, newbie. You can sleep on the floor,' said Wolle.

'Is there a mattress?'

'Can you see one?'

Jesse shook his head.

Alois raised his eyebrows. 'Then don't ask such stupid questions. When Mr M does his nightly rounds–'

'Who's Mr M?'

'Messner, the head, of course. Anyway, when he comes around on his nightly rounds you'll be in Richard's bed, and then when he's locked us in you'll get back on the floor. Got it?'

Jesse nodded apprehensively.

'Any more questions?'

'Um, Messner, I mean, Mr M,' Jesse corrected himself, 'locks us in here?'

The boys smirked at each other. 'So what?' Alois asked. 'Scared you'll shit your pants because you can't go to the toilet?'

Jesse gritted his teeth and shook his head.

'Mr M locks the boy's block,' Wolle explained, 'not the rooms. Got it?'

'Got it.'

'Oh, and another thing,' said Markus, who hadn't spoken for a while. 'Whatever happens here at night, you keep your mouth shut. Don't say a word to Mr M.'

Jesse nodded again.

'If you say so much as one word, or if one of us ends up in the hole because of you, we'll open the window and chuck you out of it,' Alois added. The way he smiled was a clear sign that he was being entirely serious.

'And if anyone asks, we'll just say it was an accident. We'll say we warned you, but you took no notice and climbed out anyway,' Mattheo squawked. The words sounded strange coming from him, like someone else had put them in his mouth and he was repeating something he'd heard the others saying a thousand times before.

Chapter 22

Artur Messner stared at the hatch in the centre of the attic. The sound of boots walking up a wooden staircase resonated through the slats on the floor. Isabelle had cautiously shuffled back to the gable end and was crouched down on her mattress with her back against the wall.

He was sitting on his own mattress, with the bars of a warm radiator pressing into the small of his back. He contemplated putting up a fight and attacking the man making his way up the stairs. He kept imagining, if just for a second, that he was young and in full possession of his faculties. When that feeling came over him, he felt compelled to hatch a crazy plan, but it fell to pieces as soon as the delusion wore off.

No, at his age it was better to just wait it out. Wasn't that what he had always done? Wait for things to sort themselves out? The most hideous thing about old age was the clarity of one's self perception. When you got old, there were fewer things to obscure the truth.

Whoever it was pulled back two bolts under the hatch. The noise travelled through the wooden slats and filled the attic. Then the hatch sprung open and hit the floor with a loud bang, stirring up a cloud of dust as it slammed onto the wooden slats. A head appeared through the opening. Whoever it was, he was wearing a black mask. A gas mask. Artur gulped. It was true, the man did look like an insect. Dark eyes glowered at him from behind the slanted oval discs, piercing him with their stare. He thought about the silhouette in the beam of the headlights and wondered whether this was the same man. He wished that none of this was really happening, or at least that his worst fears wouldn't come true. It was just too ... too *what*? He couldn't even put his finger on that.

The man glanced at Isabelle, then he climbed up the last steps and shut the hatch, clearly without a thought for the noise he was making in the process. A bad sign. Obviously, there was nobody nearby who might hear what he was up to.

'Excuse me, what do you want from us?' Artur croaked. He thought it would be safer to be polite to the insect man.

The man put down the sports bag he'd been holding. A wooden handle was sticking out from between the zippers. He opened the bag with his gloved hands without saying a word, then he took out a rope.

'Over there, to the table,' he ordered Artur. His voice sounded hollow and metallic beneath the mask. It also sounded sort of fuzzy, like it had been deliberately distorted or there was some-thing in the man's mouth preventing him from speaking clearly. If it was the man from the gatehouse, then he was obviously going to great lengths to make sure he wouldn't be recognised. 'Now put your right hand flat on the table.'

Artur did as he was told.

'Hey, you. Can you tie a knot?'

Isabelle nodded anxiously.

The man walked over to her and passed her the rope. 'Tie this around his wrist and fasten it.'

Isabelle looked at Artur hesitantly.

What the hell was he planning?

'Hurry up!' The man whacked Isabelle hard in the face with the back of his hand. The little girl grabbed hold of her cheek and stumbled over to Artur in a hurry.

The rope was about half a centimetre thick and made of modern synthetic fibres which made it so flexible that Isabelle's knot virtually tied itself. It dug into his skin. Isabelle looked at him apologetically. Her cheeks were glistening wet.

'Now tie his hand to the table top.'

'How?'

'You're a big girl, aren't you?'

Artur could see that Isabelle really wanted to shake her head, but instead she pressed her lips together and took the rope, then crawled under the table and wrapped it around Artur's hand.

'Tighter.'

Isabelle pulled on the rope, and it pressed Artur's hand onto the top of the table.

'And another knot.'

Her little fingers were trembling. Wisps of her blond hair fell onto her face and she blew them away.

Artur bit his tongue to fight the pain the rope was causing him. What was this all about? He glanced again at the man's holdall and the worn wooden handle sticking out of it, and instantly he understood. Horrified by the realisation, he tried to pull his hand away from the table, but it was too late.

'Stand next to the table,' the man ordered Isabelle.

'No,' Artur whimpered. 'Please, no!'

The man reached for the wooden handle sticking out of the sports bag and pulled out an axe.

There was a look of sheer dread in Isabelle's eyes. Artur was dizzy with fear. He had often worried that his past would come back to bite him, but it had always been a vague, nagging feeling – background noise that he had managed to drown out over the years. The nightly visits from ghosts were the price he'd had to pay, and now one of his ghosts was standing right here in front of him. He pushed against the solid oak table in a senseless, desperate attempt to flee, but it just juddered and grazed the floor, halted by the first little bump it encountered.

'If you move you'll only make it worse,' the man said.

Isabelle screwed her eyes up and shrank back.

'Look at it!'

She shook her head.

'Look, or you're next.'

She quickly opened her eyes, her face white as a sheet, then looked at the table and the hand tied to it.

The man spread his legs out to get a firm footing. He gauged the distance.

'No! Please don't!' Artur begged.

The man slowly took aim and lifted the axe over his head, keeping his eyes on Artur's hand. His unwavering breath hissed faintly through the filter on the gas mask.

Then the axe fell in a swooping arc.

Chapter 23

Jesse and Jule followed Philippa through the corridors. Adlershof was in remarkably good condition compared to what Jesse remembered. The walls must have been freshly painted – there were no signs whatsoever of flaking paint from the impact of doors or windows. The worn herringbone oak floor was sanded and had the deep, dark grain that only shows with a touch of fresh wood oil. They used to call it the 'Nazi floor' when they were kids; not just because of the building's past, but also because the right angles in the parquet bore a slight resemblance to swastikas.

The walls and floor seemed to whisper with every step. Each two sets of oak slats produced an angle like an arrow pointing forward, then the angle of the pair next to it pointed backwards. *This way. Go away. This way. Go away.*

'Where is everyone?' Jule asked.

'Classes only start back next week,' Philippa said. She had just stopped and was opening the door at the end of the hall. 'Here we are.'

Jesse didn't recognise the room, but he did know that the hallway leading to his old room was above them. The distant pattering of feet overhead told him that upstairs was still in use.

Whoever this Kristina woman was, her room was spacious. It had two large windows to the back of Adlershof and was home to a massive double bed with twisted mahogany posts, which sat on the left-hand side of the room. The bulky chest of drawers and the bedside tables matched the bed. All the furniture in the room was covered in a thick layer of dust, and there were spider's webs dangling from the lampshades. A silver frame with an oil painting in it was hanging against the green wallpaper above the bed. It had been drawn with excessively thick brushstrokes and depicted Adlershof in the snow; a similar scene to the one they'd seen just a few minutes ago. The building was as radiant from the outside as it was oppressive on the inside. The parquet in the room was dried out and pale; it clearly hadn't been oiled like the flooring in the corridor. A concealed door to the left of the bed led to a narrow bathroom with misted windows.

'You'll find linen in the chest of drawers,' Philippa said.

Jule gave a deep sigh and cautiously sat down on the mattress, as if she was trying her best not to disturb too much dust. The springs creaked. Jesse stared out of the window without uttering a word and took in the mountain, the sky and the immutable coniferous forest. Only its smell and cushioned floor changed with the seasons. He couldn't see the clearing from where he was standing, but it was there. It too whispered, like the walls and the Nazi floorboards. Adlershof had risen from the depths like Moby Dick and now it was threatening to devour him.

'Now I understand Sandra,' Jule mumbled.

Jesse knew he needed some rest. His forehead was burning, and he felt slightly dizzy. But he knew as well that it was going to be twice as hard to stand back up again if he let himself lie down.

He blinked a couple of times to try to clear his vision, then he rummaged around in his pocket until he found the packet of Ibuprofen. He pressed two tablets out and swallowed them dry, deciding to trust in their antipyretic properties and the anti-inflammatory effect, then he put the rest of the tablets into his trouser pocket. Time was of the essence and Isa was still in the hands of the kidnapper. 'Let's go for a little walk.'

'Walk? Where on earth do you want to go? Have you even looked in the mirror recently?'

'I need to find Artur and Markus.'

'Markus won't be back until tonight, and from what I heard, Artur still hasn't turned up. And you know, we could both benefit from some time out.'

'I don't believe a word Richard says. He just doesn't want any hassle. If he needed to, he'd try to convince me that the pope lives in a chapel on a mountain around this way.'

'I get where you're coming from, Jesse. I want to find Isa too. But it's not going to help if you're totally exhausted—'

'Just leave the knife in next time, will you?'

Jule bit her tongue. She was angry and certainly had every reason to be. But with the best will in the world, he couldn't afford to be understanding at this point. 'You can always make the bed if you want to stay here.'

He turned his back to Jule, knowing full well that she was exploding inwardly at his display of machismo. There was no way she'd give in to that kind of behaviour.

'Forget it, I'm coming with you.'

He resisted the urge to grin. The dizziness grew stronger as he opened the door, but thankfully the handle was a good support.

'I hate being so predictable,' said Jule.

'I'd have thought you'd know all about how predictable people can be, what with being a psychologist and all.'

'Well yes, when it comes to other people, but not myself,' Jule grumbled.

For a split second, things seemed almost normal. A bit of light-hearted banter. Then the dizziness came back with a vengeance when they were on the stairs.

'You OK?'

'Pretty crappy,' Jesse grumbled.

Jule smiled at him. He wasn't sure how to interpret her smile, how much honesty, compassion or encouragement it was meant to convey. But it felt good to be on the receiving end of a smile in circumstances like these, where it seemed almost impossible to feel good. 'We have to go down to the second floor.'

'Jesse, I—'

'Second floor.'

It didn't take them long to make it to Artur's door. Jesse felt like he'd walked there in his sleep. He pushed the handle without a moment's hesitation and was genuinely surprised to discover that the door was locked.

'Jesse, look.'

Jule pointed at the polished brass plaque by the door. *Dr Richard Messner, Principal. Adlershof Children's Home and Boarding School.* Apparently, Richard hadn't just taken over the reins of Adlershof from his father, but he had also moved into his living quarters.

'So where next?' Jule asked.

'Maybe down to the ground floor. There's got to be someone who knows where Artur lives. Maybe someone in the kitchen will know. And I could really use a coffee.'

They made their way back to the staircase. The steps creaked as they always had, and Jesse wondered if he could still hit just the quiet parts, but he was too tired to try it now.

The kitchen was deserted. He expected it to be different somehow, yet apart from a couple of updated appliances with spotless stainless-steel surfaces, it looked much the same as it had done all those years ago. The only sign of life was the dishwasher whirring. It was still the school holidays, so breakfast had finished bright and early. Even the Thermos jugs had been washed and set aside to dry. No sign of any coffee. He blinked involuntarily again. His forehead still felt hot.

Finally, he found a filter coffee machine on the worktop and located the ground coffee in the same tall cupboard Dante had kept it in all those years ago. He reached up to take the container out of the cupboard, but had to lean on the stainless-steel surface when another strong wave of dizziness came over him.

'Are you OK?' Jule asked.

'It'll be fine,' he muttered.

A short while later, the coffee maker was gurgling away in the kitchen and Jule had pulled up a couple of stools so that she and Jesse could take a seat. It was blissful relief for Jesse's leaden limbs. He wondered when on earth the painkillers were going to kick in, and felt his eyes closing. He let the coffee aroma seep in through his nostrils and felt himself drifting off. *Just for a couple of seconds*, he thought, *just give in to the tiredness for a few seconds*.

Then he toppled over.

He was still aware of the limpness in his limbs. Jule's body was a warm cushion until finally he hit the cold floor. And there she was, anxiously tapping him on his cheeks. She must have done her first-aid training. Always call the patient by their name, maintain eye contact, talk to them and, and, and . . . He was a doctor, but man was it different being on the other side. He just wanted some rest. His head was so delightfully empty. Even Isa had faded into the distance. The last thing he felt was a hand, Jule's hand, rummaging around in his trouser pocket. He thought about the car key and could see her right there in front of him, getting into the car and driving away. And she should. He wouldn't stop her.

He could hear Jule's voice somewhere far in the distances. She was talking again, saying something like 'dia—' – dia-something.

He sank back onto the floor of the Adlershof kitchen and the lights went out.

Chapter 24

Tuesday, 8 January 2013

The table top shook under the impact of the axe and Isabelle cried out. Artur let out a moan and started whimpering. The blade had sunk deep into the wood right in front of his fingertips.

The man prised the blade out of the table top without saying a word. Artur's whole body trembled, and his old heart was pumping in stops and starts. He knew he wouldn't survive the ordeal a second time. He wanted to keep his hand, but if he really had to lose it, he would have preferred it to be over with.

The man lowered the axe from the table, holding it loosely so that the handle dangled by his side, like an extension of his arm, with the blade pointing at the floor. 'If either of you cause me any trouble,' he said to Artur, 'then it won't be the table I hit next time.'

It took a second for Artur's frazzled brain to understand what that meant. He was going to keep his hand. He felt dizzy with relief.

'Are you going to cause trouble?'

They both shook their heads silently.

'Good. Here are the rules: when you hear me coming, you move away from the hatch and back to the wall. I'll bring you food and drink once a day. The bucket is your toilet. I'll change that once a day too. Keep quiet. Is that clear?'

They nodded.

The dark eyes gazed at them unflinchingly from behind the oval glass discs on the gas mask, with the same eerie calmness that had deeply unsettled Artur when he first spoke to the man on the phone. The strange way of talking and the mask through which his voice was being filtered made everything seem even more surreal.

'What do you want from us?' Artur asked timidly.

'What were you doing at the gatehouse?' the man replied.

Artur hesitated and thought about the container with the hand in it. He had left the plastic bag somewhere near the bin. Perhaps he had been lucky. Maybe someone had found the container and phoned the police?

'I was just being nosy,' Artur said. 'I often end up wandering around when I can't sleep. Adlershof – the main building, the corridors, the cellar – it's all like part of me. Pacing around the place is the only thing that helps when I'm feeling restless. Then I saw the light in the house and it surprised me. I thought I'd check if everything was OK.' He cleared his throat. 'Old habits, I guess.'

'Light? What light?'

'Um, it wasn't on for long. On the ground floor.'

The man went quiet for a moment, like he was mulling over what Artur had said. 'What did you do with the hand?'

Artur had been proud of his shrewd mix of truth and lies, but now he could feel the blood rushing to his cheeks. How did the man know about the hand?

The man adjusted his grip, making the handle of the axe swing a little.

'I hid it,' he admitted.

'Hid it where?'

'I . . . um—'

The axe's movement became more pronounced.

'In my kitchen, in the freezer compartment.'

The man gave a nod. A cold shiver ran down Artur's back. Did this man also know where he lived?

The man in the gas mask reached into his holdall and took out two buckets that were stacked together, along with two water bottles, two spoons and a large plastic container. Artur noticed the container resembled the one with the hand in it. As hungry as he was, he wasn't convinced he'd be able to eat anything out of a container like that. The man put the axe back in the bag. The zip buzzed loudly as he closed it, then he opened the hatch, climbed in and closed it without so much as a parting glance in their direction. Artur thought he could feel the floor shaking as the two bolts slid forward.

'Sorry,' Isabelle whispered. She moved closer and tried to undo the knot around his hand. Artur felt her fingers trembling, cold against his skin. The knot proved unyielding; his attempt at an escape had only served to pull the synthetic rope even tighter.

Artur smiled at her gratefully.

'Do you think my dad's going to call the police?'

'Are you scared he will?'

'I'm scared that man will find out if he does. I don't want to die.' For a second Artur thought she was going to burst into tears. 'But I'm also scared of nobody calling the police.'

'I don't think you have to worry about your dad calling the police.'

'How come?'

'Because he doesn't want anything to happen to you. Anyway, if I know your dad, he's bound to come looking for you himself.'

'You know my dad?' Isabelle let go of the knot and looked at him, her eyes wide and innocent, deep blue, like Sandra's were when she was little. She had Jesse's curls. He had met a lot of children, but there had always been something special about those two. That became even clearer with the benefit of hindsight. His eyes welled up with tears. 'I know both of them. Your dad and your mum.'

'Are you from the children's home?'

'Did they tell you about the home?'

'Not much. But they talk about it sometimes.'

Artur sighed, partly out of relief because he hoped that meant they had resisted telling Isabelle any horror stories about him, but also with a twinge of wistful melancholy. 'That makes sense. People who have grown up in children's homes often prefer not to think about their time there. And they never want to go back. Except for when everything in the outside world is even worse.'

Isabelle looked down and fiddled with the knot again. 'What about you? Did you go back?'

'I never left. I used to be the principal.'

'Really?' She stared right through him. 'You're Mr M?'

Artur twisted his mouth into a sad expression. 'I see, so he told you about me?'

'Uh-huh,' Isabelle said, now fully immersed in her efforts to undo the knot. 'Now who's the loser?'

'Pardon me?' Artur asked, confused.

'That's what dad always says when he solves a problem.' She pulled on the cord and the rope slithered through the knot as it came undone. Artur pulled his hand out of the loop and gave a sigh of relief. A ring of dark bruising ran around his wrist. 'Thank you,' he mumbled faintly, but he got the feeling that wasn't good enough. Praising and thanking people had never come naturally to him; sometimes he wondered how much Richard had suffered because of his shortcomings in that area.

'You did a good job there,' he said. It sounded awfully wooden, like something he'd learned by heart. Still, that didn't seem to bother Isabelle. She smiled back at him.

Artur carefully made his way back to his mattress and let out a deep groan as he sat himself down. He pulled himself over to the radiator attached to the brickwork at the gable end, using his back to wiggle along the wall. The heat soothed his back.

'Can I come and sit with you?' Isabelle asked.

Artur didn't know what to say. Isabelle obviously took his silence for acceptance and promptly slid in next to him. She placed her hand in his. Artur was lost for words. How long had it been since he'd held another person's hand?

'You're all right,' Isabelle declared. 'Definitely nicer than Mum made out, anyway.'

His eyes welled up again. His whole life seemed to have boiled down to a big fat nothing, and this fleeting moment here with Jesse's daughter was threatening to provide more closeness than anything else he'd experienced in recent decades.

'Why are you crying? Are you scared of dying too?'

Artur swiftly wiped the tears from his cheeks. What was he supposed to say to that? A 'no' would certainly be lying. But he also knew that there were other things far more terrifying than dying. And not knowing what the insect man was planning to do with the two of them shook him to his core.

'So what do you reckon? How will he go about it?' Isabelle asked.

'What?'

'My dad. How do you reckon he'll find me?

'I've no idea. But I'm sure he'll search high and low until he does.'

They sat in silence for a moment.

'Artur?' By now Isabelle's voice was almost a whisper.

'Hmm?'

'Do you think the man will let us live?'

Chapter 25

Diazepam? Jule read the tiny letters printed on the silver side of the packet. She had just fished it out of Jesse's trouser pocket along with the car key. It appeared that Jesse had swallowed a sedative, but she couldn't understand for the life of her why. How many tablets had he taken? Two? And in such a state of exhaustion! Surely a doctor like him would know that this dose alone was enough to knock out a gorilla. Had he just grabbed the wrong packet when he reached into his doctor's bag?

The coffee maker rattled away loudly as it blasted the last of the water into the filter. Jesse was lying on the cold floor like he had been knocked out in a boxing ring.

The car key in her hand was still hot from Jesse's trouser pocket. If she wanted to get out of here, now was the perfect time to make a run for it. But did she really want to? She would have done anything to get away from Jesse last night in the car park, but she had changed her mind.

She had watched from the driver's cab as the Polish guy shoved Jesse backwards and finally clobbered him. But now everything felt different and she was starting to doubt herself.

She realised, of course, that she might just be feeling sorry for him because of the pain he was in. Maybe she was even feeling guilty. It also occurred to her that she could be experiencing a touch of Stockholm syndrome and might be beginning to sympathise with her kidnapper. But for all she tried to reason with herself, the nagging doubts were too hard to ignore. Not to mention the thing Jesse said about her being frightened, which was still gnawing away at her.

Sandra had said she wanted to talk to her about Jesse, and even over the phone it was clear that she was agitated. But when Jule gave it some more thought, she realised that didn't necessarily mean she was afraid of Jesse. Perhaps she'd also feared *for* Jesse. There was a huge difference. When she saw Jesse there stooped over Sandra's body, the shock was so overpowering that she couldn't think straight. She couldn't rule out the possibility that she'd misinterpreted Sandra's vague insinuations.

Tiny beads of cold sweat gathered on Jesse's forehead. He'd been at the point of collapsing several times in the last hour, but his sights were so set on not losing Isa that he'd just kept going.

She slipped the Volvo key into her pocket and decided to go for help. There was no way she'd be able to move Jesse by herself, and the cold floor was only going to aggravate his burning fever. As she stood up, she noticed a metallic-looking door at the back of the kitchen. It was slightly ajar and moving ever so slightly in the draught. The door to the cellar steps, no doubt. A blond shock of hair appeared from behind the free-standing kitchenette.

'Hello-o?' Jule said.

The cellar door gave a faint creak.

'I've seen you, you can come out.'

No movement.

'I could do with your help over here.'

Round, light-blue eyes peered out over the steel edge of the kitchen unit. A girl, maybe ten or eleven years old, with messy flaxen hair.

'What's your name?' Jule asked.

The girl said nothing, but at least dared to move a little further forward. She was pretty, in a nondescript sort of way, with skin even paler than her freckles. 'I've never seen you here before,' she said.

'It's my first time,' said Jule. 'What about you?'

'Not my first time.'

'I thought there were no classes on this week?'

'No. It's the holidays.'

'So what are you doing here?

'The homies are always here.'

'I see. And what were you up to down there?' Jule immediately kicked herself for the hint of accusation in her words.

The girl hesitated and shifted from one foot to the other. It seemed Jule had hit a nerve, like she had caught the girl doing something naughty. Maybe she'd stolen some sweets.

'It's OK,' Jule said. 'You don't have to tell me. But maybe you could help me by fetching somebody. My friend here,' she pointed at Jesse, 'he needs to go to bed. I need one or two strong people to help me shift him.'

The girl got up on her tiptoes, but stayed in the same spot.

'Would you go and tell someone, please?'

She gave a brusque shake of the head. Her hair looked greasy, like it hadn't been washed for a long time. Jule noticed for the first time that her left jawbone was slightly crooked. 'Why not?'

'I can't let them know where I am.'

'Are you in trouble?'

She shook her head again. 'Who's that?'

'A friend of mine. His name is Jesse.'

She chewed her lips and stood on her tiptoes again, but she still couldn't see Jesse from where she was standing. The two kitchen units either side of Jesse were like walls. She cautiously crept around the unit to the corner, like she was scared of falling into a trap. 'He's spooky,' she whispered.

'Spooky? What do you mean?'

It looked like the girl was trying to find the right words. The look in her eyes was more reticent than before, like Jesse's spookiness might be contagious. Suddenly she craned her neck like a startled bird. Soft creaking footsteps echoed behind Jule. Clearly the girl had extremely sharp hearing.

'Hello? Alois?' A man called out from the hall.

The girl's eyes widened with fear, and she put her index finger on her lips. 'Don't tell on me,' she whispered and then swiftly disappeared, slipping through the narrow crack in the cellar doorway like a lithe fox. It seemed she could find her way back down there blindfolded. The sound of her footsteps quickly faded into the darkness.

'Alois?'

Jule blinked.

Standing there in the kitchen doorway was a stocky man with a straight back and a slight tilt in the hips.

His eyes were disconcertingly dark and large, the bags under his eyes were puffy and surrounded by bluish-black shadows. 'Who are you? What are you doing here?' he asked.

'I . . . um, I'm here with my friend,' said Jule. 'Do you think you can help me?'

'Where's Alois?'

'I don't know who Alois is, but—'

'Our cook.'

'There's nobody here. Can you help me, please?'

'Why should I help you?' The man turned to leave.

'It's not me you should help, it's my friend Mr Berg.'

He stopped dead. 'Sorry, who?'

'Mr Berg. Jesse Berg.'

'Jesse's here? He turned around to face her. His dark eyes had narrowed, and a streak of light was shining on his face from one of the light fittings. 'Where?'

Jule shrank back instinctively and stared into his eyes. They weren't just dark; his pupils were so unnaturally dilated that a thin border was all that remained of the brown iris. 'Who are you?'

'The caretaker. And you?'

'*You're* Markus?'

The man sneered. 'Apparently Jesse's told you about me, then.'

Chapter 26

1979, Garmisch-Partenkirchen

Jesse always had to lend a hand in the kitchen on Sundays. The homies were responsible for the washing-up. They had to earn their keep, unlike the boarders, whose parents paid for them to stay at Adlershof. The chores weren't just limited to school time either; they also had to help in the holidays, when the boarders went home to their parents. Homies didn't have parents. Or the ones who did had been saved from them.

Jesse didn't mind initially; after all, he was used to keeping a stinking two-bedroom flat clean. At least down here in the kitchen he had Dante, the grouch of a cook, for company. At two metres tall, Dante was always stooped over because the doors were too low for him. The corners of his mouth pointed downwards like his drooping shoulders. A wreath of grey hair ran around a gleaming bald spot, which was hardly ever visible because of his looming proportions. At least Dante spoke now and again, so on his first Sunday in the kitchen, Jesse learned a few things about Adlershof. He also discovered that Dante liked to drink out of a brown bottle with no label, and when Jesse accidentally dropped that same bottle on the floor, Dante's expression turned so angry that Jesse feared he was about to be on the receiving end of a blow from those shovel-like hands. 'Useless little urchin,' Dante growled. He hit his head on one of the low-hanging tin lamps, making the light dance wildly on his face and the stainless-steel kitchen surfaces. 'Go and get me another one.'

Jesse looked at him. How was he supposed to know where to find another beer? He got a hefty slap on the face for not knowing. And perhaps for looking cheeky too.

His cheek burned as he made his way down to the cellar. He followed Dante's directions: down the stone staircase, then take the corridor on the right. Every couple of metres there was a tin lamp hanging on the red brick walls. Jesse was reminded of the cellar in the house back in Kiel. It had the same kind of heavy wooden doors. The revolving postcard stand hovered as his mind zeroed in on the image of his mother underneath the brown coat. Her legs sticking out from underneath it. Her hand, grasping at nothing.

It wasn't just that she'd gone. Even when she'd been around, he had always been pushed out, always came second place. He choked back the bitter memory.

What was it Dante said? Which door did he have to open? The fifth one on the right. His fingers were still trembling slightly as he put the key in the lock. The bolt creaked as it slid back. There was another noise too. Jesse froze. Was it music? It sounded tinny, but muffled at the same time. But yes, it was definitely music.

He pulled the key out of the lock and followed the trail of music. He wandered further down the hall, then around a bend until he found himself standing in front of another wooden door. It was exactly the same as the others in every way, apart from the thin strip of light shining through the edge of the door between the wall and the oak. Mesmerised, he leaned forward and held his breath as he glimpsed the most beautiful and surreal sight he'd ever seen in his life. There on the cellar floor was a large makeshift square made of gently shimmering wooden floorboards and, in the light of a cellar lamp with a wire mesh guard, a girl was dancing in front a line of three mirrors. He guessed she must be about the same age as him. She was wearing a sort of black swimming costume with long sleeves and her blond hair was tied in a plait that rose and drew a curve when she spun around. Some of her movements were jerky; others were flowing. She seemed to be experimenting unselfconsciously with movement. He had watched a ballet performance at school once and had seen a clip on TV, but he hadn't witnessed anything like this before in his life.

The girl's movements were so honest and full of intensity! He could feel the goose pimples bubbling up on his arms. She was everything he wasn't. She was so happy and focused on her movements. Her face gleamed, and there was something so . . . so pure about the way she danced. He felt idiotic thinking such things. But pure was exactly the right word!

Suddenly a fist collided with his cheekbone, sending him flying onto the rough cold concrete of the cellar floor. He doubled over when a foot struck the pit of his stomach, then a pair of hands grabbed his shirt and pulled him away from the door, to the next side corridor, where his attacker pushed him against the wall. 'What are you doing sniffing around down here?'

Jesse stared into the furious face of a boy he guessed was around twelve years old. 'Nothing . . . I just heard music and wanted—'

'To perv on Sandra?'

Perv. Was that what he was doing – perving? When he was in the room when Father had been doing it with a woman, the woman had called it perving. He remembered how she grinned, splayed her legs, spat on her fingers and rubbed the slightly open mound between her legs. Perving must have meant watching something dirty. Or did they also call it perving when you were dirty and watching something beautiful? 'I was just curious.'

'About what Sandra looks likes when she gets changed, yeah?' The boy punched him in the stomach again.

'I was just watching her dancing, nothing else,' he gasped.

'That's bad enough, you little arsehole. This is my cellar, OK?'

My room. My bed. My cellar. Everything here belonged to some-body. But none of it belonged to Jesse. He didn't even have his own mattress. He nodded. 'What's your name?'

The boy stared at him with a furious look on his face. 'Richard. And make sure you remember that.'

Jesse nodded again. So this was Richard. 'I'll remember,' he answered in a strained voice.

Richard stared at him for a while, unsure whether he should take Jesse's answer as an admission of defeat.

'What's she doing dancing down here?' Jesse asked.

'What's that it got to do with you?'

Jesse shrugged. His right cheek was burning, and he felt a dull throbbing pain in his stomach. Richard let him go and wiped his hands on his woollen jumper, as if he was trying to get rid of some dirt. 'Dante set it all up for her. He's got a real soft spot for her. He watches her sometimes too.' Judging by Richard's expression, it looked like he wanted to sock him one too. Obviously that was out of the question though. 'Stay away from Sandra. Do you hear me?'

More nodding. Always more nodding. It usually helped things, at least for a while. But lately he found all this nodding so damn hard. 'Are you a homie too?'

'Me?' Richard's laugh was full of contempt. He seemed like he didn't really know the answer to that question. 'I'm not one or the other. Now piss off, you weirdo!'

Jesse didn't need telling twice. He pushed himself away from the wall and made his way over to the door he had closed on his way in.

'Not that way,' Richard snarled, blocking his path. 'Over there!'

Jesse bit his lip, then turned around and plodded back along the hall. He could feel Richard's eyes burning into his back. When he made it back up to the kitchen, Dante gave him a series of sharp slaps. One on his right cheek because he was so late coming back. One on the left because he had come back without the key. And finally, a second on the right – particularly forceful this time – because he hadn't brought the bottle with him.

'Pull another stunt like that and you'll be spending two weeks in the hole,' Dante hissed.

Jesse nodded. Despite the pain, there was only one thing on his mind. The girl in the black swimming costume.

Chapter 27

Markus Kawczynski was standing beside Jule and leaning forward slightly. His dark, dilated pupils moved quickly, and he blinked repeatedly as he took a good look at Jesse lying there on the kitchen floor. Jule wondered if he was on drugs; his eyes suggested as much. The right side of his face was like that of a stroke victim – it seemed strangely rigid and gave him an air of insensitivity and coolness. The left corner of his mouth had contorted into a smile.

'What's up with him?' Markus asked.

'He's taken a strong sedative.'

'Did you give it to him?'

'What makes you think that? No.'

'Why did he take it?'

'He . . . well, he's not doing too great.'

The smile on Markus' face turned mistrustful, and the rage beneath it was palpable. Clearly there was no 'we're quits' for Markus Kawczynski.

'Is Sandra here too?' he asked.

The way he asked about Sandra made her ears prick up. He obviously meant for the question to sound casual, but he failed miserably.

'Sandra's . . . in Berlin.'

'In Berlin. Well, how about that! And so why has Jesse dragged you with him here instead of her?'

'It's a long story,' Jule replied.

'Jesse's stories are always long. And they usually end badly. Especially for other people.'

Jule had nothing to say.

'So do you want to shift him?'

Charming! He made him sound like a piece of meat. Markus looked at her expectantly, his head slightly tilted.

'The floor's too cold,' said Jule. 'He's got a fever.'

'Are you a doctor like him?'

'No, a psychologist.'

'A psychologist. Very nice!' Markus's stare was piercing and sinister. She felt the key to the Volvo in her trouser pocket. It was her ticket to freedom, far away from all this. But even if she could have brought herself to abandon Jesse, she owed it to Sandra to stay, and that was much more important.

'OK,' Markus mumbled, then wandered past her to the cellar door. He opened it and hit the switch with the back of his hand, illuminating the gloomy exit with yellow light.

'You grab his feet, I'll take his shoulders.'

'Down there?' Jule shook her head. 'I think it's better if we get him to a bed, don't you?'

Suddenly Markus's smile hardened and then a boyish look crept onto his exhausted features.

'I'm not going to do anything to you. This is just the quickest way to get him to a bed, that's all. The kitchen assistant's lodgings are down there. In the basement. It's not a luxury hotel, but it'll do.' He pulled a crooked smile, noticed that Jule was having reservations, and added: 'Listen, I'm not Jesse's biggest fan. The bastard cost me a kidney and that's not even all of it. But I'm not mad or stupid. Why would I want to do anything to you?'

'I . . . um . . .'

Jule brushed a wisp of hair out of her face. She was embarrassed that he'd seen through her. 'I just don't think I can manage to carry Jesse down the stairs. Maybe we should get help.'

Markus pushed the cellar door again. It opened wider, revealing a stairlift mounted on the brick wall. The grey plastic seat shone in the hallway light. Markus smiled. 'Just a couple of metres.'

Jule nodded and smiled like she always did. She didn't know what to think. Markus suddenly seemed more awkward than he did creepy.

'You don't have to help me. I can manage it by myself if I need to,' Markus said. He purposefully grabbed Jesse under his armpits and heaved him up. Jule remembered the fresh stitches and the wound in Jesse's side. She quickly jumped up to Markus and grabbed hold of Jesse's feet. Jesse moaned gruffly as they heaved him onto the seat, but he still didn't open his eyes.

'You have to make sure he doesn't fall off the seat,' Markus ordered her.

He pressed the button before Jule had time to object. The seat gave a jolt and slid down the stairs on the rail. Jule followed, trying her best to keep Jesse in his seat. His body jerked slightly as the lift reached the bottom of the stairs.

'There you are,' Markus mumbled. His footsteps creaked on the stairs. He was wearing battered black work boots, no doubt with steel toe caps.

'You take his feet, I'll grab his top half.'

Markus grabbed hold of Jesse under his armpits again. Jule put her arms around Jesse's calves and did what she could to help.

'We need to go over there,' Markus puffed, pointing behind her with a nod of the head. 'It's best if you go backwards.' Jule could feel herself starting to sweat even though the air was cold. The floor was made of concrete, the walls of old brick. Old wooden floorboards had been used for the doors, with planks nailed to them in a cross shape for stability. Cellar lamps were positioned at regular intervals on the wall. Jule wondered where the outside wall could be. She hadn't noticed a basement at the front of the building.

'A bit further to the right so you don't hit the doorpost,' Markus said.

Christ almighty! Why was Jesse so heavy? She paced backwards through one of the doors, then looked to the left and right of the door frame and noticed that the walls had been crudely panelled with wooden planks.

'Just a few more steps,' puffed Markus, who was clearly taking more of the strain. 'And now here we go, onto the bed.' They heaved Jesse sideways onto a mattress in an iron frame. The springs grated as they bent under the weight of his body. Markus unhooked a karabiner from his belt with a movement he had no doubt done a thousand times before. The keys jangled lightly. He purposefully inserted one of them into the lock on the door, then pulled it shut and locked it from the inside.

Jule stared at him.

'Being the caretaker has its perks,' he smiled.

Chapter 28

Jule could have slapped herself for being so stupid. She took a quick glance around the room and became acutely aware of how claustrophobic it was. It was narrow, the size of a cell, and lined on all sides with old wooden planks. Floor, walls, ceiling – the whole lot. Even the door was made of the same wood – it was hard to tell it apart from the wall now that it was closed. The room didn't have a single window, in fact it didn't have any openings or ventilation at all – only the gaps in the door frame. A sliver of light entered the room from the hall, but other than that the only light was a ceiling lamp with a lattice guard. Jule couldn't see the switch for it anywhere.

'Take a seat,' Markus said. His voice sounded dull and lifeless. He fiddled with the bundle of keys with his rough, calloused fingers, pushing them back and forth on the key ring like rosary beads on a chain.

'I'd prefer to stand up, thanks.'

'Your knees,' Markus pointed to her legs, 'they're shaking.'

'Why did you lock the door?'

'Why did you come here?'

'Tell me why you've locked us in first.'

Markus smiled patiently and his dark pupils glimmered. 'Are *you* the one holding the keys, or am I?'

Jule pursed her lips and said nothing.

If he was on drugs, then they definitely weren't making him think any slower. On the other hand, his dilated pupils could always be the after-effects of the night before.

'So, why are you here?'

'As I already told you, I'm a psychologist and I work with kids. I'm working on a study on adolescents in children's homes, investigating their development up until adulthood. Jesse offered to show me the home where he grew up, so here I am.'

'Study. I see. And the sedative? Is that part of the study too?'

'He took it accidentally. I think he mistook it for a painkiller.'

'Accidentally, you say?' Markus snorted. 'A doctor?'

'He's . . . like I said, he's not doing too well at the moment. He's injured.'

'What kind of injury?'

Jule pointed at Jesse's waist and, without saying a word, Markus pulled up his shirt and looked at the bandage.

'What happened?

'Like I said, he got hurt.'

'Did he attack someone?'

'No, it's not what you think.'

'OK, so what do I think?'

Jule said nothing.

'I take it you know what happened here?'

'I . . .' Jule hesitated a moment. Markus stopped flipping the key over the ring in his right hand for a second. 'I only know what Jesse's told me,' said Jule.

'Jesse's side of the story, of course,' Markus laughed bitterly.

'Then tell me your version,' Jule suggested.

'There's nothing to tell. Nothing happened. I would have thought you'd have realised that by now, being a psychologist and all. At least if you're any good, I guess.'

'You're saying you think Jesse has mental health issues?'

'Think? I know it.'

'Well, what about you? Don't you have some as well?'

The only sound to be heard was Jesse letting out a sigh.

'You overestimate yourself,' said Markus. A thin veil of sweat glistened on his forehead.

'What's that supposed to mean?' she asked, her voice quieter than before.

'If you think you have any control over Jesse, then you're massively overestimating yourself.' His fingers got back to work again, and the keys started clinking on the ring.

'This is ridiculous. What do you want from me?'

'Tell me what's going on with Jesse. Why is he doing all this?'

'I really don't have a clue what you're talking about. And even if I did, I wouldn't tell you anything.'

'So you do know what's going on with him,' Markus prodded her for information again. The keys flew through his hand. The spinning was like a twitch. Click. Click-click.

'For God's sake, no! That's not what I said.'

'You're keeping your mouth shut because of patient confidentiality, aren't you?'

'If he was my patient, then yes, I would be! But he isn't my patient, for crying out loud!'

Click-click, click-click.

'Do you want a piece of advice?'

'What kind of advice?'

'About your patient – I mean, not your patient.'

'Advice about psychology? From you?'

'Get him out of here. Take him as far away from here as you can. The best thing you could do is have him locked up somewhere in a loony bin miles away. I don't want him hanging around here at night any more.'

'I beg your pardon?'

'You heard me.'

'What do you mean, hanging around the place at night?'

Markus blinked three times, in tempo with the clicking of the keys. 'What do you think I mean? I've seen him here. I told Sandra about it too. Maybe you should speak to her. You all know each other, don't you?'

Jule looked at him in shock. 'You spoke to Sandra?'

'Yes. She came here the last Saturday in December.'

The Saturday after Christmas. Jule thought about what he'd said. That was less than two weeks ago. Jesse was right after all: Sandra *had* been in Adlershof. 'So when exactly did you see Jesse here? And where?'

'A few weeks back, around mid-November. I only ever saw him at night.' He stood in silence for a moment, like he was racking his brain to try and remember something. Or maybe he was trying to come up with a story? 'One time I saw him walking up the stairs in the main building, then another time I saw him right at the top, under the roof. In the part where the children from the home sleep. He came out of the girls' toilets covered in dirt.'

Jule stared at Markus and felt her old anti-Jesse reflexes kicking in, although she should really know better. Markus

Kawczynski was clearly a drug user – it didn't matter whether he was on them right now or had taken them last night. And the longer she listened to him, the more paranoid his behaviour seemed. 'Did you speak to Jesse? When he was here, I mean?'

'No way. I stayed away from him. We're done with each other.'

'And what did Sandra have to say about it?'

'She looked at me in the same way you are now. She couldn't fathom how he could have been here. That's why I sent her to see Wolle.'

'Wolle? Who's that?'

'Wolfgang Seifert. The owner of Wolle's Tavern, the pub down on Klammstrasse. Jesse and I shared a room with him when we were kids.'

'What's this got to do with him?'

'I thought if she was going to believe anyone, then maybe she'd believe him. Sandra had a bit of a thing with him once. Only very briefly though. Before she started going on about Jesse all the time. She was still fond of him later on. Wolle never got worked up about it like the others.'

'So did Wolle see Jesse here too?'

'No, he didn't. But Wolle always saw through Jesse. He never believed anything they said after the accident. Jesse, the poor victim. He'd really nailed the whole coming off unscathed thing. But Wolle knew better.'

'What did Wolle know better?'

'He hinted that something didn't quite add up with Jesse. He'd seen it for himself. He told me about it one time after a few beers. But when I tried to get him to tell me more, he made this huge secret out of it. He kept saying he'd had to promise the principal that he wouldn't say anything about it to anyone.'

'And what might he have seen?'

Markus raised his shoulders. 'Whatever it was, it must have spooked him. He was really edgy about it. All he would say was that Jesse gave him the creeps.'

'The creeps? And you think that justifies getting someone locked up?'

'Jesse has no reason to be sniffing around here. Why is he wandering around at night like a ghost? Tell me that much.'

Jule snorted. 'Why don't you tell me what *you*'re up to, wandering the building at night?'

'I'm the caretaker.'

'Oh, so you repair the girls' toilets at night, do you?'

Markus glowered. His fingers were frantically sliding the keys around the ring. 'It's up to you who you believe. But I can't put up with Jesse playing his little games. He should be locked up.'

'If he was awake right now he'd probably be saying the same about you.'

Markus glanced coolly at Jesse. He blinked, then shrugged his shoulders. 'But he's not.'

'So now what? You're going to lock us in here? You can't do that.'

Markus had been standing slightly stooped all this time. Finally, he stood up straight. His black eyes glinted, and his fist closed around the keys. 'Who's going to stop me?'

Jule felt a chill run down her spine.

'Nobody I can think of,' said Markus. He stepped out into the corridor, pressed a switch, and the light in the room went out. The door closed with a creak behind him. Jule held her breath as she sat there in the darkness, waiting for the inevitable noise from the door. But all she could hear was her beating heart, Jesse's deep breathing and a pair of footsteps moving further away.

Markus hadn't locked the door.

Chapter 29

Tuesday, 8 January 2013

Artur had managed to get some sleep for a change – a deep slumber, without any ghosts. He rubbed his face, confused. Here he was, being held captive in an attic, and suddenly he could sleep again? Perhaps it was just sheer exhaustion. The past few hours had taken more out of him than he could possibly handle.

Isabelle was sitting across from him on her mattress. Her legs were crossed, like she had ligaments and tendons made of rubber. He remembered her hand and the way she had sat next to him while he fell asleep. Suddenly he was desperate to turn back time a few hours.

'At last,' Isabelle said. She sounded a touch on the grumpy side.

'Was I asleep for long?'

'Ages.'

He pulled himself up. 'Did anything happen?'

She shook her head, sending her blond ringlets swinging back and forth.

Artur rubbed his wrist. The mark wasn't quite as dark now, but it hadn't completely disappeared either. Nothing completely faded any more. Every bit of pain clung to the body at his age, like it had been bathed in adhesive.

'Are you going to eat something too?' Isabelle was waving the Tupperware box at him.

Artur grumbled. The container was like the pain – he just couldn't shake it. No matter what he did, he just couldn't get the image of the hand out of his head.

'But you have to eat something,' she insisted. Artur could easily imagine how many times Sandra must have said the same thing to her.

'Later,' he mumbled. Isabelle went quiet for a while, but her restlessness was clear to see.

'He-ey?'

Artur smiled.

'What do you think the insect man is going to do to us?

Artur's smile faded. The mere mention of the insect man was enough to make him shudder. It was like the man was right there in the room with them. 'I don't know.'

Isabelle nodded silently. She gulped, pressed her lips together and composed herself, despite the threat lurking in the air. Of all the children he had met in the past few decades, Isabelle was definitely the most courageous. He wished he had something comforting to say to her, but what could he possibly have to offer? So instead he decided to take advantage of feeling reasonably refreshed and try to order his thoughts.

The first thought that sprung to mind was revenge. There were a lot of people who'd had it in for Jesse before the accident. The masked man was clearly gunning for him, otherwise why would he have kidnapped Isabelle? The only question was how far he would go.

Then what about Wilbert? Why did he have to die? And what did Artur have to do with it? There could only really be one explanation for it all, but it was so outlandish, so insane, that it didn't make any sense. That would have taken everything to absurd extremes. The accident, the time after it. Everything!

He found himself thinking about Wilbert again.

The last time he'd shaken the hand with that familiar scar was back in 1981. Dante had woken him up in the middle of the night, and his friend Wilbert was standing there when he opened the door. The man was a picture of misery. Artur was still ashamed of how he had behaved that night. He had been afraid, and he still didn't know if that made it any more excusable. It had been bugging him for years. Sometimes he wondered if the exact opposite was true: maybe it only served to make things even worse. He glanced at Isabelle. She was rubbing her cheek with her hand, and once again he found himself marvelling at how brave she was. He wished that he could find some of that courage inside himself. He didn't like who he was. But what could he do about that now? He wasn't a superhero by any stretch of the imagination – he'd never been sporty or strong, and now he was just an old, doddering lump.

'Isabelle?'

She sniffed and stuck out her chin defiantly. 'Yes.'

'Come over here and sit with me.'

Before he knew it, she was right there. It was like she'd just been waiting for an invitation – from him, this feeble old man. For the first time he felt like he didn't need to hide his trembling hands. 'What do you think of us cooking up a plan?'

'What kind of plan?'

He smiled conspiratorially. 'An escape plan.'

Her eyes widened. 'But how can we do that?'

'I've no idea,' Artur admitted. But he swore to himself that he would get her out of there before he let anything happen to her.

Chapter 30

Everything was different today. It seemed to be all about the plan.

Jesse had slept on the floor every night for seven weeks now, and the bed behind him was always empty. It was four of them against one of him. There was no point in putting up a fight. Especially as the empty bed belonged to Richard, who also just so happened to be Mr M's son.

But the one thing Jesse didn't understand was why he couldn't use the bed if it was sitting there unoccupied night after night. Richard had only sat on it twice so far, both times in the afternoon when it was raining outside. Jesse had been made to leave the room because they were hatching some sort of plan.

This was the only time there had been any change to the routine. While Jesse was lying in bed for Mr M's nightly rounds, Richard was secretly hiding on the floor underneath his bed. Jesse's thoughts began to wander. He started imagining himself jumping around on the bed and Richard having the slats repeatedly pressed into his face.

But of course, that was just the work of his imagination, and instead, he lay quietly in the bed while Artur Messner went on his rounds. And of course, he obediently vacated it for Richard when

Mr M locked the boys' block at around half past eight. He lay on the floor as far away as possible from the bed, fully aware that the other boys thought they had him right where they wanted him: on the floor, like a dog. But deep down, he was really lurking like a wolf. With glowing eyes and pricked-up ears, ready to pounce.

Half an hour went by, and still nothing happened.

Finally he heard Alois's husky voice: 'What's up, scared shitless?'

'Don't talk shit,' Richard replied. It was probably intended as an aggressive remark, but his voice sounded high-pitched and childish in the darkness. Scared shitless? Jesse wondered of what exactly?

'You can tell your girlfriend Sandra all about it after,' Wolle whispered.

'She's not my girlfriend,' Richard hissed, although it certainly sounded like he wished she was. Jesse knew just how he felt. He wished he could sneak down into the cellar to watch again, but he didn't want to push his luck just yet. One thing was for sure though: he'd be back down there eventually.

'Maybe then she'll hold hands with you,' Alois murmured. 'Or let you kiss her.'

Mattheo and Wolle sniggered away in the background, unlike Markus, who was as quiet as ever. He only spoke when he had something to say, otherwise he just kept himself to himself. And he was always tight-lipped when conversation turned to Sandra.

It seemed like they waited for ever, but finally there was a rustling sound. Alois stuck his feet out of the bed and threw his duvet off. 'Go on, then, open the window.'

Richard got out of his bed and made his way over to the window. Now there were movements coming from the other boys' beds. Cool air rushed into the stuffy room as Richard opened the window. His silhouette stood out against the moonlit sky, then a second silhouette moved towards him. 'It's a bit different going down that way, isn't it?' Alois asked in a soft voice.

'Not all that different.'

'Oh really? Then you go first.'

'I'm no chicken, but I'm not stupid either. You go first.' Alois's grin glinted in the moonlight.

Jesse got up, being careful not to make a sound.

'So you need me to show you how it's done, eh?' Alois teased.

'Don't be so full of yourself. You were worried the first time too.'

'And you always get to go through the front door, principal's boy. Your door's never locked, is it?'

'I'm trapped in here just like you. When will you get that into your head?'

'Give it a rest,' Markus said, before Alois had a chance to respond.

'Can we go now?' Mattheo whispered eagerly.

'There's no way you're coming,' said Markus.

'Why not?'

'You're too small. Your legs aren't long enough to get from the gutter to the window ledge yet.'

'But I'm old enough now.'

'Age has nothing to do with it, Mattheo. You're just too small. Sorry.'

'You stay here,' Alois chimed in, although everything had already been decided. 'You can keep an eye on the new boy and make sure he doesn't screw things up.'

'I'm not staying with him. I'm part of the group.'

'Of course you are – that's why we need you to keep an eye on him,' Alois said, swinging one of his legs over the windowsill. Suddenly he was outside the widow on the narrow stretch of roof

in front of the gutter, then in the blink of an eye he seemed to disappear over the edge. The others could hear his hands sliding along the tin on the rain guttering. 'Are you coming?'

He was asking Richard, who climbed onto the roof after him and peered over the edge, clearly impressed by Alois. Then he made his way down, followed by Markus and lastly Wolle.

'Dickheads,' Mattheo whispered. He was careful to make his voice quiet enough so that the others outside wouldn't hear him. As he took a step towards the window, he noticed that Jesse had got up. 'Don't move an inch, newbie – do you hear me?'

'Don't you ever go with them?' Jesse asked in a hushed voice.

'Shut your trap.'

Jesse did as he was told and stayed quiet. He could still hear faint noises coming through the open window, but after a while they faded to nothing.

'What are they up to?'

'I said shut it.'

Jesse went over to Mattheo at the window, undeterred. He grabbed hold of Jesse's arm to try and hold him back, but he just shook him off and looked out into the night. Four shadows were scurrying across the courtyard towards the woods. He leaned forward and looked out onto the roof. He couldn't identify any footholds on the outside wall. Had the four of them climbed in through a window and then walked down? Jesse's heart was pounding as he plucked up the courage to leap onto the roof.

'Hey, newbie! You're not supposed to go out there,' Mattheo moaned.

Jesse stopped and looked into the room. 'My name is Jesse, you little prick. And I'm the one who decides what I can and can't do.'

'The others aren't going to like it. You'll be in trouble. You don't want to mess with Markus.'

'You're pretty scared of Markus, aren't you?'

'Me? No!'

Jesse grabbed Mattheo by the collar and pulled him towards him, so far that Mattheo's legs dangled helplessly over the windowsill. With just another small movement of his hand, Mattheo would surely fall off the edge of the roof. 'If you snitch on me,' he hissed, 'then I'll throw you down there – do you hear me?'

Mattheo stared at him with bulging eyes.

'It's about fourteen metres down, isn't it?'

Jesse let go without warning, making it difficult for Mattheo to keep his balance. He quickly backed into the room and away from the window.

Quietly triumphant, and with Mattheo's pale, anxious face staring at him from behind the window, Jesse finally made his getaway. He slid over the rain gutter, then dangled his body over it while hanging on to the metal. Now he could see the outside wall – and the window below. It was closed.

For a fraction of a second he contemplated giving up and using his strength to pull himself back up instead. But then if he did that, not even Mattheo would take him seriously.

He aimed for the narrow ledge with his feet, then grabbed hold of the edge of the roof from underneath, got a good grip and managed to crouch down on the ledge in front of the closed window. His heart was pounding wildly. He couldn't stay here. He felt around for something to hold on to and finally felt the shutters on the wall. Then he remembered the carved stone coat of arms protruding from the centre of the façade. It was about seven metres to the right and a metre and a half below him. He would be able to reach the lower balcony from there.

Wrought-iron wind restraints were sticking out of the wall by the windowsill, preventing the shutters from slamming against the wall. Jesse carefully straightened himself up and reached for the upper edge of the right shutter, hoping that the hinges would hold his weight, then he placed his foot on the wind restraint and scrambled onward to the adjacent shutter and finally to the window above the coat of arms. A gentle breeze blew along the façade and started rattling one of the shutters. Jesse could feel himself sweating. He paused for a second to press his forehead against the cool windowpane, then with his hands on the window ledge, he scrambled down to the coat of arms.

He felt like king of the world when he reached the balcony below. And when he finally got to the bottom, he felt like the whole universe was his. Now all he had to do was conquer the forest. And find out what the four boys were up to.

Chapter 31

Before he even opened his eyes, Jesse recognised the distinctive scent that wood acquires when left in an old, damp cellar. Musty and oppressive. Memories of his past barged into his consciousness. The narrow cell. Dark, except for a couple of slivers of light. Helplessness.

Although he never admitted it, the hole was always more of an ordeal for him than it was for the others. As soon as Dante closed the door and the light went out, he felt like he had been buried alive. The place stank of mould and the odour of damp earth crept into his mouth and nose, making it hard to breathe.

One time, when the hole was empty, he snuck into the cellar and rubbed the wooden walls with vinegar, trying to kill the bacteria causing the smell. He wore a gas mask he found in an unused part of the cellar vault so that he wouldn't have to inhale the vinegar.

The stench of vinegar rose all the way up the kitchen, alerting Dante, who caught Jesse in the act. The acrid smell lingered in the cellar for weeks, but as soon as the worst of it had worn off, Dante locked him up in the hole for three days. The acetic acid made him wretch and upset his stomach and throat so much that he was ill for almost three weeks.

He opened his eyes and blinked. He was surrounded by wooden walls, but it was light. Thank God. He sat up – much too quickly, he realised, as the dizziness struck. The nagging pain in his waist brought him to his senses. Sandra's death, Isa's abduction, the last few hours – it all came rushing back to him. He was overcome with feelings of guilt. He'd lost control. Shit, how long had he been asleep? And what was he doing in the hole?

Jule was on the wooden floor next to the bed. She was sleeping on a couple of discoloured cushions from the chair, her legs sticking out through the doorway, as though she was trying to make sure that no one closed it.

'Jule! Wake up!' He shook her shoulders, and she came to with a start.

'What? Jesse?'

He noticed the slight smell of sweat, not unpleasant, but it seemed the events of the last few hours were clinging to her skin.

'What time is it?' he asked.

'What?' She brushed her blond hair out of eyes with a puzzled look on her face.

'What's the time?'

Jule took a deep breath and tried to shake off the groggy feeling. 'For God's sake, Jesse, you scared me.'

Jesse rubbed his temples. His head was heavy, and his mind felt slow and cloudy. 'How long was I asleep?'

'No idea. Quite a while though.'

Jesse pulled his phone out of his back pocket and pressed the home button. The screen didn't light up. Great. That was the last thing he needed. He shot a quick glance in Jule's direction.

'Don't look at me like that,' she said. 'Think what you like, but this definitely wasn't my idea.'

Jesse hesitated. He needed someone he could trust right now and wished it could be her, but even though she had stuck around, he just wasn't sure he could. 'How on earth did we end up in the hole, of all places?'

'The hole?' Jule looked around the cell. 'This is the hole?'

'Didn't Sandra tell you about it?'

'Yes, but . . . I guess I imagined it differently.'

'What happened? Why are we here?'

Jule told him about the diazepam tablets, her encounter with Markus and the secret that Wolle Seifert had apparently shared with Artur.

'So Sandra really was here.' Jesse wrinkled his forehead. 'I just don't understand why Markus is saying that he's seen me as well. I haven't been anywhere near this place in years.'

'And what about Wolle? Did you know that Wolle and Sandra—?'

'No.'

Jule went quiet for a moment, as if *she* was embarrassed that Sandra hadn't told him anything about it.

'It looks like Sandra had her own secrets, doesn't it?' Jesse observed.

'Did you know that Sandra was supposed to meet me the night she was killed?' Jule asked in a soft tone.

Jesse looked at her in surprise. 'No. She told me she was going to look at a dance studio.'

'We were supposed to meet at Einstein for a coffee. Sandra wanted to see me because there was something she desperately wanted to tell me. She said it had to do with you and Adlershof.

I waited for ages for her, then eventually I got worried and drove over to the flat—'

It took Jesse a moment to get his head around Sandra's lie. Now suddenly he understood what she had been trying to tell him the day before. Markus had obviously managed to get to her; that's why she asked him if he'd been to Adlershof recently. 'Is that all she said? Nothing else? No hint about what Wolle might have said?'

'We only spoke on the phone very briefly. But she was really worried.' Jule looked at him and added: 'The thing that really surprises me is that Markus doesn't necessarily seem like the most trustworthy person.'

'What do you mean?'

'When I met him I was convinced he'd taken something. Coke, marijuana, I don't know what exactly. I don't know enough about that sort of thing, but his eyes were like saucers. Everything about the way he behaved was just a bit . . . I don't know, nervous – manic.'

Jesse frowned, trying to reconcile the picture of the Markus he knew with a person who took drugs. It would have made sense if it was Mattheo or Alois. Maybe even Wolle. But Markus?

'I can't imagine,' said Jule, 'that Sandra would have sounded so on edge unless she had a good reason to be worried.'

'If Markus is as unconvincing as you say he is, then she must have been worried because of something that Wolle said to her.'

'So Wolle is the best person to ask, don't you think?' said Jule. 'Markus says Wolle's Tavern is on Klammstrasse. Do you know it?'

Jesse didn't know whether to be grateful or wary of her motivations. Jule seemed to sense his doubts and smiled at him. Not a fake smile, but a lopsided, honest one. 'Of course I do. It's near Marienplatz. And Klammstrasse isn't that long, so it should be pretty easy to find Wolle's Tavern. Jesse rummaged around in his trouser pocket for the car key and came away empty-handed. 'Where's the—' He looked at Jule. She was dangling the Volvo key from her finger. The smile on her face had gone, giving way to a determined expression much more in keeping with those green eyes and that hoarse voice. 'I don't think you're quite with it enough to drive yet,' she said.

The snow had started again. Small flakes spaced far apart were playfully fluttering down from the dark sky. Jule was a little shaky behind the wheel. The snow chains were irritating her, but at least they made sure the Volvo stayed on the road. The headlights swept over the angel gate, then left it standing in the shadows. Only a few of the windows in the building were lit. They sank behind the horizon in the rear-view mirror as they drove away from Adlershof.

'Just who is this Wolle guy?' Jule asked.

'His full name is Wolfgang Seifert. He shared a room with me and the others in the home. From what I can remember, his dad took off when he was little and his mum ended up in prison for some stupid reason – embezzling money, I think. Then something happened to her when she was in prison. Wolle always had that kind of look about him, you know, like he was haunted by something that had happened. He had this long, dark hair. He was secretive and quite sensitive. But at the same time he seemed tough enough not to let anything get to him. Everyone liked him, but he was always sort of in the background.

'And now he's a pub landlord?'

'Is that what Markus said?'

'Well, Wolle's Tavern sounds like the name of a pub to me.'

The headlights skated across the snow on the hairpin bend. The chains rattled under the wheel arches. Garmisch was like a field of lights on the ground below. Brake lights glowed on the roads.

'Looks pretty busy down there,' Jule mumbled.

'It's ski season,' Jesse said. 'We're in ski heaven.'

As if to underscore his statement, the Volvo suddenly skidded on a patch of ice. Jule steered into the skid, gritting her teeth. Jesse let her take a moment to calm down, and then asked: 'Do you think Markus has got something to do with Isa's disappearance?'

'I'm not sure. He was behaving pretty strangely though. And "You don't deserve her" sounds like something he'd say. But if it was him, surely he would have taken the opportunity to lock us in the hole.'

Jesse nodded. But Markus was a tough one to figure out. 'How did he seem to you?'

Jule's answer came quickly, without hesitation. 'Mistrustful. And sort of cold, although there's obviously a lot going on there. It's like he's spent a long time trying not to feel anything.' She stopped for a second, then added: 'Definitely someone who is socially awkward.'

Yet again, Jesse found himself wondering what she would say if someone asked her the same thing about him.

'Sooner or later people like him need some kind of outlet,' Jule continued. 'But something must have happened to make him do something so . . . so awful.'

They spent the rest of the journey in silence.

Upon arriving in Garmisch, they were welcomed by brightly lit windows in the first houses and a scattering of stray Christmas lights. The roadsides were lined with cars with roof racks and ski boxes. All the guest houses seemed to be full, and the tourists were wandering around in all directions on the pavements. Some of them were still in their snowsuits with their skis thrown over their shoulders, unsteady on their feet because of their hefty ski boots or a few too many après-ski drinks. Others were freshly showered and had changed their clothes, ready to fill their bellies in the restaurants around Marienplatz. The supermarket and McDonald's were bustling with activity.

They pulled into a parking space outside the cinema on Forstamtweg. Daniel Craig was staring at them from a poster, gun in hand. Jesse was jealous, even though he hated guns. He was constantly witnessing the damage they could do when he was in Sudan. But now things were different, and he wished he had his own.

The cold air bit their skin. Jesse marched on ahead, wondering what Wolle looked like these days. The image he had in his head was that of a boy with shoulder-length dark curls and eyebrows that resembled the two sides of a pointed roof trying to meet in the middle. He only slowed his pace when he reached Klammstrasse. Just behind the Wildschütz, a packed, brightly lit restaurant, he noticed a wide two-storey building with a large, low-pitched roof, dark wooden gables and huge rafter beams. The white façade was unassuming and slightly grubby, but the colourful stucco-style embellishments around the windows made the building look quite the Bavarian gem.

A sign with the words *Wolle's Tavern* on it and two brewery logos on either side was illuminated by spotlights above the entrance.

How on earth had Wolle ended up with a tavern of this size?

'Look,' Jule pointed at a board by the entrance. *Winners of the Garmisch-Partenkirchen Sled Race, 2001, 2004 and 2005: Wolfgang Seifert, Ricci Kolbert, Alois Fürtner, Anton Schaffner.* 'Looks like someone's pretty settled here,' she said.

Jesse nodded. 'Let's go in and ask for him.'

A wall of sound hit them as soon as Jesse opened the door. The pub was warm and bustling with people. About seventy or eighty punters were gathered around low-hanging lamps or standing at the bar; some of them had sweaty hair and snowsuits on, with their tops tied loosely around their hips. The place smelled of people, sausages, sauerkraut and Hefeweizen.

'Doesn't get more stereotypically Bavarian than this, does it?' Jule smirked.

'Do I detect a touch of northern snobbery?'

'Well, you know, we don't all go around wearing sailor's caps in Hamburg either.'

They wrestled their way through the crowds and were greeted by a rotund man in his mid-fifties who was standing behind the bar. He had a well-groomed goatee and was wearing a Lacoste polo shirt. 'What'll it be?' he asked in a thick Bavarian accent.

'Two Hefeweizens,' Jesse answered.

The man nodded and called out 'Two Hefe, Anna' in his broad dialect. Then he vanished into a passage behind the bar and resurfaced carrying several steaming dishes while Anna, a twenty-year-old with dark curly hair, poured the beers.

'We're looking for the landlord,' Jesse said. 'Wolfgang Seifert. Is he around?'

The young woman grimaced. The sad, strained expression on her face clashed with her colourful dirndl dress. 'Dad doesn't want to be disturbed. Can I give him a message?'

Jesse looked at her, stunned. Did he think he was the only one of them who had a kid? 'I'm Jesse Berg, I went to Adlershof with your dad. We haven't seen each other for ages.'

Anna's face brightened up a bit, albeit only momentarily. 'He said he wants to be left alone, doesn't matter who comes in. He couldn't help himself: he just had to have another go at the sled race and ended up bruising a rib. Now he's in a state. But he won't have anyone feeling sorry for him. It's best nobody sees him when he's in one of his moods.'

'I see.' Jesse wondered what exactly she meant by one of his moods. 'Where does he live these days?'

'He moved back in here after Mum died.' She pointed towards the ceiling with her thumb. 'It's easier that way, or so he likes to think. All he has to do is come down the stairs and there's something happening.'

'I desperately need to talk to him about something,' Jesse said. 'It won't take long. Do you think you could let me see him for a few minutes?'

'I can't let you in from down here. But if you want to try outside, be my guest. Go around the house and ring the bell next to Seifert. As far as I know he's disconnected the doorbell though. I haven't seen him myself since the day before yesterday.

'Don't you live with him?'

'Me? With Dad?' Her laugh was anything but cheerful. 'He's a bit of a loner. You don't really notice it when he's down here – he's fine with company. But it's a different story when you're alone with him.'

Jesse didn't know what to say.

'Maybe it's best if you come back in a couple of days.'

A couple of days. He didn't have that much time. Jesse noticed a big bunch of keys hanging from a board on the wall right next to the cash register and a doorway to the kitchen area. He guessed the stairwell must be over there too. He suddenly found himself thinking about his own keys and the fact that Marta still had his wallet.

'Here you go. Your beers.' Condensation coated the glasses as she pushed the beers across the counter. A big group of punters burst into deafening laughter behind them. Jesse's attempt at a 'thank you' was drowned out by the noise. He clinked glasses with Jule and raised his glass at Anna. 'So how did your dad end up owning this pub?'

'What?' She leaned forward so she could hear him better.

'How did he end up with this place?' Jesse raised his voice over the din.

Anna snorted. 'He never told you the story? Wow, you really haven't seen each other in a long time.' Her eyes flashed with amusement. Jesse remembered that Wolle used laugh like that – just not very often. Jesse had always liked Wolle, but he never knew quite where he stood with him.

'He inherited it. Like something out of a film. Totally mental story. A lawyer called from San Jose in California. I was seven at the time, I think. He said one of Dad's aunts had died and left him some money. A lot, actually. He bought this with it,' she pointed around her, 'and turned it into Wolle's Tavern. Or should I say, Mum did.'

'Anna!' another thickly accented voice called out from behind Jesse, 'What're you waiting for?'

'Sorry. I'd better—' Anna said, then rushed out from behind the bar to a table full of people.

Jesse glanced at Jule and gestured towards the cash register.

'Do you see that bunch of keys?'

'What are you thinking?'

'I've got to speak to Wolle. I need to know what he said to Sandra.'

'You want to . . . How do you think you'll manage that? This place is full of people.'

'With your help?'

She looked at him disapprovingly.

'Maybe you could knock your beer over or accidently bang into Anna when she's carrying a tray full of glasses. The louder the distraction the better.'

Jule said nothing and looked at the beer in her hand. 'Is that really necessary?' she asked. 'Shouldn't we try ringing the bell first?'

'You heard what Anna said. That'll be a waste of time. He won't answer. He won't even hear us if he's disconnected the doorbell.'

'Honestly, Jesse, I think you're jumping the gun.'

'Why glue the wound if it clearly needs stitches?'

'That's hardly the best comparison,' Jule objected. She put her glass down. 'I have to go to the toilet.'

Jesse resisted the urge to argue. He eyed up the bunch of keys while Jule made her way through the crowd.

Five minutes later Jule came back with flushed cheeks. She took a swig of her beer, and the froth clung to her upper lip. 'She's right: he won't answer,' she said.

'What do you mean?'

'I rang the doorbell. Wolle didn't answer.'

'Now what?'

'When I've knocked the tray over, I'll say sorry, then I'll pay and leave. Just please don't drag me into it if they catch you with the key. I'll be waiting outside in the car.'

Chapter 32

Garmisch-Partenkirchen – Tuesday, 8 January 2013, 7.58 p.m.

Anna's tray was loaded with a mineral water, three beers, two colas and four shots of schnapps. When it crashed to the ground, the beer glasses shattered, and the schnapps glasses clinked as they bounced along the floor, drink splattering the shoes and trousers of the bystanders. All conversation stopped dead for a moment, like someone had pushed the pause button. All eyes were on Anna and the shards of glass around her.

'Ah . . . I'm so sorry,' Jule spluttered. 'Was that me?'

Jesse couldn't hear Anna's response. He pocketed the keys on his way past and slipped into the passage behind the bar. Dishes were clattering noisily in the kitchen and a ventilation system was roaring away in the background. He guessed the door to the left of him was the one that led to the stairwell. He'd been afraid he might have to try several keys, but the door wasn't even locked. He slipped through and found himself standing in a clean white stairwell lined with tiles, completely out of keeping with the rest of the building. He hurried up the stairs to another door on the first floor. Lined up next to the door was an impressive collection of pricey yet neglected-looking men's hiking boots.

Jesse knocked on the door. He tapped gently to begin with, then started banging impatiently.

Still no noise from behind the door.

He twirled the bunch of keys in his hand. Maybe he should just open the door? He shouldn't have even taken the keys in the first place, so what difference would it make? It wouldn't be the first line he'd crossed in the last two days.

The third key he tried fitted the lock.

The door swung open. It was dark inside.

'Wolle?'

He stepped inside and flicked the light on, then closed the door behind him. Was Wolle asleep already? He peered into the first room. A kitchen, one that didn't look like it was used much – some empty schnapps and wine bottles were all he could see on the worktop. Long strands of hair clung to the bathroom sink along with traces of soap and toothpaste. The bed sheets were churned up in the bedroom, and there were two empty screw-top wine bottles on the bedside table. There were no glasses in sight. Now he knew what Anna meant when she had talked about his 'moods'.

The living room was unusually large and housed a hotch-potch of bulky Bavarian softwood furniture, a scattering of dark antiques in woeful condition, and a modern table with grooved metal legs. A spiral staircase twisted its way up through the ceiling and into the attic.

'Wolle?'

Still no answer.

The staircase shook under Jesse's weight as he climbed all the way up, almost to the rafters. There were only two doors on the tiny landing. He pushed the one he guessed led to the larger room. A gust of ice-cold air blew into his face. Although the room itself was dark, all the windows were open, letting the light from the street lamps shine into the room.

Jesse gasped.

Hanging from a rope around one of the struts of the roof beam was the body of a man. The open windows to the left and right of him looked like wings. A dark patch of pungent-smelling liquid had spread over the floor next to the overturned stool beneath the man's bare, limp feet. Stray snowflakes fell past the dark, lifeless figure, melting into puddles as they hit the ground.

'Oh God,' Jesse whispered. He forced himself to turn the light on. Wolle's eyes bulged out of his pale, bloated face. Those full curls had turned straggly and grey, but his hair was still as long as ever. His clothes looked neglected, and when Jesse moved closer he noticed his dirty, badly trimmed fingernails and toenails. The skin around Wolle's wrists was red, almost like chafe marks from restraints of some kind. Now Jesse felt cold on the inside too.

He rushed into the kitchen and searched the drawers for a cotton towel, then he soaked it with water and washing-up liquid and started systematically wiping all the light switches, the handrail in the spiral staircase, the drawer handle and the tap in the kitchen. He even wiped away the traces of his damp footprints.

He quietly left the apartment, walked down the stairs and closed the back door behind him. The air was freezing. His pulse raced while the snow fell thick and calm from the sky. He wiped the bunch of keys clean with the towel, then threw them into the hallway and pulled the door shut.

Jesse tramped back to the car, leaving footprints in the fresh snow that would disappear before long. But the image of Wolle's limp body hanging from the roof beam was still lingering in his mind. He wondered what to tell Jule. The truth? That somebody had probably killed Wolle? Not all that long ago, Jule had taken him for Sandra's murderer. She'd only just started to trust him. Another murder would just ruin all that; the secret between Wolle and Artur was about him, after all.

Chapter 33

1979, Garmisch-Partenkirchen

Finally, something had happened. The night in the woods was like a baptism of fire for him. Sure, the others hadn't noticed him lurking in the undergrowth, but just knowing what they were up to changed everything for Jesse. And apparently for others too.

There had been something in the air for days. The other boys had a different look in their eyes. More guarded, somehow. More evasive. They watched him in secret. And not just Richard – Markus, Alois, Wolle, Mattheo, all the other homies too. He didn't care how the boarders looked at them. They had nothing for contempt for the homies, anyway.

When Jesse was busy doing his chores in the kitchen after lunch that Friday, Dante left him and wandered off to smoke in the courtyard without saying a word. Sandra appeared just as he was leaving and scurried past Jesse on her way to the cellar. As she did she brushed against him ever so lightly, like a whispered 'hello'. He turned around and looked at her. She stood in the doorway to the cellar, switched the light on and stared at him. 'What are you looking at?'

'You're looking at me too.'

'I'm only looking because you're looking.'

Jesse couldn't help but smirk. 'I don't believe you.'

She went quiet for a moment, then brushed the stray hairs away from her face and stuck out her chin. It looked as though light was flowing through her veins. As if she was dancing.

'I keep catching the others looking at me too,' Jesse said.

'Are you surprised?' Sandra asked.

'Nobody understands what went on with the window.'

'Which window?'

'The window was closed.' She looked at him for a long time, her dark-blue eyes waiting for an explanation.

It slowly dawned on him. Mattheo had snitched on him. His expression turned darker.

'How did you get down there?' Sandra asked.

'Well, I climbed, didn't I?'

She giggled. 'That's what I said to them. But Richard said that was impossible, and Alois didn't say anything at all.'

'And I'm guessing Markus didn't say anything, either.'

'Markus hardly ever says anything.'

Jesse nodded. 'You know, Richard sometimes watches you too,' Jesse rasped.

'Watches me? Doing what?'

Jesse gave a nod in the direction of the cellar. Sandra instantly turned red and started twisting her hands. 'Did he . . . did he say something to you?'

'No. I . . . um . . . '

'What?'

Now Jesse started blushing, and suddenly Sandra understood. Her face changed to a deeper shade of red to match her rage. 'So you've watched me too,' she hissed.

'I . . . I only watched you dancing. It was,' he gulped, 'really sexy.'

Shit! Did he really just say that?

Sandra's blue eyes instantly turned ice cold. 'The others were right about you. You're just a horible pig,' she blurted out, then spun around and headed for the cellar before having a change of heart and rushing back the other way. She touched him on her way past again, but this time, instead of a whispered hello, she bashed into him so hard it almost made him topple over. Then she was gone.

Jesse felt dirty. Not only because of what had just happened, but because of the thoughts he'd been having recently whenever he saw Sandra. Those thoughts had made those words slip out of his mouth and upset her. He turned to face the filthy dishes. A short while later a cloud of cigarette smoke wafted into the room. Dante was back.

That night he climbed into bed as usual in time for the principal's nightly rounds. Artur Messner's eyes briefly rested on Jesse as he surveyed the dorm. Jesse got the feeling he could see all the filth inside him – everything that was wrong with him, everything that he was not and would never be.

'Sexy.' That was what he'd said. Almost as if his dad had been talking for him! Wasn't Sandra's purity the thing that was so great about her? So then why did his mouth go dry whenever he thought about doing something dirty with her? What would his brother have said to her instead? Maybe: 'It looked nice.' That would have been more appropriate. Nicer. Better.

But he wasn't his brother. He wasn't this better version of himself.

The truth was, he did find it sexy. Even if it was wrong to think that way.

Jesse stayed in bed when Messner closed the door to the homies' dorm. He didn't care what they did to him. They could pull him out of the bed, beat him up – whatever they wanted. Maybe he would fight back. Maybe not.

But nobody said anything. And nobody disturbed him.

That night he dreamed he was stuck in a filthy, cramped cave. His father was with him, and the remnants of a fire was still smouldering. The back of the cave had vanished in the darkness. He didn't dare to go back there, because that was where his mother's body was lying. The invisible, better version of himself was keeping watch over her. And the odious man with the scar was somewhere outside in the black, rainy night, running away from him. At some point he was going to catch him and kill him, he told himself. And he vowed that he was going to take down the better version of himself while he was at it.

Chapter 34

Garmisch-Partenkirchen – Tuesday, 8 January 2013, 9.19 p.m.

Jule had seen him coming. She was waiting in the car with the engine running. Jesse leaped onto the passenger seat and snow fell from his jacket when he slammed the door shut.

'So?' she asked.

'Let's go,' Jessie replied.

'Why? Did something happen?'

'No, no,' he said, making light of the situation. 'But the weather isn't showing signs of getting any better. And the snow is piling up on the roads.'

Jule hit the accelerator and the car jolted out of the parking space.

'Turn right ahead and then right again onto Zugspitzstrasse,' Jesse said.

Jule focused on steering between the closely parked cars, which were partly obscured by the snow. Jesse was glad it was dark. It was going to be difficult enough to lie to her as it was, but he couldn't afford any more conversations about calling the police. He had to prioritise – that much he'd learned during his time with Doctors Without Borders. The dead were gone; Isa was the only one who mattered now.

'So, did you find him?'

'I ran into him, yes.' He took a deep breath. 'But I'm none the wiser.'

'Didn't he tell you anything? But Markus said he knew something. The only issue was that Artur had asked him to stay quiet.'

'*Asked*,' Jesse mumbled. 'More like made him keep his mouth shut.'

'So Artur must have a lot to lose, then.'

Jesse nodded. That was if there was still anything left for Artur to lose. Perhaps Artur hadn't just disappeared. Perhaps he was dead, just like Wolle and Sandra. His heart tied itself up in knots when he thought about Isa.

'And you think that's why Wolle is still acting like he knows nothing after all this time?'

'Wolle was always good at keeping secrets. And who knows what Artur did to pressure him into it.' Jesse looked through the windscreen onto the road as they drove past Marienplatz on the left. A couple of youths crossed the street and Jule had to brake suddenly. 'Idiots,' she grumbled under her breath. Someone beeped a horn behind them, but they drove on. 'But he must have told you something. What did Sandra want from him?'

'The same thing I want. To find out what else there is to this secret. Something that apparently only Wolle knows. And Artur. That's why she went to see him.'

'And he didn't tell her anything?'

'That's what he's saying.' Jesse shifted about in his seat, feeling uneasy. 'I mean, maybe he did say something to her but just didn't tell me.'

'Why do you think that?'

'Isn't it obvious? He liked Sandra, but he was never keen on me.'

'Did you tell him she's dead? And that you think her death might have something to do with this old business?'

'And make him suspect me and go running to the police? No.'

Jesse was waiting for a lecture from Jule, but it didn't come. For a moment all was silent except for the jangling of the snow chains.

'You have to take a left up there,' Jesse rasped in between breaths. Lying was taking it out of him, and the interior of the car felt claustrophobic. Jule manoeuvred the car without saying a word, and he wondered if she sensed something was wrong. Everything suddenly went dark when they passed the last of the buildings just outside Garmisch. Snowflakes drifted into the beam of the headlights. Jesse saw Wolle's lifeless figure hanging from the roof beam and he couldn't help but think of his daughter.

'Now Artur is the only one who can help us,' Jule said quietly, snapping him out of his thoughts.

'Yes. Where could he have gone?' Jesse muttered, distracted. 'Maybe he's back in his room.'

'But we haven't got a clue where that is.'

'Maybe we do though,' Jesse mumbled. 'I just thought of something.' Although Artur's room could obviously be anywhere in that vast building, if he knew Richard – and he thought he did – there was only one place it could be. Richard would have no doubt wanted his father out of the way when he took over Adlershof. As far as he was concerned, there was nothing worse than standing in his father's shadow. And there was only one corner of the whole building where Artur would be so far removed from everything that his shadow would no longer touch anyone or anything there. It had to be the old attic room in the west wing.

They parked the Volvo on the fir-lined square near the gate-house. For some reason, Jesse decided he didn't want to park the car in front of the main building for all to see. It seemed that somebody had made a crude attempt to clear the driveway. Jesse recalled them clearing the path with a snow plough attached to an old Hanomag tractor when he was a kid.

They rang the doorbell. After they had waited for what seemed like a small eternity, Philippa opened the door with a sour expression on her face. She was wearing a roll-neck jumper with a towelling dressing grown over the top. 'Didn't Mr Messner give you a key?'

'No, it seems he didn't think of that. Maybe you could give me one?'

'You'll have to ask him.'

'I probably will, then,' Jesse said. 'Do you know if Artur's back yet?'

'Artur Messner?' Philippa hesitated before quickly regaining her composure. 'He wasn't around at lunch. But then I was in the east wing for the rest of the day. I've got too much to do to keep looking for him, you know.'

'He's an old man, for God's sake. And he's been missing for a long time,' Jesse said.

'I'm not his carer,' Philippa replied, but Jesse thought he saw a faint hint of guilt flash over her face.

'He lives in the west wing, in the attic room, doesn't he?'

'Why are you asking me if you know already?'

'Thanks, then we'll go and look for him ourselves.' Jesse kicked the snow off his boots and walked past Philippa.

The staircase was deserted, and there wasn't a soul to be seen outside. A solitary street lamp shone in the courtyard, turning the snowflakes a luminous yellow as they fell through its beam. Jule followed him up in silence as they climbed the wide, creaky wooden stairs. They walked along the hall to the west wing and climbed another much narrower staircase until they reached the highest, most remote corner of the building. The steps on the last flight of stairs were as wonky and steep as he remembered. They would have been a challenge even for a man much younger than Artur. The renovations obviously hadn't made it this far. The Bakelite rotary switches came from the pre-war period and there were cracks in the wallpaper. The occasional wooden slat wobbled as they walked over the Nazi floorboards. At the end of the hall was a door with a white scrap of paper on it. The name *A. Messner* was written on it in erratic handwriting.

Jesse thought about the polished brass plaque and the freshly painted door to the principal's room on the second floor. Gratitude had never been Richard's strong point. He always bided his time before taking exactly what he wanted. Granted, Artur might not have always treated him with love and affection, and sometimes he was perhaps even overly strict with him, but that had just been to prove to everyone else that his son didn't get special treatment. This, on the other hand, was disgraceful.

Jule didn't say anything, but she seemed to be thinking the same thing. 'Do you think he's asleep?'

'Artur's never been to bed early in his whole life. We always had to wait until well after midnight for his lights to go out.'

'Wait? To do what?'

Jesse waved dismissively and knocked on the door.

Still no noise from inside.

Please, not again. The hairs on the back of his neck stood up. He knocked again. Then when nothing happened he pushed the handle, and much to his surprise, the door opened. It was dark in the room, like it had been in Sandra's flat. Like it had been at Wolle's. The reflection of the light from the courtyard outside the window made the falling snow dance like flecks of white dust. The hallway light shone into the room, creating silhouettes of Jesse and Jule on a tatty oriental rug.

'Artur?'

No reply.

'So maybe he's not in?' Jule whispered.

Jesse hesitated. He was afraid to turn the light on. He straightened his shoulders and felt around for a switch, but all he found when he touched the wall was the rippled wallpaper. Just then, something knocked into him with such great force that he fell and banged his head against the door. Jule screamed. Jesse saw a fist rapidly moving towards him from his right and instinctively turned his head to the side so that it caught his jawbone. His head slammed against the door again. Bright spots waltzed before his eyes. Someone rushed past him, then ran out into the hall before heading down the steep staircase.

Jesse tried to regain enough composure to run after the figure, but he was in too much of a daze to compose himself. He stood still and breathed heavily, leaning against the wall.

'Are you OK?'

He felt Jule's warm hand on his back. He nodded, even though his head was pounding.

'You sure?'

More nodding. Like the old days. Nodding always meant things were OK, even though they really weren't. But they had to be OK. 'Did you see him?'

'No. All I could see from behind was a woolly hat. I couldn't make out a face. It all happened too fast,' said Jule. 'But judging by the build I'd say it was a man. Did you see him? Or recognise him?'

'No.'

'What do you think he was doing in Artur's room?'

Jesse took his hands off the wall. The dizziness gradually subsided 'We should check it out.'

Jule nodded apprehensively. The memory of the night before was nagging her as well. She stepped into the room hesitantly.

'The light switch should be somewhere on the right,' Jesse said. A moment later, the ceiling light went on. The energy-saving bulbs in the three-armed art nouveau light fixture glimmered and slowly came to life.

The furniture in the room was an odd mixture: some of it was too old; some of it was clearly too cheap. Over by the window was an ancient burgundy wing chair, and beside it was a standard lamp and a small table with a cheap mosaic pattern on it. The dining table was nondescript, with two simple wooden chairs, and the carefully made bed had a headboard and a footrest decorated with Bavarian wood carvings. The tiny kitchen unit must have been there for about forty years. Jesse quickly made his way over to a narrow door and peered into the bathroom. It was green with shoddy tiling and smelled of old man, like the rest of the place. Only the old man wasn't there.

'God, it's depressing,' Jule mumbled.

'I doubt he chooses to live like this,' Jesse said, wondering if Artur could even get into the bath by himself these days.

'There's a photo of you here,' Jule called out from the next room.

Jesse walked over to her. She was standing in front of three pictures, and he instantly recognised his face in the one in the middle. He even knew when Artur had taken the picture: it was just after he'd finished his final exams, when he was about eighteen. Artur had given him the watch that day. The look on Richard's face had spoken volumes.

The picture on the right was of a boy holding his mother's hand. Richard. He must have been around thirteen at the time.

'Ah, here you are again,' Jule pointed at the photo on the left with the whole gang standing outside in the fresh snow. 'He seems to really care about you. He's got your picture hanging here almost like you were his son, not Richard.'

'Perhaps that's part of the problem,' Jesse said. He looked around the bare bedroom, but his eyes returned to the group picture in the snow. He couldn't remember it being taken – he was sure it must have been before the accident.

'What's that?'

Jesse followed the direction of Jule's gaze. The fridge door was slightly ajar, as if Artur had forgotten to close it. Jesse looked inside. The only thing inside was a half-empty bottle of water, some bits of food and a startling collection of cortisone-based medicines. But the strange thing was that the door to the freezer compartment was also open. He looked inside, but all he could see was a thick layer of ice on the inner walls.

'Does Artur have dementia?' Jule asked.

'You think he forgot to close the fridge door?'

'That'd be pretty typical.'

Jesse shook his head. 'The water's still cold and the ice hasn't thawed yet.' He looked around the room. There were a few bits and bobs lying around, but everything looked like it had some kind of order to it. The organised chaos of a lonely old man. There was nothing to suggest that someone had been through Artur's belongings. 'I think it's more likely that we caught the guy off guard while he was rifling through the fridge. It looks like, for some reason, he thought there was something in the fridge or the freezer compartment. The only question is, what could he have been looking for?' He closed the door and stared at the outside of the fridge, deep in thought. It had a large, flat, square-shaped handle, and the side by the hinge sported the old Siemens logo: a long 'S' intersected by an 'I'. The kitchen still looked like something from the sixties. He opened the door and scanned the fridge again but found nothing of any significance.

He flopped into the burgundy wing chair, exhausted. The worn-out springs creaked in protest. His jaw ached, and his head was throbbing. He was desperate. Isa was still missing, and he still wasn't any closer to finding her. If only he could talk to Artur. Jesse knew he knew something. And not only since he'd heard Markus's insinuations. Jesse blamed himself for not doing something about it long ago. He should have forced Artur to speak up years ago. But Artur had always been stubborn and secretive. Jule was right. He must have had a lot to lose.

'Where the hell are you, old man?' he mumbled. 'I need your help.'

Chapter 35

Artur lay on his mattress, staring at the dark space where the roof ridge was hiding. Was it late enough yet?

He had been racking his brains all day, trying to come up with an escape plan. Most of his ideas had ended up on the reject pile, generally because he lacked the energy to see them through.

Isabelle was sleeping beside him. She had dragged her mattress over to his and now she was lying there, whistling gently as she exhaled. He kept feeling the urge to stroke the silky hairs on her little head, but he was worried he might frighten her. He didn't want to break her trust. Anyway, wasn't there a rule about old men touching little children? At least he was sure that was what all mothers drilled into their children at an increasing rate these days.

He had promised he would wake her up soon. He would have to keep his word.

The only means of escape appeared to be the window in the gable end, but their kidnapper had bolted a horizontal row of boards in front of the window so that they couldn't open it or smash it in. Only a scant amount of light shone through the cracks in the boards and into the room.

Of course it was crazy for an old man like him to think he could escape through a gable window, but all that mattered for now was finding a way out of this attic, no matter how outlandish the plan.

His thoughts were revolving around one chink in the room's armour: the screws the kidnapper had used to attach the boards to the wood panels around the window. They had a slotted hemispherical head, which was perfect, as a cross-head countersunk screw would have ruined the plan. Obviously the bastard in the gas mask hadn't thought about that when he boarded the place up.

He tried using the blue cap from the plastic water bottle to start with, but he soon discovered that the rim was too thick and the edges were too rounded to fit into the screw slot. Then he tried the bottle instead. Unlike the lid, the bottle neck fitted the slot when he squeezed it, but annoyingly the plastic was too soft to loosen the screw.

Just before the sun went down his eyes fell on the tin bucket. Or more specifically, the bottom edge of the bucket. Protruding from under the base of the bucket was a narrow rim, like a large circular biscuit cutter. All he had to do was somehow manage to bend this edge straight, then perhaps he would be able to turn the bucket into a kind of primitive screwdriver. The main issue was the noise. He was nowhere near strong enough to bend the tin with his bare hands, so he would have to keep working away at the bottom of the bucket until it was at least reasonably straight. And he guessed the best time for that was at night, when the kidnapper wouldn't overhear him.

He reached out for Isabelle's shoulder and shook her gently. 'I think it's time,' he whispered.

She woke up as soon as she heard him. 'Why are you whispering? We're going to be making noise anyway, aren't we?'

Artur couldn't help but smile. He had spent a long time closing his mind to children's logic. It would have only been a hindrance in his line of work, especially in his role as principal. Where would being understanding have got him?

But this situation was something completely different.

'Well,' he said softly, 'you never know, do you?'

'What do you think the insect man will do to us if he hears?'

Artur gulped. 'He won't hear.'

'But I'm scared,' Isabelle whispered.

'If he comes up here, I'll tell him I tripped over the bucket in the dark.'

'O . . . K,' said Isabelle, but she didn't sound convinced.

'Here goes. Don't be scared, now.'

Artur grabbed the bucket with both of his hands and banged it against the floor with all his might. The wooden boards vibrated, and the racket soared up to the roof and lingered there, like it was caught in an echo chamber. He wished he could cover his ears, but there was no time and instead he banged the bucket on the floor again. Twice, three times, four times – focused movements, always hitting the same spot. He banged the bucket in quick succession, going as fast as he could in the hope that the noise would be less noticeable if it was over swiftly.

When he finally stopped the silence burned Artur's ears.

Neither of them dared to breathe. They listened out in case they could hear footsteps darting up the stairs – or any other noise, for that matter.

Eventually Isabelle couldn't bear to stay quiet any longer.

'Do you think he noticed anything?'

'He'd be here by now if he'd heard us,' Artur murmured.

'What if he's still thinking about how he's going to punish us?'

'He'd want to know what we were up to first. I don't think he's here.'

'You mean you think we're all alone?' Isabelle suddenly seemed unsure which was the scarier prospect: being left all alone, or the kidnapper being there. 'What if he's forgotten about us?'

'Sadly I'm afraid he'll be back.'

'I hope he has a nasty accident,' Isabelle muttered.

But people like him never have accidents, Artur thought, bitter with contempt. It's always other people who have accidents. He took hold of the tin bucket and felt the bottom rim. He'd managed to bend it after all. A small section was almost straight now.

'Did it work?' Isabelle asked.

'We'll have to wait until tomorrow morning to know for sure. I'll need some light.'

Isabelle sighed. The springs creaked as they lay down on their mattresses. The woollen blankets were surprisingly clean, maybe even new. It was like they had been bought especially for the occasion.

'Artur?'

'Hmm.'

'What was my dad like back then?'

'Hm. That's a tricky one.'

'Why?'

He went quiet for a moment. Dangerous territory.

'Did you like him?'

'Yes, I did.'

'And the others? Did they like him too?'

'Well, your mother, for example – she always liked him a lot,' Artur said, dodging the question.

'Well, she didn't like him that much at first. Or, she did in the beginning, but then she didn't, but then she did,' Isabelle said. 'That's what she said, anyway.'

'That all sounds very complicated,' Artur grumbled.

'But what about the others?' Isabelle insisted.

Artur sighed. 'Jesse wasn't always the easiest person to deal with.'

Isabelle giggled in the dark. 'That's what Mum always says too. "There are two sides to him", she says.' She paused: '"And I only know one of them."'

'That's a good thing,' Artur mumbled. 'Let's try to get some sleep. I'm tired.'

'O . . . K,' Isabelle said. She sounded disappointed, but at least she seemed to have forgotten about her fears for the time being. Artur closed his eyes. His mind was racing. Not even the pain he'd kept in check with the cortisone was enough to distract him. The ghosts were more threatening than ever. He tried to concentrate on the next morning: on the screws, the bucket and the boards. There wasn't much chance of him escaping through a gable window. Maybe Isabelle could manage it though. She was Jesse's daughter, after all, so maybe climbing was in her blood. He wondered how old Jesse must have been the first time he climbed down the façade with the others.

He'd often wondered whether he should have kept a closer eye on things. Yes, he'd always had his suspicions about what the boys were up to climbing onto the roof, but he never really gave it too much thought. He'd figured it was a better way for them to let off steam than some others.

But somehow, they still found other ways . . .

Chapter 36

1980, Garmisch-Partenkirchen

It was March and the snow was still falling. These days, Jesse slept in the bed every night. The others still snubbed him, but at least they'd stopped hassling him. Nobody had climbed out of the window since that last time, probably because it was too cold to venture out. The roof was their only escape route, and as long as it was frozen they had no choice but to stay put. But now finally it was thawing, and change was in the air.

He gazed out of the window as Messner closed the door from the outside. He was getting increasingly irritated with the principal always acting like he had this impressive classical education. Jesse didn't buy it. Sometimes he suspected the reason they kept getting summoned to the principal's office was just so that Messner could show off his books. He didn't believe that Messner read a lot. Or if he did, he didn't have all that much to say for himself.

When the old man had finally left, a tense silence filled the room. The full moon looked like it had been cut out of the night sky with a razor blade. Not a single star was in the shadows. The Milky Way resembled a dusty cloud of light.

The conditions couldn't have been better. Jesse knew what they had planned for tonight. He'd seen the others whispering in secret and Sandra gesturing at Richard to tell him she thought he was nuts. He saw Richard acknowledging the gesture with a grin, seeming to mistake her criticism for admiration. And though Sandra would never have admitted it, there was a hint of both in her eyes. She looked at him often. The principal's son. The golden boy. Life just wasn't fair. Richard had everything. A family, plenty of money and his own clique of homies. He could go wherever he wanted, whenever he wanted. He was even on a par with the boarders.

Jesse, on the other hand, was never on a par with anyone. And he definitely couldn't go wherever he wanted. No wonder Sandra looked at Richard instead of at him. Both of them had watched her dancing, but it was him she held it against, not Richard.

It was time to do something to change all that. He hated how other people were always getting ahead of him. First invisible brothers, then golden boys.

'I'm coming with you tonight,' he declared, punctuating the silence.

No reaction. Had he made a mistake?

'Oh right, where are we going?' Alois asked.

'To the woods, where else?' Jesse replied.

'Forget it. You're off your head.'

'I'm coming with you,' Jesse insisted.

'No!' Alois glared at him.

'Shh,' Markus hissed. 'You'll wake everyone up.'

'If he's coming, so am I,' Mattheo grumbled.

'Shut it,' Alois barked. 'He isn't coming with us so forget about it.'

'And you're definitely not coming,' Markus said, reminding Mattheo where he stood.

'There's nothing you can do to stop me,' said Jesse. 'I won't let you.'

Alois was raging. He darted over to Jesse. 'Markus, Wolle, come and give me a hand.' Suddenly, he was standing next to Jesse's bed. Wolle was almost as quick. The two of them grabbed Jesse. 'Markus,' Alois panted, 'I need something to tie him up with.'

Jesse fought back. He had never been in a fight, but he had taken his fair share of beatings, usually from his father. He used to be good at putting up and shutting up. But this was different. A fire was raging in his stomach. He waved his arms back and forth, then he somehow managed to free his right arm and punch Alois in the pit of his stomach. Alois doubled over, groaning, then suddenly hit back in a rage and dealt a blow to Jesse's chin. Jesse tasted blood, but he didn't make a sound. Instead, he just kicked at Wolle, who was still trying to hold on to him.

'Quit it, you morons! Stop it!' Markus yelled. 'Do you want to wake the whole building up?

They all backed off. For a fleeting moment, the only sound to be heard was the three of them huffing and puffing.

'Just leave him, for God's sake. There's no point.'

'Of course there's a point!' Alois sneered. 'If you'd help us, we could tie the prick up and just get on with it.'

'And let him go running to Mr M's office to tell on us?'

'Well, if he does that then we'll just throw him out of the window,' Mattheo chimed in.

The others stayed quiet.

'You've said it yourselves.'

'Nobody's getting thrown out of the window here,' Markus said, trying his best to sound calm. 'And you keep your mouth shut, you little squirt.'

Mattheo bit his lip.

Jesse stood up, went to the bathroom and washed the blood out of his mouth with cold water. Then he planted himself in front of the others and said: 'I don't care what you say or do; I'm coming, end of story.'

'Fine by me,' said Markus.

'Are you being serious?' Alois snapped.

'He knows about everything anyway.'

Silence.

'Fine,' Alois said, clearly feeling bitter about the whole thing. 'He'll just miss anyway. I mean, what else would you expect from the son of an alky?' The anger came over him like a wave. In the space of a split second, Jesse had lunged at Alois and punched him in the face. Alois gave a muffled cry, then staggered backwards clutching his nose. Just as Jesse was about to pounce on Alois a second time, he felt Markus's arm on his. 'That's enough.'

Jesse backed away. He was breathing so heavily it was almost like he had run all the way down to Garmisch and back again. Alois sat on the edge of the bed moaning and holding his face. Jesse was lost for words. He felt a deep satisfaction. So this was how it felt to take what he wanted. 'I'm coming with you,' he said one last time.

'Fine,' Markus grumbled. 'But for now let's just lie down in case anyone heard us. It's still far too early to go.'

In no time at all, they were all back in their beds. The fight played over and over again in Jesse's head.

Two hours later, they finally climbed out of the window. Everyone except for Mattheo, who cried in disappointment at being the only one left behind.

It was easier to scramble down the side of the building this time around. They only had to go one floor down to the window

Richard had opened for them earlier, then they climbed in and crept along the hall, making sure not to tread on the creaky parts of the old parquet, and finally down the staircase. Richard was waiting by the back door of the kitchen. He stared at Jesse like he had seen a ghost. 'What's going on?'

'Don't ask.' Alois glared at Jesse, his eyes full of hatred. Under his nostrils there was a wide patch of dry blood that he had smeared across his cheek with the back of his hand.

'Jesse's coming too,' Markus said firmly, resolutely.

Richard raised his eyebrows in disapproval and scowled at Jesse, but instead of arguing with Markus, he just opened the door with a sullen look on his face. The whole group ran over to the shed, then Richard unlocked the padlock and vanished into the darkness before reappearing with two pairs of leather gloves and the rest of the kit.

They marched through the snow behind the shed and then turned off into the woods. It was freezing cold, and as they walked away from Adlershof, the back of the building rose up like a fortress behind them. For a second Jesse thought he could see Mattheo behind one of the roof windows. But that was impossible: their room faced toward the front.

After a while they arrived at a small clearing in the woods. Richard took the crossbow out of the case, revealing the clearly defined contours of the matt-black steel against the snowy backdrop. Richard put his foot in the stirrup at the front end of the stock, held the crossbow upright and leaned his chest against the butt end of the stock to keep it steady with his weight. Markus and Wolle were wearing the leather gloves. They had grabbed hold of the left and right sides of the bowstring and now they were using their combined strength to pull it up until the string engaged on the trigger catch.

'You first,' Markus said, handing Jesse the tensioned crossbow and a bolt. Jesse was overcome with excitement as he lined the bolt up with the slot and lifted the heavy piece of weaponry. A solitary tree in the clearing towered up out of the snow like a demon with twisted arms. The moon bathed everything in a silvery light.

'The light spot there,' Markus pointed at the wide tree trunk. A branch had been sawn off it some time ago and the surface where it had been cut off was about the size of a plate. 'Three shots. If you hit the target every time, then you get another shot – and it's up to you to decide who has to stand under the target when you take the fourth shot.'

'I know,' Jesse hissed. 'I saw you last time.' His arms shook as he took aim. The crossbow was heavy – much heavier than he'd expected – and a frosty wind was blowing over the clearing.

'Just imagine it's someone you hate,' Richard whispered. 'Your dad or someone like that.'

Jesse blinked. How come everyone knew about his dad? How had they all found out? And how come they had got it so wrong! He wished he could scream at the top of his lungs. He'd say: 'You know nothing, nothing at all!' He closed his eyes for a second. His father's face flashed in front of him – but not the face he knew now. Not the face of that drunkard. Not the face of that brutal, desperate man he'd had to run away from. No, the face he saw was the one he used to know. The one from the postcard. The beaming face of a proud man, like in the Superman advert he'd seen in a magazine. This beaming Superman whispered in his ear: 'You've betrayed me! Your own father. You're a nobody, nothing but a disappointment. HE would never have done that!'

Jesse bit his bottom lip and opened his eyes again. He raised the crossbow a little higher, then moved it into a better position *slightly to the left. Yes, he could imagine someone standing there in front of the tree, their face the target. It was the face of his better self. The branches on the tree were his arms, and the shabby bark was his clothing*

'Can you see him, your dad?' Alois whispered.

'It's not my father,' Jesse muttered. The shoulder stock felt freezing cold against his cheek.

'And your mum? What about her?'

The wind blowing in Jesse's face was as cold as the metal of the crossbow. Tears welled up in his eyes. He bent his finger. The bolt buzzed as he fired it and hit the target.

He was so excited to hit the target that the second shot landed above it and slightly to one side.

When he was taking aim for the third time, he noticed a faint movement in the bushes behind the tree trunk. It was a tall, lithe four-legged creature. A baby deer, perhaps. Suddenly his fingers were tingling with excitement. None of the others seemed to notice the animal. Without a second thought, he adjusted his position and aimed a little to the left, towards the animal. A rustling sound came from the woods as he fired the shot, then the deer promptly disappeared. He was disappointed. After misfiring on his second shot, he wished the third one would have at least hit the target.

Alois's grinning mouth lit up in the moonlight as he took hold of the crossbow. He hit the target three times in a row. 'I pick Jesse,' he said, sounding extremely pleased with himself.

Jesse slowly walked over to the tree. The snow crunched under his feet. He pressed his back into the tree trunk. The spot where the branch had been sawn off was about thirty centimetres above his head. He wished he could close his eyes while Alois took aim. But no, he wasn't going to grant him that satisfaction, so instead *he stood there with his eyes wide open, waiting. He felt the blood pumping through his veins. Every thought was clearer than ever before.*

If Alois hit him now, maybe that would be his punishment for having aimed at the baby deer.

The bolt flew towards him and everything stopped for a moment. Nothing but silence. The wind held its breath. His head was completely empty.

The bolt bored right into the tree.

No punishment.

What's one baby deer, anyway?

Chapter 37

Garmisch-Partenkirchen – Tuesday, 8 January 2013, 11.06 p.m.

What a contrast. Jesse swallowed his anger. He tried his best to avert his gaze from the shiny brass plaque, but it was almost impossible to ignore.

He banged on the door with his knuckles. It took a while for the key on the inside to finally turn. Same as ever. The Messners were never ones for closing the door without locking it. Artur used to lock their door when they were kids, and now apparently Richard was in the habit of locking himself in too. The weary face of his former schoolmate appeared though the crack in the door. Even though he had obviously been asleep, his hair still looked freshly combed.

'You again?' Richard glanced from Jesse to Jule and back again. 'What do you want?'

'It's about your dad,' Jesse said. 'We have to talk.'

Richard frowned and opened the door, then without saying a word he showed them into his adjoining study.

The principal's office was just as Jesse remembered it. The mahogany panelling didn't quite match up with the British style of the building. Like the floor, it had been fitted by a Nazi bigwig and gave the room an almost oppressive feel. The rows of books and files behind the glass panels on the recessed shelves conveyed an air of culture and sophistication, hinting at a level of education neither Artur nor Richard had ever been able to attain. Still, it had profoundly impressed Jesse when he was a child.

Richard was wearing a dressing gown over a pair of striped pyjamas, and his felt slippers gently padded across the parquet as he walked. Richard sat down in Artur's beloved leather chair behind the bulky desk, scrutinising the two of them like a couple of insects that were disturbing his sleep. 'So, what's this about the old man?'

Jesse and Jule sat down at the desk without waiting for an invitation. 'Didn't you say he wasn't around earlier today?' Jesse asked.

'Yes, that's right. But he isn't senile, you know. And he doesn't have to check in and out every time he goes anywhere. He isn't a prisoner here.'

Maybe not in a strict sense, Jesse thought to himself, yet he couldn't help but feel that it was almost the same thing. 'This morning I got the impression you were worried about him and you were going to look for him.'

'Of course.' Richard spread his arms out. 'He's my father. I'm always worried about him. I probably spend far too much time worrying about him. But come on, don't beat around the bush. Why have you dragged me out of bed at this hour?'

'We went to see Artur just now, but he wasn't in. His door wasn't locked either.'

'And?' Richard frowned again and gave a rather condescending smile. He clearly wasn't taking them seriously.

'We wanted to make sure that nothing had happened to him, so we looked—' Jule paused for a second '—and instead of finding Artur we caught a man rummaging through your father's room. He knocked Jesse over and ran off.'

'Good heavens!' Richard stared at Jesse. Only now did he seem to notice the slight swelling on his jawbone. 'Did you recognise him? Could you describe him?'

'It all happened much too quickly,' Jule said. 'He was wearing a black hat and he was about the same size as Jesse.'

Now Richard looked genuinely stunned. 'Do you have any idea what this man might have been looking for?'

'No,' Jule said. 'But—'

Jesse stopped her mid-sentence with a dismissive gesture. He thought it was best not to mention the freezer compartment. 'Whatever he was after, he didn't completely ransack the room,' he said. 'I think we disturbed him.'

Richard raised his eyebrows. They were gradually getting as unruly as his father's. 'What could Dad possibly be hiding up there?'

Jesse looked at Richard and didn't say a word. A tense silence dominated the room, broken only by the creaking of the wooden panelling by the heater.

'You can't seriously be saying,' Richard said, adopting a deliberately derisive tone, 'that you think my old man is hiding some kind of secret—'

'To be completely honest,' Jesse replied, 'I'd prefer to ask Artur that myself. But he isn't around and I'm starting to worry about him.'

Richard snorted and shrugged it off. 'Bah, the old guy can handle himself. He's got a mind of his own with a whole load of mischief in it. He's always playing tricks on me. And always at the worst times. He even pilfers the odd bottle of wine from me at night sometimes, even though he can't really handle the alcohol with his rheumatism drugs. I almost feel like we've switched roles, like he's the kid and I'm the grown-up.'

For a moment Richard almost sounded sympathetic, as if he found his old man's quirks annoying but also quite endearing at the same time.

'So you think he's just going to turn up?' Jesse asked.

Richard shrugged. 'Of course.'

Jesse found his remark implausible in view of the two deaths. But what was he supposed to say? Richard didn't know anything about the murders, and that was how it had to be. At least for now. 'And the guy in Artur's room?' Jesse asked. 'You've got no idea who that could be?'

'Me? Not the foggiest. But to be totally honest, I do find it extremely troubling – the thought of someone creeping around here, rummaging through other people's rooms and hitting you when you disturbed him.'

'Don't you think we should call the police?' Jule chimed in.

Jesse shot her a sharp sideways glance. Richard's eyes had become smaller too. He seemed to be as keen on the idea of calling the police as Jesse was. 'That would probably be a bit hasty,' he said. 'Who knows what's behind all this? It could turn out to be something totally harmless. Perhaps Alois was bringing him something up from the kitchen and you startled him.'

'Harmless?' Jule looked at Richard in disbelief. 'But the man—'

'Alois?' Jesse interrupted her. 'Which Alois?

'Fürtner. Our Alois,' Richard smiled. 'He's the cook here now. He trained in a hotel and moved around a lot. He popped up here at just the right time three years ago when I had just had to fire the old cook.'

Jesse looked at Richard with a baffled expression. 'Almost all the old homies from our room are back together here. You've got Alois as the cook and Markus as the caretaker, then there's Wolle with his pub down in Garmisch.'

'Not everyone wants to get away from here.'

'And what about Mattheo? Does he live around here too?'

'Mattheo works in Garmisch. He's a postman. He comes up here once every day, except Sundays.'

Richard watched Jesse intently. He seemed to be waiting for a reaction, but when it failed to materialise, he just shrugged. 'It wasn't all that great here when Dad was in charge. But it seems that for some people it was enough. Alois and the others didn't exactly get the best grades, so they had to take what they could get. Mailman, cook . . . those were the options.'

'Markus could have definitely gone on to study something.'

'Well, Markus . . . he's a special case.'

'What do you mean by special?'

'I only know one person who's as attached to this old place as my dad, and that's Markus. It's like he's part of the furniture. But where else can you go when you've grown up in the mountains? The city? Are *you* happy there, where you live now?'

'It's OK.'

'So no, then.'

'Like I said, it's OK.'

'And you took the best that this place had to offer with you.'

Jesse said nothing. Every conversation with Richard some-how led to them talking about Sandra. That's how it had always been. Only this time it might be a useful opening. 'How long has it been since you last saw Sandra?'

'Why?'

'She was here recently, wasn't she?'

'Not that I'm aware of.' Richard pursed his lips and shook his head. Jesse couldn't tell if he was lying.

'Listen, does Alois live up here nowadays?'

'Yes. Just like Markus. They both live in the north wing, on the second floor.'

Jesse promised himself he'd be paying Markus a visit in the north wing as soon as he got the chance. He wondered whether it was wise to talk about the accident too. But Richard was probably the last person who would tell him anything voluntarily. The impression he had given so far was that he had no interest whatsoever in entertaining a frank, open conversation. The old wall of silence was back up again. 'I meant to ask: how's the boarding school going? It looks like you're not doing too badly financially.'

'Let's just say I can't complain. Why do you ask?'

'Oh, just out of interest.'

'Honestly, Jesse,' Richard said. 'I'd love to stay and chat with you. Really, I would. But I've got an early start tomorrow and I need to get some sleep.' He yawned, although the tiredness in his face seemed to have magically vanished since he first opened the door. 'We'll have another look for Dad tomorrow. No doubt we'll find him snoring away in his bed.' He stood up and smoothed down his dressing gown. Meeting adjourned.

Just as they were leaving, Richard quietly called out from the doorway: 'Oh, before I forget: if you speak to Sandra on the phone, tell her I said hi. Same goes for your daughter too. Even though we haven't met yet.'

Jesse gritted his teeth so tightly it made his jaw ache. Richard quietly locked the door behind them and the sound echoed in the empty hall. The two of them made their way down the corridor to the staircase. Snowflakes the size of feathers were falling to the ground outside the window.

'God, talk about dancing around the subject,' Jule said quietly.

Jesse put his finger to his lips and guided her around the corner into a dark classroom. The silhouettes of two dozen upturned chairs on the tables flashed up against the windows. Somebody had scribbled something nonsensical on the board.

'Richard has good ears.' Jesse closed the door, making the classroom ever darker than before.

'Look, I know you don't want to call the police,' Jule started to say.

'Is that right? So then why do you keep suggesting it?' Jesse snapped.

'I wanted to see Richard's reaction. He looked like he wanted to avoid a visit from the police like the plague. That was strange, don't you think?'

'Yes and no,' Jesse said. 'He has his reputation to think of. That's how it was when Artur was in charge of Adlershof, too, and it's probably even harder these days. You know, because of the public scandals surrounding youth camps and boarding schools – like with that old sex abuse scandal at Odenwaldschule. Sometimes calling the police is the right thing to do, but it always has its consequences. It makes it look like something's not right. It doesn't matter if everything's fine, something always sticks in these situations.'

'It seems you and Richard are of the same mind when it comes to keeping quiet.'

'What's that supposed to mean?' Jesse snapped.

'Maybe it wouldn't have hurt you to be a bit more open with him.'

'I see. More open. So how do you suppose that would work? Hi, Richard, my daughter's been abducted and Sandra's dead. But please don't call the police, we need to chat about it first . . . something like that?'

'Don't be so touchy. I just mean you could have asked him about the accident. Or about Wolle and Markus.'

'Didn't you notice how he jumped on the subject of Artur and his secret? He wanted to know if *we* knew anything.'

'Do you still think it's all tied in with your accident?'

Jesse went quiet. He went over to one of the windows and looked out of it thoughtfully.

'Well, whatever it is, we're not getting any further right now,' Jule said.

The twirling snowflakes reminded Jesse of the mess in his head. 'It's all connected somehow. Sandra, Isa—' – and Wolle, he added silently – '—and then Artur's disappearance. Richard's strange behaviour. And that man in Artur's room.'

'At least if the man in Artur's room has something to do with Isa's kidnapping, he knows you're closing in on him now.'

And that just puts Isa in even more danger, Jesse thought to himself. He felt hot and cold all at once. He thought about the drained battery in his phone. The kidnapper had his number!

Maybe there would be another warning from him or some sign of life from Isa.

'Jesse?'

'Hm?'

'What do we do now?'

'Time for a detour to our room. I need a charger.'

Chapter 38

Wednesday, 9 January 2013

It was dark, and it would be that way for a while yet. Artur knew from countless past experiences that not sleeping or sleeping badly always made the night unbearably long. And being held captive just made it twice as bad.

He couldn't stop thinking about the hole. He had never dared to lock the boarders in there, although a couple of those spoiled brats certainly could have done with it. The fear of the children's parents cancelling their contracts always held him back. He couldn't risk losing a single cent. But he was less concerned about repercussions when it came to the children from the home, or the 'homies', as Richard used to call them out of his childish enthusiasm for all things American. The subsidies from the child welfare office were more or less set in stone, so who was going to have anything so say about it there? Wisselsmeier? Unlikely. As much as she looked like a shapeless lump of dough, on the inside she was made of Krupp's steel. Sending those kids to the hole was just part and parcel of keeping them in check. Apart from detention, what other threat could he use?

Back then he had no idea how it felt to be locked up. Now here he was, in a hole of his own, and suddenly he was kicking himself for the things he had done. Guilt: another ghost that haunted him. Sometimes he wondered why he saw everything so differently these days. It was almost like he'd undergone some sort of transformation – like Jesse, the only child who ever *really* deserved his stint in the hole. At least before the accident anyway.

Now the only question was what accident had caused him, Artur, to change.

Richard, perhaps?

He tried to distract himself by listening to Isabelle's peaceful breathing and let himself sink into her soft inhalations and exhalations.

The sound of footsteps on the stairs startled him. It had been hours since they had made a racket with the bucket and they had been completely quiet ever since, so why did the footsteps sound so loud and angry?

The hatch sprang open and crashed onto the floorboards. A blaze of bright light from a lamp that swayed in the darkness as it came to rest on the ground dazzled Artur and Isabelle and shone on the man climbing through the hatch towards them. His shadow grew ominously and hovered in the acute angle of the roof truss. With the gas mask over his head, the man was transformed into a creature from some feverish nightmare. The insect man. The sight of the man openly holding the rope and the axe in his hand filled Artur with dread. Isabelle had woken with a shock and now she was clinging on to him for protection.

The man came towards them without saying a word, then he grabbed Isabelle by the hair and hoisted her up. Isabelle's scream rang out in Artur's ears.

'Watch carefully, Artur Messner. This is all your fault,' the man said with a snarl. 'This is just a taste of what's to come.' His voice sounded hollow under the mask.

Rigid with fear, Artur watched as the insect man dragged Isabelle over to the table by her hair and tied her arm to the table.

'Oww!' Isabelle screamed.

'Please, don't,' Artur moaned. It occurred to him that he should offer himself instead, but the words wouldn't come out.

'It didn't have to come to this, really it didn't. But you asked for it.'

'Why, for God's sake? How?'

The insect eyes flashed in the light. The man raised the axe.

Isabelle screamed again, pulling her head between her shoulders and screwing her eyes up. 'No, please! No, no, no!'

Artur couldn't bear it. 'Why are you doing this?' he screamed. 'What did I do wrong?'

'Where's the hand I sent you?'

In that second, Artur understood. It was about the freezer compartment. The man had been at Adlershof, looking for the hand with the scar on the back. It *really was* his fault. Why had he lied about that damn hand? Well of course he knew why: it was because he had been foolishly hoping that someone would find it next to the bin and call the police. He had been stupidly clutching at straws and now the man had found him out. Oh, how he used to laugh and scoff at all the simple-minded lies the pupils told in the old days. He always acted so superior when he was the principal. And now look at him. He was just the same as them.

'I . . . I'm sorry,' he stammered. 'It's . . . it's by the bin. The bin by the gatehouse. Please, please leave her alone. You're right. It's—' – he had to cough when the bitter stomach acid welled up into his throat – '—it's my fault.'

'Think carefully about what you're saying. If you lie to me again—'

'No, please! I swear I'm telling the truth,' Artur begged. 'It's there. Honest to God.'

The man let go of the axe. He breathed softly through the filter on the mask. Flecks of dust hovered around his silhouette in the harsh light of the lamp on the floor.

Isabelle trembled as she sniffed and opened her eyes. She directed her first fearful glance at the axe. Her hunched shoulders eased back down a little. Then she looked at Artur with eyes so full of pleading and desperation they made him feel completely wretched.

'You care about the kid, don't you?'

Artur looked down and said nothing.

'That makes me hate you even more,' the man shouted.

Artur winced and stared at him in confusion. 'Who are you?' The words just slipped out of him.

The man didn't convey the slightest emotion from behind the gas mask. His whole body froze, like he was regretting having expressed his hatred.

'What do you want with the hand?' Artur asked.

The silence that followed was so oppressive that Artur wished he'd kept his question to himself. The man dangled the axe limply and twirled the handle in semicircular motions, causing the blade to spin erratically.

'Forget about the hand,' the man said. 'The fact that you lied to me is much worse. You already lied to me once. And you'll both have to pay for that.'

Artur winced. *Pay. Both.* All this time he'd been kidding himself there might be a way out of all this, deluding himself that he might get out at least partly unscathed because it had nothing to do with him. Wasn't this about Jesse and Isa? He thought he'd just got caught up in it because of a stupid coincidence at the gatehouse!

And now *he* had to pay for it?

And Isabelle too? For *his* lies?

The insect man grabbed the lamp and headed back down the stairs. The light swayed from side to side and vanished down the hole with him. The hatch slammed shut, plunging them into complete darkness.

Even though it was pitch black, it was like he could still feel Isabelle's eyes on him. He was so overcome with shame he wished the ground would open up and swallow him. It was like those eyes could look right through to the pit of his soul and see everything he was – and everything he wasn't.

'I'll help you,' he whispered. 'With the rope.'

No response.

He winced as he slowly stood up, then he fumbled with the knot, trying to steady his trembling fingers. The occasional waft of Isabelle's breath brushed against his cheek. It was like the ghosts were surrounding him in the darkness, all standing around him pointing their fingers at him. He wished he was sitting in his room with that stupid old rug and his worn-out bed. He wished he had a bottle of Riesling or, better still, two bottles. He could have done with some cortisone at the very least, just to ease the rheumatism. This attic was the essence of everything he had become. This was where he had ended up. This was where *running away* had got him. But he was done with all that now. His fingers picked at the knot. Isabelle sniffed in the darkness right by his ear. She didn't say a word.

Yes, this was about Jesse. And it was about his friend. In fact, no, he couldn't call himself a friend any more. It was about

Wilbert, someone who really had been a friend at one time. And it was about Isabelle. And it was about him! The knot inside Artur's brain suddenly came loose while he was still holding Isabelle's knot between his fingers. Just like that, it all made sense. For the first time he thought clearly about what he had been refusing to see all this time. Because he'd thought it impossible. Crazy. He knew who the insect man was. There was only person it could be. He just didn't understand what he wanted.

'Thank you,' Isabelle mumbled. Her cold fingers grazed his as she pulled her hand out of the loop.

'I'm sorry,' Artur rasped. He was too weak to feel his way over to his mattress in the darkness, so instead he just sank to the floor next to the table and sat there with his legs out in front of him.

Suddenly he sensed Isabelle grasping around, trying to locate him in the dark. She found his legs and slid a little closer, then she threw her little arms around him and squeezed him tight. He could feel her tears running down to his collar as she pressed her cheek against his neck. 'Artur, I want to get out of here. Please, please get me out of here.'

He gulped and bit back his tears. 'I'm sorry, I really am.'

At that moment he realised that without him, this wonderful little girl would never have existed. And although maybe it helped to ease his guilty conscience a touch, he now felt more responsible than ever for making sure that she at least came out of this.

Chapter 39

1981, Garmisch-Partenkirchen

It was too dark, too wet and too slippery. More than a year had passed since Jesse's first night in the clearing. Spring was a non-event and the full moon was hiding behind a wall of rain. Nobody would be climbing out of the window tonight. With nowhere to go, he just lay there with the black hole in his chest like he did so often, listening to the rain as it pattered down on the roof tiles.

Every drop was like a bolt from a crossbow.

Thunk. Thunk-thunk. Thunk-thunk-thunk . . .

The noise the arrows made when they hit the wood over his head was equal parts threat and a relief. It was exactly the same for the other boys. None of them got out of playing this dangerous game. They made an agreement to push things as far as they could go. To feel something for a moment, even if it was just fear and pain.

Markus still refused to let Mattheo go with them, unlike Jesse, who was now part of it in his own way. He had a bed, and now, for the first time, he had something resembling a group of friends. Strictly speaking he had a new life, perhaps even something like a home. But the black hole was still there. He could feel the hatred gnawing away at him and the hole getting bigger. It was like someone had cut him long ago, removing any real chance he ever had of a better life.

He got up and walked over to the toilet, trying to shake the feeling that had taken hold of him. The wooden floor creaked as he crossed the hall. The locked door to the staircase was to his right, and there was a light on in the bathroom opposite. Three washbasins, three showers, three toilets, all lined up in a row on one side of the room. The other side had a sloping roof that began about a metre and a half above the floor.

He squinted in the glaring light, stopped in front of the middle sink and ran his wrists under a stream of cold water. Instead of looking at himself in the mirror, he avoided his face and stared into the space behind it instead. Finally his eyes rested on the access panel under the sloping roof. It was inconspicuous and about the size of a cellar window, but he couldn't help thinking it looked like a poorly disguised secret door. He turned around, curious. Just what was behind that panel?

Jesse looked at the four screws holding the panel in place on the wall. Slotted screws. He was going to need a screwdriver, but he was so curious he just couldn't wait. How about the plug? He pulled the long metal stopper out of the sink and noticed the flat-headed metal screw sticking out of the bottom. Probably thin enough to loosen the screws.

The inner catch came loose after just half a turn on each side, then the panel came away from the wall. It was only fastened with four rotating hooks. Jesse knelt down and poked his head through the hole. The sloping roof and the cladding formed a triangular passage that trailed off into the darkness under the eaves on either side. The air was stuffy and the sound of water falling onto the roof tiles was considerably louder under the eaves.

Jesse took a close look at his surroundings.

Then he pushed himself into the passageway with his back against the wall, lifted the panel back onto the gap in the wall from inside, and turned the hooks into position. The bathroom light punched a frame of bright lines into the darkness. His heart was pounding as he crept away on all fours. With a bit of luck, the passageway would go past the locked door to the boy's block. And it would be pretty surprising if there wasn't another access panel on the other side of the door.

Progress was slow in the pitch darkness. The occasional spider's web planted itself on his face and unravelled as he crawled forward. His hands shuffled along on the dusty wooden floor. They must be black by now. Shouldn't he have gone past the closed door a while ago?

He paused for a moment. It was pitch black all around him. How was he going to see an access panel if there wasn't a light shining through behind it? And most importantly, what would he do if one of his roommates turned the light off in the bathroom? How would he find his way back then?

He decided to turn around and come back the next night with a torch. As he crawled along under the eaves, he fantasised about his new-found freedom. This was his way out of Alcatraz, the legendary prison from that film Richard had bragged about seeing. The most escape-proof prison in all of America. And although Jesse might only have been twelve, he was the smartest of all the inmates. The king of the jailbreakers.

But where the hell was the panel with the border of bright light framing the edges? Shouldn't he be back there by now? Jesse froze. Had somebody turned out the light?

He turned around again and tried to feel for the cladding with his fingers. Surely he could find the panel this way if the light had gone out. He slowly crawled further along the passageway, keeping his fingertips on the wall at all times. As he moved along, he could feel the old wooden laths supporting the cladding. He paid attention to every recess or bulge in the spaces between them until he finally came across a slight groove in the surface. Feeling relieved, he eagerly fumbled around until he found the hooks at the corners, then loosened them and climbed into the bathroom. He caught sight of himself in the mirror: a shadow against the dark wall. Then, just as he was about to turn the light on, he noticed something wasn't quite right.

There were four sinks on the wall. Not three.

Where on earth—?

He was startled by a noise from outside the bathroom. Bare feet approaching on wooden floorboards. The door creaked, and a thin, shadowy figure came in from the hall. Any second now the light was going to go on and he was going to be caught in the middle of the wrong bathroom like a complete idiot. He silently darted over to the door and threw his right arm around the figure from behind, then put his left hand over the mouth and hissed 'Sssshhh!' A stifled scream resonated through his hand. The slender body was stiff with fear.

'Don't be scared!' Jesse whispered. 'I'm not going to hurt you.' Whoever it was he was holding, they showed no signs of emotion. The only giveaway was their heart. He could feel it beating hard and fast under their ribcage.

'Do you promise not to scream if I take my hand away?'

A tentative nod.

Jesse carefully let go and felt the long strands of hair brush against his hand as he pulled it away. 'Who are you?'

'Sandra,' the figure whispered.

Oh God, of course! So that was what had happened. He had somehow ended up in the girl's block on the other side of the staircase. Sandra's heart was still racing, and suddenly he realised where his hand was. He quickly moved it, glad that it was dark and she couldn't see how red he was. 'I . . . um . . . I didn't mean to frighten you,' *he mumbled.*

'Is that you, Jesse?'

'Yes.'

'Have you gone mad? How did you get in here?

'I found a passage.'

'You do realise what Messner will do if he catches you here?'

'And how's he going to catch me?' *Jesse asked, defiantly.* 'He wouldn't come up here even if there was a fire.'

Sandra went quiet. And she seemed to be considering what he had said. 'What kind of passage?'

Jesse took hold of her arm and pulled her over to the wall. 'You have to kneel down.'

She put her hands on the hole in the wall. The rain sounded like it was trying to slash its way through the roof tiles. 'That's mad,' *she whispered.* 'And you came through there?'

'Of course,' *Jesse replied, every inch the king of the jailbreakers. Sandra hopped into the passageway. Then suddenly a light went on in the hall and they heard footsteps approaching. Without hesitating for even a second, Jesse followed her into the hole, then pulled it shut and locked it from the inside.* 'Psst,' *he whispered. Sandra didn't make a sound.*

The light went on in the bathroom. Sandra looked at the bright border around the panel, and a shimmer of light fell on her face.

The skin around her lips was smudged with dirt from Jesse's hand, and she had a dark mark on her light-coloured nightgown, right on her chest.

A resounding fart broke the silence. They couldn't help but giggle.

The sound of the toilet flushing was followed by the light going out, leaving them in the dark. Now the pattering rain was the only thing they could hear.

'Are you scared?' Jesse asked.

'No,' Sandra said, but Jesse didn't believe her.

'I always thought you climbed down the side of the building. But you went through the passageway, didn't you?'

'Nope. I only just found it.' He neglected to mention that he didn't know where else the passage led or where the other exits were. But then he realised that Sandra might think he was just bragging about it and lying to her so that she'd keep believing he had climbed down the side of the building. 'Honestly, I really did just find it. I have no idea where else it goes.'

They stayed quiet in the darkness for a while.

'Crazy.'

'What?'

'Everything. The passage. The fact that you climbed down the side of the building.

Jesse's chest felt like it was about to burst with pride.

'Does Richard know about the passage?'

'Why would he? Anyway, I told you I only just found it.'

'I just thought . . .' She seemed embarrassed all of a sudden.

'Go on.' Jesse insisted.

'It doesn't matter.'

'Tell me.'

'I . . .' Sandra squirmed, 'well, we're together.'

Jesse gulped. Together. *How ridiculous it sounded! So bloody stupid and grown up. The proud feeling in his chest was ousted by the black hole that was always lurking there and just kept growing. Richard already had everything. And now he had Sandra too. Stupid bloody second place.* 'I don't want Richard to find out about the passage,' *he snapped.*

There was silence apart from the sound of the rain falling.

A cool draught rushed towards him through the darkness and brushed over his skin. 'This is *my secret. I mean . . . our secret.'*

'It's OK,' *Sandra said softly.* 'I have secrets too.'

Jesse felt calmer. There was something about Sandra that made him believe she really would keep quiet about it. 'What kind of secrets?'

'Hmm, secrets are secrets because you don't tell anyone, aren't they?'

'Are you talking about your dancing?'

She went quiet.

'How come you dance so well?'

'Did you really like it?' *she asked quietly.*

'It was beautiful,' *Jesse said. The words slipped out of his mouth. He instantly felt the heat in his face. He was grateful once again for the darkness.*

'Not sort of . . . indecent?'

Jesse instantly knew why she'd asked him that. 'No,' *he lied. He wasn't going to say 'sexy' a second time. You didn't always have to tell people what you were feeling. Most importantly, he didn't want her to feel dirty. He knew what it was like to feel dirty.* 'Not at all.'

Sandra said nothing, but it was clear that she was relieved.

'My mum taught me,' *she finally confessed.* 'I mean, she taught me how to dance.'

Images of a stage in a big white theatre with pillars and sculptures shot through Jesse's mind. 'Where did she dance?' he asked, curious.

Sandra said nothing for a strangely long time.

'Is she still alive?' he finally asked in a soft voice, although he had already guessed the answer. He could see her shaking her head in the darkness.

'She's dead.'

'What about your dad?'

'He ran off. A long time ago.'

More silence, and more rain.

'How about you?' Sandra whispered. 'What happened to your mum?'

He always knew this question would crop up at some point. Now it was out there, and he couldn't block it out any longer. That old shitty postcard flashed up before his eyes: the one with the brown coat and the legs sticking out from underneath the hem.

Jesse gulped. 'She's dead. Like yours.'

'I'm sorry,' Sandra said.

'She was murdered,' he blurted out.

'Oh no! Who did it?'

Jesse felt a fleeting urge to tell her everything. His earliest memories, the things he knew about his father, everything. But he stayed quiet, perhaps because he was scared to talk about what happened with his father when he got older. He didn't want to sully her with the dirt. Everything that happened later was between him and his father. He couldn't help what he had become, but nobody would understand that. Everyone around here thought of his father as nothing more than an insufferable drunk, and God knows what else they said about him. No, this was his secret. And anyway, Sandra had hardly been forthcoming about her mother.

'Is he . . . in prison?'

'You mean the guy who did it?'

'The murderer.' The word sounded even more monstrous when somebody said it out loud. 'No. He's dead,' he said. What he really meant was that he wanted to see him dead.

'Are you glad? I mean, are you happy he's dead? I would be, I think.'

'No,' Jesse answered instinctively. He wasn't dead yet. He could only really be happy when it finally happened.

'I would be really happy,' Sandra said. Her voice was very close now. Her breath felt warm on his face. 'I'm impressed,' she whispered.

'Why?'

'I mean, if somebody had killed my mother, I would want to see them dead. But you say it doesn't make you happy to know he's dead. I honestly don't know anybody who would see it that way. Nobody at all!'

Jesse was confused by the misunderstanding. Her fingers tentatively moved towards his face, then ran down his forehead, over his nose and eyelids, and finally down to his mouth. He could smell her breath. Remnants of toothpaste and milk. Her fingers left a fleck of dust on his lips. Suddenly something hard yet also soft and damp pressed against his mouth. For a split second, a beat of wings, their lips seemed to be stuck together inextricably. It was a strange and unfamiliar feeling, yet so clear that something inside of him lit up, like his whole life changed in this moment.

He felt the first pang of pain little more than a second after her lips parted from his.

The silence lasted too long. Her silence. And his too.

'Sorry,' she finally whispered.

'What for?'

'I . . . let's keep this as our secret, yeah?'

He didn't know what to say.

'I'm with Richard.'

Richard. How could he forget?

There was someone better than him.

These guys like Richard, they had it all.

'But we can still meet here and talk, can't we?' Her voice sounded tense, as if she was afraid he might say no. 'Maybe next Friday?'

Almost everything! *Jesse thought to himself. Richard had almost *everything.*

Chapter 40

Garmisch-Partenkirchen – Wednesday, 9 January 2013, 12:14 a.m.

It smelled like the room had been left without the heating on for a long time. The old damp air from the walls had crept all the way into the bed, and the musty smell still lingered even though the mattress felt dry. Jesse wondered how long ago Kristina had lived here.

He sat on the edge of the bed. There were two bedside lamps, but only one of them was on, shining its harsh light onto the green wall from the yellow shade. Jesse had unplugged the other lamp so that he could charge his phone. Now they just had to wait. Jesse saw his face reflected as a yellow shadow on the blank screen. He couldn't stop thinking about Isa. He reached into his doctor's bag for the little stuffed lion, then he unhooked it from the key ring and started stroking the clumps of blond mane with his thumb.

The beep from his phone snapped Jesse out of his daze. He put the lion in his trouser pocket and typed in the four-digit code. The network operator's logo appeared in the corner of the screen. It was showing three bars out of a possible five.

'So?' Jule asked, sitting on a plain wooden chair next to the chest of drawers. She didn't seem much calmer than he was.

'Nothing. No message, no missed calls.' Jess rubbed the back of his neck. An oppressive headache lurked behind his eyelids. 'Is that a good thing or a bad thing?'

'If it was the kidnapper we ran into earlier, at least he's had his warning. I find it strange he hasn't been in touch though. You would expect him to really start laying on the threats now.'

'I'd almost prefer him to do that – at least that way I'd be sure it was him.'

'Well, then, maybe that's why he's lying low.'

'Or maybe there's no connection.'

'A coincidence?' Jule looked at him sceptically. 'Do you really believe that?'

'Not really. You?'

'Come on, I'm a psychologist.'

'What's that supposed to mean?'

'Psychologists are even less inclined to believe in coincidences than doctors.'

'So then why hasn't he made contact?'

Jule let her eyes wander over to the painting above the bed, the one with Adlershof aglow in the morning light. 'What if he was never intending to get in touch? What if he just wants to disappear with Isa?'

'But he did contact me. And if it's the same man from Artur's room then why is he still here?'

'You're right, it doesn't add up,' Jule said.

'So what could he want if he's not getting in touch? What's he planning?'

'The only thing I can think of is that he wants revenge. "You don't deserve her". You should feel guilty. And all these doubts about what's happening to Isa are more agonising than anything else.'

Jesse said nothing, dejected. They both stood staring at the picture for a while.

'The man who knocked you for six in Artur's room seemed to have this overwhelming anger towards you,' Jule finally said. 'He was trying to run off without being recognised but at the same time he also took a swing at you right in the middle of your face. See what I mean? He wasn't just trying to immobilise you; he wanted to hurt you.'

Jesse looked at her sceptically. 'And you're saying you noticed all this in that moment?'

'Believe me, I've seen a lot of punch-ups between young people in my work. I know how people fight when they're really wrapped up in their rage. Remember how the Polish guy in the car park squared up to you? He was more calculated, even though he was probably drunk. The way he hit out at you was controlled, like he just wanted to put you out of action.'

'So then, anger and revenge,' Jesse concluded.

'But for what?'

'We're just going around in circles now. It's got to have something to do with the part of my childhood I can't remember, the time before the accident.'

'Or it might have something to do with the accident itself. There must be a reason why Markus thinks you're mentally ill.'

'Did he really say that?'

'He said I should have you sectioned.'

'OK,' Jesse said, trying hard to keep himself in check even though he was seething on the inside. 'That's enough.' He got up so quickly that he felt a stabbing pain in his side from the wound. He winced, opened his doctor's bag and took out two tablets. The right ones this time. 'I want the bastard to say that to my face. And I bet he does know something about Wolle and Artur.'

Jule raised her hands. 'Whoa, slow down. I'm not sure that kind of tactic's going to get you anywhere with him.'

'What's that supposed to mean'?

Jule stayed quiet and took a long look at him.

'OK, OK! I'll pull myself together.'

It was clear to see that she didn't feel good about it. But by this point she was too deeply committed to the search for Isa to let him go alone.

It didn't take them long to cover the distance to the second floor of the north wing. The hallway outside the rooms where the teachers and staff lived was lined with a row of identical doors. One of them had a brass-coloured piece of plastic on it reading 'Caretaker'.

Jesse tried to slow his pulse rate. He knocked on the door.

He almost had to laugh when nobody answered. Wherever he was, and regardless of whether he rang the bell or knocked on the door, the outcome always seemed to be the same. He knocked again. This time loudly and with purpose.

When he knocked on the door for the third time, the next door along was suddenly flung open and an angry bearded face peered out from behind it. 'What on earth is all this racket? Do you know what time—' The man stopped mid-sentence when saw Jesse and squinted at him. 'Is that you, Jesse?'

'Hello, Alois,' Jesse said.

'Holy shit. I don't believe it.' Alois stepped out of the door-way into the hallway light. He was wearing boxer shorts, and the dark hair spreading from his tank top became thinner as it crept over his shoulders and all the way down to the backs of his hands. His chin was covered by a bushy salt-and-pepper beard, unlike his head, which was as bald as a freshly shelled egg. He looked at Jule, who had inched back a little. 'And . . . bloody hell! Sandra! I almost didn't recognise you. Did you dye your hair?' He gave a strained grin. Then he realised that the two of them were standing in front of his neighbour's door. 'Are you looking for Markus? He left.'

'Left?' Jesse asked.

'I mean he's out. I heard the door at about ten thirty. He hasn't been back since.' He looked from Jesse to Jule and squinted again. 'You're not Sandra, are you?'

'No. This is Jule, a friend of mine. Jule, Alois,' Jesse introduced the two of them. Alois reached out to Jule, and she shook his hand reluctantly. He seemed entirely comfortable standing opposite a completely unknown woman in his smalls. Jesse couldn't help thinking he might even be enjoying it. 'If you want to wait for him,' he pointed at the open door behind him with his thumb. 'Be my guests.'

Alois's abode consisted of two rooms: one bedroom and a living room with a small kitchen unit. He fetched three half-litre cans of beer from the fridge, then opened them and set them down on the tiled coffee table under the sticky flycatcher that was dangling from the ceiling. Jule was sitting in a heavy fabric chair with a Bavarian pattern on it. Alois let out a sigh as he flopped onto the couch beside Jesse and scratched his bare thigh. The heating was roaring away and turned their cheeks rosy red.

'So, what brings you here?' A quick sideways glance from Alois to Jule confirmed Jesse's suspicions. He had taken a liking to her. Jesse wasn't sure how much he could trust Alois – of all the guys from the children's home, he was the one he hadn't seen for the longest. Alois had thrown himself into an apprenticeship at the age of sixteen, before he had all that hair on his body. But although Jesse had lost touch with him, he was the only one here who had given him a reasonably friendly welcome. 'I've been having trouble sleeping—' Jesse began.

Alois sniffed. 'Same here.' He took a big swig out of the beer can. 'As you can see.'

'—because of the accident.'

'Does it still hurt, the wound?'

'I'm more bothered about the fact that I still don't know what happened. And I can't stop thinking about it.'

Alois raised his eyebrows, puffed up his cheeks and blew out a stream of air. 'Bit late for that, isn't it? And you're wanting to talk to Markus about it? He's hardly your biggest fan after what happened back then.'

'You mean what happened in the dining hall.'

'I was talking about Sandra, actually.' Alois looked over at Jule, as if to check whether he had riled her at all. 'He was totally fuming about Sandra. But really,' he winked at Jule, 'we were all just jealous.' He grinned.

'All right, Alois, we get the picture.'

'All right, all right,' Alois mimicked, shaking his head. 'He gets the best bird and acts like it was nothing.' He turned to Jesse. 'And you know, you really weren't her favourite person.'

Jesse knew what was coming. God, Sandra was the last thing in the world he wanted to think about right now. He wished he could shut Alois up, but he seemed to be in the mood for talking. And maybe if he let him talk for long enough, eventually he would find out something about the accident and the time before it.

'Sandra used to have a necklace like this.' Alois drew a 'V' on his hairy chest with his fleshy fingers. 'She got it as a birthday present from her mother. Her mother was—' He looked at Jesse and cleared his throat. 'Well, it doesn't matter. Anyway, she somehow managed to lose the necklace one day when she was swimming in the lake. I'm telling you,' he said, lowering his head and looking deep into Jule's eyes, 'we all dived in to look for the thing. All of us boys.'

Jule nodded obligingly.

'But none of us found it. And then this guy comes along.' Alois jerked his head in Jesse's direction. 'Four months later it was. Somehow Jesse managed to find the chain. I'm telling you, Sandra didn't let on when he gave it to her, but I caught her smiling away half an hour later. Her eyes were red and she was beaming.'

Jesse felt Jule looking at him and avoided making eye contact. He found himself picturing that rainy day in the shed. Sandra had dragged him in between the skis and kissed him. It all happened so suddenly, as if she had even taken herself by surprise. Her cheeks were glowing and she looked nervous, like she had done something naughty. It seemed like she was waiting for something bad to happen the whole time, but the only thing that happened was more kissing. Later on, Mattheo asked him accusingly where he'd been for those three hours, knowing full well. After all, he was the one who eventually told Markus.

'But do you know what the strange thing was?' Alois asked.

Jule shook her head and leaned forward inquisitively. Alois let his eyes wander down to Jule's chest for a moment. It seemed her jumper wasn't low-cut enough for his liking.

'Well, this was after the accident. And Jesse had forgotten how to swim. I mean, he forgot just about everything after the accident.'

Jule frowned.

'Strange, don't you think? The boy can't swim but, somehow, he manages to fetch the necklace from the lake. A few of us were puzzled by that. But guess what? I eventually worked out how he did it.' He drew a rectangle in the air with his fingers and grinned slyly. 'A photo. He went down to Garmisch with a photo of Sandra, showed it to Fliehinger – he was the jeweller – and pointed to the chain around her neck.' Alois grinned triumphantly. 'Fliehinger told me himself. He made a copy of it based on the photo. The one thing he didn't tell me was where Jesse got the money from.' He looked at Jesse probingly. 'But maybe there are some things you just shouldn't ask, is that right?'

'It wasn't gold. The necklace wasn't real,' Jesse said. 'Sandra realised later on. It was really embarrassing.'

All three of them went quiet for a moment.

Jesse could still picture the chain with the small gold sun-shaped setting and the single pearl. In the end, Sandra actually preferred wearing it to the original. Even after they separated, he saw her wearing it one time when he bumped into her at the French bakery. She tried to pull her jacket together to cover it up, but he'd already seen the two gold-coloured lines as they disappeared into her décolletage.

'How did you pay for the necklace?' Jule asked.

'I played piano.'

'You did what?'

'Fliehinger's wife was ill, bedridden. She used to play the piano and loved it. I went there once a week and played for her. He was happy, and I got my necklace.'

'You play the piano?' Alois looked at him like he was an alien. 'How is that possible? There's no piano here.'

Jesse shrugged. 'I could only play a couple of tunes, but they weren't bad.'

Alois shook his head and took a quick look at Jesse's fingers, as if trying to work out whether he was telling the truth. 'Well.' He wiped the whole story off the table with one brisk swipe of the hand. 'Back then we all thought Jesse stole the necklace so that he could make it magically reappear later. We had our reasons. There was the whole thing with the accident and the fact that you always said it was Markus who did it, but Markus was also angry back then because of the incident with Sandra and the necklace.'

'I was angry too,' Jesse said. 'Because he wouldn't admit that he'd aimed at me. Maybe he didn't want to shoot; maybe it really was an accident. But he could have at least admitted it. He was just a coward, spineless. He said nothing, nothing at all. *None of you* said anything.'

'What if there was nothing to say?'

'Oh, please!'

'I just mean, why are you so sure that it was him? And the past is the past – why can't you just forget about it? You've achieved more than any of us. Look at yourself. You're a doctor. You wear fancy clothes.' He pulled at Jesse's jumper and twisted it with two of his fingers. Alois looked over at Jule, then winked at her and said: 'I honestly couldn't stand him before the accident. He was such a stubborn little prick before it happened. Then he chilled out a bit and he was easier to be around. Well, not always,' He grinned and took another swig of his beer. 'And not to everyone.'

'To be totally honest, I still don't really understand what happened,' Jule said. 'I just know that something got Jesse in his back. An arrow, a knife, whatever.'

'A bolt. It was a crossbow bolt. That's all anybody knows,' Alois said.

'Well, that's all anybody *says*,' Jesse corrected him.

Jule looked at Alois in disbelief. 'A teenager gets shot in the back with a crossbow bolt, and nobody knows anything? Those things are pretty easy to spot.'

Alois rotated the beer can in his hand and looked into it as if he was trying to see something at the bottom.

'There was a crossbow in Artur's shed,' Jesse said.

'Why did Artur have a crossbow?'

'No idea. Anyway, Richard always used to steal the key.'

'What do you mean always?' Jule asked.

Jesse shrugged. 'We used to go shooting in the woods at night. Always at full moon.'

'With the crossbow?'

'Of course. There was nothing else to do,' Alois mumbled.

'And what did you fire it at?'

'A tree, out there in the clearing. And one of us would always have to stand against the tree for fun, under the target,' Alois said, but avoided lifting his eyes.

'You shot *at each other*?' Jule's eyes flitted back and forth between them, aghast.

'Not *at* each other. We always aimed just above.'

It was quiet in the room except for the hissing coming from the heating. The twisted flycatcher gently turned in the rising warm air.

'We were kids. Teenagers,' Alois said defensively. 'You do stuff like that when you're that age.' He lowered his head and took another sip of beer. Remnants of foam glistened in his beard as he put the can down.

It took Jule a moment to get her head around the rather terse explanation he had given her. 'Who do you mean by *we*?'

'Markus, Richard, Wolle, Alois, Mattheo and me,' Jesse said.

'Not Mattheo, actually. He only joined us right at the end,' Alois added.

'Oh really?' Jesse asked.

'Can't you remember the night he came with us?' Alois asked, baffled.

Jesse had tried a thousand times to remember what happened each night they ventured out, but all he could picture was a gang of boys heading out to the clearing to shoot in the moonlight. He could see the crossbow and the pale faces of each boy in the glow of the moon, but apart from these fleeting images, he couldn't remember what had happened. As time went on, he repeatedly snuck out to the clearing by himself at night, spending hours there in the hopes of salvaging at least some of his memories. But he only ever found loose fragments, like random photos with no labels. Why did his stupid damn memory always fail him like that? He pressed the cold beer can against his temples. He was bothered by the excessive heat and the stress. 'Can we open a window?'

'In the middle of winter?' Alois exclaimed, horrified. 'It's cold enough to freeze the balls off a brass monkey out there.'

'Can you remember now or not?' Jule probed.

'I can't remember the night Alois is talking about. But I know we always used to go there.'

'Did you ever go out shooting again after the accident?'

They both shook their heads.

'So who told you about what you used to get up to out there?'

It didn't take Jesse long to answer that question. 'Artur. When I was in the hospital.'

'Artur knew about our nights in the clearing?' Alois asked in disbelief.

'More or less. I guess he figured it out somehow. And maybe Richard told him something. I begged him to tell me what happened. He said he wasn't totally sure, but he thought it was an accident. He said that's what happens when you sneak out of the building at night and mess around with things you're not supposed to touch. Mattheo filled me in on the details later on.'

'Mattheo,' Alois snorted. 'God, he was so desperate. The guy comes along once and totally shits himself, then he goes around mouthing off about it.'

'And what made you think Markus was the one who fired the shot on the night of the accident? Did Mattheo tell you that too?'

'He said he wasn't there, just like everybody else. Like they were trying to make out I'd wandered out to the woods by myself and somehow mysteriously ended up with an arrow in my back!' Jesse glowered out of the window and took a swig out of the can. The beer ran down his throat. 'He just told me about the other times we went shooting, before the accident happened. And he told me about how I'd antagonised Markus.

I can still remember exactly what he said: "You shouldn't be surprised if it's the end of a friendship when you point right at someone instead of aiming above their head."'

'You aimed at Markus?'

'I might have aimed at him, but I never shot him.'

'But what would have made him shoot at you?'

'Either it really was an accident, or it was about Sandra,' Jesse said.

'You think he wanted to kill you because he was smitten with Sandra?'

'He was more than smitten.'

'How do you know that? Did Mattheo tell you?'

'Yes, but that wasn't the only reason. We were constantly clashing after the accident. Markus only had eyes for Sandra. He never so much as looked at another woman all his life. I'm guessing that's still the case – am I right, Alois?'

Alois looked up from his empty beer can. He nodded silently. The conversation seemed to have taken a turn he didn't like, and he had gone noticeably quiet. He got up and took another can out of the fridge.

'Can you remember Jesse aiming at Markus or shooting him?' Jule asked. 'That must have been the same night Mattheo was there.'

Foam spurted out of the can when Alois opened the beer. 'It's so long ago I can't remember. We all aimed at each other.'

'That's not how it sounded before,' Jesse said. 'You seemed to remember very clearly.'

'I can distinctly remember that Mattheo only came with us the one time, because that's what happened.' Alois took a big swig from the can, as if underlining his position. Then he wiped his lips with the back of his hand. 'And I know that Mattheo talks a lot of shit sometimes.'

'What kind of shit?'

Alois shrugged. 'Ask him yourself. He'll be bringing the mail tomorrow morning. If he can make it up here in the snow.'

'You know something. Why won't you just say it?'

'It's too complicated.'

Jesse stared at him. 'You can't be serious.'

'You know what your problem is?' Alois asked. 'You always make a big deal out of any little thing. And then you just go running around accusing people.'

'You've got no idea how important this is, Alois. Please.'

'If you want to sleep soundly again, you should talk to Mattheo. Or just sort it out with Markus. I'm not getting myself into hot water. Now please just go and let me get some sleep.'

Jesse watched as Alois got up and walked away. He looked as helpless as he did stoic in his boxers and his tank top. Now he had clammed up and was as impenetrable as ever. Jesse was at a loss. Everyone was doing the same thing: keeping their mouth shut and pointing the finger at someone else. Each person he spoke to just pointed at the next.

They all act like none of them were there, he thought to himself, fuming.

Chapter 41

1981, Garmisch-Partenkirchen

Mattheo was going to join them this time. This had been decided in the notes they passed around under the table during maths lesson. Jesse couldn't care less; he was too busy watching Richard exchanging glances with Sandra. Each look he sent her way was one too many for him.

Jesse and the other homies often had to help out with the chores when the last class finished, unlike Sandra and Richard. Richard got out of it because he was the son of the principal, whereas Sandra was excused because Dante, the eternally grumpy chef, had a soft spot for her. Instead of working with Jesse in the kitchen, Sandra slinked off down the stairs to dance in the vaulted cellar as usual.

A few moments later, Dante muttered something about needing to fetch a drink. The lintel above the steps to the cellar was much too low for the two metre tall cook, so he awkwardly ducked down, revealing the sweaty patch of bald skin inside the circle of grey hair on his head. Then he disappeared inside the vault.

Jesse furiously scrubbed the pots and pans clean. Inside his head, he was up under the eaves with Sandra. They had met there in secret three more times since their first encounter, but she hadn't kissed him again. Still, he was sure that by now he knew just as much about Sandra as Richard did. Sandra seemed to trust Jesse more and more, and she became increasingly uncomfortable whenever Richard came up in conversation.

Every one of these meetings was special to Jesse, albeit none of them quite as special as their first encounter. He missed the loud pattering of the rain on the roof tiles. They'd had to move closer together to hear each other better.

'Hey, take it easy! Are you trying to scrub it to pieces?'

Jesse was caught off guard. Richard was standing next to him with rosy cheeks and slightly damp hair. He looked like he'd just come out of the shower.

'You could help, you know. It'd be done quicker if you did.'

Richard shrugged and watched as Jesse angrily scoured the inside of the pot. 'Thanks, but I've got better things to do.' His grin left Jesse in no doubt that he had noticed the longing looks he directed at Sandra.

'Don't you feel pathetic always standing there gawping through the cracks?'

Richard's grin became flatter. 'She usually lets me in afterwards. She knows I'm there, she just likes to dance by herself.'

'Maybe she wishes she really was alone. And as long as you're not in there with her, she can pretend she is by herself.'

'What makes you say that?'

'Maybe she told me,' Jesse lied.

'Told you? When?'

'We talk a lot.' Jesse tried his best to be evasive.

Richard snorted with contempt. 'Sure. When you're not scrubbing pots and pans. But even then, you've still got your family's dirt sticking to your fingers.'

'It's still better than having bad breath,' Jesse replied.

Richard stared at him. 'Bad breath?'

'That's what Sandra said.'

Richard turned red and clenched his fists, but he didn't dare pounce on Jesse. Richard knew by now that Jesse was in good shape, and he wasn't one to take unnecessary risks when it came to fights. He had other, more effective, weapons at his disposal.

'Maybe you're as much of a waster as your dad and just as sick in the head as him,' Richard hissed. 'So let me spell it out for you again: She wants me to watch. I reckon I know that better than you!'

'You haven't got a clue,' Jesse blurted out. He was seething.

'No, you moron. You haven't got a clue. She totally loves it when I watch her through the slit because she's just like her mum. It turns her on, do you understand?

'What . . . what do you mean?'

'Well, what do you think? Her mum was a whore. She used to dance for blokes. Naked.' He wiggled his chest in Jesse's direction and licked his lips with his tongue.

'You're lying!'

'She told me herself, you moron.'

'No.'

'It's true.'

'No!' Jesse was beside himself with rage. He yelled and hurled the pot into the steel cabinet opposite along with the pots he had already washed. There was a deafening crash, and the dishwater splashed all over the place.

Richard shrank back. His face was pale yet triumphant. He knew he'd won.

'What's going on, goddam it?' a loud voice growled. Jesse spun around. Dante was standing in the doorway to the cellar red in

the face and with fever-bright eyes. His stained white trousers were sitting crookedly on his shapeless hips and the buttons were in the wrong holes.

Jesse stared at his trousers, realisation setting in.

'What the hell's going on in here?' Dante bellowed. He pointed towards the mess of pots and pans with his shovel-like hand.

'He just flipped out,' Richard said calmly, nodding in Jesse's direction. 'He wanted me to help but I explained to him that I do a lot to help Dad out and this isn't my responsibility.'

Dante locked eyes with Jesse. 'You're going to clean every single one of these pans. Spick and span. And when you're done with them, you're going to smear them in rubbish from the kitchen bin and start again from the beginning.

Jesse's mouth opened and closed again.

Sandra wandered up the stairs behind him, clearly alarmed by the noise. She looked around and then quickly down at the ground and weaved her way between the puddles of dishwater on the floor, heading for the door towards the main building. Her blond ponytail bobbed up and down as she turned the corner.

'Can I go?' Richard asked.

'Of course you can go,' Dante grunted. 'Oi, you,' he snarled at Jesse. 'What are you gawping at? Get on with it!'

Five hours later, Jesse stomped up the stairs to the attic. His hands were burning from all the scrubbing and his arms ached from his wrists to his shoulders. But the discomfort was nothing compared to the rage bubbling up inside of him. He'd been able to accept that Sandra was with Richard. He'd reasoned that maybe she had to be with him because she had no other choice. She was a homie like him. If she ever wanted to get out of this place, Richard was her passport. And passports didn't come for free. Still, why did this have to be the price? He still couldn't quite believe it, even though the look in her eyes had confirmed it all. The look in her eyes and the buttons on Dante's trousers. He would have killed Dante and Richard if he'd had the chance.

Why on earth had she opened up to Richard? Why had she told him, of all people, about her mother? Didn't she know how little respect Richard had for secrets?

Artur Messner closed the door as soon as he got to the homies' block. Jesse shot another hateful glance in his direction, then he quickly washed his face in the bathroom, grimaced at himself in the mirror and collapsed into his bed, exhausted. Nobody said a word. They all knew the score. Jesse stared at the full moon. He could hardly wait to climb out of the window.

The clearing was a field of cold silver, the tree a skeleton. Mattheo was giddy with excitement and trembling with fear at the same time. His teeth chattered, and the crossbow was shaking so much in his hands that he didn't even manage to hit the target once. Jesse snatched the crossbow from him and tensioned it without any help from the others, then he aimed at the tree with grim concentration, hit the target and took aim again, like someone in a trance. The third bolt hit the light mark on the tree. He lowered the crossbow. 'I choose Richard,' he said. His voice was icy and cut into the tense silence.

Mattheo gave a sigh of relief as he watched Richard trudging over to the tree with a dark, vengeful scowl on his face.

'Stand up straight,' Jesse hissed.

Richard made a point of taking his time to position himself with his back against the trunk and his face turned to Jesse. He had grown, and the light section where the branch had been hacked off started barely fifty centimetres above his head. His sombre expression gave way to a look of feigned indifference.

Jesse tensioned the crossbow for the fourth time. The string clicked as it sprung over the catch. He tried to breathe calmly as he put the bolt in the slot, but his fingers were trembling. He lifted the crossbow and took aim. This time he didn't have to imagine someone standing by the tree; he was looking straight into Richard's face, staring at the spot right between his eyes. People like him had everything!

Richard was just like the invisible brother he hated so much. The better version of himself, the one he had obliterated with a single shot to this very tree.

And yet he hadn't managed to kill him, had he? It was impossible to kill someone so damn invisible, something buried so deep inside.

But there was someone just like him standing right where he wanted him. A real target, in the flesh. Someone who was standing in his way. Someone whom the others preferred. Someone who imagined he was better. They were all the same, these guys who always came first. And the others were always taken in by them. His mother. His father. Sandra . . .

'Jesse?' Markus muttered. 'You have to aim higher, are you listening to me?'

All the indifference had vanished from Richard's eyes. He was staring straight at the arrow.

What did this shitbag expect? Did he think it was going to go on like this for ever? Did he really think he'd never have to pay the price for anything? Did he think he could just go around doing whatever he wanted? That he could just take whatever he wanted?

He had exactly the right person in front of him. The one who had taken his mother away and his father – and now he was going to take Sandra too . . .

'Jesse! Higher, for God's sake!' Markus yelled.

'If you're feeling sorry for him, you can always switch places,' Jesse snarled.

Suddenly it had turned even quieter than before. The wind blew across the grass on the clearing. A cloud pushed in front of the moon, blocking Jesse's line of vision and leaving just two light, round shadows, one just above the other. He continued aiming at the lower one.

'Jesse,' Richard yelled. His voice fearful and high-pitched. 'I'm sorry!'

Jesse didn't budge, not even a millimetre. He had taken aim, and if he didn't shoot then nothing would change. It was always business as usual unless you did something about it. With no mother, no father and no family, he was all alone in the world. People like this guy had everything and didn't give two shits about it.

'Jesse!'

He couldn't tell who was yelling his name any more. It didn't matter anyway.

The cloud drifted past and light poured from the moon. He saw Richard's sweaty face and his eyes, wide with fear. He was slipping further and further down the trunk, his clothes rubbing against the bark as he sank centimetre by centimetre.

'Jesse, please!

How far had Richard slipped down the trunk already? Far enough? Was it worth adjusting? He bent his finger, knowing that the other boys' mouths were opening instinctively although they didn't dare breathe. Richard sobbed and sank even further down. 'Please! Please, no!'

Jesse wondered whether his mother had pleaded for her life too. Had Wilbert given her enough time? Wilbert was another one of those guys who always came in first place. They'd kill you if you didn't stop them.

His mother's face flashed before his eyes again. No, she wouldn't have begged for mercy. She had too much pride. She was too radiant. Nothing like as pathetic as the whimpering lump standing by the tree, scared shitless.

He pulled the trigger.

The bolt shot out of the groove with a dry popping sound and hurtled towards Richard. No one had time to scream. The bow was still vibrating when the bolt hit the tree just a few centimetres above Richard's head.

A prolonged silence filled the air after the shot sounded.

Jesse rushed over to the tree, Markus following him with a scared look on his face. Richard was sitting on the ground, breathing heavily and sobbing. Jesse hoped he'd wet himself with fear. He stared down at him with the eyes of a wolf. 'You don't deserve her,' he snarled. Before Markus could step in, he hurled the crossbow into Richard's lap. 'Pretty crap game, huh?'

He turned on his heel and trotted off back to Adlershof. The woods seemed to fly past him, like it was time to run away. Not time for him to run from the woods though. Time for the woods to flee from him, the wolf.

Chapter 42

Wednesday, 9 January 2013

The first light of the day seeped through the cracks between the boards. Artur slept through it. He had been awake for most of the night, so the tiredness was catching up with him. Eventually he was awoken by a kick from Isabelle. He grumbled and opened his eyes but stayed where he was, not moving his aching limbs.

'Sorry,' Isabelle whispered. She didn't look at him. She was standing directly above him, eagerly fiddling with the bucket in front of the boarded-up gable window. It seemed the part at the edge that had been bent into shape didn't quite fit the slot of her chosen screw. Her mouth was tense and twisted. She seemed annoyed, as if she'd been working away at it for a while. Her blond hair was ruffled up into a tousled mane, lending a touch of wildness to her appearance. Specks of dust danced in the pale light in front of her face.

Like a little lioness, Artur thought to himself. He couldn't help but think about her father.

Still, lioness or not, he decided he wasn't going to tell her who he thought was behind all this yet. It was better if she didn't know for the time being. Getting out of here was far more important.

'Why don't you let me have a stab at it?' Artur offered tentatively.

Isabelle didn't react. Instead, she pressed the bucket against the screw head and tried to turn it, growling fiercely from the exertion. The rim of the bucket gave a loud click as it slipped out of the slot on the screw. She lost her balance and almost fell on top of Artur.

'Oh shit!' Isabelle blurted out. Artur raised his hands defensively when he saw her about to hurl the bucket to the ground. His arthritic joints meant he wasn't exactly the quickest. Thank God she was still holding the bucket in her hand.

'Whoa, little lady. Patience is a virtue,' Artur said.

Isabelle was on the verge of tears. 'But this is shit!'

'Did you hear me complaining?' Artur asked.

'Mum *always* complains when I say that word.'

'Does she now?'

'Yeah, she does!' Isabelle replied.

'Then you should tell her that you met somebody who remembers her from a long time ago. When she was a little girl, she said "shit" so much it beggared belief.'

Isabelle's face lightened up ever so slightly. 'Really?'

'Really,' Artur said. He kept talking: 'When something's *really* shit, you have to let it out, don't you?'

'Shitty screw,' Isabelle said. 'Shitty bucket, shitty kidnapper, shitty day, shitty attic—'

—and shit-scared, Artur added inwardly. 'The bucket,' he said, 'is one thing I'd be tempted to leave off your list. Look.' Artur lifted up a small silver piece of metal. 'This just fell off the bottom of it.'

Isabelle sniffed and surveyed the fragment with a furrowed brow.

'Let's divide up the tasks,' Artur said. 'You and your young ears can listen out for anyone coming. And I'll try to get this screw out.'

Isabelle nodded and stepped away from the space in front of the boards. She watched as Artur manoeuvred the long piece of metal into the screw head with trembling fingers. It fitted the slot. But turning it was a harder and far more uncomfortable job than Artur had anticipated. The sharp edges of the piece of metal cut into his fingers and made them bleed. He cursed and let go.

'Does it hurt?' Isabelle asked.

'There are more painful things,' Artur grumbled and shook his hand. They weren't going to get very far like this. 'Could you pass me the *shitty* bucket again?'

Isabelle grinned ever so slightly and handed him the bucket. Artur examined the cracked, weathered rim. The bucket must have been left outside for a long time to end up in such a state. Only a piece of the edge was still hanging on to a small ridge. He held it between his thumb and index finger and turned it until the ridge was so thin that it snapped. Now he had a strip several centimetres long, which he bent in the middle and clamped over the first piece of metal to create a kind of mini screwdriver with a flat handle.

His cheeks were glowing. When he pulled the first screw out of the wood, he held it up in the air by the tip. 'Ta-daaa!'

'Cool,' Isabelle whispered.

Cool. Artur couldn't stand that word. He thought it was way too much of an understatement to express a triumph like this. Frankly, he found these Americanisms stupid. Perhaps part of the reason the lads had thought up names like *homies* and *Mr M* was because they knew they would wind him up. He would have forgiven Isabelle for using any word though, especially in these circumstances.

Artur set to work on the next screw, feeling exhilarated. All his efforts paid off when he eventually managed to remove the first board. Light streamed into the attic. To their disappointment, however, the window was dull and cloudy, so they couldn't see what was behind it.

Artur kept on working at the screws. Even though he got cramp in his fingers and they ached from the hard work, giving up was out of the question. His mood almost went through the roof when he loosened the second board. Now if he wanted to make it easier to get out, the boards at the top would have to come off too. He got back to work, but for some reason the screws in the top boards were so tight that he couldn't unscrew them. Finally he gave up. Not bad though. The gap with the two boards missing from it was about thirty centimetres high and as wide as the window.

'That might be enough,' he mumbled, sounding considerably less enthusiastic than before.

'For what?'

'Listen,' he whispered, even more quietly than before. 'I'm going to smash the window now. I don't know if he's going to hear, so we have to be quick. You go first. Then I'll follow. Got it?'

'Why do I have to go first?' Isabelle asked. She suddenly looked very uncomfortable at the prospect.

'You're much quicker than me. I'd just hold you back if I went first. And we're in the attic here, so we'll probably have to climb.'

Isabelle gulped. 'Climb?'

'It's got to be better than this, hasn't it?'

She nodded anxiously and kept quiet.

Artur grabbed one of the loose boards, then he took aim and rammed it against the glass in the gap between the boards. The window only shattered the third time he hit it. Shards of glass fell to the ground and silently sank into the blanket of snow. An icy wind blew towards them. The sharp, jagged edges of the hole made the window look like a mouth with fangs. Artur quickly cleared the rest of the glass from the window frame with the board, or at least as much of it as he could. He turned back and looked at Isabelle, who was anxiously staring over at the hatch. Artur lowered the board and listened.

No footsteps. No crashing or thudding.

Just the whispering of snowflakes.

He beckoned Isabelle over to him. The two of them stood together gazing through the broken window at the landscape. It was a single mass of white with no outlines. The snow was falling so heavily that they could only just see the edge of the woods about fifty paces away from them. *A house in the middle of nowhere*, Artur thought to himself. No streets, no lights, no pylons and no buildings as far as the eye could see. It was impossible to tell whether there were any mountains behind the woods. There wasn't the slightest clue as to where their prison was located.

'But we're pretty high up,' Isabelle whispered. She had rested her forehead against the top board and was peering down below. Her breath rose in clouds of steam that quickly got lost amongst the snowflakes.

Artur had to agree with her. It was *much* too high up. He'd been hoping they were perhaps four or five metres up. That would have been dangerous enough, but they were actually more like seven or eight metres from the ground.

'Now what?' Isabelle asked.

Artur put his index finger on his lips. He could hear the muffled crescendos and diminuendos of a powerful diesel engine plouhing through the snow in the distance.

Chapter 43

Isa pressed her back against the tree trunk and cried. Bare black branches were reaching out in all directions. The winter sky was as pale as the ground. The man with the crossbow seemed to be rooted in the soil like a gnarled oak tree. His arms were so strong that he managed to tension the steel bow single-handedly. He snapped a sharp branch off the tree, straight as an arrow, and placed it in the shimmering groove.

Jesse held his breath as he lay on his back in the pit. He tried to get up and run over to Isa, but a black, armoured insect shovelled a heap of soil on top of him, forcing him down onto the bottom of the pit. Desperately he stretched his hand out in Isa's direction, but she was out of reach. The insect stared down at him. He recognised himself in its dead, blank eyes. He looked over towards Isa, horrified.

The man with the crossbow and roots for feet had the same build as Markus – oh God, no, it *was* Markus – and he was aiming the loaded crossbow at Isa. He had to get out of there and save her! And he'd kill Markus if he had to. But the walls of the pit were getting higher and higher. Suddenly the insect had multiple arms and shovels. The soil rained down on him, burying him alive. Everything was black, he couldn't move a single limb and he couldn't breathe. Then someone picked a tiny hole in the soil, right in front of his eye. It was summer and night-time. Markus was still standing on the grass, aiming at Isa. The moon was dazzling like the sun. He begged the heavens to send clouds; maybe then Markus would miss. He screamed Isa's name, and then suddenly, like it was the most natural thing in the world, her warm hand was on his waist. It had gone numb with pain. It was only then that he noticed the bloody arrow sticking into his side.

The bowstring clicked. Thwap.

Jesse opened his eyes.

His heart was racing.

It was dark in Kristina's room, and Jesse was lying on his side. Jule was sleeping next to him – with her hand on his waist. He didn't want to risk moving. The physical contact was radiating through his whole body, making him feel at peace for a moment. Suddenly, Jule took her hand away and turned onto her other side without saying a word. He stared into the darkness and listened to her breathing.

Feeling exhausted after their conversation with Alois, Jesse and Jule had retreated to Kristina's room. Jesse tended to his wound and cleaned the specks of blood off his shirt while Jule scrubbed her knickers and her top with soap and hung them up to dry over the radiator. There was just one duvet, so they both got into bed in their jumpers and trousers.

The touch of Jule's hand lingered. Jesse found himself wondering for a moment what would happen if he let himself put his arms around her. The thought that she wasn't wearing any underwear struck him like a drop of hot wax on his skin.

But in the next moment he couldn't help but think of Sandra lying there dead on the balcony in the freezing cold with the flokati rug from the living room as her only protection. He knew he had to think on his feet. The doctor in him knew she wasn't in pain any more. But all the same, it still felt wrong.

He didn't sleep for the rest of the night.

He got up at 5.30 and roamed the building like a ghost, then he tried to cool down by walking to the gatehouse and back. He felt like he was losing his mind worrying about Isa.

In the hours that followed, he found himself repeatedly standing in front of Artur's door and Markus's door, but always with the same disappointing result. Mattheo didn't appear either – hardly a surprise given the deep covering of fresh snow and the time of day. The mail would be stored in the office until the mountain road was more passable.

Jesse ran into Philippa in the lobby a short while later. She was carrying a clipboard and her thin lips were pressed together like a line drawn by the stroke of a pencil. What car did Markus drive? She gave a sour nod in the direction of the kitchen and said it was a black VW pick-up. Sure enough, there was a VW Amarok in the back yard next to the tall fence surrounding the bins. Fresh snow had piled up around the four-wheel-drive vehicle, right the way up to the Adlershof logo on the door. Richard's green Toyota was parked right next to it. Neither of the cars appeared to have been moved during the night, but there were some tyre tracks covered in fresh snow leading away from one of the free parking spaces.

Philippa shrugged when he asked her about it. Did she look like she was in charge of a fleet of cars? It was enough that she already had to check on the old curmudgeon upstairs and all the little rascals in the children's home without having to worry about the cars as well.

He decided to wake Jule at a quarter past ten. He didn't know what his next move was going to be, and he needed someone to talk to. When he opened the door to the room, she was standing naked in front of the radiator with her back to him, balancing on one leg as she put on her underwear. He stood there, glued to the spot. Jule glanced over her shoulder, pulled up her knickers and shrugged. 'It's fine, don't worry. Come in.'

Jesse walked into the room, agitated, and closed the door behind him. Jule kept her back to him and took her bra off the heater, then slipped it on and fastened the clasp, completely unfazed.

It was only when Jule turned around to face him that Jesse noticed he was still standing by the door, staring at her. Her underwear was sheer, and her nipples were clearly visible under the material, but his eyes had homed in on the pale, elongated scar directly above the waistband of her knickers. A clear sign of abdominal surgery.

'What?' Jule laughed. She looked exhausted and weary. 'I hope this isn't the first time you've seen a woman in her underwear?' Her smile disappeared when she realised where he was looking. She instinctively covered the scar with her hand.

'Hardly,' Jesse replied. 'I'm just having trouble trying to match up the Jule I knew with the Jule I'm getting to know right now.'

She stepped into her jeans and the scar disappeared. 'I was on tour with a band for four years. Loud young men. Cheap shared hotel rooms. Getting changed backstage. The whole shebang.'

'I see,' Jesse said. Although he wasn't entirely sure what 'the whole shebang' entailed.

'It's not what you're thinking,' Jule said.

'Of course.'

She rolled her eyes. 'I was in my mid-twenties.'

'I was in my mid-twenties once too.'

Jule looked at him. She was obviously trying to figure out what he meant but failed to arrive at a clear conclusion. 'Have you been awake for long?'

'Way too long.' Jesse sat down opposite the bed on an elaborately shaped, horribly uncomfortable chair. Sticking to the facts, he quickly told her that neither Mattheo, Markus or Artur had made an appearance.

Jule was now fully dressed, and standing in front of him deep in thought. 'I've been thinking about Markus and your accident this whole time. Didn't you say you thought you were quits?'

'After what Alois told us last night I'm not so sure any more. I mean, we might not be as far as Markus is concerned,' Jesse admitted.

'Exactly, that's my point. Maybe the accident really is the key, but in a completely different way to what we've been thinking.'

'What do you mean?'

'What if your suspicions about Markus causing the accident are completely wrong?'

He felt the resistance surging inside of him. 'You think it's just conjecture?'

'Well, that's quite possible. One of my psychology professors always used to cite this guy Wolfgang Singer who called memories "data-based inventions".'

'I don't have any memories. And I haven't invented any either.'

'Maybe you have no real, tangible memories because of the amnesia. But maybe you're so eager to remember the past that you've pieced together something that resembles a memory. This American psychologist, Elizabeth Loftus, did an interesting study where she showed adult test subjects pictures of themselves as children on a balloon ride with their parents. About half of them could suddenly remember this balloon ride, right down to the little details, even though it never actually happened. The pictures had all been Photoshopped.'

Jesse raised his eyebrows.

'The brain's an opportunist,' Jule continued. 'If certain facts are available to us, we take them for granted and just play along. Then we supplement this supposed knowledge by filling in the gaps. Preferably with something personal or emotional. Something we're afraid of, maybe, or something that we long for. Like the fear of falling out of the basket under the hot air balloon or a longing to experience a great adventure with our parents. In the end the picture we form has very little to do with reality.'

'And you think that this is how I've ended up convincing myself that Markus is responsible for the accident, by piecing the bits of information together?'

'Yes, more or less. Like I said, you have absolutely no recollection of the accident because of your amnesia. But still you've created a sort of replacement memory based on what Artur and the others told you. It's like building with cement. You lay the bricks and grout the cracks. Eventually you have a solid wall.'

'So you mean to say that everything I think I know about the time before the accident is wrong?'

'Well no, just that it *could* be wrong. It isn't *necessarily* wrong.'

Jesse said nothing while he tried to get his head around what Jule was saying.

'What do you think would happen,' Jule said, 'if it wasn't actually Markus who caused the accident? What if he had absolutely nothing to do with it?'

'Then I guess he'd think I'm pretty nuts,' Jesse admitted.

'Paranoid or delusional. Or just plain mentally ill. You two had a difficult relationship anyway, didn't you? Now, on top of that, you're constantly suspecting him, trying to make him confess to something he didn't do. And because you make such a convincing case, the others start suspecting him too. Even his friends suddenly start looking at him differently. Then there's this stabbing in the dining hall and he ends up losing a kidney. And the girl he loves ends up with the one who did all this to him. Now *that* could be a motive, couldn't it?'

'"You don't deserve her",' Jesse mumbled. His stomach tied up in knots. And all this because he'd 'remembered' things wrongly? All this because he'd suspected Markus unduly? Heat rushed to his head and he suddenly felt like getting up and running away from himself.

'It's not your fault.' Jule looked at him like he was made of glass: fragile and transparent. 'Even if that is what happened, you lost your memory and nobody helped you. They all kept you in the dark. I think I'd have searched and speculated too, if I were you.'

'That doesn't make things any better.' The old chair creaked as Jesse leaned forward with his elbows resting on his knees. He rubbed his face. Up to now he'd managed to hold back the feeling that he was to blame for all this, but suddenly it was all getting too overwhelming, and he couldn't help but feel guilty. He felt Jule's hand on his hair. She had moved closer to him and his forehead was now touching her stomach. He wished he could burrow away and hide somewhere! He leaned back so forcefully that the chair banged against the wall. 'The worst thing,' he said, 'is that I feel like I can't believe anything or anyone any more. Least of all myself.'

Jule tried to take hold of his hand, but he shook her off.

'So why did he kill Sandra? Why the hell would he do that?' he asked.

'Maybe for the same reason so many jealous men kill their wives: they'd prefer to kill them than to lose to another man,' Jule said. 'You know: if she can't belong to me, she can't belong to anyone.'

'But after so much time has gone by?'

Jule glanced at the window, then over to the door. Her eyes flitted in all directions as she thought it over. 'Sandra was here not long since. Maybe that triggered something in him.'

'And what about Isa?'

'To hurt you. Maybe he wants a little Sandra of his own too. A little Sandra would be easier to control than a fully grown woman. More obedient. Just—' she stopped talking all of a sudden. Her eyes stilled, no longer moving with every little thought.

'What?'

'I . . . well, if that was the scenario then Isa would be in really serious danger. Not only is she like Sandra, but she's like you too. She'll remind him of you.'

Jesse had a flashback to his nightmare from just a few hours ago: Markus was shooting at Isa and all he could do was watch, helpless. 'And Artur?' he asked. 'How would you explain Artur's disappearance?'

Jule shrugged. 'Because he's involved somehow?'

'What about the freezer and the man in his room? Was that Markus too?'

Jule shrugged again. 'Whoever that was, he definitely knew his way around here. He ran down the stairs like the clappers even though they're crooked and steep. At the very least, that would suggest it's someone from here.'

'Do you think Alois was keeping quiet because he's scared of Markus?'

'Possibly. The two of them get along living side by side, don't they?' Jule glanced over to the window. Snow was still falling from the sky. 'Where would you hide Isa if you were him?'

Jesse thought about it for a moment. 'Not here, anyway.'

'But if it had to be here? He can't keep travelling back and forth over long distances.'

'Maybe in the gatehouse. But the tracks in the snow would be too conspicuous.'

'Where else?'

'Somewhere under the roof. Or in the cellar vault. In the back, maybe.'

Jule nodded and looked at him.

Jesse clenched his fists. 'Right, well that's exactly where we'll start looking: in the cellar.' Suddenly all his doubts about Markus being to blame vanished into thin air. 'From the hole to every nook and cranny. And then we'll look through every bit of the attic.'

Chapter 44

'Oh no!' Isabelle murmured. 'Is that him?'

Artur stood like a statue. The sound of a diesel engine was approaching. He squinted into the snowstorm but couldn't make out any headlights. All he could see was the dark shadows lining the edge of the woods. The car must be coming from the other side of the building.

Artur stuck his head out of the window and felt the cold air stinging his thin, dry skin. The shards of glass had left small gouges in the pristine cover of snow. If the man looked up from there it would be hard for him to miss the broken window, even if Artur screwed the boards back on from inside.

Isabelle was sticking her head out of the opening next to him. Her lips were trembling. She did as he did and looked down the side of the building.

The gable was made of stained wood, a style typical of the Alpine region. An ornamental beam roughly the width of a child's foot ran along the border between the attic and the top floor.

Artur gulped. He had to make a quick decision, but his ability to think had slowed down over the years and his thought processes weren't as smooth as they used to be.

He glanced at the ornamental beam before turning to look at Isabelle. He was sure of it now: she would have to go, and he would have to stay. It didn't matter what might happen to him after she had gone. The appearance of the insect man had brought back the terrible memory of the SS captain from just before the end of the war. He remembered how the SS officer had aimed the barrel of the gun right at the back of his brother's head, amongst his blond curls. Werner was on his knees, just two steps away from his father's body. The SS man had executed his father with a shot to the back of the head. He was merciless and moved at lightning speed. He could have waited after he'd shot their father. He could have asked again, and she would have told him everything without hesitation. But he didn't *want* to wait. The SS captain only gave their mother a second chance to answer the question correctly when Werner was already dead.

And now?

Artur had seen what a bullet did when it went through someone's head. And he had seen what an axe could do to piece of wood, a chicken's throat or an arm. There was no doubt about it: if he let Isa go and the man found him alone in the attic, he would have to suffer the consequences. Was this his punishment? His penance for being a coward? For always making himself so comfortable and covering up the 'accident' out of blatant self-preservation?'

Isabelle's hair flew up in a gust of wind. 'Artur, what do we do now?'

Maybe it wasn't a punishment, Artur reflected. Maybe it was more like a test. One last chance. Wasn't it funny how things changed when time was running out? Suddenly you wanted to feel good, pure. But who was pure anyway? Not him – that much was clear. Still, maybe this was his chance to redeem himself a little and do something for those whose fates he had turned around, first for the better and then for the worst.

'Artur!' Isabelle was getting impatient.

A little hint of redemption, he thought. Snowflakes fluttered around his head. Isabelle shook him his shoulder.

'Isabelle?' Artur cleared his throat, then quickly took off his coat and passed it to her. 'Put this on. Hurry, now.'

She looked at him blankly.

Artur took hold of her by the shoulders with both hands and stooped down to her height. He spoke quickly and with a clear sense of urgency. 'I want you to climb out of the window now. You'll have to put your feet on the beam and use your hands to hold on to the moulding along the window ledge. Make your way over to the side, where the rain guttering is. You'll be able to get to the roof from there. With a bit of luck, there should be cross beams and stones there to stop the snow falling from the roof and to keep it secure. Just hold on tight and make sure you don't cause an avalanche – do you hear me?'

Isabelle nodded with wide eyes. Artur didn't know if she had any idea what he meant by an avalanche, but there was no time to explain it to her now. 'Keep an eye out for a dormer or any other kind of window. You might be able to smash it in and get inside. My coat will protect you. Even better: look for a snowdrift, where the snow is as deep as possible.'

That blank look again. She clearly didn't have a clue. Certainly not about snow, anyway. Good grief, these city kids!

'The important thing is that the snowdrift should look like a wave with really soft, flowing shapes. Don't go for any snowdrifts that look like there might be something underneath them – you know, a wheelbarrow, a barrel, anything like that. And when you've found a good snowdrift, jump.'

Isabelle's eyes grew wider still. She nodded. She probably understood what he was saying.

'Don't jump feet first, OK? Your back, your arms and your legs all have to land at the same time, like you're making a snow angel. Do you know what a snow angel is?'

She nodded again, then spread her arms and legs out wide.

'The snow will protect you. But whatever you do, don't jump in front of here! The snow isn't deep enough here – this side isn't as exposed to the weather, you see. And there are shards of glass in the snow below us. Do you think you can do it?'

'Why aren't you coming with me?' Isabelle asked instead of answering him.

Artur shook his head. 'Look at me. Do I look like a mountain goat?'

'No. But neither do I.'

'But you're a lioness. A *young* lioness.'

Isabelle nodded and squared her shoulders. Silence filled the air and they looked at each other for a moment. The engine was getting much louder now.

Isabelle put Artur's coat on. It was far too big for her. Artur rolled the sleeves up, fastened the zipper right the way up to her chin and tried to crack a smile. Isabelle hurled herself against him and hugged him with all her might, so tightly that she almost took the wind out of him. Good lord, how much energy that little girl had! 'You're the best,' she whispered. She looked up at him. 'Lion-pa.'

Artur's eyes welled up with tears. 'You have to go now,' he rasped. 'Be quick. And tell your dad to forgive me.'

'For what?' Isabelle asked, surprised.

'Quick now.' Artur waved his hand energetically.

'Can you help me?'

He nodded. He interlaced his cold, screw-torn hands and stood right next to the window. He hadn't given anyone a leg-up in sixty years.

Isabelle stepped into his hand with her left boot and then climbed out of the window.

'When you get down to the bottom, make sure that nobody sees you. Look for a road. Make sure you walk alongside it, not directly on it. Keep a bit of distance. And just keep walking downhill until you reach the next village.'

Isabelle nodded one last time. She had made it outside and seemed to have a sure footing. She scrambled to the right, keeping hold of the moulding with her hands, and kept going until finally she disappeared from Artur's line of vision. 'Good luck, Isabelle,' he whispered. Artur quickly reached for the board he'd used to smash the window, then he lined it up in front of the window and pushed a screw into the top and bottom. His thumbs were hurting but he didn't care. The most important thing was to make sure the board stayed there for a while. He proceeded in a similar fashion with the second board.

He listened to see if he could hear anything when he'd finished. The engine had gone quiet, but now he could hear the sound of footsteps crunching in the snow on the roof. Isabelle must have made it to the rain gutter, and now it sounded like she was moving towards the edge of the roof.

He realised that he'd neglected to mention that it would be possible to hear her climbing over the roof from inside here. He anxiously glanced at the hatch, expecting to hear footsteps thudding up the stairs any second. Expecting to hear *him* coming. Artur silently cursed himself and wondered how he could have let him go so easily back then. At least in those days he might have been strong enough to stand up to this monster.

The fear was like a rock in his stomach. What would he say when the man asked about Isabelle? Should he just stay quiet? Should he say that he'd fallen asleep and she was gone when he woke up?

He groaned. Nothing was going to help. There was no way he was going to escape his wrath.

Artur closed his eyes, and at that very second a harsh grinding sound shook the whole roof. It was the kind of noise that only an avalanche could make. He thought maybe he had heard a scream too, but he couldn't be sure. Judging by the noise a huge amount of snow had fallen from the roof. Enough to carry a child away and bury her underneath it.

He held his breath and pinned back his ears.

Nothing. Nothing at all.

Oh God, Artur pleaded. Please open the hatch. Make him appear right now. Then maybe Isabelle will still have a chance.

Chapter 45

Garmisch-Partenkirchen – Wednesday, 9 January 2013, 10.51 a.m.

On their way to the cellar they passed through the dining hall and the kitchen, where apparently cleaning was the order of the day. Jesse saw children in the building for the first time since they'd arrived. Homies. So they still had the old cheap labour, then. There was an anaemic-looking boy of about twelve years of age with an angry look in his eyes, and a chubby girl, perhaps fourteen years old, whose pretty features got lost in her puffed-up face. The boy kept calling her 'Tinkerbell' and was trying to annoy her, but her only response was deep-rooted sadness. Jesse noticed that Jule was watching her with concern. The girl looked almost broken. Jule seemed to be thinking the same as him.

Alois was wearing high-necked kitchen whites. He was dishing out orders, which kept Jesse and Jule from proceeding directly through the kitchen to the cellar. Jesse kept seeing flashes of his bald skull and heard him shouting at Tinkerbell to scrub the worktop. Finally Alois came out of the kitchen, uttered a brief 'good morning', and disappeared in the direction of the hall.

Not a minute later, Jesse and Jule were on their way down to the cellar, accompanied by the curious glances from the boy in the kitchen. Tinkerbell, on the other hand, didn't seem to be interested in anything and carried on scrubbing.

Jesse and Jule began by systematically searching the front of the cellar. It didn't take them long to realise that quite a few of the doors were locked. They banged on every door, but not a single one opened. It was pretty unlikely they were going to stumble upon a secret hiding place in the front part of the cellar, anyway. This was the place for storing supplies, tools, chairs, school desks and other things they used in the classrooms. The door to the back part of the cellar was locked.

'End of the line,' Jule mumbled.

Jesse stayed by the door, wavering. Were they going to let a bit of wood stop them going any further? 'Wait a minute,' he said.

Jesse stumbled upon a crowbar in the room two doors back. It was about eighty centimetres long, perfect for the job. Without saying a word, he wedged the iron claw between the lock and the door frame. He was convinced that Jule would object, but instead she just watched in silence. The wood split with a crack and the door burst open.

Jule shrugged and took a quick look around.

Jesse pushed the door open and stepped into the darkness. He could still remember the layout from when he was younger. Ahead of him was a tunnel-like passage, almost thirty metres long, with two corridors branching off on either side. Cold air rushed towards them, and the smell of mould crept into his nose. The weak light from the front part of the cellar faded away behind the door, just by the old Bauhaus rotary switch on the wall. Jesse turned it, but nothing happened.

'Shh,' Jule hissed and pressed his arm. She pointed into the darkness with her other hand.

'What is it?' Jesse whispered.

'I saw something behind there. A glimmer of light. Really faint.'

'Are you sure?'

'Just before you flicked the switch. It was like someone closed a door or turned a torch off.'

'I didn't see anything.'

'But it was there.'

Jesse nodded. 'OK. We need some light.' He quickly crept back to where he'd found the crowbar. The shelf was a complete mess. Tools, old pans, loose power sockets, tangled-up power cables, a disused sandwich meat slicer and lots of crates. Two mousetraps were set up next to the door, one with a taut string, the other one with a dead rat in it. He found a torch with a leaking battery next to a bottle of turps. The brownish-red liquid from the battery had eaten through the screw-on cover.

'Shit,' he cursed under his breath. He heard footsteps approaching and spun around. Jule was standing in the doorway, staring at the defective torch in his hand.

'What about the kitchen?' she suggested. 'Maybe there's something there. I could ask one of the kids.'

'Just be quick. If there is somebody down here, I don't want them doing a runner.' He grabbed the crowbar like a club. Cold, strong iron. It felt good in his hand. 'I'll wait by the entrance to the back.'

Jule gulped and nodded. The whole place looked like one big black hole from where she was standing. 'I'll be right back.'

Jule showed him her meagre haul when she returned. No torch, just two half-empty disposable lighters and a box of matches.

'That'll have to do,' Jesse said, grimly. He pushed down on the gas release and flicked the flint wheel. The lighter reluctantly spat out a couple of sparks and a puny flame, half the length of his little finger. Jule's lighter was no better. 'Where did you see the light?' He asked.

'Right back there. It disappeared off to the left.'

'Let's go,' Jesse whispered.

The flames from their lighters illuminated barely two metres, and the draught was threatening to put the flames out with every overly hasty step they took. They crept along, even though Jesse would have liked to run. Small stones and porous joint mortar from the ceiling crunched under their feet as they walked. A drop of water fell on Jesse's forehead. The yellowish glow of the lighters flitted over the walls and closed doors, making their shadows dance. Old cables ran along the wall just above their heads. Some of them were corroded and covered in chalky residue, and only one of them looked new. Plastic tubing as thick as a thumb, the kind usually used for power cables. A track of light grey in the darkness.

'What about the doors?' Jule whispered. 'What if someone's hiding behind one of them?'

'We would have heard them. The doors down here are so old, they always make a sound when they move.'

'Maybe somebody has greased them.'

Jesse looked up at the clean light-grey plastic cable and had to admit she could be right. They had made it to the first set of side passages and were standing in the middle, surrounded by silence and the meagre glow from their lighters. The open door was illuminated in the distance behind them. Jesse could still remember that it was about fifteen paces in each direction from where they were standing. He could still have drawn a map of most of the corridors in Adlershof if someone had asked him to. 'What do you think?' he whispered. 'Was it here or was it further back?

Jule glanced backwards to gauge the distance. 'Further back.'

Jesse leaned over to Jule, so close that he could feel the stray hairs by her ear tickling his nose. 'Just in case the person you saw is actually hiding in the first passageway and planning to make a run for it, can you look behind us and keep an eye on the door?'

Jule glanced at the rectangle of light. 'OK.'

They made their way deeper into the cellar. Jule put her hand on Jesse's shoulder to stop herself from stumbling while she kept her eyes on the door behind them. The hallway ended in a T-junction. They took the left fork, where Jule had seen the beam of light heading. Jesse stopped just around the corner. Did he hear footsteps?

He listened. No, nothing but silence. He turned around, caught Jule's eye and pressed his finger to his lips. Then he took two steps and stopped abruptly in his tracks. He turned around and looked towards the bend. Whoever was there, they would be able to see him and Jule. He quickly took his thumb off the gas release and blew Jule's flame out. They were just a few steps away from the bend. He slid along the wall until he reached the T-junction, then he glanced over at the door he had pried open at the other end of the corridor. A small, shapeless shadow was leaning against the wall on the right-hand side, clearly visible against the rectangle of light punched out of the darkness by the doorway. He ran towards it with the crowbar in his left hand and the hot, flameless lighter in the other. The shadow broke away with a swift motion and started running towards the door. The tip of the crowbar got caught on a doorjamb, snatching it out of Jesse's hand. It crashed to the floor with a loud clang. Jesse kept running, chasing the shadow. The figure got to the door with the broken lock just before him and promptly slammed it shut.

Suddenly it was dark. Jesse stormed on, reaching out in front of him with his hands. He collided with the door with a painful bang. It flew open, rebounded and caught him on the shoulder. Now the light in the front of the cellar was off too. Whoever was down here, they were quick and smart. Jesse followed the sounds of puffing and swift footsteps, hoping that he wasn't going to end up hurling himself against a wall at full pelt. He reached out in front of him. The other person was so close he could almost feel their body heat. He grabbed a lump of hair and yanked at it. A high-pitched scream rang out in his ears. He banged his shoulder against the wall, tossed his arm around the figure and threw them both to the ground. Warm breath hit him in the face. Unbrushed teeth. Two fists were pummelling him. He pushed the hands away, surprised at the lack of resistance, and pinned his opponent to the ground. 'Jule,' he yelled. 'Over here.'

The space behind him brightened; there was a flicker of light but then it went out again.

'Here, Jule, over here!'

Suddenly her footsteps were beside him and he could hear the spark wheel rasping right by his ear. The flame shone a flickering light on a tangled mass of blond hair around a girl's face, her skin white as a sheet.

Jesse let go of the girl, startled.

'It's you?' Jule said automatically. The girl suddenly stopped struggling and was now staring at the two of them.

'Do you know her? Who is she?' Jesse turned from Jule to the girl. 'And why are you hiding here?'

'Shh, don't be so loud,' the girl whispered. 'They hear everything.'

Jesse stood up, confused.

'I've only seen her once before,' Jule muttered under her breath. 'In the kitchen. She ran off into the cellar. I thought she'd maybe stolen some food or something.'

'Who are *they*?' Jesse asked the girl. She said nothing.

'I see,' Jesse said. 'And who are *you*?'

More silence. Their shadows flickered on the girl's orange-red face in the glow of the lighter.

'I want to know who you are,' Jesse snapped.

She took fright and buried her head in her chest. 'Charly,' she confessed, reluctantly. Jesse thought he could remember hearing that name before. Hadn't Richard mentioned it? 'Have you run away?'

Charly stood up straight and rubbed the bits of gravel off the palms of her hands. 'Are you one of them?'

'Would I be asking you if I was?' he snapped. 'For goodness' sake, I don't even know who *they* are!'

'Jesse.' Jule's hand was on his shoulder.

'Fine,' he said. 'Why are you hiding down here?'

'Are you the one who always comes through the corridor?'

'Which corridor are you talking about?'

Charly looked at him warily and shrank back.

'I recognise you.'

'She saw you in the kitchen when you were unconscious,' Jule murmured in Jesse's ear.

'OK. Let's take it slow,' Jesse said. 'Your name is Charly and you're from the home.'

She nodded.

'And you're hiding down here.'

More nodding. Only this time he got the impression that she was hiding something from him.

'Who are you afraid of?'

'I'm not afraid. Not of anybody,' she said defiantly, but with a weak, nervous undertone to her voice.

'What's this about a man going through the corridor? Who is he?'

Charly looked at him like she was questioning his sanity. The flame from the lighter was reflected in her pupils. 'I don't know. I don't know him. I just saw him on a photo here.'

'What photo, Charly? It's important, really important.'

The same odd look, like it was strange that he had asked her that question. 'In the principal's office.'

Jesse's heart was beating faster. He started mentally searching through the photos in Richard's office. He could still remember them. He had a few hanging up there, most of them depicting the whole gang from the old days. 'Where was the photo, can you remember?'

'No. It's been a while.'

'Then we should go and have a look.'

Charly's eyes widened. She shook her head and backed off until she was almost out of the light from the flame, then she seemed to vanish into thin air in the darkness. 'I'm not going up there. Not during the day. Not if they're going to see me.'

'Charly, please. It's really important. You have to show me that photo.'

'I don't understand,' she muttered under her breath and took another step back. 'I don't understand why it's such a big deal.'

'Listen, Charly. This is about my daughter. She's a bit younger than you are. Her name is Isabelle and I'm looking for her. She might be with the man you've seen down here. Do you understand? Don't worry about getting into trouble because you've run away. Mr Messner and I go way back. He's an old friend of mine. I'll talk to him, you won't be in trouble.'

Charly bit her lip. Every fibre in her body showed that she was on the defensive. Her eyes glistened with tears. Something seemed to be troubling her so much that she was lost for words.

'Hey, Charly,' Jule said. She was standing next to Jesse and speaking in a soft, hushed voice. 'I'm Jule, remember? You don't need to be scared of us. We won't tell on you. I didn't say anything the other time I saw you. And we're not going to do anything to hurt you. But it's really important. Maybe you'd like to show me the photo?'

No reaction. Her eyes flitted back and forth between the two of them.

'Didn't you say that the man came through a corridor? Can you show me?'

Another shake of the head, this time more vigorous than before.

'Is that because that's where your hiding place is?' Jule asked gently.

The head shaking became frantic.

'OK, Charly. What do you say to showing me this corridor? Just me? Jesse can stay here.'

Charly's eyes flitted back and forth between them again, as if she was trying to figure out how they were connected to each other. Finally she gave a resigned nod.

Jule held her hand out and Charly took hold of it, but not without first glancing nervously at Jesse, like she was worried he might object to them leaving.

Jesse sighed, half relieved and half anxious. He exchanged a brief consensual glance with Jule and then watched as the two of them made their way through the door with the broken lock. The glow from the lighter shrouded them in a quivering aura of yellowish light that was slowly getting smaller and smaller as they walked away from him. When they got a little bit further away, Charly tugged on Jule's hand and they stopped in their tracks. Charly stood on her tiptoes and whispered something into Jule's ear. The flame died out.

Jesse waited. He didn't dare spark the lighter. He was hoping that Charly was going to confide in Jule. His heart was beating twice as loudly in the darkness. He couldn't shake the image of Jule and Charly, hand in hand. He imagined Isa standing next to him, with her hand in his.

Eventually he couldn't wait any longer and decided to press the light switch. The dark hole behind the broken door stared back at him. How long had they been gone? Five minutes? Seven? It seemed like an eternity. He didn't want to call out, but he couldn't wait any longer either. Treading lightly, he set off with the lighter in front of him and Isa in his mind. At the first junction, he decided to turn left. He didn't know why. The flame from the lighter leaned in the direction he was heading in. He took ten steps, then he bumped into something. Charly ran past him.

'Charly! Stay here!'

The darkness swallowed her up like a ravenous animal. He heard the sound of her scampering away, then it went quiet.

'Jule?'

He lifted the lighter and ran to the end of the corridor. The light shone on the spot where an old solid brick wall used to be. The bricks had been re-laid and freshly grouted, and they framed a robust metal door. It was open. Jule was standing in front of it, staring at him.

'Jule. Is everything OK?'

She nodded, but her eyes said the opposite.

'Where does this lead?'

'Charly says it goes to the gatehouse,' Jule said.

Jesse took a step past her. 'What took you so long? Is everything OK?' When he got no response from Jule, he reached behind the door and flicked a light switch, and a row of cellar lights came on. The corridor ran in a straight line from the main building and was definitely leading towards the gatehouse. The walls looked old and weathered, like they had been built some time before the First World War.

'Come on, let's go,' Jesse said.

Jule followed him. He could clearly see how afraid she was, but he didn't have time to deal with that right now. Finally they had something to go on. They should have taken a good look at the gatehouse long ago. What was it Richard said? They were renovating it?

At the end of the tunnel, they came across a vaulted room full of sacks of cement, stacks of wood, a bunch of tools and a raised platform. The door was unlocked and well oiled. An exposed, freshly concreted staircase led up to the tiny corridor on the ground floor. Jesse kicked the door to the gatehouse living room open. It was sparsely furnished, with curtains covering the windows. There was a heavy wooden table in the middle of the room. Jesse froze. Jule cried out behind him.

The top of the table was soaked in fresh blood. Somebody had wound a rope around the table top with loops knotted into it. There were deep indentations in the wood. The smell of metal and urine filled the air. A thin line of dark specks adorned the ceiling above the table. The floor was covered in chaotic spray patterns punctuated by footprints. But not a single one of the footprints led out of the room.

Jesse's heart was pounding. He tried to push the thoughts of Isa out of his mind. It couldn't be true. This couldn't possibly have been Isa! He touched the table top with trembling fingers. The blood was still sticky. Whatever had gone on here, it hadn't happened long ago.

Chapter 46

1981, Garmisch-Partenkirchen

The night he fired the shot at Richard, Jesse slept in the passageway beneath the sloping roof. Two blankets and an old cushion were all he needed. He was used to sleeping on the floor. He woke up before the others, crept back into the bathroom through the access panel and washed his face.

The scene at breakfast took him by surprise.

Alois, Wolle, Markus, Mattheo and Richard were pale-faced and quiet, but they didn't snub him like they usually did. They all nodded at him – well, everyone except for Richard, who looked away. Their gazes were serious, with a hint of respect and perhaps a touch of silent hostility. There was complicity in their eyes. None of them were going to say anything. Maybe they were just trying to lull him into a sense of security so that they could push him off the roof at the next opportune moment. He had humiliated the golden boy, after all. Then again, one or two of them might have secretly enjoyed it. Even Richard had his enemies, and there were definitely people who envied him.

He could even see the approval in Markus's eyes. In fact, he tapped him on the shoulder twice – very out of character. The second time Markus tapped his shoulder, Sandra stepped into the room. Jesse didn't know why he hadn't noticed earlier, but Markus reacted to Sandra much like he did. Now he understood what Markus must think of Richard.

Sandra was the same as ever: happy and animated, but at the same time delightfully coy. The breakfast hall was her stage and she was in the limelight, even though she had no need to perform. She danced into the room and everyone turned to watch.

As they were on their way to class, she suddenly appeared next to Jesse and gestured at him. Jesse hung back a little, trying to be discreet. 'Meet me tonight in the passage?' she whispered, her eyes glued to the floor.

He had a lump in his throat. He nodded. Was it a trap? 'About twelve,' he replied, peering at the others. Nobody seemed to notice them.

'Thanks,' she said softly.

Just the sound of her voice gave him goose pimples.

The hours that followed seemed like an eternity: time was dripping like resin from a tree. Jesse did his schoolwork, ate his food, scrubbed the pans without any hassle from Dante or seeing Richard or Sandra resurfacing from the cellar. He slipped into bed and said the bare minimum, not wasting any energy on pitying Mattheo, who was clearly unhappy with how the previous night had ended. He couldn't be sure he would get another chance; they needed Richard and his key for the shed, but he was definitely sick and tired of all the bullshit now.

He crept into the bathroom just before twelve, made sure that nobody was there, climbed under the eaves and locked the passage *from the inside. Then he jammed the torch in his mouth and crawled along on all fours until he reached the girls' bathroom. Just after twelve he heard a gentle knock on the panel. He opened the catch and let Sandra in.*

'Hi,' she whispered. That voice again. She smelled of milk and something else. Something unfamiliar. A good smell. Exciting.

He couldn't help but think of what Richard had said about her mother. God, maybe he was right about her?

'Hi,' he responded in a gravelly voice, closing the panel behind her. They crept on another couple of metres until they reached the blankets. Jesse put the lit torch on the old floorboards with the reflector pointing upwards. Sandra's nose cast a long, dark shadow between her eyes. Her neck was lit up to her chin and the skin below her ears looked like velvet. Her long blond hair shimmered different hues in the light.

'Can you turn the torch off?' she asked.

Jesse shook his head. He wanted to be prepared in case it was a trap. He also liked being able to see Sandra and what she was wearing: a baggy light-blue pyjama top and white underwear.

'What's the matter?' he asked, trying hard to sound cool.

She sighed, crossed her legs and leaned back against the wall. 'Richard,' she groaned.

'Hmm,' Jesse muttered. He was lying on his back right in front of her, in the acute angle between the sloping roof and the floor. His head was just two palm widths away from her lap. It was exciting being so close to her. The only way they could have been further apart would be to crouch down side by side, but he didn't want that. He took a quick glance at her pale legs.

Sandra reached for the torch. She was about to switch it off, but then Jesse took it out of her hand and put it back.

'Hey, you can see my knickers,' she protested, her voice almost a whisper.

'So what? It's not the first time I've seen a pair of knickers,' he boasted. And it wasn't a lie if he counted all the sightings in his dad's flat.

She giggled and adjusted her pyjama top between her legs to cover up her pants.

'So, what about Richard?' he asked casually.

Sandra hesitated for a moment and looked down at him. 'I . . . I think he's gross.'

Jesse was surprised. He'd expected anything but that. He thought maybe Richard had put her up to talking to him or she wanted to defend him. But gross? He looked at her and asked: 'Why?'

'Well, you know him,' she squirmed.

Jesse was confused. 'Of course I know him,' he said. 'But what exactly do you find gross about him?'

'His mouth,' she confessed.

Jesse had been secretly hoping for more than that. He found his mind going to the women his father had brought to the house. Many of them had been truly vile, with hair not only under their bellies, but also under their arms, and a smell that made him recoil in disgust. Still, that didn't stop his father. 'What disgusting thing does he do with his mouth?'

She turned bright red and looked away.

He took advantage of this moment to try and catch a glimpse between her legs. He felt compelled to do it, especially now that her pyjama top had shifted ever so slightly. He became aware of a very familiar smell, just a whiff of it, but it was unmistakeable. He didn't dare think of the word, but his father had said it at the time, and he could hear him whispering it to him now: pussy.

Jesse knew how dirty it sounded. Not just how it sounded, but how dirty it was. His mouth went dry.

Their eyes met. She'd had plenty of time to adjust her pyjama top, but she hadn't. She was sitting there with a bright red face, not moving a muscle. Richard was right. It turned her on. That much was obvious.

He turned onto his side and put one hand on her bare leg. She flinched but stayed where she was. 'Careful,' she whispered.

Women want you to take them, but they'll never tell you that. His father had impressed that upon him when he was younger, but Jesse had never understood what he meant. What did the beatings and the furious clapping about on top of each other have to do with satisfying a woman's secret desires? Especially as the women usually groaned in pain or even ended up with tears running down their cheeks. Maybe he was just too young to understand. They have to feel how much you want them, his father used to say. That turns them on.

Richard popped into his head again. And Sandra's remark about being careful. He was careful. Much more careful than Father. He straightened himself as best he could under the sloping roof, then knelt down in front of her and moved his hand closer to her lap. Sandra's eyes glinted. She raised her hand self-consciously and stroked his hair.

No, Richard didn't have it all! Richard didn't have Sandra, Jesse thought. He was going to lose her.

Sandra's mouth opened into a startled, horrified circle when he slid his hand into her knickers. It was warm beneath the cotton. Was that sweat from his fingers? Was it wet between her legs? Was that what Richard meant when he talked about being turned on?

He grabbed hold with both hands and pulled on the waistband of his knickers, fumbling with the elastic as he pulled the pants down off her hips and out from underneath her bottom while Sandra squirmed and wriggled. 'Jesse, no . . .' she groaned. She was breathing fast and the heat of her breath struck him in the face. He let go of her knickers and left them dangling from the back of her knees. He pushed himself up against her and gave her a wary kiss, or at least what he thought was a kiss. Nobody had taught him how to do it.

She gave a bashful smile and ran her hand through his hair again. Pulled him closer and put her arms around him. Her mouth was by his ear. 'I like you. Not Richard. I like you!' A powerful sensation ran through his body, from his ear to his loins. He wished he could spend his whole life like this. In Sandra's arms. Close to her. But he wanted to get even closer. He moved away slightly and opened the first button of her pyjama top, then fumbled with the next one down.

'Jesse, no . . . please.'

He couldn't get the third button open as it was fastened too tightly. He ripped it off with a single tug, then he reached for the next one. 'Jesse, no, please wait.'

He'd waited long enough already. He'd waited every time she'd been down in the cellar and put on her show and God knows what else for Richard.

He pulled her pyjama top as far down her shoulders as he could. The torch wobbled over and banged on the floor, shining a harsh beam of light onto her bare chest. Her breasts looked nothing like the ones he'd seen on his father's women. They were round, firm and pert – not big and heavy. The excitement came over him in ripples. He pressed his mouth against hers. She tried to say some-thing, but he drowned out every sound with his tongue. She gave in for a moment, playing along with her lips and her tongue. A wave of heat rushed through his body. So that's what Father had talked about. Now he understood! Like someone possessed, he pushed her to the ground and pulled her knickers all the way down until they slid off her ankles. She started thrashing about and trying to get him off her. 'Don't. Please, no! No!'

He stared at the fleshy groove between her legs under the mer-ciless glow of the torch. He didn't know why he was doing it or if he was imitating something he'd seen before. He didn't know what was driving him to it. This pussy didn't have any hair like the ones he'd seen on the other women. Delicate blond fuzz tickled his tongue. There was a brief moment when she stopped struggling, just froze and groaned. Maybe just like her mother. And him? Was he just like his father?

Suddenly she grabbed hold of his hair, forcing him to let go. She quickly pressed her legs together. He tried his best to part them again. 'Don't! No! No!' She wasn't groaning any more. Her voice sounded desperate. She waved her arms about and kicked him off her. Tears glistened on her face in the beam of the torch.

Jesse panted. 'Why not?'

'I can't! Why did you do that?'

'Come on, you know what you're doing.'

'I . . . what?'

'Oh come on. What was all that with Richard and Dante?'

She stared at him in amazement. 'What are you talking about?'

'I know all about your mum. You're always playing the inno-cent with me but putting on a show for Dante and the golden boy in the cellar.'

'What kind of show?' she asked, her voice trembling.

'The last time Dante came up out of the cellar when you were down there, his dick was almost hanging out of his pants.'

Sandra looked at him in disbelief.

Jesse wondered where the words were coming from. But they just flew out of his mouth.

'What do you know about my mum?'

Jesse hesitated. 'Well, that she was a whore.'

Fresh tears ran down Sandra's cheeks. 'Who told you that?'

'Richard. You told him everything.'

Her lips were trembling. She pulled her pyjama top over her chest and folded her arms. 'I really don't know where you got that idea from.' Her chest rose and sank erratically as she spoke. 'But Richard is the last person I would have told that to. I might have told you, but definitely not him.'

Jesse gave her an incredulous look.

'And I have no idea what you're on about with Dante. He likes the way I dance. He said I can practice in the cellar if I want to. He was probably watching me while he was drunk. I have no idea if he did something disgusting while he watched me. I couldn't care less what goes on in his head. Or in Richard's. Or yours.'

Jesse sat frozen stiff like the wind had been taken out of him. A wave of shame came over him. He wished it would wash him away, wash him clean. He sat there feeling more and more ashamed, having to look at Sandra's tearstained face. Richard had lied to him. Maybe Mr M had told him about Sandra's mother. But that didn't matter any more. The worst thing was that he'd believed him, that he'd believed even for a second that Sandra was like her mother. He wasn't like his father either. Or was he? Wasn't that exactly why he'd just behaved as he had? And hadn't he enjoyed it?

He gulped. He felt dangerously close to something really evil, like that night in the clearing when he'd fired the crossbow at Richard.

'I want to get out of here,' Sandra said. Her voice sounded weak and hollow.

Jesse wished he could beg for her forgiveness. But how could she excuse his behaviour? How could he excuse it?

Without saying another word, Sandra turned around and crept towards the girls' bathroom on all fours. Her knickers were still on the floor and her pyjama top provided an open view of her bottom – and a touch more. The last thing he saw that night was the thing that had driven him wild. He couldn't help but stare at her until she disappeared through the access panel.

He sat there transfixed for several minutes.

Then he crawled after her and closed the panel from the inside.

He wanted to scream. He wanted to roar his way out of the dirt he had just fallen into. It seemed like his father was pulling away from the darkness and moving towards him, reaching out to him with his hand. Jesse gave a swipe and knocked the hand away. But how much longer would he be able to keep fighting him off?

He climbed into the boys' block, closed the access panel and crept back over to the dormer window in his room, his shoulders drooping and his heart running riot. The rest of the boys were asleep.

He quietly opened the window and climbed onto the roof. The cold wind clawed at him, making him feel marginally better. Bare feet first, he climbed down the side of the building like someone in a trance.

The pebbles outside the building pricked the soles of his feet like needles. His nerves were frayed. His whole body was raging.

Nothing made sense any more. He had to get to the clearing. He had the tree in his sights, the one the others had made him stand against. The one he himself had shot at so many times.

He was just about to make a dash for it when he heard a car coming up the path. The yellow beam of light shone on the main building, and at the last second, he jumped for cover behind the edge of the wide staircase at the entrance to the building. He tried to calm his rapid breathing. Whoever it was, they would be gone soon. Then he could leave.

The engine noise ceased and a car door slammed shut. Then he heard heavy footsteps on the stone staircase – sluggish, tired footsteps that sounded like they belonged to a large man. Dante, perhaps? But then why wasn't he going to the back entrance? And Dante didn't have a car, just that stupid moped. Suddenly the doorbell rang. It sounded like an alarm. A sharp jangling sound that pierced his already frayed nerves. Jesse had always hated that sound. He considered running away, but the risk of getting caught was just too high. So he stayed there while the bell rang on and on. Finally someone opened the door. 'What on earth are you doing here? Do you know what time it is?' a voice snarled indignantly. It sounded a lot like Dante.

'I want to speak to Artur Messner.' The voice was deep, dark and slightly breathless. Jesse couldn't tell whether he'd heard it before.

'Then come back tomorrow.'

'No. I have to speak to him now,' the man insisted.

Dante seemed to be hesitating. Curious, Jesse stretched his back and peered over the side of the stone staircase. The stranger was tall – very tall – and Jesse couldn't see his face. But the one thing he could see was his large, fleshy hand.

He gasped.

Closed his eyes.

Opened them again.

On the back of the hand was an unmistakable crescent-shaped scar. The last time he had seen it had been ten years before.

Chapter 47

The horrible scene they witnessed in the room in the gatehouse seared itself into Jule's mind. Her imagination immediately started filling in the blanks. Loops of rope . . . notches in the table . . . specks of blood on the ceiling . . .

She watched as Jesse touched the table with his hand and the blood stuck to his fingertips. She couldn't help but think of Isa. She stared at the floor and the footprints which suggested somebody had staggered through the room. Somebody with big feet – bigger than hers anyway, and definitely bigger than Isa's. Should she find that reassuring? Well, only if the person who had left the footprints behind was the victim. And how could the victim have walked through their own blood?

She glanced over at Jesse, who was also sizing up the footprints. She wanted to say something comforting. But it was as if the secret Charly had told her in the darkness of the cellar was blocking her throat.

Charly had reluctantly led her over to the door and turned the key in the lock. She didn't say where she had got it. No doubt she had pilfered it from somewhere. And yes, the gatehouse had been her hiding place for the last few days. There was heating, and she'd found a bed to sleep on. She thought nobody lived there. Or at least, not until *he* came.

Jule asked her who this *he* was.

Charly stood on her tiptoes in the darkness and whispered in her ear: 'Your friend. The one called Jesse.'

Jule froze, hoping that she'd misunderstood Charly. 'Jesse? Are you sure?'

'Yes,' she said breathily in the darkness.

Jule wished she could see Charly's face. Everything was so unreal down there in the darkness. But she didn't dare use the lighter. 'So when did you see him for the first time?'

'Yesterday morning.'

'Yesterday?' The hairs on the back of Jule's neck stood on end. 'How early?'

'I don't know. Pretty early.'

'Was it still dark?'

'I don't know. You can't tell from down here.'

Her breath faltered as she thought back to when they arrived in Adlershof. She tried to work out what time it must have been. How deeply had she slept in the car? Suddenly she got the creeping feeling that Markus's warnings might make sense. Maybe Jesse really was unpredictable. Uncontrollable. Maybe even mentally ill.

She hadn't believed Markus when he said he'd seen Jesse here recently. But now, after what Charly had told her, everything looked different.

She went through the full spectrum of personality disorders in her mind, or at least the ones she could still remember from her studies. Until recently she thought that Jesse's memory loss was because of the accident, but now she had to consider something else, such as a dissociative identity disorder. Maybe he had a split personality – a different side of him that acted completely independently of the Jesse she knew. A personality with completely different morals and priorities. She knew how rare this form of identity disorder was, even if so-called 'multiple personalities' were a common theme in films and books these days.

She would have asked Charly so many more questions, but then Jesse had arrived, and she had run away before she got a chance.

And now here she was, standing with Jesse in the middle of this room, the site of something truly horrific. Did Charly know about it? Unlikely. Surely she would have said something or seemed even more distraught if she had seen it.

'We have to search the rest of the place,' Jesse said.

Jule snapped out of her thoughts. Yes, he was right. But what was he hoping to achieve?

'I'll look in the attic.' His voice was rough and breathy and sounded deeply troubled. 'Should I check the ground floor too?'

Jule nodded stiffly.

Jesse left without saying another word. She heard him pacing through the ground floor, followed by the sound of the wooden staircase creaking under his footsteps. She felt sick. She had to get some fresh air. But wasn't the front door boarded up? She made her way across the small corridor and got a fright when she saw her own reflection in an open wardrobe door, then she stepped into the kitchen.

The kitchen unit was painted in off-white and the gold knobs on the drawers looked like they had been sanded down. The plastic worktop was covered with a thin layer of dust with fresh marks in it. Clear water was dripping into the scuffed sink. To

Jule's surprise, the back door to the kitchen opened with a gentle push. Cold air whipped against her face and she shivered as she exhaled light clouds of breath. The flat roof of the carport stretched out overhead. There was no knob or door handle on the outside of the door, which explained why nobody had closed it.

She guzzled up the fresh mountain air, hoping that it would help to make her thoughts clearer. What the hell was she supposed to do?

Snow was still falling, and the dirty ground beneath the carport stood out in the white landscape. A shapeless wall of snow had formed at the back of the parking space. Jule stood staring absent-mindedly at the tall white mound until she realised that something wasn't quite right. Where had it come from? The carport had a flat roof. Snow definitely wouldn't have fallen from it.

She approached the long white wall with caution and glanced up at the vertical gable end of the gatehouse. The snow probably couldn't have come from there either. It would have had to slide sideways down the surface of the roof.

Her eyes fell on the shovel propped against the side of the building between the door and the rubbish bins. The handle was large and bits of snow were stuck to the blade. She carefully reached out and ran her finger along the top of the wall of snow. It was loose, like it had just fallen. The snow underneath felt more solid. She glanced up above. The edge of the carport roof looked like it had been cleared, like somebody had raked the snow down with the shovel.

She dug a hole in the snow with both her hands. Her fingers turned red and her cheeks were glowing. About nine inches deep, she felt something hard beneath the snow. It rustled. A thin, black film, like a bin bag. She made the hole wider, then wiped away the rest of the snow. There was something large and undefined down there. She kept digging frantically and hooked her index finger into the stiff film, then pulled on it until the plastic gave way with a sigh, making a hole. She ripped the plastic bag open with both her hands. Two dull eyes were staring into the sky. A snowflake twirled down and landed in the frozen eyelashes on the ashen man's face. It took her a moment to recognise him.

It was Markus.

She quickly let go of the plastic bag, like it had given her an electric shock, and staggered back until she felt the wall of the building behind her. She looked around to see if there was anyone nearby. She was alone, except for Jesse, who was still wandering around the building.

What the hell had happened here?

Jesse. Her thoughts were running wild. Sandra flashed before her eyes: Sandra wrapped up in a rug on the balcony, frozen. And now this. What time had she woken up that morning? About ten, wasn't it? Jesse had already been up for a while by that time.

Suddenly it all made sense. The two corpses in the snow. Jesse's hatred for Markus. His frustrated love for Sandra. Charly, who had seen Jesse in the corridor. And Markus, who had seen him in the girls' toilet. She felt sick. How come Markus had seen Jesse in the girls' toilet of all places? Hadn't he said that Jesse's clothes had been dusty? This particular detail had seemed so unbelievable when she first heard it. But now she was wondering if there might be a very specific reason for it. A hiding place, perhaps? Or the entrance to a hiding place?

Was one of the Jesses looking for Isa while the other Jesse hid her? Isa would have had to be in the car with them when they came to Garmisch if that was the case. But then again, Jesse was a doctor, so he probably had anaesthetic on him. She hadn't looked in the boot of the Volvo either.

Had she figured it all out? Wasn't it possible that she was just filling in the gaps between the facts? Jesse had seemed so honest and so lost. It wasn't long since he'd sat there in front of her, distraught, with his forehead against her belly. Was he such a perfect liar? Or was he completely oblivious to what he was doing?

She glanced at the back exit, then away from the gatehouse to the street. Then she ran.

The sky was like milk and lead. The main building towered up between infinite falling snowflakes. The mountain range behind the building was submerged under a huge wall of snow. Not long now and she'd be snowed in here. The path from the gatehouse to the road was barely visible; yesterday's tyre tracks had been reduced to two blurry grooves. She looked over her shoulder, afraid that Jesse might burst out of the building and start running after her. She tried to move faster. She had to get to the main building. She had to find a phone before Jesse found her.

She sank knee-deep into the snow with every step, and she was freezing cold by the time she reached the road to the main building. Now her progress was faster. She could hear the deep throttle of a diesel engine and the jangling of snow chains approaching on the road behind her. A pair of bright headlights skimmed the final crest on the mountain road and pierced the grey daylight, then finally Richard Messner's Toyota appeared.

She stood still.

She waved at Messner and hoped Jesse wouldn't see her. But there was still no noise from the gatehouse. It was deserted and looked peaceful in the snow. Surely Jesse had noticed that she had disappeared by now? Maybe he was running through the corridor back to the main building that very second.

The Toyota edged closer and the chains rattled as the car pulled up next to Jule. The snow growled under the weight of the heavy SUV. Richard Messner rolled down the window and gave a greasy smile. 'What are you doing out here dressed like that? Trying to catch your death?'

'Thank God it's you,' Jule gasped. 'Could you tell me if there's a police station nearby?'

Messner's smile froze. 'Of course. Why do you ask?'

'Somebody has killed your caretaker. He's up there behind the gatehouse.'

Messner's expression was blank, like hadn't understood what Jule had just said. 'Markus Kawczynski? Are you sure?'

Jule nodded. Her ribcage heaved. She was exhausted after running though the deep snow. It was all too much for her.

Messner unfastened his seat belt. He turned the engine off and climbed out of the car. 'I want to see him. Show me.'

'I don't think that's a good idea,' Jule snapped. 'The murderer's probably still in the gatehouse.'

Messner's eyes darted over to the house. 'Did you see him?'

'I think it's Jesse. And I think he killed Sandra too.'

For the first time, Richard looked genuinely dismayed. Red blotches emerged from his clean-shaven jowls. A fuzzy covering of snow crystals was accumulating on the shoulders of his dark green coat. 'Sandra's dead? Since when?'

'Please, we really should call the police.'

'Yes, we probably should,' Messner mumbled and glanced back over at the gatehouse. 'Get in.'

It was warm in the car. Still, Jule could barely feel the heat with all the coldness coming from inside. She perched on the seat and shivered. She could still see Markus's pale face and the bloody table top with the notches in it. She was trying hard not to think about exactly what had happened to him. Messner eased onto the accelerator, and the chains burrowed into the snow as they crept forward. The snowflakes were falling thick and fast, and the sky was low and heavy, like it was trying to devour them. Richard Messner tapped the display on the dashboard with his right hand and navigated to the phone menu on the hands-free kit. He held on to the steering wheel with his left hand to stop the car swerving. 'Are you sure it was Jesse?'

'I don't know. I think so. A girl saw him walking through the underground passage in the cellar. She also saw him in the gatehouse. It all seems to add up. I can't explain it now, please just call the police, I—'

'What girl?

Jule paused for a second and thought about whether she should keep Charly's name to herself, but the little girl couldn't just keep rattling around the cellar for ever. 'She's called Charly.'

Messner's finger froze and hovered over the screen. 'You spoke to Charly?'

'Yes. She's been hiding down there – sometimes in the cellar, sometimes in the gatehouse.'

A pale-faced Messner started tapping a number into the screen. Jule sank into her seat in relief. Finally somebody was seeing sense and calling the police.

Three ringing tones later, an old but forceful female voice answered the phone. 'Hello?'

'You have to come here, we have a problem,' Messner said.

'Now? Are you being serious?'

'Yes. Completely serious.'

The woman went quiet for a short while. Jule looked at Messner in disbelief. Who the hell was he calling?

'Did you hear about Wolle Seifert?' the woman asked.

'No. What about him?'

'He hung himself. In his room above the pub.'

The ground opened up beneath Jule. The events from the night before came rushing back to her, like images in a time lapse: Jesse getting into the car, clearly agitated, saying they should get a move on; his vague remarks and how he said that Wolle couldn't tell him anything. Did Jesse have Wolle's blood on his hands too? Had she spent all this time in the company of a serial killer? Her hands were shaking uncontrollably. She swiftly folded her arms to retain at least an ounce of her composure.

'Shit,' Messner mumbled.

'I thought you knew,' said the woman on the other end of the line.

'This is all getting way out of hand.'

'All right. I'll come over,' the woman snapped irritably.

Jule looked at Messner, baffled. Instead of dialling again, he put his hand back on the steering wheel.

'Who was that?'

'Somebody who's coming to help,' Messner said.

'Why don't you call the police?'

'There's still time.' Messner stared vacantly through the windscreen, his lips still moving.

'But—'

'Leave it to me. Adlershof is my responsibility, not yours. Don't worry.'

'But I *am* worried,' Jule replied. 'If you'd seen the blood in the gatehouse, then you'd understand. It looks like . . . an abattoir.'

Richard's hands clenched the steering wheel. His larynx twitched over the starched shirt collar with the embroidered edelweiss blossoms on it. Even though his hair had gone grey, he suddenly looked like the young boy Jule had seen in the photo in Artur Messner's room. 'Believe me, I know what he's capable of,' Messner said quietly. The greasy tone had completely vanished from his voice. 'I've known him for longer than you.'

Messner parked the car at the back of the house, near the entrance to the kitchen. Before Jule could say anything else, he leaped out of the car and opened the boot. Icy air whipped at the nape of her neck. She got out of the car and watched Messner pull a shotgun out of an olive-green case. He quickly inspected it, his fingers trembling, and then he put it back in the cover but kept the zip undone so he could keep his hand on the trigger. 'Come with me.'

Jule shook her head. 'I don't know what you're planning to do, but you should be letting the police handle this.'

'It wasn't a request.'

Chapter 48

The steps creaked under Jesse's footsteps as he made his way up to the top of the gatehouse. He couldn't help but think of Wolle hanging from the roof beam. He could taste iron on his tongue. The stench of the blood from the ground floor filled the air. There was another body around here somewhere. And his fear of finding it was as strong as his need to. On his Doctors Without Borders missions, he often saw people pacing along the rows of dead bodies looking for their fathers, mothers or children. Bodies suddenly became beacons of hope: a sign that the one person you were looking for was still alive.

The stairs led through a kind of open hatch to a small landing with two doors. He opened the one on the right and stepped into an attic with a sloping roof. He gasped despite the comfortable warmth.

Five beds were arranged in a row under a sloping roof with two dormer windows. The floorboards had been freshly varnished with oxblood and the walls were covered with stripy green, white and brown wallpaper. The room was a carbon copy of his old dormitory in the main building. Even the bed linen was the same. Everything just seemed slightly smaller than before.

Who in their right mind had put this room together? And why? When he thought about it, this room could only really mean something to five men. He didn't count himself, which just left Markus, Alois, Richard, Mattheo and Wolle. And, of course, anyone else who stayed in the room after them. But they had nothing to do with this.

He took a quick glimpse into the next room. It was empty.

'Jule!' he yelled down the stairs.

No response.

He was about to go down the stairs and look for her when his phone rang. The name on the screen struck him like a lightning bolt. *Isabelle.*

He accepted the call and pressed his phone to his ear. 'Isa, sweetheart! Where are you? Are you OK?'

The other end of the line was completely silent. Jesse's stomach tied up in knots.

'Do you want to see her?' a man's voice asked.

'Who are you? What have you done with her?'

'Nothing you wouldn't have done too.'

'What . . . what's that supposed to mean?'

'I've stolen her, just like you always stole everything.'

'Who the hell are you?'

'And now you're alone. How does that feel?'

'I want to speak to my daughter right now!'

'Just like I was alone.'

'I want to speak to my daughter!'

'Of course you do.'

Jesse stopped talking. The conversation had taken a strange turn, like he was talking to somebody who never intended to answer any of his questions. Somebody who was talking to himself more than anyone else.

'Are you ready?' the man asked.

'For what?'

'I still can't believe you haven't got a clue.'

'What have you done with Isa?'

'It's impossible to forget as much as you have.'

'If you've so much as touched a hair on her head, I'll kill you.'

'Come on, then.'

'Pass the phone to her, I want to speak to her. I'm not going anywhere until I've heard her voice.'

'You'll come anyway. You'd do anything for her.'

Jesse felt dizzy with rage and fear. 'Tell me where I have to go.'

'Over the border. To Austria, near the Zugspitze. Ehrwald. The house by Lake Seeben.' The line went quiet for a moment. 'The weather's getting worse. You should get a move on. Oh, and make sure you're alone. Otherwise you'll never see her again.'

Then the line went dead.

The address reverberated in Jesse's head, like somebody had shouted it to him from down a dark well shaft. And that definitely wasn't Markus's voice on the other end of the line.

Chapter 49

'All right,' Dante grumbled. He glanced into the darkness again, like he was making sure there were no unwanted spectators around. 'Wait here.'

He closed the door in the man's face and went away to fetch Artur Messner.

Jesse was huddled in his hiding place right next to the steps. His heart was pounding.

Standing less than three metres away was the man who was responsible for all his misfortune. The one to blame for his mother's death, for tearing his family apart, and for his father's miserable demise. He had this man to thank for everything he was, maybe even for everything he wasn't. He had almost killed him in a hundred different ways in a hundred different dreams, but he had always woken up to the disappointment of knowing he was still too young and he would have to put it off. He never knew how to find him anyway.

And now here he was: Uncle Wilbert, in the flesh.

The door opened. Artur Messner spoke like someone who had been rudely awoken and had found himself faced with something extremely unpleasant. 'What are you doing here?'

'Why the hell didn't you call me?' Wilbert Berg asked.

'Why the hell should I have called? We haven't spoken for almost ten years,' Messner barked.

'Because he's dead, for God's sake!'

'Who's dead?'

It was quiet for a moment. A little owl shrieked. A light gust of wind blew into the nearby trees, rustling the leaves.

'You haven't heard?'

'What on earth are you talking about?' Messner sounded wide awake now. His voice was impatient, perhaps even a touch anxious.

'My brother Herman is dead.'

Jesse went numb. All the strength drained from his limbs, like there was suddenly no blood left in his veins. Now Father too!

He'd always known that his father wouldn't live for long. Looking back, it almost seemed like he had been determined to die. An image flashed into his head: his father's haggard face as he lay there in an open casket in his gleaming white uniform. He stood by the coffin with a huge lump in his throat. Then his father suddenly opened his eyes and asked him what he was looking for and where the hell his brother was.

'Bloody hell,' Messner mumbled. 'When did it happen?'

'You didn't know?'

'No.'

Wilbert Berg took a deep breath. Tried to compose himself. 'Can I come in?'

'No.'

Jesse heard footsteps scraping the stone, followed by the noise of a lock clicking. It sounded like the principal had stepped outside and pulled the door shut behind him.

'Why did you come here?' Messner said, his voice reduced to a whisper.

'I wanted to make sure we won't have any problems.'

'Why? Because Herman's dead? He's got himself to blame for that. Or was he—?'

'No, no. Heart attack.'

'OK.'

'But what about the boy?'

Jesse flinched.

'Why would that cause us any problems?'

'Maybe Herman has some paperwork somewhere.'

They stopped talking for a moment.

'It'd surprise me if he has anything of any worth in that pigsty.' Messner shook his head while he thought about what Wilbert had said. Still, the slight hint of worry in his voice didn't escape Jesse.

'But what if he does?'

'How would that change anything? Our records are clean. That should be enough.'

'What about social services?'

Artur Messner sighed. 'Wilbert, please. I know you're upset. Your brother's dead, it's understanda—'

'I couldn't care less about Herman,' Wilbert snapped. 'Herman was a pig . . .'

You're the pig here, Jesse thought to himself. He clenched his fists tight and dug his fingernails into his palms. He fought back the urge to pounce on his uncle. He didn't have a chance in hell against this giant of a man – not right here, not right now.

'Wilbert, the records are safe. Wisselsmeier moved them into the archives ages ago. They'll just sit there gathering mould for all eternity.' Artur Messner lowered his voice to a whisper. 'And even if anyone were to go rummaging around, don't you think it'd take them for ever to notice that something's amiss?'

'Are you certain?'

Messner sighed again. 'If you really must know—'

'Yes, I must.'

'—the biggest element of uncertainty in all this is you, showing up here like this in the middle of the night—'

'We've all got a lot to lose. Especially the boy.'

'The boy's fine, there's no need to worry about him,' Messner said firmly.

Jesse's eyes flickered in the darkness. He hated it when people claimed to know how things were for him. Especially if Artur Messner was the one doing the talking. He had no idea what these two were babbling about – only that it was clearly something fishy – but whatever it was, he was deeply troubled by the fact that it also concerned him.

'I could drive over to Herman's and have a look in the flat,' Wilbert suggested.

'Don't you dare!' Messner snapped. 'Just get in your car and go back to where you came from. Then everything can stay as it was.'

Wilbert gave a reluctant sigh. Then there was a rustling sound, like he was scratching himself. 'Will you call me if you hear anything?'

'I've thrown your number away.'

Silence.

'Old friends, eh?'

'Former friends,' Messner said.

Wilbert turned on his heel, took the two steps in a single bound, and got into his car without saying another word. Jesse didn't dare to lean forward. The headlights were about to go on any second. He heard the engine splutter as Wilbert fired the car up – it sounded cheap and old – then the tyres crunched under the strain as the car quickly turned around. The beam of light he'd been expecting never went on. The oak door opened above him, then Messner disappeared into the building and locked the door from the inside.

Jesse quickly leaned forward to get one last look at the car. Perhaps he could see the number plate. But all he could see was a dark box on wheels jolting its way over towards the gatehouse before disappearing downhill into the night.

Jesse stayed still, glued to the spot. With the hole in his chest now bigger than ever, and the feeling that his soul had been torn into pieces, he didn't know which way to go.

Chapter 50

Wednesday, 9 January 2013

Still no signs of life from Isabelle.

It didn't take Artur long to make his decision. He just had to be sure when he heard the snow rushing down from the roof. He quickly set about removing one of the boards again. He pulled the screw on the left-hand side out of the wood with his bare hands. Something pricked his finger, but he didn't care. Just like he didn't care that the open window might give him away and ruin her clumsy attempt at an escape. He would take all the blame. Or at least he hoped he'd find the courage to take the blame when the time came.

The right screw took some of the board with it when he yanked it out. The wood crunched and splintered. Artur called out Isabelle's name in a low voice and peered through the opening. A gust of wind blew between the boards and into the room. Snowflakes flew towards him like cold needles. 'Isabelle? Are you there?'

Another gust of wind whistled into the building.

'Isabelle!' Artur cried out into the wind again. He felt like a coward for not yelling at the top of his voice. It was almost like he was hoping that things might not turn out too badly if he could just keep quiet enough. He called out again, this time as loud as he could. '*Isa!*' He felt a scraping in his throat as he yelled, making him cough until his eyes welled up with tears.

Still nothing.

Maybe she'd managed to escape after all? Or was there a chance she could be lying there under the snow, suffocating to death?

He had to do something! He knelt down on the floor, grabbed the bucket and started banging on the floorboards. He didn't stop, even though the vibrations set his teeth on edge. The noise filled every last corner of the attic. He must be able to hear this! Even if he was on a completely different floor or outside the building. So then why wasn't he coming?

Suddenly the hatch flew open. Small particles of dust flew into the air. Artur let go of the bucket and instinctively held his breath. Isabelle's shock of blond hair appeared. Her eyes were red. Clumps of snow had got lodged in her hair. She was still wearing Artur's coat, which was also dusted with snow. She stumbled over the last step and fell onto her knees. Thank God, she was alive!

But the relief instantly gave way to fear. There *he* was, coming through the hatch behind her. It looked like he had thrown the black gas mask on in a hurry as it wasn't sitting right. As frightening as it was, the benefit of the mask was that Artur didn't have to look right at his face. It was somehow easier to imagine him as the 'insect man' or 'the man'. Someone without a face. Someone he wished he'd never met.

'Over there,' the man said.

Isabelle listened intently, not saying a word. The look in her eyes pulled on Artur's heartstrings. 'It's not her fault,' he croaked. 'It was all my idea. I made her go out there.'

'Over there, with your back to the post,' the man ordered Artur. 'You too.'

Isabelle stood against the post.' As Artur got up with slow, strenuous movements, his eyes fell on the board he had taken off the window. The screw was sticking out of the wood. The man wrapped a rope around the post and Isabelle's neck, then he yanked it tight. Isabelle lurched forward in shock and sounded like she was choking. Her mouth opened wide and her eyes bulged out. The man tied two knots at high speed. Artur stared speechless at the rope digging into Isabelle's neck.

'That's what happens when you try to run away,' the man hissed.

Isabelle struggled and tugged at the rope in panic. Her heels banged on the floor as she kicked out and tried to break free. Artur reached for the board and grabbed hold of the end with both his hands. The brass screw gleamed at the other end like a poisoned spike.

Isabelle's desperate groans filled the room.

Artur lunged at the precise moment that the man turned to him. His insect eyes were glistening. Artur could see his own reflection in them as he lifted the board with the screw over the man's head in slow motion. The man looked up and raised his arm, and the poisonous spike scraped the glass on the mask. There was a faint thud as the board banged against the mask on the man's head.

As if nothing had happened, the man flipped the board out of Artur's hand with one swift movement of his arm. The mask stared at him, cold and devoid of emotion. Artur saw the blow coming and raised his hands to defend himself. But the board hit his leg, and the screw pierced his thigh. Artur screamed and fell. The pain in his leg was so sharp that everything went black for a moment.

The frantic stamping of Isabelle's heels on the floor brought him to his senses. 'You monster,' he rasped.

'Look who's talking,' the man said.

Isabelle's face was purple now.

'You want to save her?' the man asked. 'Go on, see if you can.'

Artur gritted his teeth and crawled over to the pole. Isabelle gasped for air. Her lips were trembling. Artur started to grope at the knot, his hands sore from loosening the screws. He could no longer feel his leg; he was just listening intently to the desperate sounds coming out of Isabelle's mouth. The waving of her arms had subsided and now her legs were jerking. The knot was so ridiculously tight . . . he grabbed hold of the loop and tugged at it, and the knot and the rope instantly loosened. Isabelle's breath rattled as she filled her lungs with air. Artur's eyes welled up with tears of relief. He quickly looked around for the man and noticed him pocketing a knife he had been holding in his hand.

Artur wheezed as he leaned against the pole.

The man moved closer, took another rope and started to tie them to the post together, sitting back to back. Isabelle was breathing uneasily. Artur couldn't see her, but he could tell that she was crying.

The insect man's eyes glinted behind the circles of glass. He was standing in front of Artur, holding the bucket in his right hand and letting it swing ever so slightly on the handle. Artur could feel the fear in his innards. The pain in his leg came back with a vengeance. Artur tried to take solace in the fact that couldn't see the axe anywhere. But what on earth was he doing with the knife? And why had he put it back in his pocket? 'It's not her fault, it really isn't,' Artur murmured.

'Which makes you all the more to blame,' the man responded, whacking Artur on the head with the empty tin bucket. Artur's head was splitting. Isabelle's scream sounded muffled. The impact from the bucket deafened him and paralysed his whole left side. He could see stars spinning in the light in front of his eyes, floating like snowflakes. The world slipped away for a couple of seconds, then he saw the bucket in the man's hand, swinging back and forth on the handle. Like looking though a magnifying glass.

'I always dreamed of doing that.'

I know, Artur thought to himself, *and that's why I was always afraid of you*. He could feel his face swelling up.

'Do you know why I'm not going to cut your hands off right now and leave you here to bleed to death?'

Artur couldn't even manage to shake his head.

'Even though you deserve it. Thieves have always had their hands cut off, I know that from my dad.'

The thought turned Artur's stomach.

'You can thank her. The girl. I have to take care of her first. Her and her father.'

Take care of her father? And her? Artur stared at him. Suddenly a truly horrifying suspicion came over him. Of course! That's why he was holding the knife in his hand before. He was going to cut Isabelle free before she suffocated. Because he had other plans for her. Something that was going to be much worse than all of this. 'No,' he groaned. 'No, please don't.'

'Everything will be just right when I get back.'

He turned around, emotionless, and went down the stairs. The hatch slammed shut behind him like a guillotine. The dull silence lingered for a while. Isabelle's soft, intermittent sobs were the only sounds to be heard.

'Artur?' she finally asked. 'What is he planning to do to me?'

Artur knew there was no turning back now. This was his final judgement. The moment of truth. His chance for redemption from a God he definitely didn't believe in but now suddenly hoped was real. He was grateful that he didn't have to look Isabelle in the eyes now. 'Isa . . . Can I call you Isa?'

Isabelle sniffed. 'Yep.' She had no idea what was coming. Or why it was coming. Or where it was coming from.

'I have to tell you something,' Artur began, 'it's about your father and your grandfather. And a man called Sebi Kochl, an old friend of mine from school. You might not believe what I'm going to tell you. I can still hardly believe it myself. It all started with Sebi Kochl and his wife. I helped them to adopt a child. His name was Raphael.'

Chapter 51

Jule sat in Artur's wingchair, stunned. She fumbled with a small hole in the scuffed material on the armrest, hoping that it would make her feel calmer somehow. Her whole body and mind had been thrown into turmoil.

Not long ago, Richard Messner had led her up the staircase, holding the gun loosely in his hand with the barrel pointing at her back. There were dishes clattering in the dining hall. Presumably everyone was eating. She knew it was probably going to be her best chance to run away. Messner was hardly likely to risk shooting her so close to so many witnesses.

'Don't even think about it,' Messner muttered. 'Nobody's on your side here. If there's any doubt, I'll just knock you down and say that you and Jesse are in cahoots.'

'What do you want from me?'

'I want you to not cause me any trouble.'

Richard Messner led her upstairs, then through the long corridor in the west wing and finally up the steep steps. She was way out of earshot up here. Messner locked her in Artur's room and walked away. She sank into the chair. It was still snowing outside. She considered opening the window to call for help, but she guessed it wouldn't take long for Messner to hear her and come rushing back to the door. What was he planning? Was he going to take matters into his own hands with Jesse? Why wasn't he calling the police? And why the hell had he locked her in here?

Her thoughts went around in circles for a while. Then she remembered the man who had bolted out of Artur's room and knocked Jesse down not that long ago.

Was it Markus? Or Messner? But why would Messner want to rummage through his father's room? And, most importantly, why had he been rifling through the fridge?

She looked at the off-white door with the square handle and the Siemens logo. She stood up, deep in thought. She opened the fridge.

There was nothing of any importance in there, was there?

She opened the door to the freezer compartment. It was empty. A layer of ice had formed on the top, the sides and the base of the freezer, making it considerably narrower inside. Her fingers stuck to the cold surface momentarily as she touched the smooth sheet of ice. How thick was it? Thick enough for someone to hide something under it?

She opened the kitchen drawer and looked for a sturdy bread knife. Then she started to pick at the ice. About five minutes later, a large section broke away from the white sheet of ice over the base. A faded light-green folder shimmered through a sheet of plastic film on the bottom of the freezer compartment. Jule's heart was beating faster. She started frantically chiselling the ice away from the bottom of the freezer. Frosty white particles spattered in her face, until finally she got to the folder and pulled it out of the compartment. It was the kind they used in old filing cabinets. She slashed it open, but the sides were stiff and stuck together. She rushed over to the bedside lamp and held the thin folder under the light bulb. The sheets of paper soon came unstuck in the warmth.

The folder contained a handwritten letter from Renate Kochl to Artur Messner, along with two thin files. The first page of the older file had a photo attached to it: two adults and a boy of roughly three years of age. It was a loveless snapshot, and the boy clearly didn't want to be photographed. He was pale with dark eyes. He looked exhausted and overwhelmed.

Chapter 52

1981, Garmisch-Partenkirchen

Everything from the night before was still eating away at Jesse. Sandra, his father's death and the fact that his uncle was alive. And then this secret, this shady story that had something to do with him . . . He couldn't think about anything else all day.

Mountainous clouds pushed eastwards through the night sky. No moon. No stars. The dynamo whined as the bike raced through the rustling trees in the wind. Jesse had 'borrowed' Richard's Hercules bike and now he was steering it downhill over the winding roads. He thought about what it must look like from above: if God was watching, he must be able to see the tiny fleck of light from the bike wobbling down the dark hillside like a lost firefly.

It was two in the morning and he didn't meet a single car on the way there. The dim street lighting shone by the sign at the entrance to Garmisch-Partenkirchen. Pale yellow. The world seemed to fade away to nothing just above the street lamps.

Jesse stopped and tilted the dynamo away from the tyre. There was light here anyway, and he definitely didn't want to be noticed.

When he got back on the bike, his thoughts turned to Sandra. Her tears, her disappointment and that deeply hurt look on her face. He held on to the handlebars so tightly that it made his knuckles turn white. He put his feet on the pedals and started moving. The shame still had a hold on him. But it turned him on to think of her crawling away from him, her butt cheeks like two halves of a moon in the torchlight, then the sight of her vagina and the soft fluff between her thighs.

Why did he always have to feel ashamed? She was the one who gave him hope! Sandra had led him on and lured him into a trap, just so she could complain about it afterwards. He pedalled faster, trying to get away from himself. The buildings whizzed by as he cycled past. Some were illuminated by the light from a street lamp. Light, shadow, light, shadow.

Olympiastrasse. Where was that again?

He told himself to keep an eye out for the street sign. It felt good to distract himself with something as simple and straightforward as looking for a street name.

Olympiastrasse was just where he thought it would be. He leaned the bike against a fence just around the corner and locked it. Richard's combination lock was a joke, but luckily most people didn't know how easy it was to pick them. All you had to do was pull tightly on both sides and turn the number rings with your thumb and index finger. Then you could feel them clicking into place under the pressure.

The building at number 10 was home to the district administrative office and the child welfare department. It was a detached building comprising three floors. Jesse thought it looked like a train station. A gaudy train station with fancy white corner pillars. The darkness washed out all the colours, yet the light-yellow façade, the sash windows and the lime-green shutters still seemed strangely inappropriate for somewhere as serious as an administrative office.

Maybe the people in charge of it wanted to seem harmless, hide their power. At least the imposing double oak doors at the entrance seemed like they were supposed to make a serious impression.

But Jesse wasn't planning to get into the building through the door.

He chose a window in the shade of a huge lime tree at the back, then he reached into his rucksack, pulled out a roll of sticky tape he'd pilfered from Dante, and covered the glass with overlapping strips of tape.

Then he smashed the window in.

He'd never broken in anywhere before, but he found it strangely easy to do. Quite a logical process, really. It felt like he was born to cross all the red lines drawn by these hypocrites.

It was just as he'd expected: there was a noise and the shards of glass crunched a little, but they stuck to the strips of tape instead of falling inside and making a huge racket.

He looked around. But just to be on the safe side, and not because he had a guilty conscience. He had every right in the world to be here. This was about him, not about some stupid office and a cheap broken window. Somebody would pay for the window. But who was paying for his broken life?

The nearby buildings remained quiet and dark. He carefully removed the sticky tape with the shards of glass attached to it and unlatched the window through the jagged hole, then he climbed into the room and pulled the curtains shut.

He shone his torch around the office. It was spotlessly clean. As well as the panorama of the Zugspitze hanging on the wall, there was a photographic calendar, two neatly arranged potted plants, a desk and, behind it, a filing cabinet. The gold frame on the table held a picture of a mature woman with glasses and a perm. Whoever worked here, it certainly wasn't Ms Wisselsmeier.

All that was inconsequential anyway. The thing he was looking for was in the archives – that was definitely what Artur Messner said. Wisselsmeier had put it there. 'We've all got a lot to lose, especially the boy.' Jesse couldn't get those words out of his head. What on earth had Messner, Wisselsmeier and his uncle done?

He rushed towards the door of the room, but it was locked.

Jesse reached into his rucksack. Along with the sticky tape and a lighter, he had packed a rusty old chisel, a firmer chisel and two screwdrivers – all tools that had been sitting unused for years in a plastic crate in the cellar under the kitchen. He chose the firmer chisel and pressed the cutting edge into the door frame. The wood creaked as he tried to lever out the metal fitting on the lock. Jesse started sweating. He now regretted leaving the hammer in the crate – he could have easily used it to push the chisel further into the wood. He cursed under his breath, battered the door frame, then banged on the chisel handle with his fists until the wood around the lock looked like a worn-out chopping block. Then he inserted the other chisel. The wood burst and the door sprang open.

The corridor in front of him was dark, like a cave.

He shone his torch around, looking for the perspex signs next to the white frame and panel doors. Central Affairs, Mr Weigand. Health Promotion, Ms Nesselwein. District Child Welfare Office, Ms Wisselsmeier, *and so on. No archives.*

He decided to try the cellar. The stairs were openly accessible, as if nobody needed protecting against an unwanted visit in this part of the building. His pulse sped up with every step he took. There were other doors leading left and right from the basement corridor, all galvanised and smooth. The metal reflected the torch like a pale, cold sun. The sign on the third door from the left read: Room 1.09, Archives. *Jesse pushed the door handle, but the room was locked. So he broke that door too.*

He frantically scanned the shelves until he found the one with the letters 'Be' on it, then he located the folder with the name Berg. His file.

He suddenly found himself hesitating. He felt that he had somehow taken a wrong turn and shouldn't really be here. There was no draught in the cellar, just a load of dusty files and a slightly damp smell that lingered in the air. Still, he got goose pimples and felt his pores tightening as if a cold waft of air was brushing against his skin. Was he just imagining it?

He stared at the file. Whatever it was that might put him in danger and whatever it was they'd done to him, this file was the key. If he didn't look at it now, the hole in his chest would just keep getting bigger, until it eventually consumed him.

He opened the file.

Rubbed his eyes.

He had to read it several times before he understood everything. And until he really believed it.

When the penny finally dropped, an incandescent rage came over him and tears began to fall from his eyes. No, damn it! He hadn't taken a wrong turn. He had been betrayed. They'd sent him down the wrong damn path.

Heaven on the right, hell on the left.

They had sent him to the left.

He wiped his tears away and stuffed the file into his rucksack, then pulled the zip closed with an angry flick of the wrist and turned around to leave. He paused in the doorway and glanced at all the files again. Then he slowly let the rucksack glide off his shoulder, opened it again, and rummaged around until his fingers located the lighter. He'd only taken it with him because he'd been worried that the batteries in the torch might die. His hand was trembling furiously as the sparks ignited the gas. He went back into the room and held the small flame at the edge of the bottom row of files. The paper caught fire instantly, and the flames quickly soared higher. Nobody was going to determine his happiness or unhappiness down in this cellar ever again.

He swiftly turned to make his getaway.

He pedalled even more furiously on the way back than he had done on the way there. He had managed to make it the first fifty metres up the steep hill towards Adlershof when he heard sirens in the distance. He stood still and looked into the valley, breathless. The glow of the fire in the heart of Garmisch was immense. It looked like the whole office was burning. Blue lights were flashing in front of the blaze. The Bible popped into his head. The wrath of God. That was how it felt inside him.

Hadn't Jesus also crossed the line? He was a rebel, a rabble-rouser. But Jesus made a mistake. Jesus only thought about other people. Not about himself.

He wasn't going to make the same mistake.

He was going to take what was rightfully his.

Chapter 53

Garmisch-Partenkirchen – Wednesday, 9 January 2013,
12.59 p.m.

Jesse stood at the top of the stairs looking down blankly, as if he had been momentarily paralysed.

Ehrwald. Lake Seeben.

Why did that sound so familiar to him?

He snapped out of it and made his way down the stairs. 'Jule?'

No reply. He reached into his trouser pocket for the Volvo key and remembered that Jule was the last one to drive. She had the key.

He rushed into the living room. 'Jule?' She wasn't there either. There was nothing in the room except for the table and the bloodstains. He went through to the kitchen, noticed that the back door was ajar, and dashed outside. The parking space under the carport was black and deserted. He saw the wall of snow and the hole inside. As he moved closer and leaned over, he found two dead eyes staring back at him through a thin, fuzzy covering of fresh snow. Jesse shrank back and gasped. It wasn't until he took another look that he realised it was Markus buried under the snow.

Suddenly everything seemed to fall to pieces. Nothing made sense any more. He felt dizzy and held on to the handle of the dark-grey bin by the back exit for support. The voice on the phone had been the first clue that Markus *wasn't* the one behind all this. Now the fact that Markus was dead was all the proof he needed.

So who was it, then? And who had dug the hole into the snow and found Markus lying there? Probably Jule. And when he looked at it through her eyes, nobody had a stronger motive to kill Markus than he did. Jesse looked out into the snowstorm. That was when he noticed the tracks in the deep snow. Small and fresh. A woman's footprints. They started at the carport by the gatehouse and led to the road.

He was sure that Jule must be trying to run away from him. But did that matter now? He had to get to Isa. That was the only thing that mattered. What he needed now more than anything else was a car. He stomped through the snow with grim resolve, following Jule's tracks until the footprints disappeared between fresh overlapping tyre tracks on the road to the main building.

Jesse lifted his head and looked up to the ashen sky. It hung low and was propelling white snowflakes into his eyes. He wasn't wearing a coat or gloves. He was freezing cold, but he barely noticed. He was going to need a four-wheel drive, preferably one with snow chains. Something like Richard's Toyota would be ideal.

He could barely see the main building in the dense snowfall. But there was one dark spot standing out against the wall of white, something with similar contours to those of Richard's Land Cruiser. As he moved closer, he realised the car was actually an old Land Rover Defender. The bonnet was still warm and turned the snow to slush as it landed.

Jesse pulled at the driver's door. Surprisingly it opened. He leaned forward, glanced under the steering wheel and tore off the flimsy trim. He was familiar with the Defender. This old model was one of the vehicles of choice in Africa and South America. It was a favourite for their Doctors Without Borders missions. The simple, purposeful design was always a major advantage when the next garage was a hundred kilometres away. He'd seen workers at the camp hot-wiring the Land Rover on multiple occasions. But the trim under the steering column was more stubborn than he'd expected. His freezing cold fingers stung when the plastic cut into his skin.

Suddenly someone yanked the passenger door open. 'Hey, what are you doing?'

Jesse was startled and banged his head on the steering wheel. A small man with a ski hat pulled right down over his forehead was staring at him with anxious grey eyes. His face was flushed, and his cheeks were as meticulously shaven as Richard's. 'This is my Land Rover. If you don't get out right now, I'll call the police.

Had Jesse been in a different frame of mind, he would have smiled when he realised who was standing in front of him. Mattheo was always making empty threats when they were kids too.

'It'll take them a fair while to get here, Mattheo.'

Mattheo stared at him with equal parts bewilderment and shock. His grey eyes scanned his adversary as he racked his brain trying to remember why he recognised him. 'Jesse?'

'If you give me the key I won't have to hot-wire it.'

'I . . . erm . . . are you crazy? What's this all about?'

Jesse leaped onto the driver's seat, grabbed Mattheo by his collar and pulled him towards him. 'Give me the key. I don't have time to chat about it.'

Mattheo's eyes glinted, but still he didn't give an inch. Jesse pulled him into the Defender by his scarf. Mattheo went to slap him with the palm of his hand. He was just the same when he was a kid – he never understood that you're supposed to use your fists to fight. Jesse had no problem understanding the basic rules of fighting. His blow to Mattheo's temple was a reflex. A powerful, albeit imprecise punch from the left. Mattheo's muscles went weak, then Jesse pulled him right onto the seat and wound the scarf around the headrest so that his torso was tied to the seat. The wound in Jesse's waist burned as he leaned over to search Mattheo's trouser pockets. He found the key in his right pocket, then he leaned over further and pulled the passenger door shut.

The engine whined as it fired up. Jesse put his foot on the accelerator in neutral, forcing a single bellowing sound from the Land Rover, then he turned the windscreen wipers on and cranked the heating right up.

The chains gripped the ground and the old Land Rover jolted over the mounds of snow on the road. The main building disappeared behind a wall of white in the rear mirror.

'What the hell, Jesse! Have you lost the plot?' groaned a dazed Mattheo.

'Shut your mouth,' Jesse barked.

Mattheo went quiet, with that same old hurt expression he always used to pull when they were kids. Back then it might have been accompanied by tears too.

A gust of wind whipped against the car like a slap in the face. Mattheo quickly located his seat belt and fastened it. They were just passing the gate. Black angel wings in a white no man's land. Jesse thought about Isa. 'Do you have a phone?' he asked Mattheo.

'Yes.'

'Don't even think about calling the police or anyone else, OK?'

Mattheo nodded nervously.

'Somebody's kidnapped my daughter. I have to find her.' Jesse took a quick sideways glimpse at Mattheo. He was staring back at him, clearly distressed. Jesse hadn't intended to explain himself; the words had just spouted out of him like steam from a kettle under excess pressure. Mattheo still said nothing. Jesse wished he could see whether he believed him or thought he was crazy, but the winding roads were commanding his full attention.

'Where?'

'What?'

'Where do you have to go to find her?' Mattheo asked.

'To Austria.'

Mattheo groaned. 'That's—'

'Don't even go there!' Jesse interrupted. 'Can you type "Lake Seeben" into your phone?'

'Is that a village?'

'No, a lake.' Jesse turned the wheel to full lock. The snow chains rattled in the wheel arch and the Defender crept around the tight bend.

'Jesse, if it's true about your daughter, you need to call the—'

'Just shut up and type it in.'

Mattheo did as he was told. His fingers automatically flitted across his smartphone. 'It's not far,' Mattheo said. 'Pretty close to the mountain, on the other side.

'Which way?'

'Past Grainau, towards the border. Then it's thirty-two kilometres from there.'

Deep in concentration, Jesse silently steered the Defender left towards the B23. Even the federal highway was covered in a blanket of snow. Every now and again single cars drove towards him through the blizzard. The visibility couldn't be more than about thirty metres. The Defender's yellow headlights were half as bright as the halogen lamps on the Volvo. The chains made their progress painfully slow, but at least they were keeping the Defender on the road.

'Mattheo?'

'Huh?'

'Do you remember how we used to go shooting with the crossbow?

'Yeah.'

'How many times did you come with us?'

'Why do you ask?'

'I just want to know.'

Mattheo went quiet for a while. 'Once,' he finally replied. And as if he had to justify himself, he added: 'You guys never let me come.'

'That's not what you told me before.'

'Really?'

'Yes.'

'Well, it was thirty years ago.'

'What's that supposed to mean?'

'Jesus! I mean I'm not twelve any more. Twelve was a shitty age.'

'And after that one time?'

'Nobody wanted to go again. Just one time, then bam, it was all over. You made a pretty good job of that,' Mattheo grumbled. 'A *really* good one.'

'Of what exactly? What did I make a good job of?'

'Do we really have to go over all that old ground?'

'Just tell me.'

'Well, you know, the thing that happened with Richard. When you fired the crossbow at him.'

'At *Richard*?'

Mattheo pressed his lips together.

'Didn't you say I—'

'Shit, yeah,' Mattheo sighed. 'Yeah, I know.'

'Why did you say I aimed at Markus?'

'I didn't. I really didn't.'

'Of course you did. I can remember what you said.'

'But that's not what I said.'

'Fine, but you let me believe that all the same,' Jesse growled.

Mattheo looked ahead through the windscreen. 'You have to stay on the B23. Just keep going straight.'

'Did Richard want you to do that?'

'Richard? Why?'

'Why?' Jesse scoffed. 'Because Richard always wanted something. And he always ended up getting what he wanted.'

'So?'

'He was embarrassed, wasn't he? Was that what it was about?'

'If you already know so much, why are you still asking?' Mattheo grumbled.

'And you played along with it as always.'

'I'd say if any of us wasn't allowed to play along, it was me.'

'Oh, for fuck's sake! Jesse bashed the steering wheel. He could see Markus's grey, lifeless face in the snow, his eyes dark like coal after a fire. Those eyes had haunted him for so many years. So much anger. And all for nothing. Jule was right after all. Markus probably had nothing to do with his accident. 'You've got no idea what you started there.'

Mattheo stayed quiet until they had crossed the border, which meant he probably did have some idea of what he started. He only regained the power of speech just before they got to Ehrwald, a small village under a thick cover of snow. 'He totally pissed his pants,' he confessed. 'We knew you'd forgotten everything after your accident. Richard wanted it to stay that way. He said if I gave you even the slightest hint of what happened that night, if I told you about how he blubbered and ... well, you know ... he said he'd play knife roulette with me until one got stuck in my hand.'

Jesse felt the anger bubbling up inside him. Suddenly he saw everything differently, like someone had drawn back a curtain. But although the curtain had finally been drawn, he still didn't understand what had happened back then.

'Turn left up ahead. Keep going along the Gaisbach.'

Jesse steered the car out of Ehrwald. There was just one set of tyre tracks on the road, which was now barely visible under the snow.

'He couldn't bear how you had put him in his place.' Mattheo continued. 'He could never deal with that. And that's why he always hated Markus too. The only difference was that Markus was smarter than you. He didn't go making an enemy of him,' Mattheo said.

The road along the river was getting narrower. It must have snowed less here, otherwise the road would be impassable by now. The higher they drove, the clearer the sky was. Snow was still falling, but the vast Zugspitze mountain was beginning to emerge from the mist on the driver's side.

'We're almost there,' Mattheo said, checking the map on his phone.

They arrived at a mountain saddle in the middle of a pine forest, then the road continued downhill. There amid the trees in front of them was a frozen lake, flat as an ironing board. Lake Seeben.

At the end of the road on the opposite side was an unusually large house that looked out onto the mountain.

Jesse stopped about three hundred metres away from the house and switched the engine off. 'Give me your coat and hat.'

'But they won't fit you,' Mattheo objected.

'Just give me them. And your scarf.'

Mattheo tugged at the knotted scarf and managed to free himself with Jesse's help. He reluctantly handed over his coat and scarf. The coat was too tight, and the sleeves were too short, but it was better than nothing. Jesse pulled out the key and got out of the vehicle.

'What about me? Am I supposed to just freeze here? You could at least leave me the key, then I can leave the engine running.'

'Too loud,' Jesse snapped.

'Shit. When are you coming back?'

'Surely you must have some blankets in the boot?'

Mattheo scowled at him. 'Is the thing you said about the kidnapping true?'

'What do you think? That I'm crazy or something?'

Mattheo refrained from answering, just to be on the safe side.

'Just be quiet, OK?' Jesse said sternly. His heart was pounding. Isa had to be here somewhere, and he didn't have the slightest urge to hang around explaining himself any longer. He gave the door a gentle shove. The air here was even colder than it was in Garmisch. He was glad he was wearing Mattheo's winter coat. He strayed from the road and stomped through the deep snow between the firs, steering clear of the icy lake. He would be far too visible if he stuck to the bare surface, and anyway, ice on top of water had always made him feel uneasy. He stopped in a thicket when he got within fifty metres of the house. There, between the ice crystals on the branches, he saw a wide wooden house. It was huge, not so much a hill farm as somewhere between a villa and a farmhouse. The outlines of the building looked strangely familiar, but he couldn't pinpoint where he'd seen one like it before.

He stood thinking about what his next move should be. Approach the house and break in? But it could all be a big trap, and someone might be there waiting for him. At least there was no light coming from any of the windows. He wondered if he would find any tools in the boot of the Defender, or maybe something he could use as a weapon. Just then, he heard the sound of footsteps crunching in the snow behind him. Mattheo mustn't have wanted to wait in the car. He never was very good at being alone. Irritated, he turned around – and froze to the spot.

Standing there, less than five metres away from him, was a man wearing a black gas mask and pointing a double-barrelled rifle in his direction. His head looked like that of a giant insect.

Jesse went weak at the knees. It was like a flashback to his nightmare. Now he realised the man was never an insect, but a man in a gas mask.

Jesse's gaze fell on the man's blue coat. It was his coat – the one that had been stolen from his locker at St Josef's hospital. He was wearing *his* boots too. A wooden handle was sticking out from behind the man's shoulder, maybe from an axe or something similar that the man had strapped to his back. Jesse remembered the indentations on the oak table.

'Do you recognise it?' The man pointed to the house behind Jesse with the barrel of the gun.

Jesse shook his head in confusion.

'I figured as much. Let's finish this, then.'

Chapter 54

1981, Ehrwald, Austria

The moon clung to the sky above the estate. The circle was incomplete, but sharply defined. A ragged cloud floated past and pushed eastwards.

It was a quarter past one. Time was running out. It was going to take him a full seventy minutes just to get back to Garmisch. Jesse stared at the dark windows. He wanted to wait a little longer yet, even though the house looked like it was in a deep slumber. The last light had only been out for half an hour. He wouldn't stand a chance unless they were fast asleep.

Lake Seeben was behind him. The wind was whipping up the ripples, making the surface resemble a shaggy rug. The southern flank of the Zugspitze towered up to three thousand metres behind him, marking the border between Germany and Austria.

Just another half-hour.

Now that the time had finally almost come, Jesse was struggling to keep his heart rate under control. The adrenalin spurred him on, kept him going. The past few weeks rushed to his head like a fever. He felt hot and cold as he went over everything again and again in his mind. Sometimes he thought about it all so much that he could no longer distinguish between his plans and reality. Lines were blurred, and it felt like everything had already happened. He felt the guilt set in on a couple of occasions. But then the anger returned with a vengeance and sent the guilt marching. The others had pushed him to this! Uncle Wilbert. His father. Artur Messner, Dante, Alois, Richard, Mattheo . . . Yes, even Sandra. Hadn't she kept building his hopes up, only to knock him back? To be totally honest, he didn't know where this ended. Even Markus had made his way into the line of people who had pushed him to this.

A week after what happened with Sandra, Markus had gone looking for him in the kitchen. Jesse hadn't been in the slightest bit wary of him; they were silent allies as they had something resembling a common enemy in Richard.

Markus planted himself in front of Jesse with that dangerous dark glint in his eyes. His black hair with its meticulous side parting sat on top of his angular skull like a helmet. 'Why did you do it?'

Jesse went pale. Markus's stance, his question and his secret passion for Sandra all boiled down to one thing: he knew about the night under the eaves.

That whole night felt like a dream to Jesse. The kind of dream you want to forget but can't. Because it was so terrible. Because it was so good. He stepped back until he felt the worktop in the small of his back. 'Did she tell you?'

'You're a giant arsehole, you know that?'

Jesse didn't contradict him. Why would he? He'd realised long ago that some people were better human beings than he was. And Markus wouldn't have understood him anyway. Nobody here was capable of understanding him.

The first blow struck him in the stomach. Jesse flopped over and gasped for air. Then Markus's fists pelted his body and head. Jesse let it happen, doubling over like he used to when father beat him. The blood in his mouth tasted of guilt. He swallowed it down. He no longer saw a reason to feel guilty. He was just the same as him.

He continued to take the blows. None of this mattered any more. He had made his decision. He knew how to escape from it all. He was going to take fate into his own hands.

Markus leaned over when he'd finished pummelling Jesse. 'The only reason I haven't told anyone is because of Sandra. But I swear, if you so much as lay a finger on her again, I'll tell the others and we'll nail you to the tree with two bolts from the crossbow, you fucking psycho.'

Markus stood up straight and towered over him like a giant. 'What was it you said to Richard? "You don't deserve her"?' Markus spat in his face. 'You're just like your dad. A sick piece of shit. You don't deserve her.'

Markus left the kitchen, and Jesse pulled himself up to the sink unit so that he could be sick. His whole body was trembling. He crept into his room, stuffed the file and a couple of other items into his rucksack and spent the next two weeks hiding under the eaves, hatching a plan. He only came out of hiding at night to steal food and batteries for the torch from the kitchen.

Messner made a huge, over-the-top fuss when Jesse reappeared. Where had he been, what was he thinking? They had turned the place upside down looking for him, they'd been worrying about him . . . and other such lies. He stayed stubbornly quiet, trying his best to grin and bear it all without jumping on Messner. When Messner grabbed Jesse and sent him into the hole, he stood there in the open doorway for a moment before turning to leave. The last look Jesse shot in Messner's direction was overflowing with his pent-up hatred. 'I'll kill you one day, old man,' he hissed. He knew it had hit home. The fear in Messner's eyes was undeniable. That was his glimmer of hope in the days he spent in the hole. Nothing else mattered to him. None of this bothered him any more.

When Jesse was allowed out of the hole, the incident was never mentioned. Clearly Mr M was a coward, just like his son. The others soon stopped gawping at him so much. Before long everything was back to normal. At least that's how it seemed from the outside.

Jesse looked at the watch he'd taken from Mattheo. Twenty to two.

He stood up. Stared at the front door. Pulled the key out. He'd had it for two weeks. The housekeeper, an overly trusting woman in her mid-fifties who wore thick-lensed glasses, had tripped over the leg he'd deliberately left sticking out. His opportunity came when he helped her up and picked her things up off the street.

Now he was standing in front of the door.

Key in the lock. Turn. Open.

The threshold was there in front of him. All he had to do was step over it. It had been easy enough in his head. But now he was hesitating. He looked at Mattheo's watch. A vision of Sandra came into his head. Then Richard, the boy who had it all. He thought about Wilbert, who had taken everything from him. And he stepped inside.

The house greeted him with silence.

It smelled of expensive furniture and freshly cut flowers. Pale evening light entered through the window and shimmered on the polished floor. The edges of the steps traced the outlines of a pale ladder reaching up into the darkness. He tiptoed up the stairs, imagining all of this was his. He had imagined the same thing the last two times he'd secretly been here. And each time it sent shivers down his spine.

The room was at the end of the landing at the top of the staircase. Time was running out, but still he pushed the handle as slowly as he could, just to make sure he wouldn't make a sound. He snuck past the door, closed it behind him and heard the sound of breathing in the room. Soft and even. Innocent, you might think.

This is madness, he thought to himself.

But he wasn't the one who'd started all this madness, was he? The madness had found him.

But then why did his footsteps feel so heavy?

He walked up to the bed. The lavish silk bedding shimmered in the moonlight, and the body beneath the sheets rose and fell rhythmically. A cloud floated past the moon and a shadow fell upon the boy sleeping peacefully in the bed. Jesse had got his hair cut three days earlier so that it would look like the boy's. 'I could be you,' he whispered coldly. 'If only he'd taken the right one.'

Jesse's breath was shallow as the air passed between his slightly parted lips.

A wolf in the undergrowth.

Eat or go hungry.

If he didn't take care of himself, then no one else would.

He reached into his rucksack and pulled out the gas mask he had found in the cellar. He felt better when he put it on.

Protected, anonymous.

Everything looked completely different through the glass. More distant. More controllable. He took the last step. Pulled the pillow out from under the sleeping boy's head. Took hold of it with both his hands and rammed it onto his face.

For a couple of drawn-out seconds, absolutely nothing happened. Then suddenly the boy's body started to stir. Languidly and sleepily to begin with, sort of confused. Jesse pressed down harder.

The body started writhing around under the pillow. Jesse quickly jumped onto the bed and straddled him. And not a second too soon, because now his whole body was rearing up in panic and his arms were waving about frantically. Stifled screams pushed through the pillow.

Jesse pressed down with resolute force.

The other boy was desperately bashing the thin air with his arms. Suddenly he felt a fist in his side. Jesse groaned and let go for a moment. The pillow fell to one side and the boy gasped as he eagerly filled his lungs with air. They lay beside each other for a split second.

Then Jesse socked him a punch to the right temple, immediately followed by another blow from the left. The boy's head wobbled back and forth once, then suddenly there was silence and the body beneath him went limp.

The boy was probably unconscious.

Jesse took a deep breath. He tried to slow his pulse down. Then he lifted the boy up and onto his shoulder, like he did with Dante's heavy sacks when he had to carry them down to the cellar. He managed to leave the room and close the door. Made it down the stairs. Opened the front door. He even managed to close it, although he got the distinct feeling that his legs could give way any second like a couple of matchsticks. If the other boy had been even slightly heavier, if he'd been just a touch taller than him, that would have ruined everything. But the other boy was just like him.

He staggered as he carried him towards the moped. The small trailer would just about suffice. Jesse removed the boy's pyjamas. Finely woven cotton that felt pleasing to the touch. He quickly folded the pyjamas and stuffed the bundle into his rucksack. Then he tied up the unconscious boy's naked body and adjusted his arms and legs so that nothing was sticking out of the trailer. He grabbed the sheet of tarpaulin with eyelets in it and lashed it down over the trailer bed.

A quick glance at his watch: five past two already.

He pulled the mask off and put the helmet on. It was old, and it didn't have a chin shield or a visor. He quickly hopped onto the silver Zündapp, the moped he'd stolen from Dante. The lumbering giant always looked like a pig on roller skates when he rode it to the shops. Jesse painstakingly pedalled the first few metres without starting the engine. The trailer felt like a box of lead now, but still he waited until he got to the next junction in the road to start the engine. The Zündapp rattled off through Ehrwald, over the 187 and along the River Loisach to the German border, then to Garmisch and up the hill to Adlershof. According to the speedometer the distance he covered was thirty-four kilometres. The reflection of the moon shimmered on the tank like a fickle companion as he rode along the stretch of road. He turned off into the woods in front of the main building at Adlershof and cycled along the narrow path until he reached the clearing. The soil was dry enough not to cause him any problems from the tyres not gripping.

He stopped at the edge of the clearing.

Swapped the helmet for the gas mask.

Untied the tarpaulin.

The naked boy was awake and staring at him in fear with his eyes wide open.

'Get out!' Jesse said.

'I can't,' the boy replied, pointing at his feet with his chin. Without saying a word, Jesse unfastened the ties around his feet and bound his legs together instead, so he could only take very small steps. Then *he stood back and watched as he struggled and stumbled his way out of the trailer with his hands tied. Jesse reached into his rucksack and pulled out the knife. 'That way,' he said.*

'What . . . what are you going to do with me?'

'Sir!'

'What?'

'You have to call me "sir"!'

The boy gulped. 'What are you going to do with me, sir?'

'Just shut up and move.'

Jesse shoved him and made him walk ahead. Leaves rustled on the ground. There was no path, just a short zigzag line through the trees. The dark outlines of Adlershof were somewhere behind him.

They walked right up to the pit Jesse had dug the day before. The boy stopped dead in his tracks. Jerked his arms helplessly.

'You want to kill me?'

'You've been dead to me for a long time.'

'What do you . . . what do you mean, sir?'

Jesse twirled the knife in his hand. He didn't know why he was doing it. Something was making him hesitate. Now he was wishing he'd followed through with the pillow.

'Please . . . let me go,' the boy whimpered.

'No,' Jesse said.

The boy gave another desperate jerk with his arms. His shoulders were hunched and shaking. He was probably crying, blubbering for his cosy little life. Suddenly the boy spun around, freed his hands and punched Jesse in the stomach. Jesse staggered backwards and dropped the knife. The boy picked it up. He looked at him like a cornered animal and hissed: 'Stay where you are.'

His hands trembled as he cut the rope around his feet.

Jesse knew this was the moment of truth. His last chance.

When the rope was fully severed, he pounced on the boy and they fell to the ground. Jesse snatched the knife right out of the boy's hand and rose up from the ground, triumphant. The boy turned away from him instinctively, but Jesse stabbed him in the back just below his heart, right by his spine. Jesse felt the warm blood on his hand. The boy groaned and contorted his face in agony. Jesse kicked him and pushed him into the pit. He flopped to the bottom and hit his head on the ground with a thud. It sounded like he had hit a stone.

He lay there motionless.

Jesse's heart skipped a beat. He was hyperventilating. He kept wiping his bloody hand on his trousers, but the blood stubbornly stuck to his fingers. He sat on the ground, trembling, and threw his head back. The trees above him were clouds of black leaves. A light went on in one of the windows at Adlershof. Whoever it was, they wouldn't be able to see all the way over here.

He had done it.

Jesse sat there for what seemed like an eternity. He looked at the moon, then at the light in the window. He looked at his watch. Almost half past three. Shit!

He jumped up and reached for the shovel, then he swiftly heaped the loose soil over the pale body. The grave wasn't particularly deep, but it would suffice. He didn't have any time left, and he couldn't tramp the ground down now.

He paused for a second when he'd finished and looked down at the grave. Here lies the body of Jesse, *he told himself, and took off the mask.*

From this day forward, Jesse was dead.

He was someone else now.

The ride back to Austria was like a journey to freedom. He rode without a helmet and felt the wind in his hair as the empty trailer shook over every bump in the road. This was the third time he'd cycled this route tonight. And it was definitely the best. He was getting away from Adlershof, away from the grave.

He had given a lot of thought to where he should bury him. Adlershof was the easiest place. All he had to do was climb out of the window, then he had all the time in the world to dig the grave. And nobody would go looking for him around the clearing. They all avoided the clearing like the plague after what had happened with Richard and the crossbow.

He made it to Ehrwald at a quarter to five. He stripped naked, tied his clothes up in his rucksack and put some stones in it to weigh it down. Then he dumped Dante's moped in Lake Seeben, along with the trailer and his rucksack.

Dante would miss the old heap of metal.

But who gave a shit?

He felt like he'd just been born. He was naked, and the brisk wind couldn't touch him. It had all been one sweet, feverish rush.

His father must have felt something like this when he screwed those whores senseless. He was only beginning to understand that now.

Finally he put on the boy's pyjamas, as if he was slipping into a new life.

He darted towards the villa, opened the door with trembling fingers, crept upstairs and disappeared into the bathroom for a while. He only started to doubt himself when he finally looked in the mirror after washing his face. In the space of a split second, he realised how crazy the whole thing was. How he was going to get found out. It was all going to go wrong. How stupid and short-sighted he'd been! He felt unsteady, and he held on to the side of the basin for support.

Still, he didn't regret it for a second. He just doubted whether it was all going to work out.

But it was too late to worry about that now. A burnt-down child welfare office, a stolen key, a bike submerged in a lake and a murder. Now it was time for him to play his starring role.

He crept into the bedroom at the end of the landing, rolled back the silky bed sheets and climbed into his twin brother's empty bed.

Man, was he happy that Jesse's grave was in Adlershof, far away across the border in a different country. In a different life. In his new life, he would call himself by his twin brother's name. From now on, he was Raphael.

From now on, he was his better self.

Chapter 55

He stared at the man in the gas mask. Not only was he wearing Jesse's stolen clothes, but his voice also reminded Jesse of his own. Stray snowflakes were scattered over the black part of the mask around his head, forming a pattern of pure, innocent white dots. His breath steamed out of the opening in front of the mouth like a hazy cloud.

'Who the hell are you?' Jesse asked.

'Do you remember Kiel?'

'Kiel?'

'Kiel – the city. We were three at the time. I know that's pretty young, but you always remember a tiny bit, don't you?'

Jesse looked at the man in confusion. 'That was when Dad suddenly appeared. Fresh off the boat in his gleaming white uniform. "The white ship of hope",' the man sneered. 'Apparently, that's what the Vietnamese called it. That's what Dad always told me when he talked about his glory days in Vietnam. But you'd already gone by then.'

'I have no idea what you're talking about.'

'Do you remember Mum? Mum and Wilbert. Or maybe how you fell into the ice? You were really young, probably about three years old.'

Jesse felt the need to hold on to something, but there was nothing to grab hold of. Just snow-covered firs and the barrel of a gun pointing at him.

'That was just before Dad came back. And do you know who pulled you out of the freezing cold lake back then? Wilbert. With that big paw of his with the scar on it. He should have just left you there to drown. But the son of a bitch was so damn taken with you.'

Jesse stared at the man in astonishment. The breaking ice, the crippling cold and the feeling that he was drowning. Then the hand with the scar pulling him out. That was *his* nightmare, and now this man was describing it. It was like he could see right into his head. Like he'd been there.

'Even that's gone? You forgot everything? Do you think you would have looked for me if not? Would you?'

Jesse shook his head in silence.

'You should have. You could have at least shown a tiny bit of interest, maybe that would have done some good. But you just lapped it all up and left me with nothing,' the man said bitterly. His right hand was on the trigger, and he was holding the butt end against his hip with his elbow.

'Who the hell are you?'

'Who am I?' The man pulled the gas mask off his head with his left hand. Short blond hair stood on end and fell back into place.

'I'm you,' he said. 'Raphael.'

Jesse couldn't believe his eyes. Standing there right in front of him was his exact mirror image. The same build, the same hair, the same face, even the same eyes. Only the look in the eyes was different. They poisoned his face.

'How can someone forget their twin brother? It's like having a piece of your body sawn off.'

Jesse didn't know what to say. He didn't even know what to call this mirror image standing in front of him. Ever since the accident, he'd asked himself countless times who he really was and where he came from. The others had told him about his father, but he knew nothing about his mother. He always tried to block out the questions. He had to block them out because there were no answers, only a couple of nasty stories. And now his twin brother was standing here in front of him?

How was that possible?

Why hadn't anyone said anything to him? Artur must have known about it at the very least. The taste of bile spread into his mouth. Was this the reason behind it all? Was this why Artur had disappeared, and the others had been killed? And, for the love of God, what was going on with Isa? 'Where is she?' Jesse asked. 'Where's Isa?'

'That doesn't matter any more.' Raphael's voice was calm. It sounded like he was used to giving orders. 'She's staying with me.'

'What's that supposed to mean?'

'She told you herself, didn't she? You've got to forget about her. That's your forte, isn't it?'

'You're insane.' Jesse's voice trembled. 'Why are you doing this? What do you want from me?'

'I want my life back. You took everything that was mine. Mum, Sandra, Isabelle . . . You didn't leave anything for me. No matter how much I tried, you were always number one. You were the hedgehog and I was the fucking hare.' Raphael's eyes were narrow and brimming with rage. 'You even waltzed out of mum's womb first. The place in the bed next to her, that was always yours. Like you had a fucking season ticket to first place.

Even when I screamed the loudest, you were the one she picked up. Wilbert told me about it. He deserved everything he got. And I bet he if it'd been me who'd fallen into the ice back then he wouldn't have been rushing to *my* rescue.'

Jesse took an involuntary step back. Snow was falling onto his neck from the branches behind him. 'I don't understand a word you're saying.'

'Because you've forgotten everything. Well, I suppose it's easier that way. Do you know what I'd give to forget about all the shit that happened?'

'Do you know what *I'd* give to remember everything?' Jesse replied, fuming. 'You talk about it like it was my decision. I had an accident.'

'Well, maybe it wasn't an accident at all,' Raphael said. 'Maybe it was your punishment. Maybe it was your time to eat dirt.'

'What do you mean?'

'That you never had to pay the price for anything. I was always the one who suffered, even when we were tiny. But then I really had to wade through it after Mum died.'

Jesse stared at Raphael standing there in the snow wearing his coat and blue jeans. He was even wearing his boots. 'After Mum died? How did she die?'

'Your uncle Wilbert couldn't keep his hands off his brother's wife. Just like you. You couldn't keep your mitts off Sandra either.'

Jesse looked at him in confusion. 'What do you mean?'

'Wilbert shot her, that's what I mean.'

The words hovered in the silence. The kind of silence that lingers in the air after shots have been fired: oppressive and charged, yet somehow also like a void has been opened. The

Zugspitze pierced through a gap in the grey clouds overhead. The sky was holding on to the snow, like it wanted to keep it to itself for a while.

'That was just after Dad came back. There was a huge row. Hardly surprising – Wilbert had tried to take Dad's place, after all. But we were Dad's kids. And Gudrun knew her place. Suddenly Wilbert was the fifth wheel. He couldn't live with it. He killed Mum, and then he abducted you. Dad ran after the two of you, but he didn't catch you.' He pulled a face. 'Even Dad loved you more. He would have given me up if he'd had the choice.'

'He kidnapped me?' Jesse felt dizzy. 'My uncle abducted me?'

'And he left me behind. From then on it was just me and Dad. There were three of us before. But you had the golden ticket. And I had a season ticket to hell and back.'

'The golden ticket? I'd lost my mum, I'd been snatched from my family, and I had to grow up in a home. At least you still had Dad.'

'Oh no,' Raphael said. 'No, no, no. *I* was in a home. You were over there, Mr Goldilocks, with your front-row seat in life and your cosy nest.' He pointed at the house behind Jesse with the barrel of the gun.

Jesse turned around and looked at the house, then turned back to face Raphael. He still didn't understand what his brother was talking about.

'And while you were there dining there on your fine silver, I had to pay for it by wading through all the shit. What do you think happened after Mum died? And after he'd lost his favourite son? The navy had sent him packing. His captain's licence: gone. His uniform never moved from the coat hanger. And he was back home, drinking all the time, trying to forget about everything but just ending up in the bathroom with his head over the toilet seat. And it got worse. When I was seven years old, he used to make me iron the uniform. Not a single crease. And I had to keep the house clean while he went on and on about how amazing my brother was. You weren't there – but somehow you were this constant presence. Like a fucking ghost. And all that time you . . .' He pointed at the house behind Jesse again.

'When I was ten years old,' Raphael continued, 'I grassed on Dad. Told social services all about him. Ironically, the one I grassed him to was the same slut who orchestrated your adoption. That fat cow, Wisselsmeier. They were all in it together. Wilbert, Artur and Wisselsmeier.'

'I was adopted?' Jesse asked, flabbergasted.

'Oh, weren't you just, Mr Goldilocks. Adopted into paradise. Soft bed sheets, clean mattress, expensive school – only the finest for you. And you never had to share with anyone. Some people can't have any children. Well, what else can they do but buy one on the black market. His brother looked at him with eyes full of hate. 'If only they'd treated you badly. But they had to be *nice* too, didn't they?

'And then guess where I ended up after I turned Dad in to Wisselsmeier? That's right. Adlershof! Nobody came to my rescue. No Artur, no Wilbert, no rich adoptive parents. I was the son of a drunk, with a murderer for an uncle and a weird look in my eyes. Damaged goods. Who would buy me?'

Chapter 56

Dear Mr Messner,

I know we agreed never to speak of the matter again, and apparently you stand by that decision as you still refuse to answer your phone, but I don't know where else to turn. My husband tells me there's no point talking to you about this. He says there's nothing you could do to help us. But I'm begging you, please at least read my letter. If not for me, then for the sake of an old friendship.

My husband and I are grateful to you for giving us the gift of such a wonderful young boy. He's so headstrong, clever and tough. He's even managed to overcome the nightmares and memories that used to bother him. He doesn't talk about those things any more – it seems the memories are getting fainter every year. Sometimes I hope that's because we've given him new memories, better ones. He doesn't ask questions all that often. And when he does, we don't answer them. That seems to make them go away.

Raphael has been with us for almost ten years now. I think I know him well, at least as well as a mother can know her child. That's why I really can't understand what's going on with him at the moment. He fell sick for two weeks in summer, one of those stomach bugs that comes and goes. Since then, I feel like I can barely recognise him. He won't let anyone get close to him any more. He's so closed off these days – he keeps shutting himself in his room and he never goes in the bathroom without locking the door. I realise how hysterical this might sound to you. He has hit puberty, after all. I thought the same thing myself. But I don't think puberty is to blame for all this. The changes are too sudden and hard to explain. Raphael always used to panic at the sight of water. He used to have this recurring dream about drowning, so we often let him skip the school swimming classes. God knows I argued with his sports teacher over it. But towards the end of this summer I kept seeing him swimming in Lake Seeben. And not just paddling either – swimming! I didn't even know that he could swim until recently.

Don't get me wrong, I'm glad he's managed to overcome his fear. I wouldn't be so worried if that was the only thing I'd seen. One day towards the end of September he came back from his swim soaking wet with his shirt sticking to his skin. I suddenly realised that he never goes swimming with his top off. He only ever takes it off in the bathroom with the door locked. You might think I'm being paranoid, but I can't stop thinking about it. I'm ashamed to tell you this, but that day when he came back from his swim, I just had to watch him through the bathroom keyhole. His torso looked so frighteningly strong. And he had this mark on his chest. It looked like a burn, but not a new one – an old scar that had stretched out with age.

How is that possible? And how come he feels on the wrong side of the wall for the light switch when he walks into the kitchen? Why does he confuse the medicine drawer for the cutlery drawer? Why doesn't he play the piano any more? A psychologist told me that the brain goes through certain adjustments in puberty, but that doesn't explain what's happening to Raphael. Sometimes I get the feeling he keeps forgetting everything and he's trying his hardest to stop us from noticing. He's got so many excuses for everything and he's told so many lies recently. It's like he's always trying to make me believe that everything is fine. He can't fool me though – I can tell that he's in a state and he's under a lot of strain. It's like he's trying hard to please me, but then when I ask him if he's all right he gets so angry it scares me. It almost feels like he could be capable of anything. I don't recognise my son any more. That's why I'm turning to you for help, Mr Messner. Can you think of any explanation for all this? Is there anything you could tell me about what Raphael went through before he came to live with us? There must be some kind of trigger for all this. I'm guessing it has something to do with his past. I can't think of any other explanation.

Please try to understand where I'm coming from. If there's any information you could give me, any tiny little detail, I would be so very grateful. Raphael's behaviour is really troubling me. I can hardly sleep at night. I feel like I'm going to go lose my mind if something doesn't happen soon. It feels like somebody has replaced my boy's soul. Please write to me as soon as you can.

Kind regards,

Renate Kochl

Jule dropped the letter into her lap. She was sitting in Artur's armchair, rubbing her arms as if she was cold, even though there was a radiator bubbling away close by. She had goose pimples and the tiny hairs on her skin were standing on end. *That's impossible*, she told herself. *You're imagining things.*

She took hold of the file containing the Kochl family's adoption application for Raphael Berg and opened it again. She looked at the photo. The file was suspiciously thin; there seemed to be parts missing. She didn't know much about the adoption process, but it seemed unlikely to her that the German social services would place a child with parents in Austria. And the idea that the red-tape-obsessed German authorities would produce a file as thin as this one – well, that was even less likely. Then there was a second file, processed by the same clerk from the Garmisch child welfare office, a Ms Wisselsmeier, with a photo that looked as if Raphael Berg's face had been scanned through one of those computer programs that simulate the ageing process.

In the interview conducted by Dr Paul Brenner, the officially appointed psychologist, Jesse Berg (11) reported having been beaten several times by his father, Herman (47, former captain, mother deceased). He described multiple acts of aggression and humiliation committed by his father. On one occasion, Herman Berg offered his son alcohol, and when the boy finally acquiesced, he was severely punished for having taken a sip. Jesse said he was afraid of his father as he had repeatedly accused him of stealing alcohol from him. Recently, Herman Berg repeatedly threatened his son with draconian punishments, referring to customs in Arab and Asian countries where (quote) 'they still cut off thieves' hands'. Given that Jesse Berg has no known living relatives and the respondent was only able to mention a twin brother who went missing at the age of three, the revocation of parental custody is hereby officially initiated, with emergency accommodation in the Adlershof Children's Home in Garmisch-Partenkirchen to be provided immediately.

Ella Wisselsmeier

Garmisch-Partenkirchen Child Welfare Office

Jule's head was spinning. Twins. That couldn't just be a coincidence. Neither could the dreadful situation that Raphael's adoptive mother, Renate Kochl, had described in her letter. And then there was the thing about Jesse playing the piano. Jesse *could* play the piano, although nobody had been able to explain to him where he'd learned it. He didn't even understand it himself. And Raphael? He should have been able to play the piano, but he had stopped for some inexplicable reason. There could only be one explanation for all this, even if it seemed crazy. Jesse and Raphael were twin brothers who must have been switched at some point. She felt cold. She rubbed her arms again, but the goose pimples wouldn't go away.

She was going to keep reading, but then she heard a key turning in the door. She quickly stuffed the papers under the seat cushion and covered it with her legs. The door was flung open.

Richard stood there in the doorway. He was still holding the case with the gun in his hand, pointing the narrow end with the muzzle at the floor. A stout older woman pushed past him through the doorway; Jule guessed she was in her late sixties or so. She was holding a walking stick in her right hand and moved with rigid, ungainly strides. A pair of heavy bosoms wobbled on top of her two belly rolls under her baggy cardigan. She glared at Jule with small eyes in a pale, doughy face.

'Is this her?' she asked Richard. Her voice sounded like she lived on cigarettes, even though she didn't smell of nicotine.

Richard nodded. His cheeks were blotchy, and he was sweating.

'And you're sure she knows?'

Knows what? Jule wondered. Her eyes anxiously wandered over to Richard's gun.

'She says she found Charly and spoke to her,' he said.

'Shit,' the woman muttered. Her little piggy eyes flitted back and forth, then suddenly came to rest between Jule's legs. She looked suspicious. 'What's that you've got there?' She pointed at the edge of the thin stack of paper peeping out between the armchair cushions.

'What do you want from me?' Jule asked. 'Who are you?'

'Give me that,' the woman said. Her left hand waved impatiently.

Jule didn't move, so Richard walked up to the chair, reached between her legs and snatched the paper out from under the cushion. 'Oi, what are you—' Jule protested. She could feel herself turning red. Richard glanced at the file, but it didn't seem to mean much to him. He passed the pieces of paper over to the woman, who grabbed them out of his hands without saying a word and squinted so she could see better. Then she raised her eyebrows, quickly leafed through the pages and turned pale. 'I'll be damned. That's impossible!' She glared at Jule. 'Where did you get this?'

'I found it,' Jule shrugged.

'Does it mean anything to you?' Richard asked.

'Does it ever,' the woman rasped. 'I wrote some of it myself.'

Jule stared at the woman. Was this Renate Kochl, the adoptive mother who wrote the letter to Artur Messner? No, that was hardly likely. Her coarse manner hardly matched the sensitive tone of the letter. So it could only be the woman from the welfare office. What was her name again? Wisselsmeier.

'So what is it, Ella?'

'It was before your time. Something your father orchestrated.'

Jule listened. Had she understood correctly? Artur Messner had set up the situation with the two boys? Did he know about the switch? Or was she just talking about the adoption?

'And how come I know nothing about it?' Richard complained.

'Does your father know about everything you get up to?'

'No, of course not, but—'

'Well then,' Ella Wisselsmeier snapped.

'We should take care of Charly,' Richard said.

'We have another entirely different problem now.'

'Huh?'

She raised her walking stick and pointed at Jule.

'What do you mean?'

'My dear, your father really does have more brains than you. Not necessarily more guts, but he was at least quick to cotton on.'

Richard's cheeks became even blotchier.

'If she's found this' – Ella Wisselsmeier rustled the papers she was holding in her hand – 'and if she's spoken to Charly, then she must know about everything.'

Jule felt uneasy. What was that supposed to mean? What did she know about? The two brothers? That they had been switched? But what did that have to do with Charly? 'I . . . um, I honestly don't know what you're talking about,' Jule said, then got up from the chair and took a step towards the door. Elle Wisselsmeier raised her walking stick and whacked her in the face with it.

'Don't lie to me,' Wisselsmeier hissed.

Jule stared at her, speechless. She grabbed her cheek and felt the blood. Her ear and the left side of her face were burning with pain.

'What should we do now?' Richard asked.

'Where's Charly?' Ella Wisselsmeier barked at Jule.

Jule bit her lips.

'In the cellar,' Richard interrupted. 'That's what she said before.'

'Is there any way we can get to the cellar without anyone seeing us? We have to take care of them both.'

Take care of us? Jule thought to herself. Oh God. What was that supposed to mean?

Richard nodded. He was clearly out of his depth. 'What if she screams?'

'Good lord! Then make sure she doesn't scream. Or do you want to spend the rest of your life in prison?'

Chapter 57

The sky seemed to break away from the ground. The clouds rose and tore into pieces. Jesse stumbled. Adopted? And the house behind him had been his childhood home? He felt like his head was about to burst.

Snowflakes aimlessly drifted to the ground. His brother caught one of them and crushed it with his left hand.

'If this was my house,' Jesse asked, 'then why did I grow up in Adlershof?'

A defiant, merciless expression had formed around Raphael's mouth. But something was hiding behind it. A feeling that Jesse knew well. It was regret: the desire to go down a different path, to turn back because everything had gone wrong. The expression on Raphael's face said he wanted to run way from all the consequences he'd failed to consider in his rage and his greed. Junkies had that same look. Drug dealers. Ivory hunters in Africa. Child soldiers in Darfur. He had that same look himself when he signed up for Doctors Without Borders and left Sandra and Isa alone because he couldn't reconcile himself with life as part of a trio because he was never 'complete' in himself.

But behind that look of regret, and as strong as the desire to turn back, was the certainty that the last train had departed long ago. All that was left was a gaping void that could only be filled with defiance; an empty feeling that could only be remedied by being tough on himself and everyone else, and by continuing in the wrong direction. To save himself, he had convinced himself that everything 'had gone wrong', that his fate was 'unfair', and the whole thing was an 'accident'.

Accident. The word reverberated inside his head.

Raphael, staring at him, smiled, but without the slightest hint of pleasure.

'The accident,' Jesse whispered. 'The wound in my back. That was you!'

'Who told you it was an accident? Artur?'

'Everyone. They all claimed they knew nothing about it.'

'It wasn't an accident.'

Jesse stared at Raphael.

'I couldn't bear it,' said Raphael. 'We were like the hare and the hedgehog from the story. You had everything I wanted. Everything I never got. Love for you; hate for me. Wealth for you; a drunk and poverty for me. Hope for you; desperation for me. How do you think I felt when I realised you were alive – and more importantly, where you lived?'

'You almost killed me—'

'Sorry about the "almost",' Raphael mocked.

'—and stole my life.'

'And you just got up and stole my life.'

'I did what?'

'Instead of dying, you crawled out of your grave. I don't know exactly how you did it. I probably couldn't finish the job. I thought it would be easier to kill you. I didn't think about how it would be, or should I say: how it would be after I did it. Well, how could I have known? I was thirteen. I was angry, and I hated you. So I came up with a plan. I took off. And then I could barely shovel the soil onto you because my hands were shaking so much.'

Jesse stared up at the sky. He couldn't bear to look him in the face any longer. The wind was pushing clouds over the peak of the Zugspitze, and the mountain seemed to be leaning the same way it was blowing.

'You think I regret it?' Raphael asked. 'I do. But not like you're thinking.'

'You're insane,' Jesse whispered.

'What do you think it was like for me, having to play your part? The brave Raphael. I didn't get a second of peace. I was always hiding. And there were always so many expectations. God, and that look in your mum's eyes – sorry, your *adoptive* mother. Like a drowning deer. She was always whining and seemed so disappointed all the time. She always wanted to help.' Raphael contorted his face and spoke in a shrill, high-pitched voice. 'What's up with you, dear? What's the matter? Oh, you seem so different, my darling.' He glared at Jesse. 'I swear she knew. She knew I wasn't you.' Tears glimmered in Raphael's angry eyes. He gritted his teeth. The barrel of the gun was twitching like a seismograph. 'Why didn't she ever scream? Or hit me? In the end I just wanted Dad back. The beatings were easier to put up with. They felt more appropriate. Same with the hole in the children's home.

'I wanted to go back. To Richard, that big-headed coward. Even Markus – at least he put up a fight. Mattheo, Alois, Wolle, Sandra. Suddenly I realised where my home was. But I couldn't go back. I was dead, for fuck's sake. Or at least I thought I was.'

Raphael's breath juddered as he inhaled. 'But then suddenly a couple of weeks ago Wilbert turned up at my house. Like a ghost. At first, I thought Dad had come back to life, but then I saw the scar on his hand. He was ill – dying, he said. And he wanted to come and visit me. To see what had become of the little boy he'd saved from his brother all those years ago. How was he supposed to know that it was me, not you, sitting across from him? And after everything else he'd done to me, now he was claiming that Dad was the one who shot Mum! The lying pig! Well, what do you think I did?'

Raphael stared at him with a knowing look on his face.

'The same thing you would have done. I smiled. I played my role nicely, right to the end, until he told me my brother was still alive, and he didn't know if I knew yet. It had been preying on his mind and he had to tell me. This brother had grown up nearby, in Adlershof, he said. He was a doctor now. He was married and had a daughter.' He wiped his eyes with the back of his left hand, still holding the gas mask. His mouth was folded into a line. 'His wife's name was Sandra.'

Jesse stared at the barrel of the gun. He was trying not to look at Raphael's tears. He didn't want to even try to understand why he'd done all this. It was too hideous, too unfathomable. He wanted to be furious and cry out with rage, but something inside him turned cold. Calm and collected, like before an operation. He watched Raphael's pupils, zoned in on his rapid breathing and looked at the gun. Tried to focus on the only thing that mattered now.

'Where's Isa?'

'She's the price.'

'What price?'

'The price you have to pay for stealing Sandra.'

'*You* left *her*.'

'You don't deserve her. You always had it easy while I always had to wade knee-deep through shit.

'What's that supposed to mean? She's the price? What are you planning?'

'I want my life back. My life from the home.'

'What's that got to do with Isa?'

'I've bought the gatehouse. Richard doesn't know about it – I bought it through a broker. But when all this is over, I'm going to live there with Isa. She's my daughter. The daughter I would've had with Sandra.'

'You're out of your mind. That will never work.'

'Why not? I look like you, don't I? I have your wallet, your passport, your credit card. God, it was so easy! Marta. Remember her? Give a girl from the street five hundred euros and she'll do anything you want. I've got your stuff, I've even had cut my hair so that it looks like yours does on your passport photo.'

'You thought it would work last time too. And now you bitterly regret it.'

'I don't regret a thing,' Raphael snapped. 'The others screwed it up for me.'

'You screwed it up. No one else. And you're about to make the same mistake again. Isabelle will hate you.'

'No,' Raphael laughed. 'She'll love me. I'm her dad, after all. I'll come and save her.' He lifted the gun and pointed it at Jesse's face. 'Put this on.' He threw the gas mask to Jesse with his left hand. 'I just have to kill the kidnapper. Then she'll love me.'

Chapter 58

Ehrwald, Austria – Wednesday, 9 January 2013, 3.24 p.m.

Mattheo sat there freezing, his teeth chattering from the cold. The heating didn't work without the key, and without any heating the draughty Defender was like a freezer. Still, he loved his Def and looked after it just like his grandfather had always looked after his old BMW R 51/2 motorbike.

Mattheo tried to peek through the windscreen, disgruntled. He could see hardly anything; it was almost completely covered in snow.

Nothing had changed. He was always left out back then, and it was just the same now. Sometimes they used to let him keep a lookout. But otherwise all he could do was wait and keep his mouth shut. Maybe that was one of the reasons he'd taken the job as a postman. The secrets, the important things, the big things: they were all inside envelopes. He was just the messenger, and he was always left out.

Richard had even turned him down when he offered to help look for Charly. He just flatly rejected his offer, even though he had gone to all the effort of traipsing out in this weather. Who else would go out of their way like that? Who else could they rely on? He was always ready for anything, but somehow he always ended up on the sidelines. He was tired of being pushed around.

He thought what Jesse had told him about the kidnapping sounded grossly exaggerated. But the rough, callous way Jesse had treated him showed that he was being deadly serious. There was one thing he'd learned about Jesse over the years: when he meant business, shit really hit the fan. Like that time in the clearing, for example. Jesse was dangerous and unpredictable, even when he was a boy. Mattheo didn't mind admitting that he was afraid of Jesse. Richard scared him too, just not as much.

Mattheo also knew that people were their most courageous when they managed to overcome their fears. He knew that when they were kids, only nobody let him face his fears back then. But who was going to stop him now? Here he was in the arse-end of beyond, sitting in the cold all alone in his Land Rover by the northern flank of the mountain.

He gently opened the door, taking care to be quiet. Then he walked over to the boot and opened it at least as quietly as he'd opened the door. He didn't want to startle Jesse – or anyone else, for that matter. He found a few blankets and an old quilted jacket that he'd completely forgotten about. It rustled as he put it on. Then he pushed the blankets to one side and looked at his pride and joy. A Darton FireForce crossbow with an AIA FRS 101 scope and a shooting accuracy of up to 180 metres.

He loved the wooden shaft of the crossbow; it reminded him of the first crossbow he ever held. He could still remember how clammy his hands were and how heavy it was. The FireForce was much easier to tension than the ancient crossbow from Artur's shed. He felt powerful every time he used the sophisticated mechanism with the smooth-running castors. He set out along Lake Seeben with a quiver of six arrows and the house firmly in his sights.

It wasn't long before he saw Jesse between the trees. He recognised him from the too-tight jacket he was wearing. He didn't know who the second man was though. He carefully inched closer, trying to be as quiet as he could despite the snow crunching beneath his feet. After about a hundred metres he stopped in his tracks and raised the crossbow. The scope brought everything within reach, even though the wind kept blowing fir branches into his field of sight and sometimes tossed the snow off the branches at him. Jesse was standing facing him. He panned the scope to the second man. He could only see his back, the back of his head and the nape of his neck. But he could clearly make out the gun in his hands. So Jesse hadn't been exaggerating. This had to be the kidnapper he'd been talking about. Jesse was in trouble, that much was clear.

He gently lowered the FireForce, just the way he'd learned to, then he put his foot in the stirrup and tensioned the crossbow until it locked into place. He slowly crept closer – not because the FireForce wouldn't shoot that far, but because if push came to shove, he would need a free line of fire. He had to make sure there were no fir branches that could deflect the arrow. Now he could see both men. He stopped thirty metres away, placed an arrow in the slot and raised the crossbow to his eye. The look in Jesse's eyes made him shudder. He looked exhausted and unusually vulnerable. This wasn't the same Jesse he knew. Was he afraid? The mere possibility made Mattheo feel more powerful. 'I'm here,' he said under his breath, so quietly that only the Fire-Force could hear him.

The man holding the gun threw something at Jesse, who then picked it up and reluctantly pulled it over his head. A black mask that was in stark contrast to the snow. The barrel of the gun was pointing directly at Jesse's head. Mattheo felt the hairs on the back of his neck stand up. He wasn't left out now. Not here. Not today!

He took off his gloves and released the safety. Pressed the crossbow shaft to his shoulder and aligned the centre of the hairline cross with the back of the man's neck. It was almost a shame how quickly it would all be over. He wished he could savour the moment, watch it being drawn out in slow motion like an action replay. He bent his index finger and felt the pressure. The cold metal of the trigger almost froze his finger.

In that very moment, Jesse looked over at him. Just for a split second, the flapping of a bird's wing. Even though he was wearing the gas mask, Mattheo thought Jesse had somehow caught sight of him between the firs.

You'll thank me for this, Mattheo thought to himself.

His finger bent further. He tried to breathe evenly, to stay calm and cool, but his heart was pounding uncontrollably.

Suddenly the man holding the gun spun his head around, following the line of Jesse's brief glance. Mattheo turned to stone. He stared through the crossbow scope in disbelief. His finger went limp and the spring pushed the trigger catch back into the original position.

The man with the gun was Jesse as well.

It had to be some kind of illusion: a hallucination. He must be seeing things. Hadn't he just seen Jesse putting the gas mask on? The man, the other Jesse, swung the gun around and aimed at him. Mattheo stared at the shotgun in disbelief. He saw the muzzle twitch. He instinctively pulled the trigger on the Fire-Force. The dry clicking of the bowstring overlapped with the sound of the shot. Then, like a hammer, it hit Mattheo in the face and tore apart everything that he used to be.

Chapter 59

Ehrwald, Austria – Wednesday, 9 January 2013, 3.39 p.m.

Jesse saw a haze of red explode between white branches. A sharp buzzing sound cut through the air between where he and Raphael were standing. Mattheo's head disappeared in the blink of an eye, as if he had managed to duck to the side at the very last moment. The shot echoed through the mountain.

Jesse pounced on Raphael just as he was turning around. He grabbed hold of the barrel of the gun and pushed it to one side. The second shot was fired. Snow fell from a tree.

The gun was now between them. Jesse had grabbed hold of it with both hands and the two of them were wrestling with it like it was a club. Raphael's face was contorted in rage. He was strong and in better shape than Jesse, and the gas mask Jesse had been forced to wear was restricting his view. It was like looking at everything through a filter. His panicked breath blew hot air into the mask. He couldn't take much more of this. The gun was still a dangerous weapon, even though it was no longer loaded.

Jesse suddenly ducked down, swiftly let go of the gun with his left arm and dived underneath it. Raphael was too slow to react. His strength suddenly had nowhere to go and he fell to the ground, taking Jesse with him. They both landed knee-deep in the snow. Jesse felt a hot shooting pain in his waist. He gritted his teeth and snatched the gun out of his brother's hand. Raphael picked himself up and stumbled a couple of steps away from Jesse through the snow. Without taking his eyes off him, he reached behind his shoulder, loosened a strap, and grabbed hold of the wooden handle that was sticking out behind him. Jesse quickly pulled the gas mask off his head and threw it at his brother. The rubber straps flapped about in the wind. The mask shot past Raphael and landed in a snowdrift.

Raphael's lips curled into a malicious smile. He raised an axe from behind his back. His fists closed around the long handle. He grasped hold of it several times, like he was trying to warm his fingers up.

Jesse grabbed the cold, smooth barrel of the gun with the butt raised like the end of a baseball bat. The hot breath steaming out of their mouths was swept away by the gentle breeze.

With a sudden sweeping motion, Raphael swung the axe down over his head in a wide arc. Jesse lifted the gun and grabbed it at both ends. The blade of the axe drove into the barrel of the gun like it was cutting a tree trunk, crashing down no more than half an arm's length above Jesse's head.

Raphael was skilled in using the heavy axe. He swung it around in a circle and struck again and again. Jesse held the barrel of the gun with his arms bent, using all his strength to keep it perpendicular to the axe flying towards it. Raphael gasped with every stroke of the axe. The sound of metal on metal echoed from the slopes of the mountain.

Jesse recoiled each time the axe struck, staggering back in the deep snow without daring to look behind him. He brushed against bushes and branches, shaking the snow from them. The barrel of the shotgun was beginning to come loose from the wooden shaft. Not long now and the gun would break apart. He broke out into a sweat, even though he was freezing cold. He moved back a step at a time. Mattheo had to be lying there somewhere behind him – and the crossbow must be there too. He knew he wouldn't have any time to load the cumbersome weapon, but a carbon arrow in his fist was almost as good as a knife.

Raphael had ceased relentlessly swinging the axe. Now he was breathing heavily and concentrating on saving his energy. He stared at Jesse coldly, holding the axe in his hands menacingly and mirroring every step he took. Suddenly Jesse felt flat ground beneath his feet. There were no trees or bushes on either side of him, just open space and snow on slick ice. Jesse chanced a quick glance to his side. He was standing on the ice over Lake Seeben. Wind was blowing against his back, driving streaks of white through the air.

Raphael stopped in his tracks and laughed. 'Scared? You don't like frozen lakes, do you?'

Jesse bit his lip and stepped back again. The ground crunched beneath his feet.

'You know what's great about this lake? I know it like the back of my hand. I know where the water's deep and where it's shallow. I used to skate here every winter. And do you know what the important difference is between shallow and deep water?'

A cold fist closed around Jesse's heart. Suddenly he knew why Raphael had stayed put.

'The depth tells you how thick the ice is.' Raphael lifted the axe and slammed it into the ice in front of him. The ground beneath Jesse's feet creaked ominously.

'You see here, where I'm standing, the lake is shallow and the ice bears weight. But where you're standing—' another blow to the ice – '—there's a sharp dip in the lake bed . . .'

Jesse glanced over to the shore, about ten metres to his left. He started moving, slowly enough not to disturb the ice, but quickly enough to reach safety. Another blow from the axe shook the ground. There was a sharp cracking sound, then the ice gave way. He dropped the gun and reached out for some kind of non-existent hold, then plunged down through the freezing water as if somebody had opened a trapdoor.

The black water sloshed over his head, paralysing him in its cold grip. Everything stopped except for the gentle gargling of the water in his ears. Then the panic set in and he remembered he couldn't swim. He started waving his arms and legs frantically in a desperate attempt to fight the crippling cold and the pull of the water. He pushed his head out and gasped for air. His chest felt so tight he could barely breathe. He clutched at the edge of the ice for safety and looked up at the bright blue sky. Raphael was towering above him a safe distance away, wearing *his* coat and *his* boots, holding the axe with both hands.

The edge of the ice broke off under Jesse's grip. The gun slipped off the ice and into the water. The wooden butt of the gun floated on the surface until the double metal barrel dragged it down into the water. *Twin barrels*, Jesse thought to himself. The sun broke through and stabbed him in the eyes. Droplets of water vibrated between his eyelashes like a thousand tiny magnifying glasses.

'No Wilbert to come and save you now,' Raphael said.

Chapter 60

Ehrwald, Austria – Wednesday, 9 January 2013, 3.39 p.m.

Artur flinched when the first bang pierced the silence. The restraints were the only thing keeping him upright against the post. His hands were tightly bound and wedged between his tail bone and the post. They had gone numb a while ago, like the left-hand side of his face. His legs were the only part of him that hadn't been tied up; he was sitting with them outstretched in front of him on the floor. His trousers had turned red in the spot where the screw had pierced his leg. He was glad he was sitting back to back with Isa with the post between them. At least that way she didn't have to see the blood.

'What was that?' Isa whispered.

The second bang resounded like an instant response and reverberated from the mountain.

'Shots,' Artur murmured, distracted.

'Is that Dad?'

'I hope so,' Artur moaned. In fact, he didn't really believe what he was saying, if he was being honest. Yes, he had promised himself he was going to be honest with Isa from now on, but how was he supposed to tell her he was worried the kidnapper was the one firing the shots?

'Do you think it could have been that . . . Raphael person?'

He instantly felt ashamed of himself. It was no use lying, because the truth always came out in the end. 'Your dad is a pretty tough guy. He won't be easy to catch.'

Isa sobbed. 'So what's my dad's name now? Jesse or Raphael? What should I call him?'

'Well, Dad, no?'

She sniffed noisily. 'Yeah, but what about his actual name?'

'I'd say,' Artur mumbled, 'his name is Jesse. Why should anybody else be allowed to take your dad's name?'

'Nobody can take my dad's name.' She went quiet for a moment. 'Artur, when did you notice?'

'Notice what?' he asked, trying to buy himself some time. But he was fully aware of what the question meant.

'The switch.'

He moaned. When he opened his mouth to speak, he tried to move his lips as little as possible. 'That wasn't until later. Our cook, Dante, found Jesse unconscious by the back door of the kitchen at the crack of dawn one day.' Artur stopped for a moment. He found it hard to keep the images out of his head. Jesse had been in a dreadful state when they found him: naked, covered in soil and blood from the wound in his back, chipped fingernails, a broken leg, and a bulge on his head. He still didn't understand how Jesse had made it to the door from wherever he had been. 'We took him straight to the hospital. I didn't get a chance to speak to him until two weeks later, and when I went to see him, he couldn't remember anything. He couldn't remember later either.' Artur looked down at his blood-soaked trouser leg and sighed. The truth was, he had actually had his suspicions right from the beginning. The Jesse lying in the hospital bed in front of him had a much narrower build than the Jesse he knew. The others didn't notice when he returned to Adlershof. Hardly surprising really, after such a long stay in the hospital.

'So when did you notice?' Isa asked.

'Maybe it was more like something I felt, you know? They're very similar, but also very ... For example, the way they can both behave when they want to get their own way—' He stopped talking. Suddenly he realised how absurd it was that they were sitting here talking while shots were being fired outside. Still, it seemed to be doing Isa some good and distracting her a little, so he kept going. 'Raphael didn't get off to such a good start. But Jesse didn't do too badly. He was always a bit of a lucky child. The whole thing with the accident – or the switch – could have changed things for him. But it didn't. Raphael was always—' He tried to find the right words. 'Raphael always wanted to go through the same door as Jesse. But everyone sort of has their own door, do you know what I mean? Jesse found his and went through it. Raphael did too, but he kept turning around, always thinking there was something much better waiting for him behind the other doors. He always had this look about him, like he thought he was always being cheated and had been dealt the wrong cards. I guess maybe that's how it was. Sometimes I felt really sorry for him. But he was pretty cunning and started to turn the tables. The only problem was he always had to push things too far. That didn't go down well with everyone else. But nobody said anything because everyone was afraid of him.'

'Including you?'

Artur thought about how the little boy had looked at him in the hole back then. Nobody had ever looked at him like that before. Such a hard expression, so full of hate. *I'll kill you one day, old man,* that's what he'd said. And he could tell from his eyes that he meant every word. It still gave him goose pimples just thinking about it. 'Maybe,' Artur mumbled.

'Why didn't you say anything when you noticed?'

'I know,' Artur muttered. 'I should have said something.' But instead he had done the opposite. Even when Wolle had come to see him and told him about the iron-shaped burn mark on Jesse's chest and the fact that the scar had now suddenly disappeared – even then, he did everything in his power to make sure Wolle kept shtum. Wolle knew that something wasn't right. He'd known it all these years. And it had cost Artur a hefty sum. Who would have thought that it would take a whole pub to make Wolle happy when he grew up?

Everything looked so different with hindsight. So unforgivable. What was the real reason for his silence? Cowardice? The relief of being rid of him? Maybe even the crazy idea that there could be some poetic justice in everything that had happened? A bit of compensation for the rotten childhood Raphael had been forced to suffer in that hellhole with his father? And ultimately, Jesse hadn't had such a terrible time in the home – did that make what he had done any better?

Just as he knew now that what he had done was terribly wrong, he had been convinced that he'd done everything for all the right reasons back then. But that didn't make it any more forgivable, especially when he saw things through Isa's eyes. 'I'm sorry,' he said softly. 'I'm so terribly sorry. But now we have to make a plan.'

'A plan? What kind of plan?'

'We need to work out what we're going to do if your dad turns up here.'

'He'll definitely come,' Isa said with conviction.

'But how will we know it's really your dad?'

Isa paused a moment. The room was so quiet you could have heard a pin drop.

'I know my dad.'

'I'm sure you do. But like I said, Raphael is clever. And he managed to make everyone believe he was his brother once before. At least for a while.'

Isa started sobbing.

'We have to prepare ourselves in case he tries to trick us. We have to make him think he's pulled the wool over our eyes because that's when he'll be at his most vulnerable.' Artur looked over at the hatch, which wasn't far from his feet. 'That's the moment we need to seize.'

Chapter 61

Jesse had been in the lake for less than half a minute. The cold had him in its grip, like an iron fist. He was clinging to the edge of the broken ice again, frantically thrashing his legs about under the water. He was amazed at how much momentum it gave him once he had recovered from the initial shock. Raphael was standing about a metre away with his legs apart, out of reach, and apparently on firm ground. He was holding the axe in front of his chest in an archaic stance, drunk on power. The gun with the buckled twin barrel was visibly sinking towards the dark bed of the lake. The butt glinted below the surface. Jesse overcame his panic, let go of the ice with one hand and reached for the wooden part of the gun, dipping his mouth and nose into the water. He got hold of the gun, sputtered uncontrollably and thrashed about even more frantically to keep from going under. He held the gun with his right hand, pointing it forward so that Raphael couldn't see it under the edge of the broken ice.

Jesse knew he only had one chance – and that he was going to be too slow. The water was slowing his movements and the cold was numbing his muscles. He looked up at Raphael. Their eyes met. He expected to see a look of triumph on his face, maybe a touch of mockery or scorn. But he saw nothing of the sort. Raphael's gaze was calm and composed. An ominous, overwhelming sense of tiredness came over Jesse, and he forced himself to do something about it. He looked past Raphael and over to the house, then opened his eyes wide. 'Isa!'

Raphael turned around.

Jesse pulled the gun out of the water, pointed it at Raphael, and rammed the muzzle of the double barrel into his crotch.

His brother let out a stifled cry, fell to his knees and slumped to the ground. The ice creaked beneath him but didn't break. Water was seeping over the surface. Raphael doubled over and groaned with pain. He managed to thrust the axe over the ice towards Jesse. Snow and bits of ice flew into the air like sparks. Jesse threw his head to one side and dived under the surface involuntarily. He floundered, pushed his head out of the water again and desperately gasped for air. The blade was caught on the edge of the broken ice. Raphael pulled on the shaft, but the axe wouldn't come loose.

Jesse swiftly grabbed hold of the other end of the shaft, just above the iron axe head, and hung on to it with his whole body weight while Raphael grimly pulled in the other direction, trying to get back on his feet. His face was pale and full of rage. The ice creaked under his weight but refused to break. Jesse's muscles were so stiff from the cold that it felt as if his tendons, joints and blood were knotted together. He just didn't have the strength. The numbingly cold water took hold of him, making him feel deathly tired. He longed for some rest. He wanted to let go. He longed for it all to end. Then suddenly, something stirred inside him and conjured up the image of Sandra lying there in her apartment, bleeding and with that blank stare on her face. And Isa: if he gave up now, she would grow up with this monster.

The thought of the two of them was the spur he needed. He pulled himself up on the shaft of the axe and lifted his shoulders up out of the water. He raised his right hand, gripped the gun like a harpoon, and then thrust the barrel right into the middle of Raphael's face. The muzzle hit his brother in the eye socket.

The scream was bloodcurdling.

Raphael let go of the axe and Jesse fell back into the lake. The water gurgled as ripples lashed over his head. Panic struck again. He thrashed about in the water, but much too slowly. The axe slid out of his hand and the gun he was still desperately holding on to scraped dully on the ice above him. Suddenly he felt his feet touching the bottom of the lake. He could stand up! He bent his knees under the water, pushed himself off the lake bed, sprung up towards the surface, and then hit his head on the ice above him. He desperately thrashed around and caught hold of the edge of the broken ice, then he pulled himself out from under it. He spluttered as his head surfaced. He clung on to the edge, gasping for air. The ice had been washed smooth by the lapping water. Now the edge was much too smooth for him to use to haul himself up.

He took the gun, muzzle first, reached out as far as he could and bashed the barrel into the icy surface, but it wouldn't stick. Raphael held his face and crawled to the shore. Jesse tried to ram the barrel of the gun into the ice again, in the same place, again and again, until the muzzle broke through the ice with a loud crunch.

He stuck the gun so far down into the hole that it got wedged in the ice, the butt sticking out like a post. He grabbed hold of it with both hands and pulled himself out of the water, then he collapsed on the ice, shivering.

When Raphael spotted Jesse on the ice, he uttered a sound that normally only an animal could make: a furious mixture of simultaneous howling and hissing. He took his hands away from his face, revealing a bloody wound in the place where his eye used to be. Jesse jumped. Raphael's fingers shook as he pulled up his jacket and fiddled with his belt. The metal of a blade flashed, reflecting the white mountainous idyll around them. Raging in pain and anger, Raphael staggered towards Jesse clutching a hunting knife in his fist.

Jesse tried to get back on his feet, leaning on the butt of the gun for support. He stumbled, stood up, saw Raphael approaching and desperately yanked at the gun that was wedged in the ice. Fuck! Why wasn't it moving? He pulled the butt left, then right. Raphael was less than five steps away from him. Turn it, try turning it!

He turned the butt clockwise. The ice crunched, and the gun came loose with a single tug. Jesse pulled it out of the hole. He saw Raphael lunging towards him with the knife. He dodged the blade, leaving Raphael stabbing into thin air. Raphael skilfully spun the knife in his hand and swiped at Jesse's neck with brisk sweeping motions. Jesse swerved to the side, grabbed the barrel of the gun and swung it horizontally through the air like a club. The droplets of water from the butt of the gun drew an arc. Then the hardwood hit Raphael's head. The blow made Jesse's arms tremble all the way to his chest.

Raphael fell without the slightest bit of resistance.

The ice shook briefly, as if a plane somewhere far in the distance had broken the sound barrier.

Jesse fell to his knees, holding on to the gun for support.

Suddenly it was quiet. A breeze blew across the ice. The fleeting blue of the sky turned to violet. Long shadows with frayed ends stretched out across the lake. Raphael's one intact eye stared blankly out into the distance. He was dead.

Jesse's teeth started chattering.

His hands didn't want to obey him. He forced himself to take off every last bit of clothing, all of it soaking wet and freezing cold. Undressing Raphael took much too long. Jesse shivered as he pulled on the dry clothes. He glanced over at the house, patted the coat pocket and found a key.

He staggered over to the building. So this had been his house at one time. He prayed he would find Isa inside. It took every last bit of strength to lift his feet in the deep snow. The image of Raphael's naked corpse at the lakeside followed him with every step he took.

Chapter 62

Richard Messner stepped into the corridor outside Artur's room, checked to see that there was nobody around, then waved at Jule to come out of the room. He waved her on ahead, at gunpoint, with the gun still inside the case. Ella Wisselsmeier followed suit, tapping her walking stick hard against the ground in time with her lumbering footsteps.

Jule's mind was racing. She could no longer make sense of it all. The only thing she understood was that Wisselsmeier had a problem with Jule and Charly and had decided to make them both disappear.

Jule grew more afraid with every step. She stepped onto the stairs in the corridor and felt Richard press the gun into the small of her back. 'Not here. Keep going until you reach the door at the end. We're taking the spiral staircase.'

Jule did as she was told. When they got to the door at the end of the hall, Richard opened it with his master key. It seemed the spiral staircase was hardly ever used. The walls were bare and there wasn't even a handrail, just dusty lamps in niches every couple of metres. Fragments of crumbling stone crunched beneath Jule's feet as she walked down the narrow winding steps. Ella Wisselsmeier was puffing and panting above her. She seemed to be struggling the most with the steps, presumably due to the excess weight she was carrying.

Jule knew she was getting closer and closer to the end of the line with every step. All the same, the spiral staircase hardly seemed her best bet for an escape attempt. She remembered a guided tour of a castle she and her family went on once. Her brother was always so fascinated by sword fights in old castles. She recalled the tour guide telling them that the reason the old spiral staircases coiled clockwise was so that attackers approaching from below would find it more difficult to wield their swords while moving upwards. Anyone defending himself from above, on the other hand, could forcefully thrust the sword around the bend with his right hand.

She glanced over her shoulder. Richard Messner's gun was swinging in sync with his footsteps. Suddenly she realised that Messner was holding the shotgun in his left hand. He can't be right-handed! The gun was much too long and unwieldy for him to accurately take aim at Jule in this narrow winding staircase. He would have to be holding the gun in his right hand if he wanted to hit his target.

Jule's heart was in her mouth.

Ella Wisselsmeier's puffing and panting echoed off the stone walls. The next lamp shone onto Jule. Her shadow grew as she passed by, blocking the light for a moment. She made her decision in a split second. She quickened her pace and took several steps at once, praying she wouldn't trip over. Messner was caught off guard. By the time he spat out a curse she was already out of the firing line.

'Stop!' Messner yelled. He sped up.

'Shoot, for God's sake!' Ella Wisselsmeier yelled.

Jule stopped suddenly, turned around and pressed herself against the wall. Messner rushed towards her. She saw the barrel of the gun poking out of the cover from behind the bend. Jule reached for it with both hands and tugged at it with all her strength. Messner screamed in shock as he fell down the stairs and landed at Jule's feet. The gun hit the steps, cushioned by the cover.

Ella Wisselsmeier roared and furiously rushed down the stairs towards her, moving at a speed that Jule would never have believed she could manage. Jule stepped over Richard Messner, who groaned as he tried to stand up. He managed to grab hold of Jule's trouser leg, but she stepped on him and he let go.

Jule bent down and tried to take hold of the gun, but Messner had managed to hook the shoulder strap and was pulling on the cover. Suddenly Ella Wisselsmeier came around the bend and swiped at her with the walking stick. Jule ducked at the last second. The hardwood bounced off the stone spindle of the staircase with a clatter. Jule let go of the gun and ran down the steps as fast as she could. She had the advantage on the narrow stairs.

'Get up, you idiot,' Wisselsmeier said, breathless. Messner seemed to be having trouble standing up. He groaned. Jule broke out into a sweat. The twisting steps were unbalancing her. She could hear footsteps somewhere overhead. They were back in pursuit of her.

When Jule got to the bottom of the stairs, she found herself standing in front of a door. She pushed the handle, hurled her weight against it and almost tripped when the door swung right open. It was dark down here and it smelled like a damp cellar. Only the sparse light from the spiral staircase shone a couple of metres into the corridor. Was this the new part of the cellar? Or was it the old part on the other side of the door that Jesse had prised open? In any case, the corridor only continued to the right; it looked like there was a dead end to the left. She shoved the door shut behind her and felt her way along the wall, moving quickly. 'Charly?' she whispered.

Charly didn't answer.

She rushed around the corner to the left at the next junction. 'Charly, where are you?'

The door flew open in the corridor behind her. 'Shit, it's dark in here,' Wisselsmeier cursed.

'Come out,' Messner shouted, 'or get caught.'

'What's with the warning? Just get on with it!'

A deafeningly loud shot reverberated through the corridor. Lead shot bounced off the walls. Jule was relieved that she'd turned left instead of continuing straight on.

'Don't try to kid yourself I don't have enough cartridges.'

Jule hurried on, desperate. Footsteps crunched behind her. Messner came through the corridor. Her eyes welled up with tears. Sooner or later he was going to hit her with a round from his shotgun. A hand reached out to her. 'Not that way!' a child's voice whispered.

'Charly!' Jule breathed.

'Shh.' The girl pulled her by the sleeve and dragged her two steps back, then to the right.

Another gunshot. The shot flew through the corridor where Jule had just been standing. Messner swore and she heard the clicking of metal. He was obviously reloading.

Charly pulled her through the dark corridor at high speed. Then she pushed a door open, stepped inside and quietly closed it behind them. A light went on. Charly quickly put the key in the lock and turned it.

'Thank God!' Jule groaned. She blinked in the light. 'Charly, I owe you big time.'

Charly gave a crooked smile and pulled her away from the door. Jule looked around and realised that they were in the corridor that led to the gatehouse. She rummaged around in her trouser pocket and gave a sigh of relief when she felt the bumpy contours of the Volvo key.

'Charly, we have to get out of here. It's not just me they're after – they're looking for you too.'

Charly didn't look the slightest bit surprised, just frightened. They hurried off in the direction of the gatehouse. As soon as they got there, Jule dragged Charly into the kitchen and then out of the back door and under the carport. She looked around the corner towards the main building, her heart pounding.

'Can you see that little patch of trees over there?' Jule pointed at the parking space. 'That's where my car is.'

Charly nodded.

One last glance, then they ran through the snow. Jule kept glancing back at the main building, expecting the door to open any second. Would Messner dare to shoot at them out here?

The parking space was covered in a deep layer of snow. The Volvo too.

'Come on, give me a hand.' She started shovelling the snow away from the car with her bare hands and arms. Charly got down on her knees and started digging right behind the wheels.

'What are you doing?' Jule asked.

'That's what the men around here always do when a car's snowed in.'

When the car was reasonably clear, they got in and quietly closed the doors. Fully aware that the sound of the engine firing up could give them away, Jule prayed the car would start straight away.

And it did.

The wheels creaked as they broke free from the snow, jangling the chains as the Cross Country jolted through the fresh snow. Jule turned onto the narrow main road. Adlershof's stone façade appeared in the rear mirror. Smoke rose from one of the chimneys. There was no sign of Messner anywhere, not even when Jule drove over the hilltop and reached the slope.

She took a deep breath and concentrated as she steered the car along the winding roads. The heating was on full blast. Her hands were shaking. 'Thank you, Charly. You really saved my life, do you know that?'

Charly nodded. Her sleeves were white with snow, like Jule's. 'Do I have to go back there?'

'No. Certainly not. But will you tell me why you were hiding?'

'Because of Messner and the woman from social services.'

'I realise that now,' Jule said. 'But *why*?'

'If they catch me, they'll sell me.'

'Sell?' Jule asked, horrified. 'What do you mean?'

'Well, they give you away to new parents. But sometimes they give you to bad parents. Or people who aren't parents at all. Like what happened to Tinkerbell.'

Jule remembered the chubby girl from the kitchen and felt a chill run down her spine. 'What happened to Tinkerbell?'

'Tinker came back. They weren't happy with her, she said; she always ate too much and was too fat. Then they gave them Thea. That was last year.'

Jule's hands clenched the steering wheel. She had to pull herself together to stop from ploughing into a tree.

'Tinker was really smart,' Charly said. 'The other ones never came back. But I didn't want to eat as much as Tinker to make them leave me alone.'

'Charly, you really are clever!'

The girl looked at her, grinned and suddenly started to cry.

'Hey, it's all right,' Jule whispered. 'I'm here with you.' She wished she could put her arm around her, but she needed to keep both hands on the wheel. 'Charly, do you know where there's a police station in Garmisch?'

She sniffed and nodded. 'Of course. I ran away before. That's where they always take you. And then the fat lady from social services comes along.'

'Well I'll tell you something,' Jule said grimly, 'she'll be coming this time too.'

'But then you'll help me?'

'You bet I'll help you!'

Chapter 63

Garmisch-Partenkirchen – Wednesday, 9 January 2013,
4.18 p.m.

'Artur,' Isa whispered.

Artur didn't respond. *Don't cry*, she told herself. If she started crying now, she might never stop.

'Ar-tur!'

She listened to the silence. Wasn't that the sound of soft breathing she could hear? If he was still breathing, he couldn't be dead! She wished she could turn around, look at him and snuggle up to him, but no matter how much she wriggled, the post and the tight fetters wouldn't let her get to him. Her neck still hurt where the rope had cut into her. It was like she was wearing an invisible choker, one that was much too tight.

How long had it been since they'd heard the shots? Half an hour? A whole hour? She had never been good at judging time. Time had this nasty habit of being unreliable. Sometimes it went slow, other times it was fast. Right now it was never-ending.

She heard a creaking sound coming from the steps. Fear took hold of her. She had no way of seeing the hatch from here. Only Artur could do that. 'Artur, he's coming.'

The footsteps were slow and quiet. So what could that mean? The insect man – or Raphael, as Artur called him – had always made a racket when he came up the steps. Was he injured?

She couldn't stop thinking about what Artur had told her before: 'Raphael has a burn on his chest from an iron. Your dad has a scar on his back. That's the only way you'll be able to tell them apart.'

It made perfect sense to her when he said it, but now the steps were getting closer, she found herself wondering how she was supposed to check for the marks. Surely this Raphael person was clever enough not to give himself away. She couldn't very well just ask him to take his jumper off. If she did, Raphael would instantly know she didn't trust him.

No, she had to find out some other way. She would have to ask him something that only her father could know. The bolts scraped against the hatch as they slowly slid back.

Please, please let it be Dad!

She heard the hatch opening behind her. Somebody was breathing heavily. It sounded like whoever it was might collapse under the weight of the door.

'Isa?'

That was Dad's voice! She had to try her best not to start crying. Artur had told her that this was how it would be. 'I'm here, Dad,' she cried anxiously.

The door of the hatch creaked open and crashed onto the floor.

'Oh God, Isa!' The footsteps sped up. Her racing heart skipped a beat when she saw him. Yes, that was definitely her father! But Artur had warned her not to jump the gun. The man knelt down in front of her. Tears ran down her face. He was wearing his coat and his boots, the same as always. There was stubble on his face, his hair was wet, and he was so pale he looked like he might pass out any second.

He carefully placed his two big hands on her cheeks and cupped her head. Now she really couldn't hold back the tears.

'Are you OK, sweetheart?'

'She nodded.

His hands were trembling and freezing cold. But her dad's hands were never that cold! 'Brr, Dad, you really are a cold man.'

'A what?' the man laughed behind his tears. Isa's heart was in her mouth. *Please, please say it!*

'A cold man,' Isa repeated. She waited for his pale lips to move.

'I thought I was your blue man?'

The floodgates suddenly opened, and Isa burst into tears. 'Dad,' she sobbed. 'I've missed you so much.' She pressed her cheeks into his freezing cold hands.

'I've missed you too, darling,' He put his arms around her and held on tight. She could feel his whole body shivering. He was freezing cold.

Jesse took his hands off her. 'Hang on.' He pulled a knife out of his coat and cut her free. As soon as the last rope fell, Isa threw her arms around him and held him as tightly as she could. Jesse groaned. Isa was startled: 'Are you hurt?'

'Don't you stop hugging me.'

She held him tight again. Her hand slipped under his jumper – *just to be on the safe side*, she thought. The scar on his back was right where it was supposed to be. 'Did you fight with Raphael?' she asked.

'You know about Raphael?'

'Artur told me.'

'You don't need to be afraid of him anymore. He's dead.'

She sniffed and nodded. 'We have to help Artur. I don't know what's happened to him.' Suddenly the fear was back. Despite all the joy and relief, the idea that something might have happened to Artur was terrible.

Jesse let go of her and checked Artur's pulse.

'Is he dead?' she asked anxiously.

He shook his head and smiled encouragingly. 'Well, he's not doing too well, but he's definitely alive.'

Isa blew the air out of her cheeks, relieved.

Jesse cut Artur free from the other side of the post, checked the wound on his leg and put him into the recovery position. Then he patted down his coat with the palm of his hand and pulled a phone out of the chest pocket.

'That isn't yours, is it?'

He shook his head but said nothing. Jesse keyed in a number and spoke into the phone with his doctor's voice, but not as confidently and quickly as she was used to hearing him talk. His lips quivered and the hand he was holding the phone in was visibly shaking.

'Are you still that cold?' Isa asked when he hung up.

He nodded.

'There's a radiator back there. I'll show you.'

Jesse couldn't stand upright anymore, so he crept over to it instead. He groaned as he leaned his back against the warm radiator. Isa sat next to him and huddled up close to him. Her narrow shoulders dug into his upper arm.

He rubbed his face wearily and smiled. 'You know something? It's not that long since the last time we sat with our backs to a radiator like this.'

'You mean at night time in the kitchen when I was supposed to be cleaning my teeth?'

He raised his eyebrows. 'You knew I was there? I thought you were sleeping.'

'I was scared I might get into trouble. Because of the Nutella,' Isa said and squeezed him even tighter.

Epilogue

The street was still wet from the rain and the sky was trying hard
to turn blue. Jule stopped near the school and got out of the car.
A man waiting to drop his kids off from a packed VW camper
honked his horn irritably. Jesse just ignored him and went to the
back door, then opened it with a faint bow.

'Da-ad, I'm not a kid anymore!'

'Who says?'

Jule turned away and stifled her grin as she leaned against the
passenger side of the car.

Isa stuck her chin out between the tips of her marine-blue coat
collar. Her face was pale and a little longer than a few months
before. She had her hair tied back in a tight, springy ponytail,
ready for her first day back at school since they'd returned to
Berlin. Time had moved so strangely in the last few weeks. The
clocks ticked more slowly, more mournfully. Sandra's funeral
was awful. Isa cried out in pain when she found out about her
mother's death. She found it difficult to let Jesse go anywhere
other than the next room for the first week. It had been a real
ordeal for her when Jesse had to leave her to make his police
statements in Garmisch and then in Berlin. She only managed

to cope with being apart from him because Jule stayed with her. The second week after the ordeal, Isa insisted on going to see her grandpa. It took Jesse a while to realise that she was talking about Artur.

The former principal of Adlershof was recovering in a private room at Garmisch-Partenkirchen hospital.

Jesse let Isa go first. He had already visited Artur a few times, and every time he stood by the hospital bed he felt like roles had been reversed from when he was the one in the hospital bed after his accident. Artur was often in a bad way when Jesse went to see him. In between the brief moments of clarity, there were times when he couldn't remember a thing. But unlike Jesse's amnesia, he mainly confused things from the recent past. Otherwise he was recovering 'as well as could be expected in the circumstances'.

Artur was in the middle of adjusting the back of the hospital bed when Isa flew into the room. He had clearly gone to an effort for the occasion; the skin on his exhausted face was covered in blotches from his recent shave. Isa flung her arms around him without bothering to wait for the backrest to stop moving into position. Jesse watched from the doorway and felt a lump in his throat. He couldn't remember ever seeing Artur look so happy. 'This is for you,' Isa said, passing him a rolled-up piece of paper.

Artur pulled a surprised face, untied the red ribbon and flattened the paper out. 'Wow,' he said, grinning. 'He doesn't have much hair, does he?'

'No,' Isa said. 'Well, he is a grandpa lion.'

'Is that me?'

'Can you see any other grandpas around here?'

He shook his head and looked at her. 'I've never been given anything this wonderful before. That's why I ask.'

Isa swung herself over to him at the edge of the bed. 'What do you do in here all day?'

'Sleep,' Artur said. 'I sleep a lot. Especially at night.'

Jesse let the two of them talk for a while. He only made a move to leave when he sensed that Artur was really getting tired.

'By the way, did you find anything out about Sebi and Renate?' Artur asked before they left.

'Not much,' Jesse said glumly. 'They both died a while ago.'

'He didn't kill them, did he?'

'Renate Kochl died of stomach cancer in 1992. Your old friend Sebastian Kochl died of heart failure eight years later.'

'Oh,' Artur said quietly. He glanced out of the window. The snow was thawing and dripping from the roof. 'I remember now. I got an invitation to the funeral. I didn't go.'

Jesse bit his lip. He found it hard to accept that he had apparently been well looked after by the Kochls for ten years of his life and yet he couldn't remember any of it. Artur had told him a few things about them. But he wished he could have spoken to them instead. 'Did you know my mother?' he asked.

'Your mother,' Artur sighed. It was clearly an effort for him to speak, but he obviously felt that he had a duty to tell Jesse anything he could. 'No. But Wilbert used to rave about her. He really loved that woman. Herman, Gudrun and Wilbert were all on the *Helgoland* together in Vietnam. Wilbert was chief mate, Herman was a captain, and Gudrun was a doctor. Women used to flock to Herman in those days, and not just because of the uniform. He always had this smile on his face, incredibly charming. He was always a hit with the girls at school too. Anyway, Wilbert never stood a chance, and Gudrun ended up falling pregnant to Herman. The war was still in full swing at the time, so Gudrun soon had to leave the ship. She went back to Kiel.'

'And my father?'

'Herman wanted to stay.'

'He only came back to Germany for our birth?'

'I'm sure he would have been granted leave to attend the birth, but he stayed in Da Nang.'

Jesse gulped and caught Isa frowning at him. 'You were at my birth, weren't you?'

'Yes,' said Jesse. 'Of course.'

'Herman was more interested in wandering around the docks. He had a thing for Vietnamese girls.' He quickly glanced at Isa, then back at Jesse. 'You already know the stories about your father and women. He was brutal, and nobody stood up to him. Being a German captain made him untouchable. There was an agreement between the governments. It was a disgrace, if you ask me. Eventually Wilbert decided he couldn't take any more, so he left the ship and came back to Germany.'

'To Kiel, as far as I know.'

'Yes. I don't know how much he told Gudrun about Herman's escapades or what Gudrun thought about Herman. But Wilbert lived with you for the first three years after you were born. He was happy in those days. He was a different person, nowhere near as melancholic. He always said he thought your mother was too good for him. Much too beautiful and clever. The fact that she chose him over his brother made a new man of him.'

'So why did he shoot her?' Jesse asked.

'Well that definitely never happened.' Artur had a sudden coughing fit. Jesse passed him a glass of water, and Artur raised the backrest a little higher.

Jesse glanced sideways at Isa. 'Maybe we should talk about this some other time,' he said.

'Why?' Artur grumbled. 'Because of Isa?'

'She's already been through enough.'

'Rubbish!' Artur protested. 'She's got a right to know. They are her grandparents, after all.'

'You already told me about it in the attic,' Isa chimed in.

'Really? Hmm. I can't really remember everything.' His eyes flitted from Isa to Jesse. 'Anyway: your daughter is braver than the two of us put together.'

The beaming smile on Isa's face was the only response Jesse needed.

'Well, there was an incident in Da Nang,' Artur continued. 'Herman was implicated in the death of a—' – he looked at Isa and chose his words carefully – '—the death of a young woman. There was no proof, but there was a lot of controversy. The German government sent him packing from the ship, and when he railed against it, they stripped him of his captain's licence. Not long after that, he turned up at Gudrun's house in Kiel. Herman was used to getting everything he wanted. He was furious when he found out that Gudrun had chosen Wilbert over him. Things quickly escalated, and in the space of a week, Herman shot Gudrun right in front of Wilbert's eyes.'

'Oh God,' Jesse murmured. Finding out about his own past felt like travelling through some strange dark tunnel.

'Wilbert got scared and ran off. He said he wanted to take both of you with him, but he was in such a hurry that he only managed to grab hold of you before he ran away. Your brother was left behind with your father.'

'Why didn't he let me stay with him?'

'How? Without any proof of what happened? He wasn't your father. Anyway, Herman had spun it so that everyone believed Wilbert was the one who had shot Gudrun. So he came to me. He knew that I'd taken over as head of Adlershof.' Artur's voice was hoarse. He cleared his throat and felt around for the remote control for the bed. The backrest buzzed back down, and Artur stopped coughing. 'Well, you know the rest of the story already.'

Jesse nodded. He still had countless questions to ask, but that was enough for today.

'Jesse,' Artur's voice was suddenly a whisper, 'listen.' He grabbed Jesse's hand and gulped. 'I—' he stopped to clear his throat. 'Do you think you'll ever be able to—'

'Forgive you?'

Artur nodded. It took a lot of effort for him to maintain eye contact.

'The man who kept me in the children's home and away from my second parents? No, I don't think so. But the man who looked after my daughter for me? Definitely.'

Artur sank back into his pillow, relieved. A nurse came into the room and they said goodbye. Isa gave Artur a kiss on his wrinkled cheek and gently stroked his face.

'Hellooo. Earth to Dad!'

'Huh?' Jesse snapped out of it.

Isa was standing in front of him. Noisy groups of children were flocking through the main gate on their way into school.

'I want to go now.'

Jesse nodded. He felt a lump in his throat.

They hugged, and Isa muttered: 'See ya, blue man.'

'See ya, Princess,' he said. Instead of the reproachful look he'd been half expecting, his accidental 'Princess' remark was welcomed with a grin.

Isa gave Jule a quick hug, then turned around and made her way over to the gate. Jesse and Jule climbed into the car and closed the doors. The noises faded away.

'I'm glad you came with us,' Jesse said.

'She's looking very pale,' Jule said.

'Yes, she is.'

They sat in the car for a while without speaking. 'Hey,' Jule said. 'Why didn't you tell me about Wolle?'

Jesse sighed. 'It was stupid of me, I know.'

'Yes, very stupid.'

'Was that what you wanted to hear?'

Jule took a moment to think. 'I think so.'

'OK, then,' Jesse nodded.

'Did you ask Artur about Wolle again?'

'Asked, yes. But he was a pretty vague with his response.'

'Because he's ashamed?'

'Yes, he is. Wolle was probably the only one apart from him who knew about Raphael's burn from the iron. Raphael never let anyone see him without his T-shirt, but Wolle must have seen it by chance at some point. And when he saw me without a burn mark, he put two and two together.'

'So Raphael killed Sandra and Wolle because they knew about the switch, but why did he kill Markus?'

'He was the one who saw Raphael in Adlershof and set the ball rolling with Sandra. I guess the thing with the girls' toilet must have alarmed him, perhaps because Markus had realised that there were dodgy dealings going on with the children in Adlershof.'

'Do you know what Raphael was doing up there?'

'Not a clue.' Jesse went quiet for a moment. 'By the way, what's going on with Charly?'

'I told you she did well answering the questions from the police, didn't I?'

'Yes, you did.'

'There's a new support worker at the child welfare office. She's young and really nice. Actually, she's almost a bit too young if you ask me. But Charly likes her. She sounded very happy the last time we spoke on the phone.'

'And the proceedings against Wisselsmeier and Richard?' Jesse asked.

'You mean the child-trafficking charge?'

'Well, the attempted murder is an open and shut case.'

'The last time I gave a statement, I found out that the police were also investigating an old case. Kristina – do you remember the name? The woman whose room we stayed in. Well, it turns out she was a teacher at Adlershof for a while. She fell into the ice in a nearby lake. I think the police received an anonymous tip-off suggesting that Richard had some part in it. Maybe she suspected something.'

Jesse shook his head, obviously affected by the news. 'And the child trafficking charges?'

'That's a tough one. They're all being pretty tight-lipped about it. So far there have been six instances of Wisselsmeier and Richard selling girls with forged adoption papers. Some of them to people with clearly dubious preferences. Tinkerbell must have been sent back, luckily for her. She might have even disappeared if things had been different. But there's still no hard evidence for anything.'

'What a disgrace.'

'You know, in a way Artur was the one who started it,' Jule said.

'Yes, but for completely different reasons. It might not have been right, but in those days Artur only made arrangements with people he was sure would look after the children. And they were always people who had very little chance of adopting legally.'

'I find it hard to believe that you, of all people, are defending him. How could he have known that these parents were really good for the children? And when you think of what he and Wisselsmeier must have raked in for it, I hardly expect that they just had the children's best interests at heart.'

'No. Probably not. But I think that what Artur started with good intentions only really turned criminal when Richard and Wisselsmeier were orchestrating it.'

There was a hard knock on the window at Jule's side. 'Hey, Isa, is everything all right?'

'Yeah. Everything's fine,' Isa answered, quickly putting them at ease. 'I just wanted to ask if you want to go to the forest this weekend?'

'Sounds good to me,' Jesse said. 'But shouldn't you be in class now?'

'Oh, that doesn't matter. They know I'm not feeling too good at the moment. Are you coming with us, Jule? To the forest this weekend, I mean?'

'Of course I'll come.'

'Great,' Isa grinned. 'I feel better now.' Then she swivelled on her heel and ran back to school.

Turn the page to read an extract from
Marc Raabe's bestselling thriller

CUT

Available in paperback and ebook now

Prologue

West Berlin – 13 October, 11.09 p.m.

Gabriel stood in the doorway and stared. The light from the hall fell down the cellar stairs and was swallowed by the brick walls.

He hated the cellar, particularly at night. Not that it would've made any difference whether it was light or dark outside. It was always night in the cellar. Then again, during the day, you could always run out into the garden, out into the light. At night, on the other hand, it was dark *everywhere*, even outside, and ghosts lurked in every corner. Ghosts that no grown-up could see. Ghosts that were just waiting to sink their claws into the neck of an eleven-year-old boy.

Still, he just couldn't help but stare, entranced, down into the far end of the cellar where the light faded away.

The door!

It was open!

There was a gaping black opening between the dark green wall and the door. And behind it was the lab, dark like Darth Vader's Death Star.

His heart beat in his throat. Gabriel wiped his clammy, trembling hands on his pyjamas – his favourite pyjamas with Luke Skywalker on the front.

The long, dark crack of the door drew him in as if by magic. He slowly placed his bare foot on the first step. The wood of the cellar stairs felt rough and creaked as if it were trying to give him away. But he knew that they wouldn't hear him. Not as long as they were fighting behind the closed kitchen door. It was a bad one. Worse than normal. And it frightened him. Good that David wasn't there, he thought. Good that he'd taken him out of harm's way. His little brother would've cried.

Then again, it would've been nice not to be alone right now in this cellar with the ghosts. Gabriel swallowed. The opening stared back at him like the gates of hell.

Go look! That's what Luke would do.

Dad would be furious if he could see him now. The lab was Dad's secret and it was secured like a fortress with a metal door and a shiny black peephole. No one else had ever seen the lab. Not even Mum.

Gabriel's feet touched the bare concrete floor of the cellar and he shuddered. First the warm wooden steps and now the cold stone.

Now or never!

Suddenly, a rumbling came through the cellar ceiling. Gabriel flinched. The noise came from the kitchen above him. It sounded like the table had been scraped across the tiles. For a moment, he considered whether he should go upstairs. Mum was up there all alone with *him* and Gabriel knew how angry he could get.

His eyes darted back to the door, glimmering in the dark. Such an opportunity might never come again.

He had stood there once before, about two years ago. That time, Dad had forgotten to lock the upper cellar door. Gabriel was nine. He had stood in the hall for a while and peered down.

In the end, curiosity triumphed. That time, he had also crept down into the cellar, entirely afraid of the ghosts, but still in complete darkness because he didn't dare turn on the light.

The peephole had glowed red like the eye of a monster.

In a mad rush, he had fled back up the stairs, back to David in their room, and crawled into his bed.

Now he was eleven. Now he stood there downstairs again and the monster eye wasn't glowing. Still, the peephole stared at him, cold and black like a dead eye. The only things reflecting in it were the dim light on the cellar stairs and him. The closer he got, the larger his face grew.

And why did it smell so disgusting?

He groped out in front of him with his bare feet and stepped in something wet and mushy. *Puke. It was puke!* That's why it smelled so disgusting. But why was there puke *here* in the first place?

He choked down his disgust and rubbed his foot clean on a dry area of the concrete floor. Some was still stuck between his toes. He would've liked a towel or a wet cloth right about now, but the lab was more important. He reached out his hand, placed it on the knob, pulled the heavy metal door open a bit more, and pressed on into the darkness. An unnatural silence enveloped him.

A deathly silence.

A sharp chemical smell crept into his nose like at the film lab where his father had once taken him after one of his days of shooting.

His heart was pounding. Much too fast, much too loud. He wished he were somewhere else, maybe with David, under the covers.

Luke Skywalker would never hide under the covers.

The trembling fingers on his left hand searched for the light switch, always expecting to find something else entirely. What if the ghosts were here? If they grabbed his arm? If he accidently reached into one's mouth and it snapped its teeth shut?

There! Cool plastic.

He flipped the switch. Three red lights lit up and bathed the room in front of him in a strange red glow. Red, like in the belly of a monster.

A chill ran up his spine all the way to the roots of his hair. He stopped at the threshold to the lab; somehow, there was a sort of invisible border that he didn't want to cross. He squinted and tried to make out the details.

The lab was larger than he had thought, a narrow space about three metres wide and seven metres deep. A heavy black curtain hung directly beside him. Someone had hastily pushed it aside.

Clothes lines were strung under the concrete ceiling with photos hanging from them. Some had been torn down and lay on the floor.

On the left stood a photo enlarger. On the right, a shelf spanned the entire wall, crammed with pieces of equipment. Gabriel's eyes widened. He recognised most of them immediately: Arri, Beaulieu, Leicina, with other, smaller cameras in between. The trade magazines that were piled up in Dad's study on the first floor were full of them. Whenever one of those magazines wound up in the bin, Gabriel fished it out, stuck it under his pillow, and read it under the covers by torchlight until his eyelids were too heavy to keep open.

Beside the cameras lay a dozen lenses, some as long as gun barrels; next to them, small cameras, cases to absorb camera operating sounds, 8- and 16-mm film cartridges, a stack of three VCRs with four monitors, and finally, two brand-new camcorders. Dad always scoffed at the things. In one of the magazines, he had read that you could film for almost two hours with the new video technology without having to change the cassette – absolutely unbelievable! On top of that, the plastic bombers didn't rattle like film cameras, but ran silently.

Gabriel's shining eyes wandered over the treasures. He wished he could show all of this to David. He immediately felt guilty. After all, this was dangerous, so it was best that he didn't get David involved. Besides, his brother had already fallen asleep. He was right to have locked the door to their room.

Suddenly, there was a loud crash. He spun around. There was no one there. No parents, no ghost. His parents were probably still quarrelling up in the kitchen.

He looked back into the lab at all of the treasures. *Come closer*, they seemed to whisper. But he was still standing on the threshold next to the curtain. Fear rose in him. He could still turn back. He had now seen the lab; he didn't have to go all the way in.

Eleven! You're eleven! Come on, don't be a chicken!

How old was Luke?

Gabriel reluctantly took two steps into the room.

What were those photos? He bent down, picked one up from the floor, and stared at the faded grainy image. A sudden feeling of disgust and a strange excitement spread through his stomach. He looked up at the photos on the clothes line. The photo directly above him attracted his eyes like a magnet. His face was hot and red, like everything else around him. He also felt a bit sick. It looked so real, so . . . or were they actors? It looked like in the movie! The columns, the walls, like in the Middle Ages, and the black clothes . . .

He tore himself away and his eyes jumped over the jumbled storage and the shelf, and finally rested on the modern VCRs with their glittering little JVC logos. The lowest one was switched on. Numbers and characters were illuminated in its shining display. Like in *Star Wars* in the cockpit of a spaceship, he thought.

As if of its own accord, Gabriel's index finger approached the buttons and pushed one. A loud click inside the device made him jump. Twice, three times, then the hum of a motor. *A cassette!* There was a cassette in the VCR! His cheeks burned. He feverishly pushed another button. The JVC responded with a rattle. Interference lines flashed across the monitor beside the VCRs. The image wobbled for a moment, and then it was there. Diffuse with flickering colour, unreal, like a window to another world.

Gabriel had been leaning forward without knowing it – and now he jerked back. His mouth went totally dry. It was the same image as in the photo! The same place, the same columns, the same people, only now they were moving. He wanted to look away, but it was impossible. He sucked the stifling air in through his gaping mouth, and then held his breath without realising it.

The images pummelled him like the popping of flashbulbs; he couldn't help but watch, mesmerised.

The cut through the black fabric of the dress.

The pale triangle on the still paler skin.

The long, tangled blond hair.

The chaos.

And then another cut – a sharp, angry motion that spread into Gabriel's guts. He suddenly felt sick and everything was spinning. The television stared at him viciously. Trembling, he found the button and switched it off.

The image collapsed with a dull thud, as if there were a black hole inside the monitor, just like in outer space. The noise was awful, but reassuring at the same time. He stared at the dark screen and the reflection of his own bright red face. A ghost stared back, eyes wide with fear.

Don't think about it! Just don't think about it . . . He stared at the photos, at the whole mess, anything but the monitor.

What you can't see isn't there!

But it was there. Somewhere in the monitor, deep inside the black hole. The VCR made a soft grinding noise. He wanted to squeeze his eyes shut and wake up somewhere else. Anywhere. Anywhere but here. He was still crouched in front of his ghostly reflection in the monitors.

Suddenly, Gabriel was overcome by the desperate desire to see something pleasant, or even just something different. As if it had a will of its own, his finger drifted towards the other monitors.

Thud. Thud. The two upper monitors flashed on. Two washed-out images crystallised, casting their steel-blue glimmer into the red light of the lab. One image showed the hall and the open cellar door; the stairs were swallowed up by darkness. The second image showed the kitchen. The kitchen – and his parents. His father's voice rasped from the speaker.

Gabriel's eyes widened.

No! Please, no!

His father shoved the kitchen table. The table legs scraped loudly across the floor. The noise carried through the ceiling, and Gabriel winced. His father threw open a drawer, reached inside and his hand re-emerged.

Gabriel stared at the monitor in horror. Blinking, he wished he were blind. Blind and deaf.

But he wasn't.

His eyes flooded with tears. The chemical smell of the lab combined with the vomit outside the door made him gag. He wished someone would come and hug him and talk it all away.

But no one would come. He was alone.

The realisation hit him with a crushing blow. *Someone had to do something.* And now *he* was the only one who could do anything.

What would Luke do?

Quietly, he crept up the cellar stairs, his bare feet no longer able to feel the cold floor. The red room behind him glowed like hell.

If only he had a lightsabre! And then, very suddenly, he thought of something much, much better than a sabre.

Chapter 1

The photo hovers like a threat in the windowless cellar. Outside, the rain is raging. The old roof of the mansion groans beneath the mass of water, and there is a dim red light rotating above the front door on the half-timbered facade, lighting up the house at brief intervals.

The torch beam darts about the dark cellar hall, revealing the slashed black fabric of a sparkling dress, which dangles from a hanger. The photo pinned onto the dress looks like a piece of wallpaper from a distance; a pale, rough scrap that has absorbed the ink from the printer, leaving the colours dull, fading away.

The dress and the photo are still swaying back and forth, as if only just hung up, and the swinging makes them seem like a decorative mobile; moving but lifeless.

The photo shows a young, very thin, heartbreakingly beautiful woman. She is slender, almost boyish, her breasts are small and flat, her face frozen, expressionless.

Her very long and very blond hair is like a crumpled yellow sheet beneath her head. She is wearing the dress to which this photo is now pinned. It seems tailor-made for her; it resembles her: flowing, extravagant, useless and costly. And the front is slashed open all the way down, as if it had an open zipper.

Beneath the dress, her skin is also slashed open – with one sharp incision starting between her legs, over her pubis and up to her chest. The abdominal wall is agape, the fleshy red of the innards veiled in merciful darkness. The black dress engulfs the body like death itself. A perfect symbol, just like the place where the dress is now hanging, waiting for him to find it: Kadettenweg 107.

The torchlight is again pointed at the bulky grey box on the wall and the tarnished lock. The key fitted, but was difficult to turn, as if it couldn't remember what it was supposed to do at first. Inside, there is a row of little red light bulbs. Three are broken, and they glow at irregular intervals. The tungsten filaments have corroded over the years. But that doesn't matter. The necessary bulb is glowing.

The torchlight hastily gropes its way back to the cellar stairs and up the steps. There are footprints in the beam of light, and that's a good thing. When he returns, they will guide him down the cellar stairs to the black dress. And to the photo.

All at once, he will remember. The hairs on the back of his neck will rise, and he will say to himself: this is impossible.

And yet: it is true. He will know it. Because of the cellar alone – even if it wasn't *this* cellar or *this* woman. And of course, it will be a different woman. *His* woman.

And on her birthday, too. A lovely detail!

But the best part is the way it all comes full circle. Everything started in a cellar, and it would end in a cellar.

Cellars are the vestibules of hell. And who should know that better than someone who has been burning in hell for an eternity.

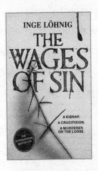

Want to read
NEW BOOKS
before anyone else?

Like getting
FREE BOOKS?

Enjoy sharing your
OPINIONS?

Discover
READERS FIRST

Read. Love. Share.

Sign up today to win your first free book:
readersfirst.co.uk